FURY *of* OBSESSION

ALSO BY COREENE CALLAHAN

Dragonfury Series

Fury of Fire
Fury of Ice
Fury of Seduction
Fury of Desire
Fury of Fate: A Dragonfury Short Story

Circle of Seven Series

Knight Awakened
Knight Avenged

Warriors of the Realm Series

Warrior's Revenge

FURY *of* OBSESSION

Coreene Callahan

Montlake Romance

This is a work of fiction. Names, characters, organizations, places, events, and incidents are either products of the author's imagination or are used fictitiously.

Published by Montlake Romance, Seattle

www.apub.com

ISBN-13: 9781477822227
ISBN-10: 1477822224

Cover design by Kerrie Robertson

Library of Congress Control Number: 2014952312

Printed in the United States of America

For Kallie Lane—thank you for always being there to steady me when I stumble.

Chapter One

Silence echoed, oozing from dark corners in the underground passageway. Beady eyes flashed red, watching him from dense shadows. Hunkered down behind a burnt-out Humvee, Venom grimaced and rechecked his position. Hemmed in underground. Alone without backup. And oh, yeah . . . rats, a whole platoon of the furry little freaks.

Terrific. Just perfect. An ugly accompaniment to an already bad night.

Swallowing his distaste, he pivoted around the back bumper and, keeping low, brushed past the wrecked SUV. He slid to a stop halfway up the dank corridor. His combat boots scuffed against cracked concrete. Uneven sound ricocheted, breaking through the silence. The rat pack scurrying along the side wall scattered, squeaking as though he'd stepped on one. Super. Another complaint to add to the pile. The disease-ridden collection of disgusting had just given away his position. Now the enemy knew exactly where he was, which left him wishing Wick would show up. Goddamn his best friend. Of all the nights for the male to leave him to his own devices. Stifling a snarl, he fired up mind-speak, sent out a mental ping, and waited. One Mississippi. Two Mississippi. Three . . .

No answer.

Not surprising. He might as well put hope away. Shelve expectation too. Wick wasn't coming. Was no doubt well occupied playing—

The rapid staccato of gunfire cracked through the quiet.

Finger curled around the trigger, Venom dodged right. Bullets flew over his head toward the Humvee. Metal ricocheted off metal. Sparks flew, lighting up the darkness as violent sound exploded around him. Teeth clenched, he pressed the butt of the Heckler & Koch to his shoulder and, leveling the weapon, changed course.

Practice made his movements efficient.

Experience sent him down an eastbound tunnel.

He needed to reacquire the target. And fast. Before the enemy regrouped and found reinforcements. One shooter was manageable. Half a dozen, however? Not great odds. So yeah, it was now or never. Time to take the male out, then relieve him of his extra ammo. Restocking would help. KO'ing the prick playing hide-and-seek in the subterranean labyrinth would be even better. Combat boots crunching over broken glass, Venom hugged the wall, rechecked his sightline, and wheeled around the next corner.

Footfalls echoed, pinging off hard surfaces.

Venom swallowed a growl. Smart move. Better strategy. With the corridor narrowing up ahead, the reason behind the male's retreat wasn't rocket science. Practicality at its best—a maneuver based in evasive tactics and rooted in the bottleneck at the far end of the tunnel. A trap, no doubt. A pretty good one too. Not that Venom cared. Eliminating the enemy, ensuring none remained, was job one. Paramount to not only the mission, but his peace of mind. So, screw it. Ambush or not, he'd walk straight into it, hope he caught a break and got out alive. Weapon at the ready, he swung into another dark hallway and—

Movement flashed in his periphery.

Venom reacted. A sideways shift, and he dodged the fist. A hard jab sent the handgun in the enemy's hand flying. The Beretta rotated end over end in mid-air. He grabbed the bastard by the throat and palmed the hilt of his hunting knife. Steel zinged against leather as he pulled the weapon free and struck. The razor-sharp blade met skin, slashing across the male's carotid. Arterial spray arced through the air and . . . oh, yeah.

Another enemy solider dead. Next level achieved and . . .

"Game Over."

Venom took his thumbs off the Xbox controls and, with a satisfied grunt, slid into a slouch against the couch back. Leather hissed in protest. Boredom slithered in, igniting a firestorm of discontent in the center of his chest. Swallowing a curse, he tipped his head back, letting it fall against the backrest, and stared at the seventy-two-inch TV through his lashes. Huge. Expensive. The best of the best. The flat screen screamed *look at me*, dominating an entire wall in his bedroom, standing alongside every video game known to mankind. The extravagance should've embarrassed him. It made him angry instead. But not for the usual reasons. He hadn't lost. Or gotten turfed by one of his Nightfury buddies in a high-octane war game. Venom huffed. Hell, getting his ass kicked in a round of imaginary combat sounded fantastic right about now.

It would've, after all, solved the greater problem.

Maybe even banished the buzz of unhappiness. Relieved him of the restlessness too—the sharp slash of isolation, the abyss called loneliness threatening to swallow him whole.

Fiddling with the gaming toggles, Venom frowned at the controller. Jesus. Labeling it like that—laying it on the line—made him feel like a pansy. Like a needy male without the wherewithal to look after himself. Like an asshole too, for wishing Wick was with him instead of across the hall, spending time with J. J.—the female his best friend not only loved, but had mated almost three weeks ago. He swallowed past the tight knot in his throat. Talk about selfish. Twisted with an extra helping of inappropriate too. Particularly since he was happy for Wick. Well okay, at least half of the time. The other half, he ended up mired in another emotion altogether. One in which the little green monster pumped envy through his veins, leaving a bad taste in his mouth and calluses on his heart.

God, it was so screwed up. A total seesaw. One that left him thrilled for Wick and J. J. one minute and jealous the next.

Rubbing his hand over his jaw, Venom tossed the controller. Its black body somersaulted. As it tumbled through the air, he stacked his bare feet on the beanbag chair doubling as a coffee table and reached for his drink. Clear liquid sloshed against the rim of the tumbler. Ice cubes clinked, sending the scent of hard alcohol into his airspace. The acrid smell singed the insides of his nostrils. Venom ignored the burn and watched the controller slide to a stop instead. It bumped into the arm of the sectional. He raised the glass and downed another mouthful.

Jägermeister. Straight up. Three shots strong.

He needed it tonight. Wanted to blunt his senses with the only thing that ever got him drunk. His curse—a terrible claim to fame—he knew. Beer didn't do it for him. Neither did wine or whiskey. Only *the Meister* would get him where he wanted to go . . . flat-out hammered with an extra helping of smashed. The reality of it burned with every ounce of rotgut he threw back. Then again, he hadn't barricaded himself behind his bedroom door seeking comfort. Or sat his ass down to KO an imaginary enemy via video game intent on feeling sorry for himself either. He'd locked himself away to face facts.

The first one was simple.

He should be thankful. Grateful something—*anything*, no matter how bad it tasted—blurred the lines, bringing the promise of oblivion. He needed the break, a way to stop his mind from churning and his heart from hurting. So yeah. A drunken stupor delivered by a bellyful of what amounted to moonshine sounded about right. Nothing else could supplant the toxic swill swimming through his veins. Not that he lamented his noxious nature. The pros of being a venomous dragon always outweighed the cons. Venom snorted, the sound half laugh, half despair, and marveled at the irony.

Another jam-up. More emotional dichotomy. Polar opposites that went something like: proud of his abilities—and the heritage that drove them—one moment, tired of all the bullshit the next.

Same story, different decade.

Anyone who touched him too long suffered the consequences—blood poisoning by way of the toxins entwined in his dragon DNA. In his blood. On his skin. Buried deep in his muscles. Which meant prolonged physical contact with anyone wasn't a good idea. Females included. A pang tightened his chest. It was intolerable. Completely unfair. He loved sex—the heat, the pleasure, the alluring sounds a female made while he stroked deep and she begged for more. He craved the connection. Liked the closeness. Enjoyed the taunt and tease and . . . hmm . . . the taste of the fairer sex, so sweet on his tongue, never failed to enthrall him.

Too bad none of the encounters ever lasted long.

Most couldn't endure his touch—the deadly effect of his skin—for more than forty minutes at a time. So he never stuck around. Or stayed the night. Never got to hold a female in the aftermath or experience the benefits that kind of intimacy wrought. Get in. Get out. Give each female all the pleasure she could handle before he took his own between her thighs. And yet, despite the contact, he still felt alone. Isolated from normal, neck-deep in deadly and not-good-enough. No doubt part of the reason he was so jealous of Wick and the other mated Nightfury warriors. He wanted what his brothers-in-arms possessed—a female to call his own. Someone to come home to after a night spent fighting the Razorback assholes he called enemy.

Someone he couldn't hurt with his touch. No matter how much time he spent with her.

With a sigh, Venom drained his glass, then reached for the chilled bottle sitting on the side table. Without looking, he poured himself another glass. Jägermeister sloshed against cut crystal. He took another pull and, sliding lower on the seat cushions, glanced at the vaulted ceiling. Two stories above him, winged angels took flight across the cupola. Painted by Wick, the fresco was a masterpiece, a testament to his friend's skill with a brush. Not that Venom had known it until recently.

He huffed at the absurdity. Sixty years spent in close quarters with the male, and he hadn't guessed. Or suspected a thing. His friend had kept that tidbit locked down tight, refusing to share anything about himself—all artist stuff included—until J. J. started hanging his paintings in her music room two weeks ago. Now Wick's art infused the space, bringing color and life to pale walls above the pile of instruments he kept buying for his mate.

Hell, she'd even hung a couple of canvases over Venom's fireplace across the room.

Turning his head, he eyed the paintings. After a minute spent staring, he swirled the ice in his glass and pushed off the couch. Unsteady from all the booze, Venom swayed on his feet.

His vision blurred for a second. He blinked. His eyes came back into focus a second before he put himself in gear. Skirting the long arm of the sectional, he strode across the room. Hardwood chilled the soles of his bare feet. Tall bookcases streamed past in the periphery. Gaze glued to the artwork, Venom barely noticed. The books were par for the course, a product of his decision to make the library inside Black Diamond—the lair he shared with the other Nightfury warriors—his bedroom five years ago.

A fantastic decision.

He loved stories of all kinds. Textbooks and treatises too. Throw in a few ancient tomes for the fun of it and . . . yeah. Pure heaven. Thanks to Daimler—the Nightfury's go-to guy—the library boasted more than its fair share of reading material. Everything he needed shelved in a large space that epitomized elegance. Dark wood. Pale walls and a river rock–clad fireplace. The incredible fresco looking down on the whole. But the pièce de résistance? The spiral staircase leading to a narrow walkway twelve feet above ground level. Two stories of absolute perfection. Each leather-bound volume just a hop, skip, and jump away from the king-size bed sitting in the center of the room.

His escape. His favorite spot, a refuge far from the perils of the world.

But not right now.

Tonight, he couldn't tear his gaze from the paintings. Precise lines. Painstaking detail. Swirling color—the muted tones of winter in Prague. Gorgeous. Every brushstroke of it. But for one thing: Despite the beauty of city streets and snowfall, the paintings reminded him too much of home. Of past abuse and present anguish. Of painful memories wrapped in a night he didn't want to remember, but couldn't forget. His conscience wouldn't let him. Guilt laid the blame on thick, reminding him of what he'd done . . .

His sire lay dead. Murdered by Venom's own hand.

Recall made his stomach clench. The need for oblivion forced him to raise his glass. Cold liquid washed into his mouth. Venom swallowed hard. And then again. Once. Twice. A third time, draining the glass dry, accepting the burn, reveling in the discomfort as the alcohol hit the bottom of his stomach. He deserved the pain. Couldn't atone for his past, never mind hope for absolution. Wishing and wanting never changed the facts. And some things—no matter how necessary the action—couldn't be forgiven.

"Goddamn it." Venom set the tumbler down on the mantle. Crystal thumped against stone. Ice rattled. Glass cracked, the sound harsh in the silence as he palmed the back of his head. He pulled down. Taut muscle squawked, protesting the stretch as agony streamed up his spine. "I need to get the hell out of here."

An excellent plan.

The best, really, but for one thing.

He wasn't supposed to leave the lair. Not tonight. Which sucked . . . in major ways. Not that it mattered. He couldn't argue with the logic behind the lockdown. Bastian was right. All of his brothers-in-arms needed the occasional night off fighting rotation. Rest. Relax. Recharge. The routine did a body good, even though it had taken time for him and his comrades to realize it.

Until four months ago, none of the Nightfury warriors had ever taken a night off. Each had been intent on one thing—hunting rogues, members of the Razorback pack preying on humankind—to the exclusion of all else. The inclusion of females in the lair, however, changed the Nightfury landscape. Now each warrior took at least one night away from fighting a week. Usually in pairs, a show of solidarity in the wingman department. Tonight was his—and Wick's—turn. More's the frigging pity, 'cause . . .

yeah. Now Venom was stuck. Under direct orders to cool his jets and—God help him—*relax.*

No way around the rules. No wingman or relief in sight either.

Cranking his hands into fists, Venom rolled his shoulders to relieve the tension, then shook his head. He wanted to go. To shift into dragon form, spread his wings, and fly. To push himself so hard exhaustion set in and the past blurred into an indistinct entity. Something to be discarded and ignored. Maybe then he'd be able to forget. Maybe then his chest would stop hurting. Maybe then he'd be able to sleep. A long shot in a losing game? No doubt, and yet, even knowing he should stay put, the temptation to leave taunted him.

Bastian wouldn't be happy about it.

Venom snorted. *Happy.* Right. Try pissed off and then some. Hell, his commander would kick his ass—and come back for seconds—the moment Venom took flight from Black Diamond alone. Not an optimal outcome. Particularly since B didn't screw around. Or give a direct order unless he believed one necessary. So yeah, leaving the lair wasn't a great idea. The entire pack would get pissy. Call him out. Put him in the hot seat. Slam him for being an idiot, but . . . whatever. He could handle the others. His commander, however, was a different story. He respected Bastian. And honestly, being turned into a Dragonkind pretzel for breaking rank didn't appear on his list of things to do—ever—but, well . . .

Tonight ignoring protocol might be worth it.

No one, after all, needed to know. He could get out—get what he craved, sex with a female—and be back before any of his buddies arrived home. Or anyone inside the lair noticed he'd gone AWOL for a couple of hours. As the realization took root, spiraling into possibility, the perfect place popped into his head . . .

the Luxmore. Venom glanced toward the sliding doors beside the fireplace. Moonlight streamed through the panes, cutting a wide swath across the hardwood floor. Venom flexed his hands. Yeah, definitely. The boutique hotel would do. Not that he'd ever visited it before. Or heard about it until a week ago. Sloan couldn't stop talking about it—or the gorgeous females who frequented the Luxmore's upscale bar, so . . .

Screw it.

He turned toward the patio door. With nothing but a thought, he flipped the lock and gave the handle a mental push. The slider retreated to one side. Chilled by winter, wind rushed in. Venom didn't hesitate. He stepped over the threshold into the cold evening air instead. With another flick of his mind, he shoved the door closed behind him, walked across the stone patio, down three steps, and . . .

Presto change-o. He shifted from human to dragon form.

Interlocking dragon skin fell like dominoes, laying a trail along his lengthening body. Armored up and buttoned down, the venomous barbs tipping his tail rattled as he unfurled his wings. Black webbing stretched, sliding into dark green scales. His sonar pinged. Sensation curled around the horns on his head, allowing him to gauge distances. Fifteen minutes tops, and he'd land at the Luxmore. So close, yet still too far away. With a growl of anticipation, Venom flexed his talons. Razor-sharp claws digging grooves in the frozen lawn, he leapt skyward and . . . hmm, baby. He was on his way. Up over the treetops. Moonlight playing against his scales. Banking toward the northeast edge of Seattle, the promise of scented female flesh and the soothing slide of relief in his future. Serious ass-kicking from his brothers be damned.

Chapter Two

Down on her luck. In hawk up to her eyeballs. Screwed six ways to Sunday and twice on Monday. Sitting inside her had-seen-better-days Volkswagen Golf, Evelyn Foxe pulled the key from the ignition and stared across the parking lot. The windshield encapsulated the Luxmore Hotel like a picture frame. A pretty view from across the avenue fifty yards away. Art deco stone facade aglow in soft light. Arched windows and gleaming steel accents. Manicured gardens curling around a wide-mouthed circular drive. And enough sharply dressed valets to make a rich man drool.

Beautiful. Sophisticated. A haven for the well-heeled and wealthy. A place most people dreamed of spending a Friday night.

Well, everyone except her.

Too bad she didn't have a choice. Do or die. Everything said and done. That's what it came down to: put her three-inch heels to work, cross the parking lot, and enter the playground for the rich . . . and sometimes famous.

Three months ago, Evelyn wouldn't have thought twice about entering the posh boutique hotel. She'd belonged in that world. Not wealthy by any standards, but respected by those in the club. Money, after all, made people—particularly CEOs of large corporations—sit up and pay attention. Ravenous greed fueled the fixation, of course. But then, that had been her job . . . to ensure the companies in her portfolio stayed honest. Creative accounting might be the norm in a dog-eat-dog world, but in the end it always equaled bad business practice.

A fact her former employer should've kept in mind inside his own walls.

Grabbing her purse from the passenger seat, Evelyn pulled the Prada into her lap. With a flick, she undid the buckle. A quick toss saw her keys disappear behind the lip of expensive leather. An even faster hunt inside her makeup bag unearthed her lipstick. She popped the top and twisted the base. Bloodred Viva Glam a la Marilyn Monroe. Evelyn's favorite lip color. Ironic in many ways, particularly since she and Marilyn had nothing else in common.

Oh, but wait. That wasn't exactly true, was it?

She and the beauty icon might not share the same skin color, but trouble didn't discriminate. Age. Race. Affluence with a heaping scoop of smart. None of the variables mattered. The norms remained the same. The world kept turning. And misfortune always took its pound of flesh. Which brought her back to the original problem, didn't it? No sidestepping the issue. No getting around the facts. Just straight-up in-her-face reality . . . her life or the money.

A shiver ghosted down her spine.

As goose bumps set up shop beneath her fancy cocktail dress, Evelyn fought to stay even. Nervousness wouldn't help. Neither would the anger bubbling inside her. Pragmatism would serve her better. But as Evelyn swallowed past the knot in her throat, glanced in the rearview mirror, and put her lipstick to work, fury tightened her chest.

How dare those assholes.

How dare they be so stupid? So self-serving? So devil-may-care with the charter of ethics . . . and other people's lives? If only the higher-ups had been responsible—instead of helping their largest client defraud investors out of millions in the Amsted scandal—the accounting firm wouldn't have folded, and she'd still have her position. Would even now be inside a struggling corporation's books, finding financial solutions as a senior insolvency and restructuring advisor for Willis, Bower & Bloom. Instead, she was out of a job she loved. And thousands were out their life savings.

Such a huge mess. Nowhere near fair either. Particularly since the scandal had left her with little recourse.

Oh, she applied for new positions all the time. At least four or five a week, interviewing with company after company. Big corporations. Small businesses. It made no difference. No matter where Evelyn went, she couldn't catch a break. Tough economic times? Sure, but that wasn't why she sat in her secondhand car in front of a fancy hotel—jobless, in trouble, and out of options. The name on her résumé made everyone run scared. A bitter pill to swallow considering her credentials and reputation. But try as she might to convince those in charge of hiring she hadn't been part of the corruption—or the subsequent cover-up unearthed by the SEC—no one wanted to give a former employee of Willis, Bower & Bloom the benefit of the doubt.

Which left her with no job. A vicious bookie on her trail. And only one way out—the Luxmore and the wealthy clientele it drew like paparazzi to a celebrity crime scene.

Her heart sank. It always did when she thought about that terrible day. *The Implosion*, as she liked to call it. The news had broken hard with a *New York Times* Op-Ed piece. She'd been in Europe, scouring an Austrian corporation's ledgers, searching for ways to save three thousand jobs by restructuring, stabilizing and—

Something rapped against her window.

Evelyn jumped in her seat. Her knees bumped the bottom of the steering wheel. Reflex snapped her focus toward the driver's door and . . .

Panic banded around her rib cage. Air left her chest in a rushing puff.

Holy God. A gun. Big, black, and ugly, the barrel hovered an inch from the glass. Another sharp rap. As she flinched, the person holding the weapon leaned down to look at her through the window. Raptor-flat, his blue eyes met hers and . . . *oh Lord, please send the swiftest of guardian angels.* Markov the Monster had found her. Hired muscle for the bookie she owed—no, strike that . . . not her, but *her mother* had owed—stood a foot away. Nothing but a flimsy door lock, tempered glass, and rusty steel between them.

Fear rattled her mental cage, making her temples throb.

A sinking feeling set in, fracturing her resolve. With a shaky breath, Evelyn struggled to control her reaction. Markov fed on fear. Which meant the second she showed any, he would press his advantage, and she'd be done. Over. Kaput with nowhere to run and even fewer places to hide. Knowing it, however, didn't lessen the pressure growing inside her head or slow the beat of her rampaging heart. She was in serious trouble. The kind she'd stayed ahead of . . .

Until now.

Dark hair gleaming in the lamp glow, Markov tapped the pistol against the window again. "Get out of the car, Ms. Foxe."

Fingertips trembling, Evelyn grasped the door handle with her left hand. White-knuckling her handbag with the other, she hesitated, debating. Options. She needed a few . . . right now.

Before fear got the better of her. Before the situation deteriorated. Before Markov decided to act, but—heaven help her. She couldn't think straight. Not with a gun pointed at her face. One thing for sure though? Driving away didn't qualify as a good idea. For one, she'd never find the keys at the bottom of her bag in time. The thug holding her hostage would shatter the glass and haul her out before she put her Golf in drive and her foot down. Which meant . . .

No hope of escape. Time to face the Monster.

Along with the Russian mob.

So tense her muscles ached, she popped the handle. Rusted-out hinges squeaked. Markov stepped back, giving her enough room to swing the door open. Taking a fortifying breath, Evelyn swiveled in the bucket seat and stepped out. The moment the soles of her black, snub-nosed stilettos touched down and she stood, Markov shifted toward her. Evelyn countered, sliding left toward the back bumper in the hopes he'd leave her untouched. No such luck. With a speed that belied his size, he slammed the car door shut and seized her wrist. His grip on her tightened. The bones in her hand protested the pressure. Pain spiraled up her forearm and streaked over her shoulder. He twisted, exposing her elbow joint to the cold night air. Her composure cracked, and she cried out as he shoved her backward.

Her back thumped against the side of her car.

The cashmere wrap she wore slipped off one shoulder, exposing a patch of bare skin. Goose bumps broke out on her upper arm. Trapped between him and the car, Evelyn bared her teeth. Showing weakness to a man who possessed none would be the kiss of death. It would only make Markov bolder and her appear more vulnerable. Not the best idea when dealing with bottom feeders who acted like great white sharks. Always on the hunt. Forever interested in finding the tastiest prey. No mercy in sight.

Clenching her free hand into a fist, she raised it in warning. "Get your hands off me, Markov."

His eyes narrowed on her knuckles, then cut back to meet her gaze. "You threatening me?"

"Injured people don't pay their bills."

"Not true, pigeon. Sometimes, they pay faster," he said, scraping her nerve endings raw with his thick Russian accent. Quiet. Calm. Controlled. His tone reminded her of a poisonous snake, coiled and ready to strike. "Isn't that so, Sergei?"

The name rippled through the quiet and landed like a threat.

A soft warning. An excellent reminder. Markov might be a sociopath, but at least he understood the concept of outstanding debt. Sergei, on the other hand? Her focus cut to the thug standing behind Markov. Boots planted in a golden pool cast by a street light, the Russian stood unmoving . . . cleaning his nails with the tip of a hunting knife. The wicked-looking blade gave Evelyn the shivers. No remorse in his expression. Not an ounce of compassion either. The Russian didn't own a conscience. She could see the truth in his eyes. The guy was a touch left of center, a blunt instrument used for one purpose.

Hurting those who didn't pay.

"*Da*. Seems to work that way." Black gaze unreadable, Sergei lifted the knife from his thumbnail. After a moment of reflection, he wiped the blade on his jean-clad thigh. "Gives 'em added incentive."

"Added incentive." Markov's mouth curved. He leaned in, dipped his head, using his size and strength to cage her. "I like that. Lovely turn of phrase."

"You do realize how wrong this is, right?" she asked without knowing why.

Reasoning with mobbed-up killers never got a person anywhere. Not when money was involved. Evelyn should know.

She'd been trying since the day Markov had shown up at her mother's funeral, insisting Evelyn assume the debt. One hundred and twenty-five grand to the penny. The mystery behind the amount wasn't difficult to figure out. A compulsive gambler, her mother had disappeared down the rabbit hole just after Evelyn's eleventh birthday.

Drugs. Alcohol. Illegal Blackjack tables. Name the vice, her mother had suffered from it.

Her dad had paid the price, working double shifts at the Seattle Port Authority, taking out loans, trying to keep his wife out of trouble with the bookie of the moment, pulling strings to get her into rehab a handful of times. Nothing had worked. No matter what Evelyn and her dad tried, the cards always proved stronger, dragging her mother in, taking both her parents before their time. Her dad of a heart attack at age fifty-nine. Her mother, just nine months ago, when she wrapped her car around a tree—accidently on purpose—on Interstate 5. The police labeled it a suicide. Open. Shut. Write the report and call it a day. And even though all the evidence supported the conclusion, Evelyn still found it difficult to accept.

Despite her mother's shortcomings, she'd loved her anyway.

"Right. Wrong . . ." Markov paused, then shrugged. "Fair's got nothing to do with it."

"It isn't my debt to pay."

"Yours? Your mother's? Makes no difference," he said. "Mr. Stampkos wants his money. We've discussed this already, Evelyn."

"It bears repeating."

His grip on her wrist tightened. "Do I need to visit your grandmother again?"

Alarm streaked through her. Dear God . . . no. No more late-night chats in Granite Falls. Mema deserved peace and couldn't handle another face-to-face with Markov. Evelyn frowned. All right, so that might not be true. At seventy-nine years young, her grandmother owned the disposition of a grizzly bear. No one pushed her around . . . Russian mobsters included. But that didn't change the facts. A repeat visit from Markov wouldn't end well. The second time was not the charm. Mema might end up in the hospital . . .

Or worse.

"No," Evelyn whispered, her throat so tight the word lacked strength. Leverage. Markov possessed all he needed. Hurt her grandmother, take the only person Evelyn loved, leave her with nothing. "Please leave her alone."

"Good," he said, nodding. "We understand each other, so . . . where's the money?"

"I have another day."

"Twenty-four hours. Not a lot of time to come up with five grand."

"I said I would get the money," she said, struggling to stay even. But God, it was hard. Especially while a thug held her hostage and terror shone a spotlight on her problems. All the nasty possibilities rose to taunt her . . . every single *what if.* What if she couldn't keep her word? What if she ran out of time? What if Markov went after her grandmother again? Terrible questions. Only one answer . . . find the money, make the next payment. Not an easy proposition. Her savings were gone. Her bank account was empty. And without a job? Forget asking a bank for a loan. Completely out of luck—the entire reason she stood here, across from a luxury hotel about to do something unconscionable. "And I will."

"Be sure that you do. Otherwise, I'll hand you over to Sergei." Pale eyes holding hers, Markov dug his nails into her arm. Blood welled on her skin. Swallowing a whimper, Evelyn shifted sideways against the car, trying to retreat as he raised his other hand.

Calloused fingers brushed over her cheekbone. She turned her face away, hating her helplessness almost as much as his proximity. With a hum of enjoyment, he traced the line of her jaw, then tapped the underside of her chin. "You've such beautiful skin, Evelyn. So soft and smooth. Far too fine to see marred by the edge of a blade."

Her stomach revolted, pitching in protest. "Let me go."

He laughed and released her wrist. "Fly away, little dove. One day 'til I see you again."

The instant Markov stepped back, Evelyn scooped her purse off the ground and escaped, slipping from between him and her car. All without looking him in the eye. The action smacked of cowardice, a condition she couldn't stand, but here . . . right this second . . . couldn't avoid either. If she met his gaze again, she'd crumble. Cry uncle. Make a fool of herself, plead for mercy and more time. Which would get her nowhere fast. Markov didn't have any mercy. He wasn't allowed to and keep his thuggish job. And honestly, Seattle didn't need another unemployed psychopath with an axe to grind.

Serial killers were born that way. Knife-wielding maniacs like Sergei too.

Another shiver rolled down her spine. Evelyn drew her shrug higher, wrapping the cashmere over her nape, crossing it over her breasts, desperate to insulate herself from the cold and the ugliness. She could feel Markov's gaze boring into the back of her head. Dangerous. Unpredictable. Barely sane. And as she crossed the road, stilettos clicking against cracked pavement, and entered the circular drive in front of the Luxmore, she wondered—not for the first time—how things had gone so horribly wrong.

She frowned. God must not like her very much.

Evidence of his disfavor peppered her life—financial ruin, emotional hardship, self-worth in shambles . . . the mob after her.

Holy hell and a hula hoop, could it get any worse? The second the question entered her mind, Evelyn shoved it away. Dumb question. Of course it could get worse. It already had. Proof positive loomed ten steps in front of her, a stretch of hotel doors and one hellish night ahead.

Taking a deep breath, she squared her shoulders and, knee-length dress pulling at her thighs, kept walking. The frostbitten plants surrounding the drive welcomed her. Deep-seated dread joined the click of her high heels on cobblestone, sounding lonely in the night air. Standing post alongside the chrome-clad doors and art deco opulence, the valets heard her coming. She put some sway into her approach, let her hips roll, kept her chin level, and stepped out of the shadows along the garden walkway. The doorman closest to her inhaled in surprise. A second later, his jaw dropped. Evelyn smiled. Good. His reaction was an excellent start. If she could wow the employees with her appearance—look rich and act the part—no one would guess the reason behind her visit tonight.

A big bonus considering her true purpose.

The pair stepped forward as she mounted the sidewalk in front of the Luxmore. Each wished her good evening. She answered with silence, opting to nod instead before gesturing toward the middle door. The duo jumped to open it, fumbling over themselves, bumping shoulders in an attempt to serve her first. Evelyn almost laughed. God, it was so easy to fool people into believing that she belonged. Inevitable, she guessed. She'd perfected the art of blending in. Had spent countless hours in high-priced boardrooms, wielding authority like an executive, subduing powerful CEOs who didn't enjoy hearing the truth about company finances.

The door opened with a whisper.

Without hesitation, Evelyn stepped over the threshold and into the grand lobby. Three stories high, the space screamed elegance. Art deco perfection with marble floors set in an intricate pattern, muted orange, sharp gray, black inlay accenting the whole. Black lacquered smooth-faced columns ran the gauntlet, standing sentry beside pale walls that showcased a sweeping staircase, delicate steel banister rising from stair treads to meet the curved railing.

Busy tonight, the lobby was full of people. Some no doubt waiting for tables in the bar and restaurant. Others content to sip their drinks and spend the night surrounded by friends and luxury. Leaving the edge of the fray, Evelyn swept the scene, searching for her contact. Not on the couches pushed up against the far wall. Not sitting in the smattering of leather armchairs clustered throughout the space either. She glanced to her left. A trio of puffs, firm circular cushions with high seat-back towers in the center, occupied the left side of the room. A twenty-something brunette, decked out in Chanel, met her gaze. Trixie, the woman she'd met two days ago in the Luxmore's bar. She'd been applying for a job as a bartender (desperation, after all, couldn't be denied) and ended up chatting with Trixie instead.

A smart woman. The calculating kind, and . . . wait for it . . . one of Seattle's most successful madams.

Not that the police knew it.

Trixie understood the terrain and knew how to fly under the radar. She accepted few women into her fold and only dealt with rich clientele. Add sophistication and oodles of charm into the mix, and . . . little doubt. The cops didn't stand a chance. No one wanted to get on Trixie's bad side, the men who enjoyed her escort service included. Evelyn had no doubt the madam would wield her little black book—and all the names inside it—to ensure protection for her girls and save her own hide.

Legs crossed, posture relaxed, confidence out in full force, Trixie smiled as she approached. She patted the seat next to her with a manicured hand. "I didn't think you would show up tonight."

Evelyn swallowed. "Neither did I."

Sliding onto the puff next to her new friend, she scanned the room. Rich men wearing expensive suits, sipping expensive drinks from VIP tumblers. Everywhere she looked she saw the divide—the have-nots serving the have-alls. It didn't seem fair. Then again, not much in life ever was—witness the fact she sat inside a posh hotel about to prostitute herself to save her own neck. Revulsion spread like poison, burning a hole in her belly. God, it was disgusting. And more than just a step down. It equaled failure on a grand scale. But the broke and halfway-to-being-murdered couldn't be picky. The deterioration of her situation demanded a quick plan and steady heart. But even as she told herself no other choice existed, dread, fear, and the inevitable questions circled.

Was she really going to do this? Could she really see it through to the end?

Markov's face morphed in her mind's eye.

Dragging her gaze away from the throng, Evelyn smoothed her palm over her skirt. Do or die. Hadn't she said that earlier? Yes. Absolutely. She was out of options and little choice remained.

"It's not forever, Trixie." Crossing her legs, she turned toward the madam. "I need the money right now, that's all."

Concern spiked in Trixie's eyes. "Someone threatening you?"

"The reasons don't matter, but fair warning," she said, deciding to be honest. "As soon as I make enough, I'm gone. As long as you understand that, we'll have no problems."

"Honest of you."

"Fair play is one of my strong suits."

"Mine as well. You'll have no trouble from me, but you have my support." Trixie gave her a pointed look. "If you have any issues—any at all—you come to me. Understood?"

Evelyn nodded.

Respect in her eyes, Trixie opened the clutch in her lap. A quick search. An even faster sleight of hand, and she slid a room keycard toward Evelyn across the upholstery between them. "Room 301 . . . take the stairs, then a left at the top. The suite is to your right, along the first corridor."

"Thank you," she whispered, and . . . ah, crap. Reduced to thanking a madam who ran a high-end escort service. One who now employed her. Forget the shame. The whole thing was a total catastrophe. Smoothing her skirt one last time, Evelyn pushed to her feet. "See you later."

"Evelyn?"

A lump in her throat, she glanced over her shoulder.

Green eyes full of understanding, Trixie met her gaze. "The first time is always the hardest, my dear. It gets easier with time."

Dear God, she hoped not.

Evelyn didn't want it to get any easier. She wanted to remember this feeling, the one rooted in self-loathing and hardship. Time wouldn't blunt it. Neither would the idea of necessity. And as she walked across the lobby, around rich patrons, past beautiful furniture, and climbed the stairs, she knew the ugliness would stay with her forever. It had come down to this . . . to her and the awfulness of the moment. Her life or her virtue. Sad to say, but right now she couldn't have both.

Chapter Three

Cloaked in magic, invisible to human eyes, Venom walked into the Luxmore looking for three things. A drink, a beautiful female, and sex. The hit list equaled sanity on a large scale. And the upscale boutique hotel? He smiled. Sheer perfection. The first item on his list would be simple enough to acquire. Jägermeister on ice, three shots straight up. The promise of it lay one right turn and fifty ground-eating strides across the lobby, a wide, single archway between him and the Triton Bar & Grill. An easy walk under normal circumstances. Tonight, though, didn't fall into that category.

Easy had nothing to do with it. Not while out in the city . . .

Without a wingman to watch his six.

Slipping into the shadows beside the front doors, he set up shop next to a potted plant and, pressing his shoulder blades to the wall, shoved his hands into his jean pockets. Probably not the best way to go. The Levi's, along with his T-shirt and leather jacket, screamed underdressed. Venom didn't care. He hadn't made the trip into Seattle to socialize with the city's elite. He'd done enough of that while living in Prague with his sire . . . before his *change*. Before his dragon DNA activated, allowing him to shift from human to dragon form. The memories weren't good ones. His father had seen to it. Meant to belittle and hurt him . . . break him—no matter how well dressed or behaved he'd been.

Sadistic males were like that, brutalizing those they deemed unworthy. Trumped-up charges. Imagined offenses. Unfounded accusations. All came part and parcel with the package. Nothing Venom could've done to stem the tide of his sire's rage. The general hadn't needed a reason to hurt him. His own amusement had been reason enough.

The thought made his throat tighten.

Venom shook his head. He needed to stop thinking about it. About the thick post standing upright on the beachhead. About being tied to it at low tide—hands bound by heavy rope, spine flush against the wooden pole, heart hammering as salt water washed around his feet, then rose above his head. Shit, he'd only been nine years old when his sire started the punishment. Too young to understand. Far too vulnerable to fight back. Unable to protect himself from the one male who should've shielded him, not hurt him.

All right, so the beatings hadn't killed him.

And he'd never drowned.

But it had been close more than once. He relived the horror of it every time he closed his eyes. Had nightmares of the world going dark, of doctors rushing to revive him, of his sire reprimanding him for his lack of stamina—his inability to hold his breath and stay afloat in the cold ocean froth. Venom shivered. He could still smell the brine. Still felt the water in his mouth, rolling down his throat, filling up his lungs. No matter how much he tried to put it behind him, the ugliness continued to taunt him. He'd never been good enough. Not for his sire, never mind the Dragonkind aristocracy he'd been born into, so . . .

Screw the Luxmore fat cats in their expensive suits and shiny shoes.

He didn't give a shit about etiquette. Or toeing the line in the human world. The self-important assholes could all go straight to hell. No passing *GO*. No collecting their money on the way out.

Eyes narrowed on the crowd, Venom lifted the cloaking spell, allowing the shadows free rein as he stared at the entrance into the bar area. Yeah. No sweat. A simple hop, skip, and jump away from an establishment full of females. Dragging his gaze from Triton's, he swept the lobby again, hopscotching over human heads. Fluted wall sconces and chrome chandeliers threw illumination like dice, enveloping the circular space in a warm glow. Chatter rose around him, male voices mixing with female, sound rising to meet the ceiling three stories up. Habit made him search for trouble. Instinct told him there wasn't any to be found. His dragon senses pinged, backing up intuition. No danger on the wide mezzanine at the top of the stairs. No Razorbacks hiding in the throng of humans. Nothing out of the ordinary at all.

Venom nodded. Excellent. All clear. Time to go to work.

And yet, he didn't move.

Flexing his hands, he shifted his shoulders against the wall. Being here alone wasn't the best move. Then again, he'd known that before flying away from the lair. And no matter how much his conscience squawked and the past taunted, his intentions hadn't changed. He needed a distraction. Something to hold his attention long enough to alleviate the tension. Venom could feel the pressure building. The dangerous swell dragged him closer to the edge, making discontent seethe just beneath the surface of his skin.

By no means a great way to start the night. Seduction required patience and a gentle hand. Which necessitated keeping his cool long enough to achieve his goal. A good plan all the way around. Particularly since females ran scared at the first hint of his temper, so . . . yeah. Time to shut down the bullshit. Otherwise he wouldn't get what he craved—connection and closeness, the slick, creamy slide between a female's thighs.

The thought sent a thrum of anticipation through him.

Reality leaned in to rain on his parade.

Goddamned limitations. Forty minutes with a female wasn't going to be enough. He needed more tonight. More time. More than a brief taste. And a helluva lot more touch. He wanted to hold and be held in return. To talk the night away while luxuriating in a female's arms. Wishing for something, however, never made it happen. Or changed the facts. The poison in his veins wouldn't allow that kind of intimacy.

Venom swallowed the bitter taste of disappointment. Reduced to small snatches of time with the opposite sex. Such a frigging tragedy. An unchangeable one he accepted without question. Well, at least most of the time. Sometimes—like tonight . . . when his loneliness escalated—he despised the magic in his blood. And the fact he could kill a female with his touch if he wasn't careful.

The neurotoxins in his skin worked fast.

A fantastic asset in dragon form. Not so hot while standing in a lobby full of females, most of whom wouldn't survive the intensity of his touch. Low-energy females never could. So yeah. No matter how burning his need, his strategy remained the same. Seduce a female with good energy—and a strong link to the Meridian, the electrostatic bands that ringed the planet and nourished all living things—obtain what he needed to keep breathing, then get out, and go home.

Before anyone realized he was gone.

The last part of the plan was paramount. He didn't want Bastian and the boys coming after him. Particularly since he wasn't 100 percent on the physical front. The flash'n fly from the lair had drained the last of his resources. Throw in all the booze and the fact he hadn't touched a female in days and . . . no question. He needed to feed. Could feel the energy drain and accompanying muscle weakness. A shot of female energy would plug him back in—restore his core strength, nourish his body, giving him what he required to stay healthy.

A necessity considering he couldn't link into the Meridian on his own.

Cursed by the Goddess of All Things centuries ago, the connection between Dragonkind and the source of all power lay shattered. Serious damage. No hope of repairing it. A single moment in time, the totality of which equaled unfair in big ways. The fracture changed everything. Now his kind stood on the brink—outnumbered thousands to one by the human race, forced to rely on their females for survival, hemmed in by circumstance and a rift so wide magic couldn't span it. Not that he blamed the goddess for throwing the legendary hissy fit. Some things, after all, a female didn't forgive.

Infidelity appeared to be one of them.

Venom sighed. The dragon god screwed up royally that day. He flexed his hands again, itching to put his hands around the deity's throat and squeeze. What the hell had possessed the male to sleep with a wood nymph when he should've been at home—in bed—with the Goddess of All Things? The action smacked of idiocy. He frowned. Or selfishness. Venom didn't know which, but one thing for sure? Silfer had outdone himself . . . and dragged all of Dragonkind down with him.

Stupid dragon god. Dumb-ass to the next power.

Rolling his shoulders, Venom pushed away from the wall and strode toward the Triton. His eyes skipped over the crowd again. He pursed his lips. Nah. Forget the lobby. No good candidates there. Time to take a look-see inside the bar. The sooner he found a female with strong energy, the quicker he could go home.

And pretend like he'd been a good warrior, played by the rules, and stayed at Black Diamond. An excellent strategy. Particularly since it would ensure he fell into bed without any bruises.

Or a row of cracked ribs.

Halfway across the lobby, a flash of light caught his eye. Slowing his pace, Venom glanced to his right and—

He sucked in a quick breath. No way. It couldn't be, but . . . he blinked and refocused. Yup. Absolutely. No mistaking that glow. His eyes weren't deceiving him. High-energy female at three o'clock, alone, pretty, bright-yellow aura filling out the space around her. Seated in the middle of a long couch, cell phone in hand and eyes glued to the small screen, the petite brunette was the perfect mark. One more than capable of tolerating his touch while feeding him from the source. Shock spiraled deep. Interest made him tense. Venom shook off both reactions as the truth sank in. Holy shit. Silfer grant him grace—an HE female sitting in plain view, right in the middle of the Luxmore.

No wonder Sloan liked it here so much.

Boots planted fifteen feet away, he ran his gaze over her again. He wavered a moment. She wasn't his type. Not really. He preferred dark-skinned females to light, but then a hungry male couldn't be choosy. No matter his preferences, she would do. Only an idiot, after all, encountered an HE and turned away. And no wonder. High-energy females were a unique breed. So rare most males never encountered one in their lifetime. Seattle, however, seemed to be a hotspot for HEs. Which made a lot of sense considering the city sat in the middle of one of the Meridian's electrostatic bands. Theory suggested more HEs were born near the vertical strips that connected the North and South Poles.

Good for his pack. Better for him right now. Particularly since he was about to get up close and personal with the female absorbed in the contents of her iPhone.

With a quick shift, he changed trajectory, moving toward her and away from the bar. Sensing his approach, she looked up from her phone. Dark-green eyes met his, then roamed his body, assessing him from head to toe. Full lips curved in welcome. Venom swallowed a growl of anticipation. Fantastic. Her expression relayed what he needed to know. She liked what she saw. Was totally into him and up for a little fun.

Boot soles brushing over polished marble, he stopped a few feet away. She tipped her chin, indicating the club chair across from her. He stifled a surge of satisfaction. Fantastic. Just what he'd been looking for—an invitation without any of the usual chitchat. Sidestepping the coffee table, Venom sat and settled in. Leather sighed. Thick cushions acquiesced, doing their job, supporting his frame, letting him get comfortable. Silence swelled, piercing through the human chatter as she took his measure. His mouth curved. Nice. She was even prettier up close. Looked polished in her designer clothes too, but even better than that? She understood the power of a charged pause, wielding it like a homemade weapon.

"Ven," he said, supplying his name to break the ice.

"Trixie."

Shifting forward in the chair, he raised a brow. "Short for Beatrix?"

"Maybe." An amused glint in her eyes, she set the iPhone in her lap. "Fair warning, Ven. I come with conditions."

Blatant. Sexual. The double entendre wasn't lost on Venom. *Come with conditions*, indeed. The statement drew him tight. Wow, she was bold. "What kind of conditions?"

"Expensive ones."

Ah, well . . . that explained it. A call girl, a well-educated, high-end one by the sound of her. Made sense. Not much of a stretch on the connect-the-dots front. She looked the part. Trim cocktail dress made by Chanel. Thigh-high boots bought at Gucci. Sophisticated. Expensive. And by the guarded light in her eyes, worried he'd condemn her line of work as well.

"Are you worth it?" he asked, teasing her to lighten the mood. He wanted her willing, not wary. Judging another's life choices wasn't his style. God knew he didn't have a clean record . . . or an untainted past.

Her lips twitched. "Every penny."

"Then I am willing to pay." An easier solution. Much faster than seduction. Right up his alley tonight.

"A few questions first."

"Only fair." A master of the game, Venom slid to the edge of his seat. Bracing his elbows on his knees, he leaned forward, needing to get closer to the bio-energy she threw off like a supernova. Heat prickled through him. Venom locked it down. No sense scaring her . . . or losing his chance to convince Trixie he was worth the risk. Habit laced his fingers between the spread of his thighs. Experience coupled with patience helped him settle in for the chat. "Shoot."

A slight furrow between her brows, she looked away. Her gaze roamed the crowd a moment, then returned to him. Razor-sharp intellect on display, she assessed him with keen eyes. "Are you a gentle lover?"

"When a female wants me to be."

She treated him to a pointed look. "Willing to cede to a woman's wishes?"

"In bed—yes."

"A gentleman," she murmured, approval in her tone. "No means no."

"Without question."

Her eyes narrowed a second before she pursed her lips, as though unconvinced. As though testing his character. As though she owned the book cataloging the entire male species and had memorized every page by heart. After a moment's hesitation, Trixie nodded, and palming her cell phone, tapped the top of her thigh three times with her index finger, giving him a number. Venom raised a brow. Wow. Three thousand dollars for a female's time. Some might find the price steep. Not him. All things considered—her powerful connection to the Meridian included—it made for a pretty good deal.

He pretended to think about it, not wanting to seem easy. "For an hour? Or the night?"

"Stay an hour or the night . . . you decide. But by seven a.m., it's over and you're gone."

"Deal."

She blew out a long breath. "Promise to be patient."

"Of course," he said, responding to the soft plea in her voice. Venom smothered a frown as intuition whispered. Something about her request didn't ring true. It was almost as if, well . . . he didn't know exactly. She sounded uncertain and protective, as though concerned for someone other than herself. "You have my word."

"All right, then." Pausing to smooth her skirt, she uncrossed her legs and got to her feet. With a quick snap, she opened her purse, reached inside, and came away with a keycard. She hesitated a split second. Venom held his breath and, hoping she didn't back out, started to count. *One. Two. Three* . . . The card landed on the seat cushion she'd vacated. He watched it settle against the dark upholstery, then met her gaze. Trixie didn't make him wait. She gave him instructions instead. "Wait ten minutes, then go upstairs. You pay before you get started. Room 301 is on the mezzanine level."

He nodded.

Without making a sound, she walked away, leaving him tense and needy. Nerves shot to hell, he wanted to ignore the instructions and follow her retreat. He switched seats and picked up the keycard instead, settling into upholstery still warm from her body. Sensation swirled up his spine, urging him to go. Venom locked his muscles, forcing his body into submission. Rushing her wouldn't get him what he wanted—her naked . . . him deep inside her. Knowing it, however, didn't help. Anticipation tightened its grip, making impatience rise as time stretched and seconds ticked past. Turning the slim card over in his hand, he distracted himself by watching the human hive buzz a few feet away.

Ten minutes wasn't that long. Just a slice of time. Hardly worth his consideration at all and . . .

Venom shoved up the sleeve of his leather jacket. Lamplight flashed off the face of his MTM military watch. He hummed, the sound more growl than soft roll. Nine minutes down, one to go. Time to get off his duff and make his way upstairs. Pushing to his feet, he stepped around the coffee table and skirted the armchair. Footfalls silent, pace steady, he took a direct route across the lobby. His boots brushed over polished marble. The sweet scent of vermouth and twenty-dollar cocktails teased his senses. He snarled at the male closest to him. The human jumped like a jackrabbit, scurrying out of his way, causing a chain reaction as the crowd between him and the staircase scattered before he got anywhere near them. Thank God. The last thing he wanted was interference. Not with time ticking down and Trixie waiting.

Hopefully in nothing but lace panties and a push-up bra.

The image grabbed him by the balls. Venom upped the pace, eagerness playing its part as hunger overwhelmed him. He was starving, so parched he couldn't swallow anymore.

Taking the treads two at a time, he navigated the staircase. A couple of females smiled at him as he mounted, and they descended—long legs on display, high heels muffled by the carpet runner, hips swaying in challenge. He ignored the come-hither looks, and bypassing the pair, paused on the top step. His attention narrowed on the wall signs.

His gaze snapped to the left. Room 301 . . . that-a-way.

The curved banister swung him around its high-polished contour and into the double-wide corridor. Dimmed down, the wall sconces cast odd shadows across the pale carpet. Sounds drifted up from the lobby below. Venom barely noticed. Focused on the doors marching down one side of the hallway, he read the room numbers and . . .

Bingo. Objective acquired. One high-energy female on tap.

He stopped and faced the door. With a quick twist, he rotated the keycard in his hand and pushed it into the slim slot in the reader. The light on the mechanism went from red to green. Heart hammering, need set to apocalyptic, Venom unleashed his magic and, opening the door with a mental flick, stepped over the threshold. His eyes adjusted to the low light. His gaze found the female standing across the room, staring out the window and—

She turned to look at him. Dark eyes found his from across the room. Venom's breath caught in the back of his throat.

"Holy shit," he murmured, not understanding the switch-up.

Feet rooted to the floor, he swallowed and, unable to take his eyes off her, tried to make his brain work. A hard sell. One made more difficult by the fact she wasn't the female he'd met downstairs. Not Trixie. Someone else and—oh, baby—even higher energy than her friend in the lobby. Venom swallowed a growl as his dragon half rose, fixating on her, urging him to get closer and see if he got zapped by the Meridian. Eternal. Beautiful. Power pulsed in her aura, a soft green that made her glow from the inside out. Making him *want* so hard his mouth started to water.

Oh God. She was going to taste good.

Allowing his gaze to roam, he skimmed her silhouette, undressing her with his eyes. Slim but curvy. Absolute perfection with ink-black curls framing her face, falling to her shoulders, causing her to shimmer with vitality. Five feet eight—maybe five seven without her stilettos—she owned a pair of long legs, the kind made for wrapping around a male's waist. Venom frowned. No . . . strike that. Forget the generic word *male*, replace it with his name, 'cause . . . umm. He'd just hit the jackpot. The female across the room was even better than Trixie. Mocha-colored skin, gorgeous brown eyes, and a full mouth meant for kissing, she hit every note on his sliding gotta-have-her scale. Arousal hammered him like a closed fist. His body responded, absorbing the shockwave as Venom stepped farther into the room.

The door clicked shut in his wake. Silence stepped into the void, and . . .

God forgive him. So much for his promise.

He'd lied to Trixie. Patience was no longer part of the plan. He wanted the female standing across the room too much. The cascade of desire overwhelmed him. Rational thought ceased to exist. Forget the surroundings and his usual caution. Only one thing held sway. He needed to be skin-to-skin with her. And he needed it now.

She should say something. Really. She should. Right now—before the heavy silence grew any thicker. But as Evelyn held her mysterious date's gaze from across the room, words failed her. So did brainpower. Her mind had shorted out or something. Gone haywire the instant his eyes settled on her. She swallowed, trying to calm the chaotic flutter behind her breastbone, but, well . . . might as well give up the effort. Righting the arrhythmia was wishful thinking. Her heart had gone ballistic, thumping hard, making her blood rush, her ears ring, and her mind splinter. Now she couldn't catch a thought. Except for one . . .

God be good to her, he was gorgeous.

Tall. Sculpted. Big, blond, and beautiful. One of God's great gifts to womankind—the sort created for the cover of *GQ* magazine. And not the kind of man who paid for sex. Ever. Pure supposition? Evelyn released a pent-up breath. Not even close. The conclusion was bang-on accurate, supported by an inescapable fact . . .

The guy oozed sex appeal. Not the tame kind either.

His allure was more lethal than that. Pure, unapologetic animal magnetism wrapped up in an incredible package that ticked all her boxes. Well, at least, under normal circumstances. Not that it mattered. Her body was too busy reacting to his presence. To the tug and tangle of physical attraction, making her go through the usual checklist against her will. Thick, shoulder length hair—check. Biker jacket over a wide-shouldered, long-limbed, muscular body—double check. A face every male supermodel on earth would envy and . . .

Bing-bam-boom. The trifecta of sexiness was complete.

Hitch that to the hard-core vibe he threw off like pheromones and . . . holy crap. No doubt about it. Mr. Sexy didn't belong in an expensive hotel room with a desperate temporary call girl. He belonged at the center of attention. Surrounded by willing women who'd give both eyeteeth—maybe an arm and a leg too—for a chance to sleep with him. For free. Scrap the three thousand dollar price tag and—

Ah, frig. That cinched it. Something about him was all wrong.

The thought collapsed into another. Mental dominoes fell, raising serious red flags. Evelyn frowned. What the heck was going on? Was Mr. Sexy on the up-and-up? Had Trixie really sent him? Or was his arrival rooted in something more sinister—like the Russian mob and a man named Markov. A shiver rolled down her spine. Goose bumps followed, making her skin prickle and her instincts buzz. Oh, no. Not good. The power play had Markov written all over it. The psycho liked games and making other people squirm. Which meant he was more than capable of letting her go in the parking lot only to send another man after her inside the Luxmore. With one purpose in mind . . .

To catch her off guard. To get her alone. And teach her a lesson.

Lacing her fingers, Evelyn pressed her damp palms together and forced herself to think. All right. No sense letting panic out of the bag. Not yet anyway. She didn't know what she was dealing with and until she did—well, calm and collected would get her further than freaked out and fearful. Smoothing her expression, she squared her shoulders. A game plan and something to hide behind. She needed both . . . this instant. Maybe a weapon too. The ashtray sitting on the antique desk to her left, perhaps. The lamp to her right on the side table. The sharp tip of her stilettos. Anything would do, just as long as it slowed him down when he decided to come after her.

Stepping away from the window, Evelyn slid behind a couple of boxy club chairs. Her foot bumped the side table sitting between the deep-seated duo. The free-standing lamp swayed. The light shade wobbled like a bobble-head, casting odd shadows over light-green upholstery, and—

Mr. Sexy stepped away from the door and into the room.

Evelyn flinched.

"Relax, *mazleiha*." His deep voice rolled, bridging the distance between them, calming her with surprising swiftness. Strange, but . . . he sounded just right. His slight accent—eastern European maybe—along with his gentle tone tugged at her tension, urging her to do as he asked and relax. Not that she would. Sex might be part of the deal. Trust, however, was not. "Trixie sent me."

The knots in her stomach loosened a little. "Prove it."

"The keycard not enough for you?"

"No."

He grinned, the approval in his eyes unmistakable. "Good for you, love. Never take anything at face value."

Unimpressed by his praise, she gave him a pointed look.

"Green eyes. Brown hair. She's dressed to the nines in Chanel and Gucci tonight. More interested in her iPhone than the crowd. She asked me to be patient with you," he murmured, his gaze wandering over her. The slow, heated perusal made her skin prickle and . . . oh Nelly. Call her cooked and then call it a night. Mr. Sexy knew what he was doing. A master of the game, he stripped her with a look, leaving her defenseless as he undressed her with his eyes. He growled, the low purr full of promise. Evelyn tensed, finding pleasure in the soft sound against her will. "Good enough?"

"Good enough," she said, repeating his words. Unable to find her own.

With a flick, he tossed the keycard on the dresser across from the king-size bed. As it slid to a stop beneath the flat screen TV, he reached inside his jacket pocket. He fished for a moment. Her heart slammed into her breastbone. Panic thumped on her, urging her to run. And yet, she couldn't move, never mind look away. Like a spectator at a train crash, she bore witness to her doom—the reality of the horrific situation transfixing her as she watched him pull a roll of cash from behind his leather lapel. He tipped the bundle in his hand, letting her look before setting the money down beside the keycard.

Holding her gaze, he raised a brow. "Three grand—the going rate, I'm told."

Throat gone tight, Evelyn stared at the money. One-hundred dollar bills. All rolled together. Neat. Tidy. The answer to her problems and—

She smothered a cry of dismay. God forgive her. Was she really going to do this? Forsake her dignity? Forget her upbringing—all the morals her father had instilled in her—and sleep with a stranger . . . for money?

Shame tightened her chest, making it hard to breathe.

Fighting the shift toward humiliation, Evelyn reached for pragmatism. She couldn't deny the truth. Or avoid the inevitable. Much as she despised her circumstances, nothing had changed. The money or her life. Markov sat smack-dab in the middle of the mess. Wouldn't be going anywhere anytime soon either. Which meant no choice remained. Mr. Sexy was exactly what she needed—a wealthy patron willing to pay for the one thing she should be giving away for free . . .

To a man who loved her. Not a complete stranger with perfect bone structure.

He tipped his chin. "You ready?"

No. She wasn't *ready*. No matter what happened tonight—or how many times he took her—she never would be either. "Anything in particular you want?"

"For three grand, I want everything."

She shivered. "Nothing rough. I won't—"

"Nothing rough," he said, his tone soft with reassurance. With a shoulder roll, he shrugged out of his biker jacket and tossed it on the end of the bed. The white duvet sighed, giving way beneath heavy black leather. He flexed his hands, as though preparing to touch her, and took a step in her direction. "Just pleasure, *mazleiha*. For both of us. I promise."

"Okay." Unable to meet his gaze, Evelyn stepped out from behind the chair. Bowing her head, she reached for her heel. Her stiletto came off with a tug. She dropped the first to the floor and attacked the second. As the pair hit the carpet with a soft thud, nerves got the better of her. Releasing a shaky breath, Evelyn cleared her throat. "Do you want me to undress you or would you prefer—"

"What is your name?"

"Evelyn."

"Anyone ever call you Evie?"

"Sometimes."

"Then come here, Evie." Standing at the end of the bed, he held his hand palm up, inviting her to come to him. "Let me hold you for a minute."

A reasonable request. Welcome too, particularly since it bought her a little more time: to accept, to acclimatize, to get used to the idea of being stripped bare and put on display by a stranger. "Your name first."

"Venom."

She blinked. "Really?"

"Really. My sire thought it suited me."

"Oh," she whispered, her mind whirling. Strange name. Weird phrasing in the word *sire*. Not American at all. "Guess you do things differently in Europe, huh?"

"We do," he said, giving nothing away, a smile in his tone as he flicked his fingers. The movement spoke of impatience. His body language, however, said something else. He was relaxed. Prepared to be indulgent . . . but only to a point. "Now—are you done stalling?"

"No stalling. Just getting to know you better," she said, lying through her teeth. Of course she was stalling. The tactic seemed like the best option. The longer she dodged the inevitable, the less time they would spend in bed together. She gestured to the antique sideboard behind her. Crystal decanters filled with hard liquor winked in the low light. "Can I get you a drink?"

"No," he said. "Come here, Evie. Get used to me before I lay you down."

Lay you down.

The words echoed inside her head. A buzz lit off between her temples. Oh, mercy. She'd just run out of time. To be expected. Venom was right. Stalling wouldn't change a thing. Or make her feel any better about what she must do. Which meant she needed to move forward instead of away. The sooner she let him touch her, the faster the night would end. But as she crossed the room, slid her hand into his much larger one, and let him reel her in, Evelyn knew she would never be the same. She'd crossed a line. Was now in dangerous territory, a place from which she would never return.

The desire in Venom's eyes told her so.

His murmur of pleasure as she settled in his arms sealed the deal.

He would take her without mercy—use her . . . consume her—then let her go and never look back. The truth of it hit her hard, wounding her soul deep. But even as she ached for the girl she was tonight—and would no longer be tomorrow—Evelyn refused to back away. Now or never. Sink or swim. Time to throw herself into the deep end and pray she surfaced unscathed in the morning.

Chapter Four

Somewhere in Prague, Czech Republic

The sound of dripping water echoed off thick stone walls, collecting against the curved arch of an ancient ceiling. Drip-drip, pause. Drip-drip, plunk. The raindrop struck metal. A ping echoed through the quiet. Gage flinched as a droplet sizzled on electrified steel, cooking like an egg, evaporating off the crosspiece above his head. Less than an inch from where one of his wrists lay cuffed to the vertical grill.

Metal cut into his skin.

Blood rolled down the inside of his forearm.

His muscles flickered in protest. Another drop fell, missing steel to splatter across the nape of his neck. A chill worked its way down his spine, following the awful slide of cold water. Not optimal. Nowhere near good. In a perfect world, he would've broken the steel cuffs and moved. Taken self-preservation out for a spin and a giant step to his right. Out of the water's path. Out of the line of fire. Away from the entire situation—and all the pain. A lovely thought after the fact. Too little, too late as it turned out.

Rodin and his crew had done it right. Set up the ambush like pros—striking in the narrow alleyway, hitting him and Haider with forty thousand volts each, obliterating all hope of shifting into dragon form and getting airborne. A smart move on Rodin's part. A boneheaded move on Gage's. He'd known the Archguard jerkoffs would play dirty. Shit, he'd expected it. Had prepared for it, but . . .

Gage huffed. His bad along with the blame. He'd made a fatal mistake and taken the bait. One damsel in distress being attacked in a dark alley. A mere moment of distraction. A single teeny-tiny mistake and—

The assholes had struck.

Before he'd registered the threat.

If he had, he'd be halfway home by now. Hours from Seattle and the Nightfury lair. Safe. Secure. In the bosom of his family, not here: spread-eagle, hands and feet cuffed to a vertical grill, awaiting the next round of torture inside a death squad's kill room.

Multiple floor drains told the tale.

So did the scent of other warriors' blood.

Males came here to die. Got strung up inside the underground tomb all the time. Wrists and ankles shackled with steel cuffs. Limbs stretched wide across the large grate bolted to the wall. Blood flowing like rivers while electricity coursed through the metal rack. Standing with his back against the diagonal crisscross of bars, Gage tested his restraints again. No good. After three hours in hell, he was too weak. Electric shock ensured he stayed that way, stealing his strength, shutting down his magic, destroying any hope of escape.

A tough spot for any warrior to be in.

Someone turned a tap. Metal squeaked as the nozzle spun. Water drizzled into a steady sprinkle, coating his skin and the cables clamped to the sides of the rack above his head. Electricity snapped. Sparks flew, cascading into brilliant shards. The pop-pop-pop rattled the grill. Steel bars vibrated behind him, zapping Gage with another shot of high voltage. His muscles contracted as his body shuddered and his mind recoiled. He bit down on a groan, refusing to show any weakness. Or surrender. Not that his bravado mattered. Gage knew it. So did Zidane—the asshole with a nasty disposition and a whole table full of torture tools. Resistance was nothing but pride in another form. Sooner or later, the brutal claw of electrical current would become too much. He'd pass out. Lose his ability to fight, and succumb to the pain.

Just as Haider had done.

One eye swollen shut, Gage cracked the other open. The room wavered, moving into, then out of, focus. He gritted his teeth. Fucking pricks. Archguard assholes. They'd made him watch. Had kept him weak, but cognizant while Haider suffered. While Zidane—Rodin's heir—wielded brass knuckles and knives, brutalizing his best friend. The memory clawed at his heart. Watching Haider be hurt had been terrible. The worst thing he'd ever been forced to endure. Now he couldn't push the awful images from his mind. Or accept that he'd been unable to protect his friend. Add that colossal mind fuck to the fact he didn't know where Zidane had taken Haider after he'd finished torturing him and—

Anguish tightened its grip.

Gage squeezed his good eye shut and breathed through the pain. He must stay steady. Remain even and ready, able to attack fast and strike hard when the enemy least expected. Otherwise, he wouldn't make it out alive.

And neither would Haider.

Eyes closed, head bowed, Gage curled his hands into fists. The twin cuffs cut deeper. Blood trickled from his wrists, mixing with water, dribbling down the inside of his arms. He ignored the slow roll and stayed on task. Focus. Intent. Skill. Three things he owned in spades and put to work, calling on what remained of his magic. Weak, but still cognizant, his dragon half rose, sharpening his senses. Sound ricocheted inside his head. He listened harder, tracking his captors' movements inside the torture chamber. The duo stood somewhere off to his left. No doubt in front of the table laid out with sharp tools. He heard the soft rustle of clothing. Each rasp of boot soles against the concrete floor. The awful scrape of a knife being drawn over a whetstone.

He clenched his teeth. God forbid the jerkoffs use a dull blade to cut him open.

Another swipe of steel against stone. "Which do you want next, Zidane?"

"The pliers," Zidane said, an edge of anticipation in his tone. "The Nightfury has too many teeth. What say you, Ferland?"

"Start with his canines. It'll hurt more."

"No doubt. Do you want the honor of pulling the first or—"

"Go ahead." Steel teeth snapped, breaking through the quiet as Ferland tested the tool. "I enjoy watching you work. True artistry."

Zidane laughed. "Reset the camera, Ferland."

Gage tracked Ferland across the dungeon in his periphery. Blond hair glinting in the low light, the male stopped beside the tripod holding a high-tech camera. Stifling a snarl, Gage swallowed the metallic taste of his own blood. Sick bastards. The pair took cruelty to new heights, recording each session to watch later. No doubt in the comfort of whatever pleasure pavilion the duo called home. Rodin's, no doubt. The leader of the Archguard spoiled the members of his death squad and his firstborn son in particular.

Gage let his good eye drift closed again.

Just for a moment. All he needed was a second. A single slice of time to regroup and get ready. But as the pair discussed camera angles—adjusting the tripod, resetting the floodlights, lighting him up for maximum effect—his resolve slipped. Not a lot. Barely even a little. The slight shift, however, signaled trouble. Doubt pushed him off his moorings and . . . ah, shit. Not good. His defenses were starting to crack. Which led to one inescapable question. How much more could he endure? So far, he'd withstood it all without making a sound. The brutality grounded him, fed him purpose, telling him the longer he held out, the longer he and Haider would stay alive.

He frowned.

Well, at least, he hoped so. It was hard to tell. Zidane liked to color outside the lines. Usual limits didn't apply to him. He was an extremist, willing to do anything for his sire. Which meant . . . Gage swallowed in apprehension. He might've misread the situation. Maybe Zidane really was that stupid. Maybe the dickwad only planned to keep one of them alive to obtain what he wanted. He cursed under his breath. The theory made sense. Not that it mattered. Guesswork meant fuck-all while strung up and about to be filleted like a fish. And yet, even under the fog of uncertainty, the facts remained the same. Zidane might be sadistic, but he was also goal oriented. He wouldn't waste an opportunity. The song and dance inside the kill room served a purpose. The prick needed information to support his sire's mission.

The kind of intel only a Nightfury warrior could provide.

Zidane was gambling, betting big to win huge. Gage understood the game. Was even better at assessing the odds than the males holding him hostage. Which meant he already knew what Zidane didn't. He would never talk. Never give up the goods on his pack.

Or the location of his lair in Seattle.

The Nightfury pack meant everything to him: a second chance, true brotherhood, the stability of safety inside a real home with males who valued him. And whom he loved in return. So fuck it. He'd pay the ultimate price to protect his brothers. Would die in a medieval torture tomb. Amid death and squalor. Deep underground. Under the watchful eyes of a death squad commanded by Rodin—unless he found a way to turn the tables and escape.

Swallowing a mouthful of saliva, Gage lifted his head. Frayed nerve endings screamed in protest. Fatigue and blood loss converged, attacking what little remained of his strength. Reaching deep, he dredged the bottom of his energy reserves and, gritting his teeth, leveled his chin.

Blood dripped into his good eye.

Gage blinked the red ooze away and glared at the male tormenting him. "I'm going to kill you, Zidane. The second I am free, you're nothing but ash."

"Bold words, Nightfury."

"Remember them, asshole. I don't make promises I can't keep."

"Such hubris, Gage." Zidane's mouth curved a moment before he returned his attention to the tabletop. He scanned the collection of torture tools, then reached out and trailed his fingertips over a row of pliers. Serrated tips. Crooked ends. Razor-sharp blades made for cutting. His fingers danced over each implement. Eeny-meeny-miney-mo. The calculated touches spoke volumes. His enemy was savoring the moment. Wanted Gage to imagine the worst and dread its delivery. "I almost like that about you."

Pausing mid-caress, the prick picked up a pair of slim pliers. He tested the pointed tips with the pad of his thumb. As he hummed and palmed a wooden bit used to wedge a male's mouth open, Gage snarled. Bad move. He knew it the second the growl left his throat. Too bad he couldn't help it. Or call the sound back. No matter how many times he told himself not to react—that Zidane fed on fear—he admitted the bastard knew what he was doing.

Anticipation of pain, after all, always trumped its reality.

"Your choice, Nightfury." Dark eyes shimmering, Zidane turned away from the table. "A slow death—or a fast one? Give me what I want and I'll show mercy."

"Bullshit."

Zidane huffed, the beginning of a smile in his eyes. "How very astute of you. Nightfuries never lack brains, I'll give you that. Although . . ." Rotating the pliers in his palm, he raised a brow. "You may want to consider your friends. You talk, I won't take another run at them. A swift death? Or unending pain and humiliation—for each of you? You decide."

Heart thumping, Gage's breath caught in the back of his throat. Gaze narrowed on Zidane, he frowned. Friends? Had the asshole really just said *friends* . . . as in, of the plural variety? What the hell was Zidane talking about? Was he tossing out threats with no substance? Or was the news flash something to be concerned about? Hunting for the truth, he glanced at Ferland. The smug expression on the jerkoff's face gave the truth away.

Holy God. Zidane wasn't lying.

The Archguard held another warrior captive. Maybe more than one. Hell, there could be a whole host of males Gage knew and loved locked up somewhere nearby. The idea sent him into a tailspin. As the whirl got going, he dug in and stopped the mental slide. Worry wouldn't solve anything. Thinking straight and staying calm, however, just might, so . . .

Gage forced his mind away from panic. His brows collided. Wait a minute. Hold everything. The conclusion didn't make any sense. None of the other Nightfuries were in Prague. Well, at least, as far as he knew. Six days of radio silence—of being locked in a dungeon and unable to warn his brothers—didn't inspire confidence. Neither did the triumph in Zidane's eyes. Which meant—

Bastian had interfered.

Gage swallowed a curse, then started to pray, hoping Bastian had stayed out of it. Too much to wish for? Probably. No, strike that. Switch it to *definitely.* His commander never sat on the sidelines. No matter how volatile the situation, Bastian found a way to protect his pack. So yeah. Absolutely. Which meant B would never leave them behind. He was too loyal—too smart—to allow things to run their course without stacking the deck. The male always set up contingencies. A plan formed in advance—perhaps a secret alliance made in order to get them out of Prague if the situation went sideways.

"Who else do you have?" Gage asked, fighting to keep his voice even.

"Wouldn't you like to know?"

"The whole point of the question, asshole. Christ, you're a dull blade."

Fury lining his face, Zidane turned toward him. He pointed the pliers at him, threatening Gage from four feet away. "Careful, Nightfury. My patience wears thin."

Gage shrugged, raising one shoulder even though it hurt like hell. "Tell me what I want to know, and I'll give you something in return."

"And what would that be?"

"The information you need for the answer I want," Gage said, lying through his teeth. The only thing he'd be *giving* Zidane was a fist to the face followed by a broken neck. "Come on, Zidane. You like games—play."

"I do like games. Yours, however—I'm not interested in playing." Zidane tightened his grip on the pliers. Pointed teeth snapped together. The sharp sound rippled, joining the drone of dripping water as he took a step toward Gage. Anticipation in his eyes, he raised the wooden bit and smirked at him. "Prepare to lose your canines, Nightfury. Rest assured, I will enjoy hearing you scream when—"

Steel banged against stone.

The reverberation thundered through the room. A metal handle twisted, then clicked. Hinges creaked. The door swung wide, giving Gage a view into a dark corridor. A moment later, a young Dragonkind male—one yet to go through the *change*—stuck his head into the chamber. Pale eyes landed on Gage, widened in shock, then skipped away. Gage swallowed a huff. An innocent man-child in the pit of hell. Talk about ironic. It would've been laughable had he not been hurting so much. The absurdity of it, however, hardly registered on his sliding scale. He didn't give a damn about the new arrival's reaction. Or the fear he spotted in the male's gaze.

Only one thing mattered.

The interruption was a good omen. It might give him a reprieve. More time to come up with a plan. Another chance to make good on his promise to Haider and get them both out alive.

Standing on the threshold, the male swallowed. "My lord?"

"What is it?" Zidane asked, his tone sharp.

"Your sire, my lord," the newcomer whispered, head bowed, feet shuffling just outside the door. "He wishes you at the morning meal."

Zidane glanced over his shoulder. "When does he expect me?"

"Now."

With a growl, Zidane tossed the wooden bit. The mouthpiece bounced across the tabletop, jumping across razor-sharp blades. He watched it skip over the hardware a moment, then switched focus. His gaze settled back on Gage. "Saved by the breakfast bell, Nightfury. Lucky you."

"Yeah, lucky me," Gage murmured, sarcasm out in full force, even though he meant every word, 'cause . . . *thank God.* He needed a break. The universe had granted one, along with a prime nugget of information. *The morning meal.* Nine o'clock in most Dragonkind lairs. The intel gave him hope and something else too—the hour and a loose time frame. Two hours—three at most—until the meal ended. Enough time to break free, find Haider, and get the hell out of Rodin's underground lair. "Guess I'll see you later."

"Count on it." Boots thudding against concrete, Zidane strode toward the door. The man-child sidestepped, making room for his lord to cross the threshold. Zidane met the younger male's gaze. "Osgard."

"Yes, my lord?"

"Stay and help Ferland."

Osgard nodded.

Busy with the camera, Ferland looked up in surprise. "With what?"

"Turn off the electricity and get him down," Zidane said. "Put our little bird back in his cage."

Ferland frowned. "But—"

"Let him recuperate while we eat." Half in the chamber, half out, Zidane threw his friend a sidelong look, then refocused on Gage. He sighed, the sound full of longing. Gage tensed. The bastard hummed, no doubt enjoying the flex of heavy muscle. Pride in his eyes, his gaze roamed the stab wounds crisscrossing Gage's torso, strayed to the burn marks ringing the base of his throat, and took in all the blood streaking his chest. The twisted SOB smiled. "It's no fun torturing a weakling. They never scream as loud."

A truism. One Gage knew well.

He'd witnessed countless interrogations—more than one execution too—while living under his sire's roof. Enough to understand cause and effect. And what the pleasure Zidane took in hearing others scream meant. The prick was more than just cruel. He was a sexual sadist, a male who became aroused by another's pain. Terrific information to have going forward. Particularly since he wouldn't be around when Zidane returned. The plan was already in motion, taking shape inside his head. It wouldn't be long now. Mere moments until—

The hum of electricity powered down.

His muscles relaxed, making his body twitch. Gage groaned as comfort came calling and . . . oh, sweet, sweet relief. It was almost as good as revenge. Almost, but not quite. His get-even gene wouldn't give up the goods. Or concede defeat. The entire Archguard would pay for his pain, but more than that . . .

For daring to hurt Haider.

Keys jiggled as Ferland came forward to unlock his shackles.

Pretending exhaustion, Gage let his head lull and his muscles go lax. Ferland stopped in front of him and reached for the steel cuff holding his left ankle in place. The lock clicked. The first shackle swung open. One down, three more to go. His mouth curved. Fantastic. Absolutely perfect. The male might not know it yet, but Ferland wouldn't be enjoying the morning meal. Or anything else for that matter. He'd be dead long before Zidane picked up his utensils and shoveled the first bite into his fucking mouth.

Chapter Five

Wings spread wide, Bastian rocketed over thick forest. The woodlands groaned beneath him. Huge trees bowed in deference, narrow tops brushing the ground before springing into action, launching pine needles and loads of snow into the night sky. Debris mushroomed into a messy cloud behind him. A stray branch flipped up and over. He ducked, avoiding a face full of fuck you, and glanced over his shoulder. The wooden limb whirled over the spikes running along his spine and—

"Ouch!" Glued to his six, Rikar dodged right. *"What the hell, B. Have you lost your freaking mind?"*

Upping the velocity, Bastian ignored the question. He wasn't interested in conversation. Not now. Maybe not for a while either. Instead, he kept his gaze fixed on the rough terrain and blew past a cluster of ancient pines.

"Holy shit—" His first in command banked hard, dodging more debris. *"Watch it."*

Bastian didn't respond to the edge of pissed off in his friend's voice. No reason to ruin the moment and open his mouth. Or flip off his wingman through mind-speak. Rikar could handle the dustup along with the breakneck speed. So could the forest. Damage. No damage. The landscape—and any carnage left in his wake—didn't matter. Not tonight. Nature would do what it always did—so would his XO—and survive. His mind was on other things. Urgent things. Worrisome things, and the situation in Seattle.

Or rather, the non-situation.

Which meant he needed to get home. Reach the waterfall. Fly into the underground cavern. Land on the LZ, shift into human form, and beat feet toward the computer lab—the brainstem inside Black Diamond—and Sloan, faster than fast. Good intel, after all, was tricky. It only stayed current so long. So forget patient. Quick and clean. Down and dirty. Both sounded good at the moment. Either strategy would work, but only if he acquired the information he needed to fill in the blanks.

A long shot by any standards, but . . .

He needed to try. Otherwise, he'd be shit out of luck with two of his warriors MIA halfway around world.

"Fucking hell," he growled, rotating into a tight flip.

Rikar cursed and, wobbling in mid-air, unleashed his frosty side. The temperature dropped. Damp air turned into icy swirl, coating Bastian's midnight-blue scales as the terrain dipped. Thick woodland thinned as it neared a two-hundred-foot drop. Gaze on the rocky ledge, he blew past the crag. Shale rolled, tumbling toward the river below. Ignoring the splashdown, he banked hard, blasting into the next turn. Water rippled, whipping into frothy chop. His muscles squawked. He didn't care. The ball-busting flight felt good. Seemed appropriate too. Exertion brought clarity along with certain knowledge.

Set aside the problem with Gage and Haider for the moment. Something else was bothering him too—a *something* that landed a whole lot closer to home, 'cause . . . no shadow of a doubt. The vibe in the city tonight had been all wrong.

Bastian snorted. Lightning sparked from his nostrils as he shook his head. Jesus. Who was he kidding? *Wrong* didn't begin to describe the last few hours. Bizarre. Fucked up. In no way normal. Sure, use one of those. Each one applied. Particularly since he hadn't encountered a single Razorback in downtown Seattle. Not *one*. After hours spent hunting. After visiting every one of the enemies' known haunts. After he'd unleashed his magic time and again, giving away his position, inviting the enemy pack to come get him.

Usually that was all it took—an invitation to fight.

Not tonight. The usual hadn't done the trick. No matter how many pings he'd sent out, the enemy hadn't flown out to engage him.

The switch-up signaled trouble. Razorbacks didn't do different. The idiots were predictable. No deviation in behavior. No variation in ideology. Just in-your-face savagery most of the time. So yeah, the change in Razorback tactics concerned him. The reason behind the strategic shift must be significant. Huge, in fact. Big enough to keep the enemy pack inside—and out of the sky—for three straight nights. Add that worry to the situation in Prague and his problems multiplied, going global in a blink of an eye.

Which left Gage and Haider in the hot seat.

An ocean away without backup. Or the slightest hope of receiving help anytime soon.

Dread congealed in the pit of his stomach. A bad taste washed into his mouth. Bastian swallowed the burn. God. Forget *wrong*. Everything had gone sideways. Was upside down, inside out, and backward. So messed up, he didn't know where to start. Should he say the hell with it, head to Prague and challenge the Archguard? Or stay the course and trust his warriors? Instinct urged him to get involved. Experience told him to wait . . .

Just a little longer.

His warriors weren't lightweights. Each one was vicious on his own. Put them together, toss off-the-chart IQs into the equation, and . . . no question. The pair made savage look tame. And yet, Bastian couldn't shake his unease. He had a bad feeling. The kind that told him his warriors' disappearance and the Razorbacks' sudden retreat were somehow connected. Pure supposition? Guesswork without a foothold in fact? Bastian gritted his teeth. Without a doubt. He didn't have a shred of proof. Wasn't likely to get any either. Not if Ivar—leader of the Razorback nation—kept his warriors off the playing field.

"Asshole," Bastian growled, wishing Ivar would come out and play.

"You'd better not be talking to me, 'cause—" Spine flexing, Rikar rotated up and over. Frost-covered scales rattled. Halfway through the flip, he drilled Bastian with a skull-thumping look. *"You're the only asshole around here right now."*

"I'm on edge," Bastian said, by way of apology. *"Six days, Rikar. Six fucking days without word."*

"I know. I'm worried about the Metallics too, but—" Flipping right side up, his friend settled into a smooth glide off his left wing tip. *"The crazy-ass speed won't solve anything, B."*

"Maybe not, but it helps me think. I need some perspective." Or a really stiff drink. A glass filled with Johnnie Walker Blue fit the bill. Suited his mood too. Throwing back a few always smoothed out the edges. Tonight would be no different, except . . . Bastian sighed. Drinking wasn't a good idea. The guilt belonged to him along with the burden of command. So no. Whiskey wasn't in his immediate future. He needed to stay sharp. Remain focused. Be able to see the problem from every angle. Otherwise, he'd never get his warriors out of Europe in one piece. *"It's all gone to shit. I sent Gage and Haider over there, Rikar. I—"*

"It was a slam dunk . . . a good decision all the way around. We needed the intel. Now we have it and know what to expect."

Bastian understood the rationalization. Hell, he'd been the one to come up with the plan in the first place. Knowing it was the right play, though, didn't make him feel any better. *"What if they're already dead?"*

"Not a chance. Trust them, B. Gage and Haider know what they're doing." Rikar bared his fangs on a growl. *"Rodin's too greedy to kill our boys in private. The bastard needs a public stage—wants to make an example of us without jeopardizing his position."*

Bastian grunted. *"By exiling our pack."*

"A hard sell," Rikar said. "Xzinile *is tricky business. The other members of the high council remember your sire and know you. With Nian in our corner, Rodin will have a hard time convincing them to declare us outlaws, never mind sanction a hit on members of our pack."*

True enough. An excellent argument, if somewhat problematic.

Particularly since Nian had gone missing too.

Bastian grimaced. The radio silence might not mean anything. Nian could be lying low, working in the background and under the radar to get the Metallics to safety. He hoped so, but . . . one never knew with Nian. The male was power hungry and ambitious. Which made him unpredictable and by extension untrustworthy. Not the kind of warrior Bastian usually invited into his camp. And yet, he'd gotten involved with Nian anyway, agreeing to support his agenda inside the Archguard. Why? Bastian huffed. Good question. One he'd been asking himself for over a week. The question refused to leave him alone. It simply kept coming around, reappearing like an annoying person through a revolving door. But like it or not, the answer never changed.

Call it intuition. Chalk it up to experience. Label it dangerous, but Bastian saw something in the younger male. Something he liked and knew would only strengthen over time. Nian cared. He wanted to do the right thing. Yearned for change. Craved peace and a healthier path for Dragonkind—no matter how difficult the road or how many enemies he made along the way. So yeah, all things considered, Nian made a good ally.

But only if the idiot returned his calls.

Swallowing a curse, Bastian flexed his talons. He didn't like it. Gage. Haider. And now Nian. Three males missing in the space of six days. The situation carried all the markers of a plan gone wrong.

Gaze on the jagged terrain, he banked around a cliff rising from the river's edge. His mind churned. His chest tightened, squeezing his heart as instinct squawked, warning him to watch out. Rodin was behind the disappearances. Smack-dab in the middle of the power play somehow. Bastian bit down on a snarl. Not surprising. The bastard would do anything—hurt anyone—to remain in power. Manipulation. Intimidation. Murder. The male dabbled in it all. Bastian should know. He'd watched Rodin maneuver while under the Archguard's thumb as a ward of the state after his sire's death.

A murder Rodin had set in motion.

Not that Bastian could prove it. The slimy bastard was smart. Rodin never got his hands dirty. He issued orders and expected others to carry them out. Which meant Bastian still didn't know who killed his father—Sigvoid, High Chancellor of Dragonkind, the male voted in by pack commanders to oversee the Archguard and uphold Dragonkind laws. A crappy hand dealt at the eleventh hour. No matter how hard he pushed for information, no one talked. Ergo he couldn't lay the blame at Rodin's feet. That ship had sailed. No going back. No evidence to collect or guilty parties to charge. No closure of any kind. Just the pain of loss and the certain knowledge his sire had died safeguarding the future of his race.

A tough job. One made more difficult by assholes like Rodin.

To be expected. The political arena remained forever the same. Like a game of chess, the landscape never shifted, only the positions of the players on the board. Which was why he lived in Seattle, far away from all the bullshit. His sire had wanted something better—something more—for him. A real life. A chance at happiness, not the constant threat from power-hungry males who coveted his position.

The entire reason behind his promise. One he'd made to his sire before his death. Never go into politics. Or assume the role of High Chancellor. No matter how many males asked him to lead the whole of Dragonkind.

Bastian exhaled in a rush.

So many years had passed since that fateful conversation. So much pain and strife since he'd turned away from his birthright. Bastian shook his head. He'd been so young—just seventeen years old, three years from his *change* and the ability to shift into dragon form. Too naive to understand what giving his word meant. Or what it would do to his race. Complete upheaval. Total turmoil. Brother pitted against brother. Sometimes Bastian wondered whether his sire had predicted what leaving the throne empty would do, and the kind of chaos that would ensue. Maybe that's what he'd wanted. Maybe he'd known all along what his race needed . . .

Real change. Responsible government. A restructuring of Dragonkind hierarchy.

Bastian didn't know. His father was dead and gone, never to return. And worrying about what he intended? A total waste of time. Guessing games wouldn't help. He couldn't go back and change his mind. Couldn't fix two centuries' worth of problems, never mind know his sire's intentions. He lived—day in and day out—with the reality of the situation left by his father. Well, that and the memories: the cruelty he'd suffered by Rodin's command in the aftermath of his father's murder.

Sorrow tightened his throat.

His mind supplied the rest, flashing images on his mental screen, reminding him of opportunity lost and mistakes made. So many botched attempts. Far too many males interested in the throne. Sigvoid had been dead less than a week when Rodin made a play for power.

Hostile takeover at its worst.

Dissention had been the result. And the position had yet to be filled. Years spent without a true leader had fractured Dragonkind, allowing individual packs to splinter off and lay claim to different territories. Now his kind no longer lived in a central location, but all over the planet. Some still backed Rodin and his twisted aspirations. Others wanted Bastian to step into the role, just as his sire had done. And with the two camps set in direct opposition? Bastian shook his head. Political maneuvering without end. Stupidity to the next power. Jesus. No wonder it was such a mess.

No one could agree.

Or understand why he refused to become High Chancellor of Dragonkind. But the truth remained the same. His answer too—

He'd given his word and promised his sire.

Which put him in the middle of a mess, didn't it? Front and center, playing a lethal game of tug-of-war. One that went something like—keep those who supported him happy enough to accept his refusal to seize the throne while thwarting Rodin's attempts to claim it at the same time. By no means easy. Particularly when Rodin turned the political wheel, threating the Nightfury pack with *Xzinile*. Bastian growled. Fucking Archguard. The pansy-ass idiots didn't have a clue. His refusal to assume his sire's role didn't make him weak. If anything, it made him more dangerous. Toss the threat of *Xzinile* into the pile and . . .

It spelled trouble. For those on the high council, not him.

Exile—being labeled an outlaw—would unleash him. Give him the freedom to discard the law, follow his sire's example, and go after the Archguard. Eliminate them all. Dismantle an archaic system that no longer served Dragonkind interests and replace it with something better. So bring it on. Let the Archguard declare him a traitor. Bastian hoped Rodin proved to be that stupid. He really did. The second the high council voted, signed the paperwork, and put a bounty on his head . . .

Holy fuck. He couldn't wait to see what happened.

Not many males would be brave enough to come after him. Or any of his warriors from half a world away. His reputation was solid, and his methods, well known. Toss in the fact his allies would rally to support him and . . . little doubt. Rodin was headed into dangerous territory. Was risking it all to assuage his pride instead of playing it safe to keep the status quo. Which would lead to one thing . . .

War on a global scale. A chance at significant change.

"Hey, B?"

Bastian glanced at his best friend. *"Yeah?"*

"How's it going with Forge?"

"Nothing yet."

"He still doesn't remember?"

"I'm working with him." Bastian rolled his shoulders. His scales clicked together. Ice chips peeled from interlocking dragon skin, blowing behind him as he adjusted his wing speed. *"No details of that night yet, but his memory is coming back . . . slowly."*

Par for the course. And Bastian understood.

Forge didn't want to remember, never mind relive the attack. Or the resulting anguish of seeing his sire and older brothers killed. Compartmentalizing to isolate the pain, the Scot had locked the memory away inside his mind. Now he couldn't access it at all. He'd had no reason to either. Until now. Bastian wanted to know what happened that night. So cue the mind regression techniques along with the magic. He was using it all, trying to regress Forge enough to stimulate recall. It was slow going, no question, but fortune favored the patient. He refused to push Forge too hard, too fast, and damage his synapses in the process. Piecing memories together took time, and Bastian had faith. The Scot would remember—eventually—and give him what he needed.

More information. All the nitty-gritty details.

The real reason Rodin wanted the Scot dead.

But first, Bastian needed to know the *why* behind the smoke screen. The secret holding up the network of lies surrounding the leader of the Archguard. Was the bastard targeting his warrior to cover up a crime? Like oh, say, his involvement in the murder of Forge's sire—commander of the Scottish pack—years ago. A good guess. Rodin hadn't always been so careful. The bastard might like to pull strings behind the scenes, but every once in a while, he screwed up. Maybe the murder of Forge's family was one of those times. Maybe Rodin had made the trip to Scotland to coordinate the attack. Maybe . . . just *maybe* . . . Forge could place the bastard there—flying as lead dragon in the death squad.

Pure conjecture. Assumption without a shred of proof.

Bastian hummed in anticipation anyway. The theory made a certain amount of sense. It explained everything, in fact. Rodin's fixation on Forge. His willingness to risk reinstating *Xzinile* to not only hide the truth, but eliminate the only witness to his crime. A misstep that would topple Rodin and see him convicted in a Dragonkind court.

A little snippet. One jagged piece of information. Confirmation that Rodin had been there. Bastian knew what the bastard looked like in dragon form. All he needed from Forge was a description of the death squad—all the males who attacked that night. Valuable intel that could even now be locked away inside the Scot's mind. His eyes narrowed on the treetops, Bastian went over his strategy again. Slow and steady. Mind regression at its most patient. He must help Forge remember. Otherwise, he'd lose what he needed to take the leader of the Archguard down.

Once and for all.

"The sooner Forge remembers," Rikar said, deep voice rolling through mind-speak, *"the better for us."*

"I know. I might need your help with him."

Rikar frowned. *"What—tag team him? Two is better than one?"*

"Don't know—maybe. Can't hurt to try."

"Yeah, all right." Rikar nodded. *"Whatever you need."*

"I'll speak to Forge," he murmured, glad to have his friend on board. *"Get his okay before we spring you on him, then—"*

His sonar pinged.

Bastian's head snapped to the right. The tingle intensified, slithering up his spine, then shifted, colliding with the base of his skull. A prickle streamed over his horns. Gaze roaming, he searched the landscape. His ability to dissect a male's aptitude from a distance coalesced inside his head. He held on to the power for a moment, then unleashed his talent. Magic spread like a net, rushing out in front of him, blanketing treetops and sky to feed him information. He bared his fangs. Oh, goody. Dragonkind males approached from the south end of the forest. He mined the signal. Distance to target—three miles. How many in the mix—two big males. Age, skill level, and type of exhales? Bastian fine-tuned his radar. His senses contracted. One breathed fire-acid, and the other—

Ah, hell. He recognized the lethal vibe headed his way.

Mac and Forge coming in hot.

With a sigh, he threw his XO a sidelong look.

Rikar grinned, baring huge fangs. *"Wonder twins at three o'clock."*

Bastian snorted in amusement. *Wonder twins.* He liked the nickname. The handle suited the pair, fitting the newest members of the Nightfury pack like bullets in a gun. *"I was hoping for a couple of Razorbacks."*

"Wishful thinking." Rikar grumbled, the sound full of frustration. *"Bad hunting lately."*

No kidding.

Fucking Ivar. The male was screwing with his happy place, keeping his soldiers buttoned up tight. Then again, maybe he needed to readjust his expectations. Especially way out here—in the middle of nowhere. The enemy rarely left the confines of Seattle. The bastards liked the cityscape. Enjoyed the cover skyscrapers and high-rise buildings provided. A shame, really. Having a clear shot at a Razorback in open air would be a whole lot of fun. Just the kind of amusement Bastian craved tonight, but—ah, well. Better luck next time. Which meant . . .

Time to head for Black Diamond.

Some quality time with Myst would mend his mood. His female soothed him like nothing else could—knuckle-cracking, ball-busting brawls included. He was lucky to have her. Grateful too. Nothing beat coming home to his mate every morning. Or the privilege of sleeping with her in his arms every day.

Slowing his wing speed, Bastian glanced over his shoulder. Two shadows morphed on the horizon. A steep bluff rose in his periphery. One eye on the wonder twins, Bastian flew up and over, avoiding the rocky outcropping as the pair rocketed in behind him. Growling a greeting, Forge flew in on his left, taking the wingman position opposite Rikar.

Settling into a smooth glide above him, Mac opened up mind-speak. *"Anything?"*

"Nada," Rikar said, more growl than actual word. *"You?"*

"Bloody hell," Forge said, Scottish accent thicker than usual. *"Nothing. Nary an arsehole to kill. And we went all the way south to Tacoma."*

Mac shook his head. *"Something's up. The motherfuckers are hiding."*

"I know," Bastian murmured. *"I'm hoping Sloan has something new for us. Azrad's supposed to check in tonight."*

Silence met his statement. Not surprising. Azrad was a touchy subject. None of his warriors wanted to broach it, never mind float the idea Azrad might not be good for the Nightfury pack. Bastian understood his warriors' reservations. Hell, he shared them. Had a whole trunkful of concerns and more questions than he could answer.

With good reason.

Until a week ago, he hadn't known Azrad existed. Or that his father had sired another son before his death. But DNA results left no room for doubt—Azrad was his brother by blood. A long-lost one who'd finally found his way home. An odd thing to discover after so many years on his own. Dangerous too. The connection pulled at his heartstrings. Made him want to believe in miracles and family ties. All of which clouded his judgment.

Not smart or even halfway advisable. Letting his guard down before he possessed all the facts was a bad idea.

Males ended up dead that way.

One mistake led to another. Bastian knew it. And yet, he wanted to reach for the gold ring anyway. Trust instead of suspect, and invite Azrad into the fold. Which stopped him cold. Experience dictated the way forward. Caution upped the stakes. Mistrust and acceptance were opposite sides of the same coin. Flip it one way. Turn it the other. Both sides applied to the situation. Which pointed to an unavoidable truth.

He must play it smart. Ease into the role of older brother. Heed his head instead of his heart and find a way to protect his pack while doing right by his sibling. Azrad deserved a chance to prove himself . . .

Particularly since he'd gone to so much trouble to impress him.

Bastian's lip twitched. God love his little brother. Azrad was straight-up brilliant. He'd made himself useful from the get-go, providing what Bastian couldn't obtain on his own—insider information by infiltrating the Razorback pack. A spy inside the enemy camp. What a concept. One he liked without question. No one else could've slid into the enemy hive with such efficiency. Azrad had succeeded where Bastian had failed. And no wonder. After years of imprisonment inside Tanzenmed—a Dragonkind prison sanctioned by the Archguard and run by Rodin—the male didn't walk or talk like a Nightfury. No one would suspect him as long he kept his personal agenda off the table and played it smart.

A long shot. Predictability, after all, didn't apply to his brother. So nothing to do now but wait. Cross his fingers. Hope and pray Azrad kept it together long enough to get out alive.

Baring his fangs, Bastian rocketed into the last turn. Cold air rushed over the razor-sharp points of his teeth. Mist rolled into his mouth as the waterfall came into view. Falling in a straight sheet, the cascade plummeted toward the river from three hundred feet up. Wet air frothed into full bloom, rising up like a cloud to hide the half moon. The heavy vapor screwed with his visibility. Not that it mattered. His night vision sparked, and with his sonar up and running, he saw everything. The frozen reeds on the river bank. Each frost-laden pine needle. Every grain of bark on tree trunks standing too close to the water's edge.

Almost there.

Thirty—maybe forty—seconds until he went wings vertical, splashed through the cascade and into the narrow tunnel beyond. Hewn from solid granite, the jagged entrance lead to the LZ and into the underground lair. After that, he'd be home, sweet home. A hop, skip, and jump away from his female. In Myst's arms. Kissing her mouth—tasting her deep, greeting her as he always did—before heading to the computer lab to get the information he needed to round out the night. Sloan would be hard at work, mining data fields, keeping tabs on—

"Bastian." Sloan's voice came through mind-speak on a low growl.

"Whatcha got?" Water wicking off his scales, Bastian leveled out and, eyes on the waterfall, set up his final approach. *"Anything from the Metallics?"*

"Nothing yet," Sloan said. *"But I just received a message from Azrad."*

"What's it say?" Flying in from behind, Rikar bumped Mac out of the way.

"Motherfuck." Mac wobbled, seesawing mid-glide. Magic flared as the male unleashed his inner water dragon and hurled a handful of cold-wet-and-chilly at Rikar's head. The load slammed into his XO's face. Rikar sputtered. Mac bared his fangs. *"Watch it or I'll drown you."*

Wearing a shit-eating grin, Rikar retaliated, throwing flurries toward Mac. Ice and snow exploded in all directions. Forge cursed, then dodged, avoiding the whiteout. With a snarl, Mac spiraled into a flip and swiped at Rikar's tail. Scales rattled. The wind rose on a gust of icy swirl. His friend laughed at the playful attempt to maim him. Bastian sighed, then shook his head, wishing he could get in on the game. He could use the exercise along with a little stress relief right now. And a fight? Oh, man, that would feel so good. Would help release the tension before the sun chased him inside for the day. Too bad he didn't have time to mess around. Not with dawn approaching, and Gage and Haider still in the wind. So forget kicking warriors' asses in a friendly round of dragon combat training.

Or letting them blow off steam by playing pin the claw on Rikar.

Time to shut it down and get back to business.

Mac made another attempt to catch Rikar.

"Shelve it, you two. Save it for another time," he said, admonishing his warriors, killing the possibility of a wrestling match before it got serious. *"Sloan—what's the message?"*

"Two words—Granite Falls."

"What the hell is that supposed tae mean?" Twisting into a sidewinding flip, Forge fell into line, bringing up the rear of the procession. The wind kicked up, clicking against his dark-purple scales. *"Person, place, or thing, lad?"*

"Place," Mac said, putting knowledge of the state gleaned from years as an SPD homicide detective to good use. *"Small town in the Cascades, close to the Canadian border."*

"Exactly." The rapid sound of keystrokes came through mind-speak. The clickety-click-click meant one thing. Sloan was planted in front of his computer, doing what he did best—mining data, busting through firewalls, hacking into secure servers to

pull pertinent information off the cyber highway. *"Not sure what it means yet. I'm just getting into it, but that's not why I pinged you."*

Bastian tensed. The edge in Sloan's voice spelled trouble. Whenever his warrior used it, problems followed. Guaranteed. *"Tell me."*

Springs squeaked as Sloan swiveled in his chair. *"Daimler came to get me. He can't find Venom anywhere. He's gone, B."*

"What the fuck?" Blue-gray scales flashed in the gloom as Mac broke formation. He treated Bastian to a worried look. *"He left the lair alone?"*

"Yeah," Sloan said.

Rikar growled. *"Christ."*

"Shit." Oh, so not good. A total breach in protocol. One Bastian couldn't get behind. Venom knew better than to leave the lair without a wingman. Flying solo was dangerous. Alone equaled vulnerable. And vulnerable often led to dead. *"Where's Wick?"*

"With J. J."

Bastian bit down on a curse. *"Go get him."*

"No way." The click of computer keys stopped mid-stroke. The pause meant one thing. Sloan was scrambling, thinking up an excuse to stay clear of Wick. *"I'm not pulling him out of bed and away from his female on his night off. I don't have a death wish."*

With a growl, Bastian dropped another f-bomb.

Rikar sighed.

The wonder twins stayed silent for once.

Thank God. The last thing Bastian needed was more trouble. Or backlash from the pair's warped sense of humor. *"Got any ideas, Sloan?"*

"One." Leather creaked. Chair coils squeaked. The thud of boots on concrete sounded as Sloan started to pace. *"The Luxmore Hotel. Really upscale. Lots of females. Good feeding. I told him about it last week."*

Bastian nodded even though his warrior couldn't see him. *"Address?"*

Sloan rattled off a street name, pointing him toward the north end of Seattle. Putting on the brakes, Bastian wheeled around. The others followed, moving into flight formation, rocketing over the forest alongside him. Good thing too. He needed all hands on deck. The extraction would require some finesse. The kind that came with a truckload of brute force. Venom wouldn't come quietly. He never did when it came to females. His warrior loved the fairer sex too much. Liked to take his time. Enjoyed the slide into ecstasy more than most males. Wanted a female to call his own, which—ding-ding-ding, give the man a prize—was no doubt why he'd ignored the rules and flown out alone tonight.

He was hunting for a female.

A forever one? Or just sex with one of his flavors of the week?

Hard to know. But one thing for sure? The second he caught up with Venom, mayhem would ensue. And the beat-down would get under way. He swallowed a growl. Idiot male. Flying out solo. Such a dumb-ass move. One he refused to leave unchallenged. Rules existed for a reason: to ensure the warriors under his command kept on breathing. So . . . time to put the hammer down. Venom needed his ass kicked along with a reality check. Bastian snarled as he flew over Interstate 90. Just his luck. He was in the mood to give his warrior a shitload of both.

Chapter Six

Venom sighed as Evelyn settled in his arms. Hmm, she was exquisite. So warm in his embrace. So incredible pressed up against him. So beautiful with her dark hair and soft mocha skin. Everything about her lured him in. Strung him tight. Made him fixate on the smallest detail—the sensual curve of her hips, the generosity of her backside, the arousing stir of her scent. Inhaling deep, he indulged, drawing her into his lungs and . . . oh, baby. Another gift. He loved the way she smelled, summer sweet, like dew-soaked skies and warm, sultry nights.

All natural. One hundred percent female. Not a hint of perfume.

Slipping his hand beneath her shoulder-length curls, he cupped the nape of her neck and dipped his head. His jaw brushed her cheek. She gasped. The soft inhalation strung him tighter as the Meridian hummed, opening a link between them. Her bio-energy flared, expanding around her. Setting his mouth to her temple, Venom took a sip and . . . glory, glory, hallelujah. She tasted amazing. Was beyond good—everything he needed, yet hadn't expected. Not surprising. He'd never experienced anyone like Evelyn. Her uniqueness—the sheer beauty of her energy—shocked him, locking him in place against her. Her potency kept him there, tempting him to take more as he fed from the source that nourished his kind.

Unable to help himself, he indulged in another sip.

His fingertips tingled with renewed warmth.

Shivering in his embrace, Evelyn shifted against him. Tipping her chin up, she nestled closer, strengthened the connection, giving her energy and him more access. The current intensified. Venom groaned as her aura pulsed, surrounding him in glorious heat. Another round of pleasure prickled through him. His heart picked up a beat, slamming against the inside of his chest. Blood roared in his ears. The rush thrummed through his veins, pushing arousal into full-blown need.

Or toward complete desperation.

Venom didn't know which. Primal drive wiped his mind clean. Now deep-seated instinct ruled, rousing his dragon half, pushing compulsion to the forefront of his brain. He sucked in a breath. It didn't help and . . . oh, shit. Giving the beast inside him free rein wasn't a good idea. Females ended up hurt that way. At least, while standing next to him. His venomous nature didn't compromise. Neither did male needs. Both urged him to abandon his scruples, rush the foreplay and raise her skirt—spread her thighs and love her hard. Without preamble or mercy and—

Venom tensed. God help him. He wanted to do it. To touch and taste, tease until she moaned his name. Until she begged for him and all the pleasure he yearned to give her.

An excellent plan. But for one thing . . .

Rushing her would be tantamount to forcing her.

Something he refused to do.

A strange thought considering her willingness. But despite everything—his ravenous reaction to her, her profession, and the money on the table—he sensed her unease. Mistrust infused the air around her, drawing him in, making him aware of her upset. Evelyn teemed with emotion, her confusion driven by uncertainty. The tempest bubbled just beneath the surface of her skin—in the place modesty lived and integrity thrived.

Venom understood. He really did. She didn't like her reaction to him. Was fighting the push-pull of attraction. Hell, so was he. The difference between him and her? While she fought to preserve her professional veneer and stay in control, Venom wanted to accept the turmoil and let go. To be free for once. To make love to a female who made him feel something—anything—instead of indulging in a meaningless romp in a dark corner of a club somewhere. The idea grabbed hold, enslaving him with possibility.

A whole host of interesting scenarios streamed into his head.

He'd love her more than once. Twice, perhaps. Maybe even a third time before the venom in his veins took over and forced him to leave her. So, time to decide—down and dirty the first round? Or a long, luxurious loving? Both held real promise, but . . .

Venom shook his head. No. Not this time. No rushing. It wasn't going to be quick and clean. Not with Evelyn. For the first time ever, he wanted to linger and enjoy. To savor a female. To prolong her pleasure until he couldn't delay fulfillment any longer.

He growled. Oh, yeah, incendiary and slow sounded better. Like Christmas morning come early. And no wonder. Holding Evelyn was the best kind of torture. Pure bliss wrapped up in a curvy bundle. She felt so good against him. So enticing. So sweet. More than just pretty, she was sheer perfection. A feast for the senses. Without thought, he drew on her energy and, drinking deep, fingered the clasp at the back of her dress. A quick flick released the button hook. He tugged on the zipper. Metal teeth resisted a moment, then released, breaking the silence with sensual sound.

His hand slipped beneath the fabric, grazing soft skin.

Evelyn inhaled hard as his fingertips slid along her spine. He sighed and, attuned to her tension, nipped at her earlobe. She twitched, rebelling a little, resisting his touch, shifting away instead of toward him. Venom murmured her name, then waited, hoping his voice reassured her, and . . . bingo. Sweet, sweet victory. Evelyn surrendered and, exhaling a shaky breath, relaxed into his caress. And he continued, sliding the zipper all the way down. The back of her dress gaped, exposing her to the chill in the room. Goose bumps rose on her skin. Shifting focus, Venom set his mouth to the corner of hers. Her breath hitched. He tempted her with a gentle kiss. A barely there caress. Not much of a touch at all.

But it was enough.

His patience paid off. Between one moment and the next, she fell into trust and, fisting her hands in his shirt, tipped her chin up. Her lips parted. The movement told Venom all he needed to know. Evelyn wanted him. Wasn't shutting him down or tense in his arms. She'd moved past denial. Now she welcomed him, asking for more.

With a hum, Venom gave it to her, nipping her bottom lip before dipping inside. Hunger rose, urging him to deepen the contact. Venom killed the impulse. Slow and steady. A little at a time, and she would submit. Be his for the taking. One hundred percent committed to the sexual play. So he kept each caress light, brushing her mouth with each pass, tempting her to open for him, teasing her with his tongue until—

He dipped inside her mouth, and . . . oh God. She was a dream come true. His ticket to untold pleasure.

Venom's breath caught as she became the aggressor. Popping onto her tiptoes, she slipped her hands into his hair and pressed closer. Breasts brushing his chest, Evelyn grazed his scalp with her nails and kissed him back. With a groan, he opened wide, begged for more without words, praying she gave it to him, and—thank Silfer. She didn't deny him. Accepting his tongue, she deepened the contact. Her taste invaded his mouth. Desire went cataclysmic, cranking him tight and . . .

Frigging hell.

She was unbelievable. So goddamn good he needed another round. More of her skin against his. More of her taste in his mouth. More of the sexy sounds that she made. Right now. This instant. He couldn't wait a moment longer. Didn't know how to stop the sensual slide. Or slow his rapid spiral into mindless need. His brain was fried, ping-ponging all over the place, killing rational thought along with his restraint. Now he couldn't string two thoughts together, never mind control his descent into bliss-fueled oblivion.

He was losing control. Coming apart at the seams. Allowing a female to lead him.

Something he never tolerated.

Dominant in bed, he always dictated the play. The tempo too. But somehow, Evelyn pushed past his limits. Now he was lost. In a lifeboat and at sea with nothing but her to guide him home. Not a good idea. He was so much bigger—so much stronger, a Dragonkind male in control of powerful magic and a venomous nature. Which didn't bode well for her if he couldn't . . . if he didn't . . .

Goddamn it. He needed to bear down and reassert himself. Put his brain back in gear and yank Evelyn out of the driver's seat. The toxins in his veins—and the damage he could do to her without meaning to—dictated the play. He had rules. Ones he followed to the letter, no matter what when dealing with females. The first and most crucial? He kept his cool . . . at all times. The second, third, and fourth? Deliver bone-melting pleasure, receive some in return, then get out before the female ended up injured.

Tonight, however, his rules had gone to hell and not come back.

In the space of a few minutes, the landscape had shifted, dragging awareness to the forefront of realization. Evelyn did something strange to him. His reaction to her surpassed *need* and pushed passed *want*. Somehow. Some way. For some reason, his dragon half recognized her for what she was—the missing piece to an unfinished puzzle. Venom frowned as instinct screwed with his mental map, leaving him with a crazy conclusion.

Maybe the rules didn't apply to her.

Maybe . . . just maybe . . . Evelyn could take him all the way. Forget the usual forty minutes. He could take his time. Be as intense as he liked. Stay as long as he wanted. All night. Into the wee hours of the morning and throughout the day—without hurting her.

His dragon half served up the facts.

Venom kissed her again. Deeper. Harder. Taking her mouth with enough ferocity to test his theory. Paying attention to every nuance, he walked her backward. Her back bumped the wall and he pressed in, caging her in his arms. She moaned and tightened her grip in his hair. With a murmur, he cupped her backside and, hands sliding over silk, lifted her feet off the floor. A precise shift put him in front of the dresser. Tangling his tongue with hers, he set her down on the wooden edge.

The flat screen TV wobbled behind her.

Venom didn't care. The place could fall down, break into pieces around him, and he wouldn't have noticed. He was too busy with Evelyn, kissing her, shoving her skirt up, settling his hips between the spread of her thighs. Gasping his name, she hooked her knee over his hip and arched in welcome. The Meridian surged, hammering him with a pulsing wave of energy. His brain buzzed, scrambling reason, destroying restraint.

Unable to resist her, he drank deep, glutting himself on the astounding taste of her. Magic crackled in his veins. His body hummed, prickling with vitality as she moaned into his mouth. The soft sound gripped his heart. And realization struck.

She was more than just an HE female.

Evelyn was energy personified. Powerful and intense, the ideal bedmate. At least, for him. Her bio-energy—the frequency at which she connected to the Meridian—matched his . . . perfectly. No deviation in the energy fields. Not a single thread out of place. Which meant she could satisfy him. Was designed to feed him until he was full and keep him healthy. Could love him into oblivion without suffering a single side effect.

Shock struck like a closed fist.

His breath shuddered, stalling inside his chest.

He flinched, then froze. His mouth against hers, he struggled to understand. It defied reason. Simply *couldn't* be, and yet, the truth circled, refusing to be denied. Despite everything he knew about himself—and the curse of his venomous nature—she proved him wrong. The glory of her bio-energy—the absolute beauty of her—cinched it, pushing past shock to reveal the truth.

Evelyn belonged to him.

He belonged to her.

They'd been made for each other.

He'd found his mate. His equal in every way. The only female who would ever match and meet his needs . . . in a fancy hotel under unsettling circumstances. Holy shit. It was wild. Nearly incomprehensible. He'd imagined her so often. Pictured her in his mind's eye over and over. Again and again. What she would look like. How she would feel. The sound of her voice along with the unfettered intimacy she would bring into his life. Venom quivered against her. His hands started to shake. Goddamn. He'd dreamed and hoped and prayed. All without believing he had a chance of finding her. Ever. But here, in this moment, he held her in his arms. Was a breath away from claiming what he longed to possess. A female to call his own. Which meant . . .

He needed to stop. Right now.

He couldn't claim her this way. Refused to make love to her with money on the line. The claiming needed to be pure and honest, a meeting of minds, hearts, and bodies. Not like this—two strangers in a passionate exchange that meant nothing and would mean even less in the aftermath. The realization sent him spinning. Digging in, Venom stopped the mental whirl and, tucking desire back into its box, gentled the kiss.

Evelyn grumbled, protesting his retreat.

The sexy sound made him come back. He kissed her again. And then again. One more time before he pulled back to cup her cheek. Her face settled in the palm of his hand and . . . oh, man. He was an idiot. For smothering the incendiary burn of desire. For coming to his senses. For allowing Evelyn to come to hers. But with his conscience screaming and his mate in his arms, Venom couldn't fault his reasoning.

Or deny pulling back was the right thing to do.

Respect and caring ran hand in hand. He must start as he meant to go on. Do the right thing and protect his female. Even if it meant shielding her from himself.

Exhaling long and slow, he palmed her waist. "Evie, open your eyes."

Slim fingers playing in his hair, she shook her head. "Kiss me again. I forget with your mouth on mine. Please, kiss me again."

"Later—if you like."

"No." Her grip on him tightened. Shifting in suggestion, she tried to pull him closer. Venom tensed and held the line. No way would he allow her to manipulate him. No matter how much he wanted her, he wouldn't give in. He wanted to talk. Needed to know more about her before it went any further. Not that Evelyn cared. Wielding desire like a whip, she leaned in and nipped his bottom lip, lashing him with lust, using greed against him. Venom cursed. She smiled against his mouth. "Now, Venom. If you want me to stay, kiss me again."

The ultimatum firmed his resolve. Her bossy tone sealed the deal.

Little vixen. Beautiful temptress. No chance in hell he'd let her dictate the play. Not while he stood between her thighs with her half-dressed in his arms. "You're not going anywhere, Evie. Not until I let you."

She tensed. "Are you threatening me?"

"No. I would never hurt you, *mazleiha*," he murmured, calling her sweetheart in Dragonese. "Never in a million years, but I want to talk, so . . . look at me."

Her thick lashes flickered. Wary brown eyes met his. "Aren't we past talking?"

"Not by a long shot."

"Why?" she asked, sounding confused. "I thought you wanted me."

"I do want you. More than I should, but . . ." Venom trailed off, wondering how best to broach the subject. Should he come out and ask? Hope he didn't cross the line and stick his nose where it didn't belong? She might take offense. Decide he was a possessive asshole. Maybe even one of those obsessive stalker types. Venom smothered a grimace. Probably not far from the truth. At least, not for him when it came to her. "How often do you do this, Evie?"

She frowned. "Why does it matter?"

"It matters to me," he said, refusing to back down. "How often?"

"Never. You're my first client."

Venom exhaled in a rush. Thank God. Good news. She wasn't a call girl at all. At least, not yet. She wouldn't be either. Not if he had anything to say about it. A telling reaction, considering his aversion to judging others. He wasn't a saint, and it wasn't his place to decide what was right for another. Still, he couldn't deny his relief. No woman should ever have to sell her body. And like it or not, he hated that Evelyn found herself here—inside the Luxmore, forced into the arms of a stranger for money.

It wasn't her style.

Her level of polish and sophistication told him that much. Her body language—along with the uncertainty in her eyes—explained the rest. Given half a chance, she would run. Leave the swanky hotel behind and never look back. The realization unleashed his curiosity, dragging the need to know into the foreground. Now he wanted to learn everything about her—the why and how of her circumstances.

"I'm glad. I like the idea of being your first." As she huffed, he raised his hand and, unable to stop touching her, brushed an errant curl from her cheek. "Why are you doing it?"

"None of your business."

"I just made it my business."

"You have no right."

"Untrue." He had every right. More than any other male on the planet. It didn't matter that he was new to her—or that Evelyn didn't yet know she belonged to him. With a gentle touch, he shackled her wrist and turned her elbow out, exposing the inside of her forearm. Marks, the shape of fingernails, on her skin. The beginnings of bruises as well. Someone had manhandled her. Very recently too. Brushing his thumb over the nicks on her arm, Venom bit down on a snarl. "Is someone threatening you?"

She shook her head.

Intuition spiked, making his dragon senses sharpen. "I can protect you, *mazleiha*—but you have to let me."

"I'm fine."

Oh, so not true. A big lie. She was anything but *fine*. "Evie—"

"Really," she said, a stubborn lilt in her voice. "My self-defense class got a little rough, that's all."

More lies . . . or the truth?

Venom couldn't tell. Evelyn had a poker face most males would envy. Toss in her tolerance to his magic, the ability to shut him out by veiling her thoughts, and . . . yeah. No way could he get an accurate read on her. Which meant he needed to up the ante. Make her squirm a little in order to make her talk.

Gaze boring into hers, Venom pressed his hips between her thighs. Her breath caught a second before her eyes narrowed in warning. With a quick twist, she broke his hold on her wrist and laid both palms flat on his chest. Arm muscles flexing, she pushed him away. He didn't move. Evelyn shoved him again, the message clear—*back off, buddy*—as she tried to jump down from the edge of the dresser.

"How much trouble are you in?" he asked, ignoring her defiance, pissing her off by being too pushy.

Unable to budge him, she leveled her chin.

Her bravado lasted a moment. Less than an instant before shame stole into her expression. Color bloomed in her cheeks as she looked away and . . . ah, hell. There it was—the vulnerability he sensed behind the tough facade she presented to the world. Venom's throat went tight. He understood what drove her. Too much pride. Rampant mistrust. The belief safety existed in self-reliance and being alone.

"Tell me, Evie." Placing his finger beneath her chin, Venom turned her face back toward him, forcing her to meet his gaze. "I won't let you go until you do."

"It's nothing serious."

Venom gave her a no-nonsense look.

She squirmed. "Look, I really am all right. I don't need help with anything, I just . . ." Tugging on the neckline of her dress, she covered up. "God. This is so embarrassing."

"Just say it."

"I lost my job a few months ago, okay? I need the money."

"Bills to pay?" he asked, hating her discomfort as much as his high-handedness. But as much as it chafed him, getting to the truth was more important than her embarrassment. He couldn't help her, after all, if he didn't understand the problem. "Creditors?"

"Yes."

"Then I'll make you a deal."

Her brows furrowed. "What kind of deal?"

"Exclusivity. No other males but me. No more meeting strangers in hotel rooms."

"But—"

"Each time we meet, you'll get another three grand."

Reaching around her, he grabbed the roll of hundreds sitting on the dresser. Her gaze bounced from him to the cash, then back again. Perched between his fingertips, he wagged the bundle, using the money as an incentive. One designed to dial down her resistance. An excellent approach to a stubborn female. He could see it in her eyes—the need to go it alone and clean up her mess. So yeah, the bribe served a purpose. Evelyn would get to keep her pride and solve her own problems. And he'd succeed in keeping her out of another male's bed while he wooed her into acceptance.

Without having to kidnap her.

In the same way his Nightfury brothers had been forced to do with their mates.

The realization struck with the force of a dump truck at full tilt. Venom sucked in a breath. Holy shit. What an idea. A sappy one, sure, but . . . wow. It held the power to slay him. Now he couldn't deny its appeal. He longed for the experience. Wanted a chance to spend time with Evelyn outside the lair—to go on real dates, to court her, treat her right and—

"Why are you helping me?"

Her voice dragged him out of the fantasy. His gaze snapped back to hers. "Because I can. And I don't like to share."

Surprise surfaced in her eyes.

Venom raised a brow. "So . . . do we have an agreement?"

Swallowing hard, she nodded. "Okay."

"Good." Satisfaction roared as he set the money in her hand.

Looking confused—and beyond adorable—she whispered, "Thanks."

Feeling lighter than he had in ages, Venom gave her a quick kiss, caressed the outsides of her thighs one last time, then stepped back. Palming her waist, he lifted her off the wooden lip. The second her feet touched down, he turned her to face the TV. Watching her reflection in the dark pane, he zipped the back of her dress. Smooth skin disappeared behind pale silk, making regret rise and his heart throb.

Venom smothered a grimace. Had he said idiot earlier? Well, he'd meant brainless. No way he should be zipping her back up instead of stripping her bare. The image streamed into his head—of Evelyn. Naked, bowed in supplication beneath him.

His erection throbbed in protest.

Resisting the urge to adjust his button fly, Venom cleared his throat and gave her a gentle push. "Grab your things, *mazleiha*. We're done for tonight."

"And tomorrow?"

"You meet me for dinner at eight."

"Where?"

"Figorelli's . . . west side of town."

"Italian?"

"Any objections?"

She shook her head and, using one of the club chairs for balance, slipped back into her sexy stilettos. Venom breathed in through his nose, then out his mouth. Goddamn. She really did have the longest legs he'd ever seen. Evelyn straightened and shrugged into her wrap. He smoothed his expression, giving nothing away as she met his gaze from across the room.

"I'll meet you there," she whispered, walking toward him.

Enjoying the sensual sway of her hips, he nodded. "One other thing."

"What?"

"I want your full name."

Not that he needed it. She'd fed him from the Meridian—source of all living things. Now he could track the trace energy she left in her wake anywhere. The full name was for Sloan. For the information Venom wanted his buddy to pull off the web about her. He needed to know more before he came face to face with her again.

"Evelyn Victoria . . ." She paused to sling her purse over her shoulder, then sidestepped on three-inch heels, walking between him and the bed. Leaving him behind, she headed for the door. "Foxe . . . spelled F-O-X-E."

His mouth curved.

Foxe. As in foxy as hell. The name suited her better than sweetheart. Which . . . frigging hell . . . made him want to abandon his principles. Forget *right*—throw it out the nearest window while he embraced *wrong*, whisked her away to Black Diamond, and . . .

Made her his.

"Go, Evie," he said, clinging to resolve by his fingernails. "Before I change my mind and ask you to stay."

Footfalls silent on the plush carpet, she reached the door. Her hand on the knob, she paused to look over her shoulder. Uncertainty in her eyes, she met his gaze. Seconds ticked into more before her expression softened. "Hey, Venom?"

Heart thumping hard, he tipped his chin. "Yeah?"

"See you tomorrow."

"Eight o'clock."

She nodded. The lock clicked. The door swung open. Evelyn stepped over the threshold and into the corridor.

And just like that, she was gone, leaving him surrounded by silence and physical need so thick he ached for her. Releasing a rough breath, Venom bowed his head, forcing himself to stay put. To be solid and keep his word. But it was hard. He wanted to go after her. Yearned to pull her back into his arms and head for home. Clenching his hands, he shook his head. No can do. Kidnapping her was a bad idea. He must do it properly. Woo her right. Earn her trust and win her acceptance in the end.

Desiring her didn't mean crossing the line. Or disrespecting the female he wanted for his own. Claiming Evelyn as his mate would come . . . in time. But only if he eased her toward accepting him and Dragonkind. By no means an easy proposition. Venom knew it, but refused to shy away. He couldn't. His dragon half wouldn't let him. Energy-fuse—the magical bond between mates—was a powerful thing. Once activated, a Dragonkind male couldn't resist its pull. Or the female who triggered the mating instinct.

His had clicked into place the moment he saw Evelyn.

Now he was stuck. Mired waist-deep in the curse of his kind. A prisoner of desire, he'd been caged by the sheer force of her. Which meant he couldn't go back, never mind—

Venom huffed.

What a stupid thought. He didn't want to go back. He'd been lonely for so long. Had waited for Evelyn all his life. His dragon half had bonded with her in seconds. Was now locked on and tuned in—burning for her with a ferocity that startled him. Everything hinged on her and his ability to earn her love: his future, his happiness, the promise of a mate who accepted him . . . flaws and all. Flexing his fingers, Venom swallowed hard. Such high stakes. So much to lose. Everything to gain. All he could do now was hope and pray.

Hope she came to need him.

And pray she stayed when he revealed his scalier side and the truth came out.

As the door clicked closed behind her, Evelyn halted in the middle of the hallway. Probably not the wisest course of action. She shouldn't be standing still. She should be walking instead, shoulders squared, chin up, stilettos moving at a steady clip across expensive carpet, heading for the lobby and unexpected freedom. She blew out a shaky breath. Heck, forget *walking*. She should be running. Jumping for joy too. Rejoicing in ways only the victorious could—with hard liquor and a raised glass. But with shock on the rise and her feet rooted to the floor, she couldn't force herself to move.

Or keep from shaking.

A normal reaction, no doubt. Relief could do that to a girl. Wreck her composure. Devastate good sense. Make the soles of her shoes stick to the floor.

Evelyn drew another shallow breath. She needed a minute. Just a few seconds before she walked away. Maybe then she'd regain what little remained of rational thought and . . .

Another tremor rattled through her.

She shook her head. Ah well, guess that settled it. To hell with being strong. She wanted to cry instead. Let loose and allow tears to flow while she thanked God for her near miss. For pulling her out of the fire and providing an unexpected solution to a bad situation. Evelyn swallowed past the lump in her throat. Holy lord, she'd been given a gift—the best kind of reprieve. More time coupled with a way out . . .

At the eleventh hour.

Not that she cared about the time frame. Saved amounted to just that . . . *saved*. The manner of it didn't matter. Neither did the reason behind her salvation. Bowing her head, Evelyn clutched at her handbag, hugging it to her chest. The roll of cash sat inside its leather confines. Three thousand dollars, more than half her next payment to Markov. The answer to all her prayers, and—thank God. She'd done it. Found a way out of the mess. Arrived at a remedy. One that would protect her from the Russian mob.

A light at the end of the tunnel. A little bit of hope.

She'd found both tonight.

All thanks to a gorgeous guy with *sharing* issues.

Evelyn huffed, the exhalation half-laugh, half-sob. *Exclusivity.* Oh, how she loved that word. And Venom for uttering it, insisting she stay away from other men. His warning rang inside her head. *No more meeting strangers in hotel rooms.* With a single phrase, he'd turned the situation around. Returned her self-worth. Made her believe in good fortune again and . . .

Lessened her shame.

All right, so it wasn't perfect. She didn't know him. Couldn't begin to guess what he intended for her either. Add that to the fact she reacted to him in, well—she shivered . . . how best to describe it? She rubbed her lips together. Heated was a good way to explain her response to him. Passion-fueled combustion was another. Mix in desirous greed and . . . uh-huh. Evelyn blew out a long breath. All three labels worked far too well.

To perfection, actually.

Recall raked the inside of her skull, providing a visual, driving remembered sensation, making pleasure rise and her shiver. Evelyn grimaced. Dear God, she'd asked him for more. Begged for his kiss. Would've followed his lead while he laid her down, giving him everything he demanded. She frowned. There was something horribly wrong about that. Very naughty too. She didn't enjoy sleeping with strangers. Had never been the adventure-seeking sort. Or craved anonymity in the sexual arena. She liked knowing a guy before getting personal, never mind intimate. But then, extraordinary measures called for uncomfortable resolutions.

The desperate couldn't be choosy. Which meant her reaction to Venom needn't enter the equation. No matter his charms—and her interest—he was a means to an end. Pure. Simple. No reason to explore further. He offered a way out of the darkness. A chance to stay safe . . . a path back to herself and self-worth. So, no question. Even less doubt. Only an idiot would turn down his generosity.

Set aside his unbelievable looks for a moment.

Forget about his gentle touch and obvious skill with women.

Ignore that he made her tingle with a glance.

Her attraction to him could go hang itself. The facts remained the same—agree to more dates and sex with him. Or sleep with a multitude of men in Trixie's stable to make the kind of money she needed to stay alive. Fear drew an icy path down her spine. Evelyn glanced at the door behind her. Room 301. Venom was still in there and . . .

She swallowed.

Yup. It was a done deal. File agreeing to his terms under no-brainer.

Despite her unease, he was the better bet. His plans for her didn't matter. Neither should his possessiveness. Oh, she'd seen it—in his eyes, the set of his jaw, the timbre of his deep voice too. His lethal vibe said it all. After one encounter, he already considered her his. He hadn't said it, but she recognized all the *you're-mine-for-the-time-being* signs. A bad thing? A fortuitous turn of events considering her circumstances? Evelyn didn't know. But one thing for sure? Her assumptions about him were bang on. Men like him never left anything to chance, so like it or not, she was now on his hit list. A target with a bull's-eye on her back.

The realization made her nerves jangle.

Dragging her gaze away from the door, Evelyn forced herself to move. Her stilettos sank into the plush carpet, silencing her footfalls as she beat feet down the corridor. And away from Venom. An excellent strategy. One rooted in self-preservation. Not that she thought he would hurt her. He'd already proven otherwise, but . . .

She needed some time. Enough space to decide how best to deal with him. Venom wasn't a pushover. Her brief interlude with him made that all too clear. He wouldn't be swayed by an easy smile. Or manipulated by her. Instinct told her he liked his way. Probably got it more often than not too, so . . . new game plan. She required one before she met him again. Before she walked into Figorelli's—one of the most exclusive restaurants in Seattle—and sat down to share a meal with him. If she didn't, she'd end up in serious trouble. Neck-deep with no idea how to extract herself from the situation—and Venom—when their association ended.

It might not happen next week. Maybe not next month either. But it would end . . .

Eventually.

She'd told Trixie the truth. The second she raised enough money and paid off her mother's debt, she'd be gone. Back to Granite Falls with her grandmother. Back on an even keel and headed in the right direction—on her way to a new job (fingers crossed) that didn't include selling herself to the highest bidder.

Pausing at the top of the stairs, Evelyn took a moment to settle down. Charging down the steps, across the lobby and out the front door wasn't a good idea. She'd cause a stir. Disrupt the party. Draw too many looks from the crowd gathered in the foyer. The thought made her tense. She didn't want the attention. Going unnoticed—slipping under the radar instead of standing out, settling her frayed nerves instead of adding to the tension—sounded better right now.

More pride affirming too.

One hand running along the smooth curve of the banister, Evelyn descended one step at a time. No rush. No reason for anyone to look up and notice her. No reason for Trixie to end her conversation with an older man in the middle of the lobby and turn around to see her escaping the Luxmore hours earlier than planned. Evelyn swallowed the lump in her throat and, gaze riveted to the madam, kept her feet moving. No way she wanted to tangle with Trixie. Or explain why she wouldn't be increasing the brunette's revenues by taking on more clients.

Fantastic strategy.

A little sneaky, granted. But in all honesty, she couldn't handle any more upheaval. Not tonight. A phone call to Trixie in the morning would suffice. In the meantime, she must stay on task and remain calm. Otherwise she wouldn't make it down the stairs, never mind all the way to the front door.

Pace steady, Evelyn leveled her chin and continued on. One step, two steps, three steps . . . four. Not much farther now. Almost there. Half a staircase away—eight, maybe nine treads—until she reached the main lobby. Her gaze skipped over the crowd again. Drinks in hand, men laughed. Decked out in the best money could buy, women smiled. The voice-fueled din rose, happy chatter collecting against the fancy cornices three stories up as she reached the bottom stair. A quick sidestep and she slid behind a group of businessmen. Talk of the latest golf game reached her.

Evelyn's mouth curved. Mission accomplished. She'd blended in. Was now hidden in plain sight, just moments from the front doors and the refreshing chill of night air. Framed by steel and glass doors, she could see valets standing post and—

A prickle ghosted over the nape of her neck.

Halfway across the lobby, she paused to glance over her shoulder. Nothing but a sea of normal. No one followed her. Busy in conversation, those gathered paid her no mind. And yet, the strange vibration intensified. Instinct drew her attention to the mezzanine beyond the curved staircase. She frowned. Empty. Nothing and nobody. An empty stretch of railing, nothing more, but . . .

Another shiver rolled, nudging intuition.

Evelyn frowned. God, it was weird. The warm tingle kept nipping at her, raising her internal alarm system, warning her to watch out. Now she couldn't shake the feeling someone stood watching her . . . from somewhere inside the Luxmore. Evelyn scanned the mezzanine level again. Still nothing. Not a single thing out of the ordinary. Which raised the question. Had the night finally taken its toll, pushing her toward paranoia? Maybe. She huffed. Strike that. Replace it with *absolutely.* Her reaction proved the point. No one stood watching her walk across the lobby. The Luxmore's patrons were too busy drinking cocktails, laughing it up . . . impressing those in the same social circle.

The prickle nicked her again.

Evelyn put her fancy footwear to good use. Heels clicking across the marble inlay, she dug for her keys. She found a hair pick instead. With a grumble, she tossed it back into the black hole that constituted her bag and tried again. She sighed. For the love of God, what a mess. She really must do something about that. Like cull all the unnecessary stuff she carried around like flotsam inside the oversize handbag.

Or maybe buy a smaller one.

Excellent idea. Maybe she would in the not-too-distant future . . . when she could afford it again. Still digging, Evelyn shoved her wallet out of the way as she approached the front door. The doorman greeted her with a smile. She nodded back, waited for him to do his job, then stepped over the threshold. Frosty air swirled around her feet and nipped at her bare legs. She sighed in relief, welcoming the chill and—

A jangle came from the bottom of her bag. Her fingertips brushed metal. Her mouth curved. Jackpot. Car keys found and retrieved.

Pausing on the curb, Evelyn palmed her key ring. Another quick search unearthed her cell phone. She touched the screen with her thumb. No new messages. Perfect. Better than good considering she didn't want to talk to anyone. Not right now. Maybe not for a while. Well, at least, until she met Venom tomorrow night. Until then, she'd enjoy some alone time. But first things first. She had a half-hour drive to reach Granite Falls. Which meant . . .

Time to get a move on and find her car.

Without a backward glance, she stepped onto the circular drive. Lights played across stone, illuminating icy patches on the pavers. Balanced on the balls of her feet, she hopscotched, avoiding the slippery spots, and headed for the sidewalk. Night shadows lengthened, casting eerie patterns as she neared the street. The shrubbery next to her rustled. Stifling a shiver, she pulled at the edges of her cashmere shawl. The wrap-up-and-take-cover approach didn't help. The odd tingle refused to leave her alone. Now it pulled at her skin, shoving unease to the foreground, making her wonder whether Markov stood watching from somewhere.

She glanced over her shoulder again.

Still nothing. Still no one.

Heart thumping, Evelyn upped the pace, resisting the urge to look behind her a second time. She was so close now. Another minute and she'd be free. On the other side of the avenue. Mere feet from the safety of her car. Close to having her doors locked and the creep factor under control. One key turn from driving away and—

Her cell phone vibrated in her hand.

The buzz startled her.

Evelyn flinched, then stepped off the cobblestones and onto the uneven sidewalk. She teetered a second, wobbling on three-inch heels before righting her balance. The Samsung buzzed again. Settling her ragged nerves, she scanned the parking lot across the street, then glanced at her phone. Caller ID provided the name. Evelyn frowned at the screen. Weird. Very what-the-hell on a busy Friday night, considering her grandmother never called after nine p.m.

With a flick of her thumb, Evelyn answered the call. "Hi, Mema. What are you doing up so la—"

"Evelyn," a guy said, raspy voice coming through the earpiece.

She blinked in surprise. A second passed before she recognized the voice. "Dr. Milford?"

"Yes," he said, sounding out of breath. Not at all like the unflappable doctor she bumped into at the corner store on a regular basis. On the other side of seventy, Dr. Milford had seen it all as Granite Falls' long-time physician. The man deserved a medal. For bravery in the face of overwhelming odds. Evelyn should know. She'd accompanied her grandmother to more doctor appointments than she wanted to remember. Been forced to stand outside the examination room and listen to Dr. Milford argue with Mema about the dangers of high cholesterol . . . and her grandmother's fondness for butter. Slathered on everything. "Where are you?"

"In town."

"You need to come home."

"What's going on?" she asked, a death grip on her phone. "Is it Mema? Is she all right?"

"I just put your grandmother in an ambulance."

"What—"

"I'll explain when you get here." A door slammed. Men shouted nearby, the sound coming through the connection loud and clear. The police, perhaps. Paramedics maybe, the urgency in their voices unmistakable. "We're taking her to Cascade Valley in Arlington."

"Okay." Mind racing, feet already moving, Evelyn ran across the road. Gaze locked on her Volkswagen, she slid onto the walkway and into the parking lot. "I'm leaving now."

"Good," he said. "Don't doddle, Evelyn. I'll meet you at the hospital."

A siren sounded in the background.

The phone disconnected.

Fear closed her throat. Dear God. Please, let her grandmother be all right. Please, please . . . triple *please*. The litany gouged at her temples, becoming a chant inside her head. Dread joined the party, twisting her stomach into knots, asking questions like—what if Markov lied? What if the monster had paid her grandmother another visit? What if Mema didn't pull through? The raw edge in Dr. Milford's voice pointed to an inescapable fact. He was concerned. Whatever had happened was more than just serious. The situation approached life threatening. And as Evelyn unlocked the door and slid inside her car, the possibilities—each one more horrific than the last—forced her to admit the truth.

It was her fault. The circumstances along with the outcome.

Every bit of it . . . *her fault.*

If only she'd been more clever. If only she'd solved the problem faster. If only she'd found a way to pay what her mother owed. None of it would have happened. She wouldn't be in front of the Luxmore, in a godforsaken parking lot, a breath away from prostitution in the middle of the night. And Mema wouldn't be headed to the hospital, never mind fighting for her life.

Chapter Seven

One shoulder propped against the wall inside the fire station, Ivar stared out the window and scowled at the night sky. Pinpoint stars winked at him from a blanket of black above the Seattle skyline. The city's glow blurred the edges, creating a fuzzy line between light and dark. Temper getting the better of him, he frowned at that too.

Waiting sucked.

He hated it. Despised the delays. The reason behind each one too.

Ivar growled. The low rumble made the rounds, echoing off glass and unpainted gypsum. He clenched his teeth on another curse. Fucking humans. Uncooperative residents of Granite Falls. His patience thinned by the second, the need to know poking at him like a pointy stick. Like a meth addict jonesing for his next fix, he craved information. Needed statistics. Yearned for colorful pie charts full of percentages—the equations detailing infection rates of the people who lived in the small town south of the Canadian border.

Everytown USA. The perfect human petri dish. One of the best sample groups around. But only if his gamble paid off.

Too many healthy immune systems made the outcome almost impossible to predict. Which left Mother Nature out in the cold. Not that *she* cared. Or gave a damn what he wanted. The fickle witch obviously didn't appreciate bar graphs—or microbiology—the way he did. Incubation periods of powerful viruses enjoyed a different kind of symmetry. The sort that didn't include him.

Aggravation jabbed at him.

Ivar shoved at his shirt sleeve. Light from a street lamp streamed through the window, hitting the face of his watch. The expensive timepiece served up the hour—just shy of two a.m. Almost seven days without a recorded symptom. Not a single one. Ivar sighed in disappointment. Delay upon delay. Days wasted watching TV, monitoring news broadcasts, listening to annoying anchormen yammer on about nothing special. Nights spent searching the Internet, streaming live video, reading blogs, looking for something—anything—to confirm his plan was working. Or whether time marched on without him.

A good question. One that should've yielded a quick answer given the fact he'd infected Granite Falls' water supply with a superbug over a week ago. A bio-cocktail, his baby was a beaut. Nasty. Fast acting. A killer wrapped up in a lethal viral load.

Or so he'd thought.

Until tonight.

Fucking hell, it was frustrating. He should be there now, right in the middle of the action. Set up in the center of town, watching his experiment unfold while his superbug went to work and humans died. A lovely thought. Nothing but a dwindling hope right now. Evidence of the outbreak had yet to surface. Not a whisper on the nightly news. No word from Denzeil or a ripple of panic in the human population. Which *sucked* . . . big time. Particularly since he couldn't collect a single blood or tissue sample until the infection took root. Which left him where? Stuck at home. Doing what? Twiddling his thumbs—hands tied, boots planted, bad mood escalating . . .

Waiting for something to happen.

Dragging his gaze from his watch, he focused on the road snaking past 28 Walton Street. An old fire station built in the 1930s, the property suited his needs. Ivar liked the symmetry of the place—big rooms, open layout, the very essence of feng shui. Toss in the underground lair sitting beneath the thirteen acres surrounding it, and he owned a winner. All he needed to keep himself busy and out of trouble, but . . .

Not tonight.

Ivar bit down on a curse. He was bored as hell, in desperate need of a distraction. He scanned the neighborhood again. Nothing and nobody. All quiet on the suburbia front. He pursed his lips. Different night, same results. No deviation in routine. No drama after dark. Very little to write home about. Same, same, and more of the *same*. Most nights, he enjoyed that about the sleepy corner of Seattle he called home. Neighbors never knocked on his door. Cops rarely drove by. And the lights inside the tiny houses dotting both sides of the narrow avenue always went out around nine o'clock.

Nice and predictable. Safe and—Ivar sighed—completely boring.

Shifting his weight from one foot to the other, he pushed away from the wall. His reflection wavered in the dark glass. Stepping over a pile of debris, he ignored his blurry outline in the bank of windows in favor of admiring the installation. High gloss and high tech, the triple-paned quintuplets stood shoulder to shoulder—wide, tall, and church-like, with arched tops and straight bottoms: a long line of clean, clear, and fabulous. No more hairline fractures in the glass. No more heat loss or chilly breezes through rotten wood frames. Brand spanking new, just like the wide floorboards beneath his feet.

He kicked at a piece of bamboo plank left by the recent renovation. Sawdust kicked up, dusting the toe of his boot, joining the scent of fresh drywall and joint compound. He glanced at the white patch of plaster beneath one of the window's steel casing. His mouth curved.

Almost there.

Another week or two and the upper floor of the once dilapidated firehouse would be finished. Nothing left to do but furnish the rooms and enjoy the space. A pleasant notion. One that should've pleased him. Most of the time, it did. Especially while testing viral loads inside his state-of-the-art laboratory one hundred and fifty feet below his present position. Tonight, though, satisfaction remained miles away. So far from reach, he couldn't summon an ounce of pride for his new digs.

Unclenching his fists, Ivar indulged in a shoulder roll. Sore muscles squawked. No surprise there. Stiff from standing still too long, his body begged for action. Wanted him to unleash his inner beast, spread his wings, and soar above the cityscape. His dragon half perked up, liking the idea. He glanced at the ceiling. Damp plaster patches stared back, daring him to do it, but . . .

Ivar shook his head.

No way. Blasting through the roof to reach fresh air wouldn't solve anything. Sure, it would lift his mood. Might even elevate the underlying tension for a while, but the relief wouldn't last. Temporary fixes never did. He must stay on track and hold the line. Just a little while longer. A month at most and he'd have what he needed—progress on all fronts. A safe, comfortable place to land after a hard night of fighting. News about Project

Supervirus and Granite Falls. More data on his breeding program and the female captives he kept caged in his underground lair.

So many balls in the air.

He couldn't afford to drop a single one. Not if he hoped to protect Dragonkind.

Some thought his fight to end environmental erosion was a phase. Nothing more than a way for him to pass the time while he played scientist. Ivar knew better. He wasn't *playing.* His willingness to eradicate an entire species—the human race—indicated that much. His decision stemmed more from desperation than curiosity. Was a haven of last resort, one he'd reached months ago. The tipping point was coming . . . the point of no return along with it. Mother Earth couldn't handle much more of the abuse humankind doled out on a regular basis.

The idiots were killing the planet.

Slowly. Without conscience. Or an ounce of remorse.

Evidence of it dominated the headlines. Monster storms. A depleted ozone layer and poor air quality. Ravaged rainforests, poisoned groundwater, and sick kids with never-before-seen allergies. Ivar blew out a long breath. He couldn't stand it anymore. The situation was so unnecessary. A ticking time bomb. One hundred percent correctable if caught in time. He shook his head. No hope in hell of that happening. The humans refused to heed the warnings. The idiots would do what they always did—take what they wanted, be greedy morons when it came to the environment, and ignore the consequences.

Which left him one recourse. Make plans. Ensure each strategy's success. Continue to move forward on his own with fewer resources than he wanted—and more pressure from Rodin than he needed.

A pity in more ways than one.

Ambitious and power hungry, Rodin liked to meddle and never let up. He wanted regular updates and called far too often. Annoying? Absolutely. A necessary evil? Without a doubt. The constant monitoring in exchange for support from one of the most powerful males of his kind was a small price to pay. Well worth the aggravation in the long term. Ivar grimaced. All right, so he didn't enjoy the strings. Or Rodin's habit of trying to play him like a marionette. But money was just that . . . *money.* And more funds equaled greater flexibility.

The kind that would allow him to end the scourge called humankind.

Turning on his heel, Ivar strode toward the opposite side of the room. His footfalls echoed, pinging off the pitted brick walls. Bang-scrap-thump. Thud-creak-rasp. Up and back. Round and round. One circuit rolled into another . . . and then into more. His reflection flashed across the wall of glass as he skirted a plastic garbage bin. Sidestepping the table saw next to it, he halted in front of the last window. Right back where he started. Sad, but true. Ending up where he began seemed to be his MO of late.

With a long-drawn sigh, he shoved his hands into his front pockets and resettled against the frame. Steel bit into his bicep. Discomfort raced down his arm as he mimicked the sad sag of a house with ancient eaves across the street. He stared at it and the beat-up Jeep parked in the driveway. Memory clawed, then dug in, reminding him who owned the rusted-out Wrangler. His mouth went dry. Ivar swallowed as her name streamed into his head.

Sasha Cooper . . . sex kitten extraordinaire.

An image of her raked the inside of his skull, making his temples throb and the traitor behind his button fly wake up. Full-blown arousal in under a second. Devastating need. Burning desire. All-consuming *want.* Ivar closed his eyes and, giving in to recall, replayed the night he'd spent with her. The one in which Sasha had played siren to his sailor. Holy fuck, she'd been incredible. Beyond anything he'd ever experienced. Gorgeous bio-energy. Unforgettable taste. Enthralling surrender. Her beautiful brown eyes soft in welcome. The heat of her embrace. All that pale, smooth skin beneath his hands. The sound of her voice as she whispered his name, begging him to take her again. The feel of her coming around him. God. What a memory and . . .

Ivar fisted his hands in his pockets.

Shit. Not good. Or even the tiniest bit wise.

He needed to get her out of his head. Right now. Before he did something stupid—like leave the lair, cross the street, and knock on her front door. Again. Like the last time. Big mistake. Even worse results. Particularly since she'd tried to kill him in the aftermath of multiple orgasms.

Jesus, he'd almost died.

Died, for fuck's sake. And yet, here he stood . . . fantasizing about her. Recalling the touch and taste of her. Trying to figure out how to protect himself so he could visit Sasha a second time. Sleep with her again. Spend the entire night instead of just a few hours.

The idea tugged at him, urging him to find a way around the problem. So far, he hadn't come up with a single way to negate her effect on him. For obvious reasons. He'd never met a female who could counteract his magic before, never mind open a channel to the Meridian through him. Sasha had done just that, using his unique bio-signal to connect to the source and steal his core energy. She'd sapped his strength, blocked his ability to disconnect, then drained him dry. The fact he'd made it out of her house alive qualified as a miracle.

A huge one. The kind he knew wouldn't happen twice.

Too bad the scientist in him refused to let it go. He loved puzzles. Excelled at finding answers to difficult problems. Sasha represented an intriguing one. Now he wanted to know everything about her along with what kind of power she wielded. Otherwise he'd remain vulnerable, flawed by weakness instead of warrior-strong. In no way ideal. He was commander of the Razorback nation. Born and bred for war, not a sissy in need of—

"Ivar."

Couched in a thick Norwegian accent, the voice slid home like a knife blade: slick and smooth, almost soothing as it pricked across his skin. Ivar's mouth curved. Thank God. About frickin' time. A worthy distraction was headed his way.

Opening his eyes, Ivar glanced over his shoulder. Standing on the other side of the room, a six pack of Heineken in his hand, Hamersveld frowned at him. Ivar almost smiled back. *Almost*, but not quite. He was too busy looking for the male's wren. A good idea on the self-preservation front. Fen was a nasty little bugger. Devoted to the Norwegian. Great in claw-to-claw combat. Not so hot to come face to face with inside the lair. Hell, the miniature dragon had nearly taken Ivar's head off the last time he'd bumped into him.

"Where's Fen?" Ivar asked, searching the shadows behind his friend.

Hamersveld tapped his shoulder, pointing to the tattoo hidden beneath his T-shirt. "Recharging."

"Good."

"Why—you scared?"

Ivar snorted. *Scared?* Not really, although he couldn't deny his wariness. A healthy reaction driven by the need to stay alive, and yet he refused to walk away. Fen presented an interesting challenge wrapped up in a dangerous dilemma. On the one hand, the miniature dragon fascinated Ivar. And on the other?

His vicious nature made him difficult to study. Less than half Ivar's size in dragon form, Fen didn't have an ounce of human in him. Pure dragon DNA, related to Dragonkind, but genetically distinct too. Fast in flight, deadly as hell, wrens operated on a different set of magical principles. Which . . . yeah . . . qualified as a scientist's wet dream—Ivar's, in particular. Mapping the wren's chromosomal structure would take him years. Maybe even decades. A terrific opportunity, but for one thing . . .

The wren never went anywhere without Hamersveld. Why? Interesting question . . . easy answer. Fen couldn't survive on the earthly plane without the male.

Wrens didn't consume food. Or draw sustenance from human females like the rest of Dragonkind. Each wren bonded with a Dragonkind male, relying on his host to feed and keep him healthy. A unique process, one that required the miniature dragon to merge with the tribal markings on the host male's skin. The magical tattoo functioned like an electrical socket. Plug into the source. Draw the right amount of current from the electrostatic bands ringing the planet. Recharge the batteries. The instant Fen's bio-energy connected with Hamersveld's, the arcane bond clicked into place and . . .

Eureka. Two merged into one.

Well, at least for a little while. Ivar didn't know how long the recharging process lasted. It varied from week to week. Sometimes Fen disappeared inside the tattoo for days. On other occasions, for just a few hours.

Which made the wren an even more fascinating specimen.

Unable to keep his curiosity in check, Ivar tipped his chin. "How long has he been gone this time?"

"Less than a day. Five hours." Suspicion in his eyes, Hamersveld frowned. "Are you charting him?"

"The thought's crossed my mind."

"Always the scientist."

"Curiosity," he murmured, watching the male closely. "The curse of my calling."

Hamersveld rolled his eyes.

Ivar gave in to a grin. He couldn't help it. Despite Hamersveld's difficult nature, he liked the male. All right, so maybe *like* was too powerful a word. Respect might be a better one. Not that it mattered. He might not know him well yet, but Ivar had high hopes for the Norwegian. The warrior was solid, if somewhat hard to read. Accustomed to being alone, Hamersveld gave nothing away. He held his emotions in check, played his cards close to the vest, and never let anyone close.

Ivar understood the compulsion. He suffered from the same affliction. Understood the male better than most. A lifetime of mistrust took time to overcome. And friendship never came easy. Knowing that, however, didn't stop Ivar from wanting it. He craved the connection. Liked the idea of having a friend. One he could trust to help him shoulder the burden. Someone capable of becoming his first in command. Hamersveld fit the bill, ticking all the boxes on his wish list—smart, lethal, a strong male with an impressive gift.

The kind that spelled water dragon.

A serendipitous find. An even better friend to have on his side. Particularly since most Dragonkind males feared water.

Holding Hamersveld's gaze, Ivar raised a brow. "Back from your swim in Puget Sound already?"

"I didn't go."

Huh. Well, wasn't that interesting? A deviation in routine. More than a touch odd. Hamersveld never missed his midnight dip. Lake. Ocean. Small stream or Olympic-size swimming pool. The location didn't matter as long as water was involved. Which meant one of two things: either the male wasn't feeling well or he needed to talk.

Hoping for the latter, Ivar glanced at the case of Heineken. "Got one for me?"

"Maybe."

Rimmed by light blue, shark-black eyes met his. Looking a little unsure, Hamersveld hesitated. Ivar stayed silent, refusing to prompt his new friend. Talk? Refuse to confide? The decision belonged to Hamersveld, not him.

One second stretched into more before the male moved. Stepping around a stack of bamboo flooring, he strode across the room. Beer bottles rattled, shimmying inside the flimsy cardboard case. The quiet thump of heavy footfalls joined the clink of glass, then ceased as Hamersveld stopped alongside him. Cracking the top, his friend handed him a beer, took one for himself, then set the box on the floor at his feet. Finished with the buddy routine, Hamersveld propped his shoulder against the window pane a few feet away.

And Ivar waited. For Hamersveld to crack. For him to make the first move and trust him with the problem.

A furrow between his brows, Hamersveld sighed. "What the hell are you doing up here? Thought to find you in the lab."

"Finished working an hour ago." Grabbing his beer by the throat, Ivar twisted off the top. Carbonation hissed as foam bubbled up the bottle neck. Ignoring the froth, Ivar flicked the cap toward the garbage can across the room and . . . bingo. Dead center. Middle-of-the-basket accurate. Hurrah for him. A solid two points. "I'm waiting for bacteria cultures to mature."

"No word yet from Granite Falls?"

Ivar shook his head. "Not a peep."

"And now you're restless?"

"Twitchy as hell," he said, admitting the weakness even though it left a bad taste in his mouth. Ivar swallowed the burn. Humility wasn't his strong suit. Neither was copping to vulnerability—real or imagined. But bringing Hamersveld close necessitated a different approach. One that started in honesty and ended in trust. Swiping at the beer label with the pad of his thumb, he obliterated the water droplets and cleared his throat. "I hate waiting."

Hamersveld hummed in understanding. "You're impatient."

"Always have been."

"Give it time, *zi kamir*," Hamersveld said, calling him brother in Dragonese, acting like a real friend, giving Ivar hope. "The superbug you cooked up is lethal. It'll kick in."

"I know."

Ivar stifled a snort. So much for honesty. The false bravado in his tone said it all—he wasn't sure. Didn't *know* a damned thing. Not for certain anyway.

"If it doesn't take, though, we're dead in the water." Raising his hand, Ivar took a pull from the bottle. Cool and crisp, the Heineken teased his taste buds, then rolled, blazing a chilly trail down the back of his throat. "We'll have to start from scratch."

"Hasn't happened yet." Peeling the label off his bottle, Hamersveld crumpled it into a ball. A quick flick sent it flying into the open top of the six pack. "Stop dwelling on it."

"Fuck you," Ivar said, a growl in his voice. "It isn't your baby out there—not doing its job."

Hamersveld huffed. "You want a distraction while we wait for it to kill someone?"

"Please," he said, taking another sip. "Whatcha got?"

"An idea."

"About what?"

"The high-energy females you've got locked inside cell-block A."

Oh, yeah. Nice segue. An excellent turn in the conversation.

The only topic guaranteed to help him forget Granite Falls. At least, for the moment. The human females imprisoned inside his underground lair focused his attention like nothing else could. A rare breed, the HEs were the cornerstone of his breeding program. He'd hunted for months to locate each one. Now, he agonized over their well-being. Fed them gourmet meals full of protein and vitamins. Made sure each got what she needed—exercise, sunlight, as many books as she could read. Measured fertility rates too—testing for every genetic deficiency under the sun—before injecting his pretty little test subjects with the serum he'd developed in his lab.

All he could do now was wait for the Meridian to realign at the spring equinox. One of only two times during the year Dragonkind became fertile. The realignment of the electrostatic bands triggered primal drive, forcing males of his kind into the *hungering.* A frenzied sort of mating . . . a state that ensured the continuation of his species. Which meant he needed to be ready.

He had a single shot. Just *one* to get it right.

The serum was designed to alter dragon DNA. Replace the reproductive XY chromosomal pairing with an XX, breed the first Dragonkind female in over six hundred years, and break the curse plaguing his kind. A lofty goal. Incredibly difficult to achieve. He'd spent years experimenting, looking for the right sequence, the precise combination that would free him from the yoke of human dependence.

As it stood now, Dragonkind males relied on human females to propagate the continuation of his species. In less than three months, that could all change when the Meridian realigned. But only if his serum worked and he succeeded in reprogramming dragon DNA. His captives held the potential inside their wombs.

Infinite possibility. So much hope. Liberty for all of Dragonkind.

Draining his bottle, Ivar set his empty beer on the windowsill and reached for another. "What are you thinking, Sveld?"

"We should make it a competition." His mouth curved, Hamersveld tossed the beer cap like a coin. Metal spun end over end, flashing in the low light. Picking it out of mid-air, the male threw it toward the garbage can. "Don't handpick the males. Make them compete for the privilege of breeding one of the females."

"What—like some kind of Dragonkind Olympics?"

"Dragonkind Olympics . . . I like that." Hamersveld grinned. "Top five win a night with an HE female when the Meridian realigns."

"The champion gets first pick?"

The male tipped his Heineken in salute. "A once-in-a-lifetime opportunity."

Ivar's lips twitched. "You entering?"

"*Hristos*, no." With a grimace, Hamersveld threw him a disgusted look. "I don't want any offspring. I'm still trying to kill my last mistake."

"The Nightfury water-rat," Ivar said, amused by his friend's lack of paternal instinct. Talk about bizarre. Most males relished the idea of a family. Hamersveld couldn't stand the thought. He liked his one-of-a-kind water dragon status. Didn't want any competition, even if it came from his own son. "You sure you can eliminate him?"

"No question. But we're not talking about that bastard right now." Pushing away from the window, Hamersveld rolled his shoulders. Excitement sparked in his eyes, making the blue rims around his black irises shimmer. "I'll organize everything, Ivar. Set up the parameters. Find the right location for the games . . . somewhere rural with rough terrain. Lay the groundwork and invite Razorbacks to sign up for the competition. All you have to do is judge it."

Eyes narrowed, Ivar examined the possibility. The idea possessed an infinite amount of promise. Was a real no-brainer when fit into the greater scheme. The competition would drive two important outcomes. The first—ensure the strongest warriors bred his females. And second—the games would allow Ivar to assess the abilities of each Razorback. There had been an influx of new blood lately, some males arriving from Europe, others from a fractured pack in South America. Venezuela, maybe. Or Peru.

Ivar frowned. He couldn't remember. Never a good sign. Particularly since the Nightfury assholes picked his soldiers off faster than he could figure out who'd arrived from where. Now, he didn't know half the new members' names. A circumstance in need of change. He couldn't lead, after all, if he didn't know who the hell formed his pack. He wanted names. He wanted skill levels. He wanted to look each warrior in the eye and decide whether he belonged in the Razorback pack.

Which was why he'd scheduled another round of dragon combat training.

Not the most popular decision.

The lockdown meant his warriors must stay out of the city. No female company or feeding until they completed the qualifying round. No tangling with Nightfuries either. A great idea given the recent death toll. Excellent upside . . . no dead Razorbacks. The downside of his objective, however, let Bastian off the hook for the foreseeable future. The prospect didn't sit well with Ivar. But despite the disappointment, he refused to lift the lockdown.

Sequestering the Razorbacks—keeping the males in training mode and off Nightfury radar—was the smartest play.

At least, for now.

He had bigger plans. Ones that didn't include his soldiers getting KO'd by a bunch of bastards with huge chips on their shoulders. His eyes narrowed, Ivar took another drink. Fucking Nightfuries. Such a major pain in his ass. He really needed to do something about the warriors . . . like locate the Nightfury lair. Hit hard and fast. Massacre them all before Bastian knew what hit him.

Floorboards creaked beside him. "Come on, Ivar. Give it the green light."

Ivar blinked and glanced at Hamersveld.

The male's gaze bore into his. "It's a solid plan."

"A fun one too."

"Endless amounts of entertainment." Hamersveld's mouth curved. "A total win-win."

Anticipation thrummed through him. *Dragonkind Olympics.* A crazy concept with an excellent upside. "Set it up, Sveld. Let's see where it leads us, but . . ."

Hamersveld raised a brow. "But what?"

"Make sure no one dies. We can't afford to lose any more fighters."

"Not a problem." A gleam in his eyes, the Norwegian nodded. "I can work with—"

The hum of gears rattled through the quiet.

A second later, the elevator pinged. The sound of double doors opening followed, the faint hiss reaching him from the other side of the firehouse.

Ivar pushed away from the wall. "Denzeil?"

"*Ja,*" the male called from the back of the house. Footfalls echoed as his second in command trotted around the wall separating the future kitchen from the soon-to-be living room. Dark eyes alive with excitement, Denzeil wagged the tablet he held. "Got some news. Action in Granite Falls."

Thank God. Some results. It was about time.

"What kind?" he asked.

"A cluster of nine-one-one calls," Denzeil said. "Five humans have been admitted to Cascade Valley Hospital so far . . . symptoms vary, but the notes in each file indicate the humans don't have a clue what kind of infection is causing the problem."

Hamersveld hummed. "Looks like your baby's on the move, Ivar."

Meeting Denzeil halfway across the room, Ivar accepted the tablet. He tapped the screen. The first nine-one-one call became audible. He listened to the message. Total panic in the human's voice. Complete chaos in the background. A terrified husband calling on behalf of his wife.

Relief hit Ivar like a closed fist. He sucked in a quick breath. "It's working."

"Tip of the iceberg, boss man," Denzeil said, grinning at him. "It's just begun."

"Wanna go take a look-see?" Palming Ivar's shoulders from behind, Hamersveld gave him a congratulatory squeeze. "We've got a couple of hours before sunrise to—"

"Not yet. Let's give the virus more time to incubate." Twelve hours should do it. Would be long enough to monitor the activity and see how many humans became infected. Returning Denzeil's grin, Ivar listened to the next call and thumped Hamersveld with the side of his fist. The love tap connected just above the warrior's heart, making the Norwegian smile. "We leave at sundown tomorrow."

"Fantastic," Hamersveld murmured.

No kidding. *Fantastic* barely scratched the surface.

Fisting the front of Hamersveld's shirt, Ivar jostled his new friend again. God. The sweet, *sweet* taste of victory. His science hadn't failed. Wasn't flawed, after all. Which meant phase two needed to be kicked into gear. He hummed in anticipation, 'cause . . . to hell with dragon combat training. His warriors and the training op in the Cascade Mountain Range would have to wait. Tomorrow night promised excitement of another sort. He had somewhere else to be—smack-dab in the middle of a hospital, collecting samples from the infected humans who called Granite Falls home.

Chapter Eight

Head bowed, still strapped to the rack, Gage tried to be patient. Fine mist fell, mixing with his blood, trickling down his chest, toying with his willpower. Fuck. He wanted to move so badly. To unleash hell and unload on the male tormenting him. He gritted his teeth instead. Waiting it out was the better option. The second he moved, so much as twitched, Ferland would grow a brain and get a clue. And tipping his hand? Not a great idea, but . . . God. It was hard to stay still while the prick took his time unlocking the cuffs holding him against the steel grill.

Metal flashed in his periphery.

Keys jangled on the large ring.

Anticipation made his heart pound harder. The chaotic thump pushed adrenaline through his veins. Now he couldn't hear a thing, just the blood rush of cerebral burn and the threat of sensory overload. His dragon senses flexed. The magical warp skewed perception, upping the intensity. His focus narrowed. Pain gouged at his temples. Gage pushed the agony aside, refusing to feel anything, and listened to Ferland flip through the assortment of keys.

He was so close. Almost there. One shackle already open. Three more keys, two ankles, and one wrist away from complete freedom.

Long odds in a dicey game.

Gage didn't care. Unworkable situations were his specialty. He never avoided difficult assignments. Or shied away from the near impossible. Easy bored him. So did inactivity. Intrigue coupled with a healthy dose of challenge added more flavor. Like a hit of hot sauce, the promise of action jazzed him like nothing else could. The Nightfury warriors understood his propensity for violence, accepting his maniacal lean toward lethal without question. But the prick about to uncuff him? Gage cracked his uninjured eye open. He smothered a smile. Excellent. The jerkoff still didn't have a clue.

Finding the right key, the brainless wonder fit it to the lock next to his right hand and . . . umm, baby. One step closer to liberation. His quick reflexes coupled with the enemy's distraction. The perfect storm. An epic shift in circumstance. A beautiful gift in a dark place—thank God. Despite the lockdown, Ferland's ineptitude gave Gage the upper hand. Which meant he must stay still and act weak. The instant the male realized he wasn't half-dead, he'd be finished. Done. Game over. No way off the vertical rack bolted to the wall. No chance of shattering the shackles. No prospect of getting out—or helping Haider—at all.

The thought rooted him in purpose.

The threat of failure made him play the game.

With a groan, Gage sagged in the shackles, acting like a pansy too weak to hold himself upright. The move left a bad taste in his mouth but, well . . . screw it. Who the hell cared? Playing possum was a necessary evil. It would make his enemy's task more difficult. Gage's attempt at theater more convincing too, so—

Ferland cursed under his breath.

Gage swallowed a growl of satisfaction. Perfect. Right on time. His plan was working. And Ferland was officially screwed. So distracted by his weight on the rack, the prick had yet to notice his alertness. Or the fact he'd cracked his eyes open—to watch and wait. Lids at half-mast, his gaze slid to the other male in the room. Osgard stood to one side—hands folded, head bowed, shoulders hunched instead of squared—looking petrified.

Without so much as a twitch, Gage sized the kid up. Tall and gangly with too-big hands and feet, Osgard had yet to grow into his body. Sixteen—maybe seventeen—years old . . . at least three years from his *change* and first shift into dragon form, he wore vulnerability like a scent. An awful one soaked in fear, hopelessness, and . . .

Ah, hell.

The fledgling was out of his league. Completely boxed in too. Particularly since his body language indicated more than just uncertainty. It screamed abuse. The kind of beaten down and broken most males didn't come back from, never mind survive.

Regret punched through, hammering Gage like a closed fist.

Talk about unfortunate. So unlucky. For Osgard, sure, but for him too. He wasn't in the habit of killing Dragonkind infants. But then, life-threatening circumstances called for brute force driven by unerring fury. He couldn't spare Osgard and hope to get out of the death squad's underground lair alive. Everyone he encountered in the subterranean labyrinth would die. Pure and simple. Safer for him. Better for Haider. The sooner he found his friend, the more distance he'd put between them and the Archguard. The quicker he'd get word to Bastian too. A couple of hours at most before Zidane came back from the morning meal. Which meant he didn't have time for bullshit. Not an instant for mercy or the rise of a rusty conscience either, so—

A loud click echoed, bouncing off scarred stone walls.

The shackle swung open, liberating his right ankle. Both feet free, one wrist cuff to go. Gage sagged a little more, allowing his knees to dip. Ferland turned toward the last shackle. Metal scraped metal as he fit key to padlock. Another snick sounded. The Mastercraft released with a pop. The lock scraped against the steel bracket holding his arm over his head.

Gage tensed, getting ready to move.

He forced strength into his limbs. Muscles tightened over his bone. His fingertips twitched. The involuntary action signaled eagerness. Gage shut it down. He couldn't afford a single mistake. Not now, just moments away from freedom. Seconds ticked past, sliding into more. Boots rasping against the floor. Ferland shifted next to him. Gage started the countdown. Three. Two . . .

With a flick, Ferland swung the last shackle wide.

One and—

Go!

His bare feet landed on the concrete floor with a thump. Gage exploded off the rack. His skin peeled off hot steel, making pain receptors squawk along his spine. Anguish clawed around his rib cage. He ignored the sharp jab to focus on his prey. Ferland's head snapped up. Eyes widening in alarm, the male cursed.

Gage cranked his hands into twin fists.

The prick backpedaled in a hurry. With a panicked spin, he vaulted toward the wall full of torture tools. Gage snarled and lunged after him. No way. Not going to happen. A fair fight wasn't part of the plan. Neither was giving Ferland a chance to reach any of the blades laid out on the tabletop.

Rage murmured his name.

He attacked. Ferland squawked as Gage caught hold of his shirt. Cotton ripped, shredding in his hand. With a snarl, he tightened his grip, raised his fist and—

Bam!

His knuckles slammed into the side of the asshole's skull. Ferland's chin snapped to one side. The smell of blood infused the air. In a panic, the male lashed out, trying to land a punch. Gage countered and, with a yank, dragged the enemy full circle. His eyes narrowed on the torture rack. An idea sparked, hammering his temples, obliterating restraint. The fucking bastard. He'd kept him pinned for hours. Helpless in the face of pain. Locked down by electrical current. And enjoyed every second of it.

One step. A quick shift to his right, and—

Gage rammed Ferland's head into the rack.

Bone met steel. Once. Twice. A third time and . . . crack! The prick's skull split wide open. Blood gushed, splattering across the grill. Gage hammered him again. Ferland sagged in his grip. A death gurgle spilled from the male's mouth. Chest pumping, Gage loosened his hold. Matted with blood, the male's hair slid between his fingers. With a snarl, Gage twisted. Another pop echoed, reverberating against stone walls as he snapped his enemy's neck.

A quick death. Faster than Ferland deserved and Gage wanted, but . . .

Time was of the essence.

So was a quick getaway.

As Ferland's heart stopped beating, he disintegrated, muscle and bone dissolving into ash. Gray flakes floated, swirling on stale air, rising up to surround Gage. Silence descended. Relief took hold, rushing fatigue back to the forefront. His body throbbed, making him feel every cut and scrape, burn and bruise. Gritting his teeth, Gage turned toward the exit.

Pale faced, Osgard took a step back.

His gaze narrowed on the kid. "You run and you're dead."

Osgard flinched at the sound of his voice. Staring at the ash pile on the floor, the kid swallowed. As his Adam's apple bobbed, he released a shuddered breath. "I won't run. Or raise the alarm, but . . ."

"But what?"

"Take me with you. Please, my lord, take me with you."

Fear in his eyes, Osgard met him head-on, standing tall in the face of brutality. Hope mingled with terror, making the youngling's pale eyes shimmer. Gage's chest went tight. He bit down on a snarl. Goddamned son of a bitch. Of all the rotten luck. Just what he didn't need . . . a tagalong wrapped up in a kid in need of rescue. But as the kid bowed his head and knelt on the cold concrete a few feet away, Gage knew he was in trouble. He despised bullies. Disliked seeing others mistreated, and always championed the underdog. A flaw in his nature, he knew.

Too bad he couldn't seem to help it.

Every time he tried, he ended up neck-deep in dangerous territory—like now, facing off with a youngling in desperate need of help—and little hope of a better future. Which . . . just kill him now . . . set his protective nature ablaze. As the inferno got going, Osgard threw more fuel on the fire, trembling in front of him, whispering another *please*, begging Gage until his heart clenched. Now he hurt for the kid. Not a good sign. He tended to do stupid things when—

"I will be useful, I swear it," Osgard whispered, desperation in his voice. "I will serve you well if you but give me a chance to prove my—"

"I don't need a servant."

"A son, then."

A son. Gage blinked, surprise spinning him full circle.

"All warriors need a son. I know I am not of your blood, but I am strong and willing to learn. I will be a good son to you, I promise." Lifting his chin, Osgard hammered him with pleading eyes. "I know you are a worthy male . . . that you come from an honorable pack. Please, my lord, do not leave me here with Zidane."

Well, shit. A sucker punch. An excellent one too.

Smart little whelp. Osgard knew what he was doing. Particularly since his hatred of Zidane cranked Gage's need to help the kid into overdrive. Despite the seriousness of the situation, amusement streamed through him. His mouth curved. Good for Osgard. The kid played dirty. Possessed his fair share of brains . . . a truckload of potential too. Something akin to pride punched through, warming the center of his chest. Gage killed the reaction—along with the sentiment—and smoothed his expression. He didn't have time to mess around. And standing in the middle of a torture chamber chatting with a kid? Yeah, that qualified as stupid. So only one thing left to do . . .

Get a move on.

Favoring his right side, Gage tucked his elbow against his rib cage and, shoving aside discomfort, limped toward Osgard. His bare feet brushed the uneven floor. Silence expanded, throbbing through the room as he came alongside the male. Still on his knees, the kid tensed, but stayed true, allowing Gage's proximity. Uncertainty took hold, making him hesitate. He shoved it aside, then reached out. Grabbing the back of Osgard's shirt, he hauled the whelp to his feet.

Osgard's chin came up.

Gage drilled him with an intense look. "Do you know where my friend is being held?"

He nodded. "I brought him a meal an hour ago. They have him caged not far from here."

"Show me." Done with the chitchat, Gage spun the kid around. Palming his shoulder, he pushed Osgard toward the door. "We don't have much time."

"Does that mean . . ." Osgard trailed off, bright and shiny hope in his expression. "Are you—" He swallowed, the bob of his Adam's apple telling. "Taking me with you, my lord?"

Folding like a windblown reed, Gage growled. "Don't call me that. It's Gage. Call me *my lord* one more time, kid, and you won't be going anywhere. I'll rip your head off instead."

Moisture in his eyes, Osgard treated him to a wobbly smile.

Gage quelled the urge to cringe. He recognized that look. Relief times a gazillion . . . pure, unadulterated happiness. The kind that used hero worship as a launch pad. He shook his head. God, he was so screwed. Fucked six ways to Sunday. Up shit creek without a paddle. Whatever. The metaphor didn't matter. The mess he stood in the middle of, however, did . . . a whole helluva lot. Meant everything, in point of fact. Now only one truth held sway. Being injured, deep in enemy territory with fatigue gnawing on him—and a youngling to protect—wasn't optimal. But as he gave Osgard a gentle shove, limped over the threshold and into the corridor behind his new charge, Gage refused to reverse course. He'd made his decision.

And sealed his fate.

Osgard was coming with him.

Nothing left to do now but hope the whelp hadn't lied. He needed to find Haider and get out of the underground lair . . . lickety-split fast. Otherwise, he wouldn't be able to protect himself or his friend, never mind a kid in desperate need of rescue.

Chapter Nine

Hidden from view by an invisibility spell, Venom stood on the sidewalk outside the Luxmore, watching Evelyn cross the parking lot. A bad move. He'd known it five minutes ago—before he vaulted over the balcony railing, plummeting three stories to land on the garden path below. He'd known it as he trailed her across the horseshoe-shaped driveway too. In the same way he knew it now. Too bad he couldn't kill his reaction. No matter how many times he told himself to stop—to stay put and allow her to leave without interference—primal instinct grabbed hold, refusing to release him. He needed to make sure. To see her safely to her car . . . and ensure no one accosted her on the way out.

The reaction smacked of dominance. Of possessiveness and a need so profound it couldn't be denied.

Par for the course, he guessed. Energy-fuse was serious stuff. A magic-driven bond that never said quit. Or faded over time. Once triggered, a Dragonkind male couldn't resist the pull. Which explained a lot, didn't it? Like why he stood rooted to the spot, eyes trained on Evelyn, his dragon half silently protesting her retreat, heart pounding so hard Venom wondered when he'd lost his mind. Sometime in the last hour, for sure. Nothing else explained his willingness to let her go without making love to her.

Or the fact he watched from a distance while she walked away.

The action seemed unnatural. Like a huge mistake. The worst of his life. Hands flexing into fists, Venom clenched his teeth. Talk about an understatement. He'd made more than his fair share. Had screwed up so many times he'd lost count years ago. And yet as the click of her high heels grew fainter, he questioned the validity of his plan. His brows collided. Maybe he was wrong. Maybe kidnapping her was the way to go. Maybe given enough time Evelyn would come to care for him—just as the other Nightfuries' chosen females had their mates—'cause sure as shit, watching her leave felt, well . . . wrong.

All wrong.

Screwed up to the highest power or something.

Now all he wanted was to say the hell with it. Forget the plan. Bury his reasons along with the patient approach six feet under. Right. Wrong. Neither mattered anymore. Not while the urge to cross the road, pick her up, and carry her home thumped on him. Trying to loosen the tension, he rolled his shoulders. Taut muscles pulled, stretching along either side of his spine, but refused to give an inch. The ache stayed. And temptation? Venom huffed. That bastard kept poking at him, making the need to go after her hard to resist. Now he hung between two trains of thought—retrieve or let her go.

The first idea sounded better than the second.

Easy. Effective. Immediate gratification wrapped up in expediency. Abduction—a strategy loaded with real possibility. Except for one thing.

Evelyn wasn't just any female.

She belonged to him. Was the one he'd waited for all his life. His mate. His to nurture and protect. His to bring into the Nightfury fold. Which meant he couldn't rush her. He wanted her acceptance. He needed her to love him. He craved a chance at a lifetime with her, so . . .

Blowing out a long breath, Venom shook his head. No way. Not going to happen. He needed to keep it together and stick to the plan. Wooing her—putting in the necessary time—would get him further faster. Hammering the facts home, he locked his knees. His muscles twitched, protesting the clampdown. He ignored the discomfort. Moving wasn't a good idea. Not right now. The second his feet left the ground, he'd be done, halfway across the street with nothing good in mind. How fast he could get his hands on Evelyn topped the list. How much he wanted to kiss her again scored high too. How amazing it would feel to finish what they'd started in the hotel room and—

Goddamn it. Wrong thought. Again.

With a growl, Venom put a leash on desire. Restraint settled back into place, leveling him out, allowing him to take a full breath, letting logic lead. Thank God. The possessive crap wasn't much fun. Watching Evelyn move, though? Hmm baby, that was a complete pleasure.

Head bowed, feet moving at a rapid clip, Evelyn dug inside her handbag. Dragon senses keen, he heard her curse under her breath, then grumble in relief as she unearthed her keys. She rotated the set in her hand. Metal jangled against her palm. The work of seconds, she flipped the lock, popped the handle, and pulled the door wide. Rusty hinges creaked, cutting through the quiet, making Evelyn flinch. Looking a little paranoid and a lot worried, she glanced around, scanning the darkness beyond the pool of lamplight. Venom tightened the invisibility spell, ensuring he stayed out of sight. The last thing he wanted was for her to think he spied on her. He pursed his lips. All right, so he was following her around like a puppy, but that didn't mean he wanted her to know it.

Her gaze swept over the spot where he stood, then snapped back.

Dark eyes narrowed, Evelyn looked right at him. Her brows furrowed. Venom tensed. Wow, that was weird. No way she could see him. Not with his magic up and running, but her stillness said something different. She sensed him. Knew she wasn't alone and that he stood within range. He could tell by her expression. Confusion and uncertainty spiked in her scent. She whispered his name. The slight inflection in her tone made the soft volley into a question. Venom's mouth curved. Umm, such a good sign. The best of the best, really. Why? If she could sense him, the bond he shared with her ranked as strong.

Off the charts, out of this world, solid.

A good thing for him. Not so great for her right now. Evelyn was more than a touch uncertain. She was starting to freak out. Tapping into her bio-energy, he listened to her heart race. Boom-boom-throb. Slam-slam-bang. The sound carried weight, tightening his chest. Her anxiety hit him next, adding to the mix down, setting off a sound track inside his head.

Desperate to reassure her, he reached out with his mind.

"You're safe, Evie," he thought at her. A death grip on the door edge, she frowned. Her gaze swept him again. Still unable to see him, she shook her head. He sent a ghosting swirl out in a warm wave, surrounding her with certitude. *"Go home,* mazleiha."

As the endearment enveloped her, Evelyn blew out a shaky breath. Brows still drawn, she took one last look and, inky curls bobbing against the side of her throat, slipped inside the car. The hem of her dress rose, flashing a gorgeous length of thigh. Desire clawed through him and hung on hard. Venom swallowed, shutting down need, forcing himself to be patient. Not that it helped. Already jacked-up and tuned-in, he followed her every move, fixating on the details. The last scrape of her three-inch stiletto on pavement. The incredible hue of her mocha-colored skin. The innate pride that kept her shoulders square and chin level. All of it made him burn with emotion so explosive it tilted toward obsession.

Soon, his dragon half growled.

"Very, *very* soon," Venom murmured, echoing the sentiment as Evelyn turned out of the parking lot.

Gravel crunched beneath her tires.

Venom held the line, refusing to step off the curb. He must let her go . . . for now. But not for long. Tomorrow night wasn't that far away. He could do it. Stay true long enough to accomplish his goal—a dinner date with Evelyn. Maybe more than one if all went well. A string of encounters that would draw her so far into his sphere, she would accept the truth of who and what he was—a Dragonkind warrior in thrall to his mate. A male so far gone he would do whatever it took to possess and please her.

Starting with the biggest no-no of all—leaving her alone.

Both hands on the wheel, Evelyn put the pedal down and drove past him. Street lights stroked over the hatchback's faded red paint, bleeding into a pale flash of white license plate. He memorized the digits, tucking the information into the back of his brain. He might need it later. Not that he required the string of numbers to find her again. After sampling her life force, he was hooked in. So attuned to the unique frequency of her bioenergy he could track her over long distances. Sloan, though, was a different story. The more detail he fed the Nightfury computer genius, the more likely Venom would get the intel he wanted before meeting Evelyn at Figorelli's tomorrow night.

Gaze on the red flash of her taillights, Venom watched his female hang a right onto Union Avenue. The second her car disappeared around the corner, Venom unleashed his magic. With a snarl, he shifted from human to dragon form. Dark-green scales replaced his skin, sliding over his shoulders to meet the black webbing of his wings. He unfolded both, relishing the rattle of scales and stretch of stiff muscles, then stepped into the middle of the street. His razor-sharp claws clicked against the blacktop and . . . hmm, yeah. Lots of room out here. No annoying shrubs poking at his back. No electrical wires brushing his horns. No humans in sight either. Just loads of space on a deserted avenue. The perfect launchpad to get airborne, then good and gone.

Or rather, head for home.

Before anyone realized he'd been gone.

Muscles bunching, he bared his fangs and leapt skyward. His wings caught air. Heavy gusts picked up road debris. Small stones and dirt billowed in his wake, blowing a nasty cloud up the Luxmore's drive. Ignoring the dust-up, Venom ascended fast, rocketing into the night sky. The chill of midnight rushed over the horns on his head. Condensation formed on his scales, icing up the spikes along his spine. Relishing the chilly splash of release, he wheeled around a tall apartment building. His wing tip grazed a run of windows. Glass rattled, shaking the steel frames. A few lights flipped on as his brush with the building woke inhabitants inside. Senses pinpoint sharp, he heard sheets rustle a moment before human feet hit the floor.

A lock clicked. A patio door slid open behind him.

He tightened the cloaking spell, deepening the shield of invisibility. Just before he cleared the side of the high rise, Venom glanced over his shoulder. A large male stepped out onto a narrow balcony and scanned the horizon. Seeing nothing but a sky full of normal, the guy grumbled under his breath. An apt reaction. Venom grinned. He couldn't help it. The male's pissed-off expression tickled his funny bone, lightening his mood, making the last of his tension fall away, relaxing him into flight. Such a welcome reprieve. He hadn't realized how uptight releasing

Evelyn had made him. The human's reaction, though, recalibrated his internal gauge, helping him wipe away the strain.

Venom exhaled long and slow. Excellent. All clear on the emotional front. Now for the tricky part . . .

Getting into Black Diamond. Without Daimler raising the alarm.

Wings spread wide, Venom shook his head. Damned Numbai. The male had eyes in the back of his head. Add that flaw to Daimler's rigid sense of responsibility—and his need to protect the warriors he considered his—and . . . yeah. The instant he realized Venom wasn't where he was supposed to be, it would be game over. No slowing him down. No way out of the ass-kicking either. Hell, the Nightfury's go-to guy would no doubt make popcorn and settle in for the show while Bastian took a fist to his face. Although . . .

Venom frowned. That might be overstating it a bit.

Daimler might love rules, but he wasn't cruel. Nowhere near insensitive either. More astute than most, the Numbai would understand what drove him. And why he hadn't been able to sit around while Wick got his rocks off with J. J. . . . and ignored Venom. He grimaced. What an awful thought. Terrible in point of fact. He sounded like a whiny pissant—completely unworthy for being jealous of his best friend.

Evelyn's face morphed in his mind's eye.

He hummed and, settling into a smooth glide over thick forest, closed his eyes. He held on to the image of her, reveling in the fullness of her mouth. Her taste too. The way she fit in his arms, the softness of her skin and . . . ha! *Jealous.* Venom snorted. Strike that. Make it past tense. With Evelyn on his radar—and within reach—he felt less alone. Like a male on the precipice of an important event. The kind that changed everything. Purpose came home to roost, renewing belief, raising faith, preparing him for—

A cloud of static blew into his head.

Fantasyland shut down, wiping Evelyn from his mind. His dragon half rose, shoving him straight into instinct. He let the monster out of its cage as the hiss expanded between his temples. Pain clawed the inside of his skull. Experience rang his internal alarm bell. Firing up magic, Venom sent a sonar blast wide, casting a cosmic web over the treetops. Goddamn it. No magical markers of any kind, even fewer identifiers. The signal kept skipping all over the place, denying his attempt to get a lock on it. Which left him with dick-all. Nothing but ancient trees and rocky outcroppings as the terrain grew rougher.

The powerful ping came again.

Venom's gaze snapped to the right. Senses ablaze, he banked hard and headed south, hoping to access the source. The air crackled and . . . huh. Weird. He recognized the vicious vibe, and yet, couldn't place it. A smokescreen maybe, one designed to block know-how and throw him off the trail.

Lightning forked across the night sky.

The thin stream electrified, exploding into a magic-fueled fishing net in front of him.

Venom sucked in a breath. Oh, hell. Shit, shit . . . and triple *shit.* Not good. He knew what the electrical storm meant and—

He put on the brakes, wing flapping in an attempt to get out of the way. Too little, too late. The net expanded, then closed ranks, hurtling end over end, enveloping him in electrical burn. Deadly threads enveloped his scales, then contracted, blocking all chance of escape as electricity yanked him out of the night sky.

Rocketing over the clearing, Bastian cringed as Venom slammed into the ground. Tangled up in the electrical web, his warrior slid into a skull-splitting skid. Tall grass and topsoil flew skyward. Venom's spiked tail whipped around. Saplings went airborne like a cluster of heat-seeking missiles. Brutal sound cracked through the quiet, exploding across the dell. Ruby-red eyes aglow, Venom cursed and bore down. His huge claws bit, ripping into rock, digging trenches in dirt as he spun into another body-torqueing rotation. Moon-glow flashed off his green scales, joining the blue crackle of the net. Bastian grimaced. Again. For what seemed like the umpteenth time.

Well, hell. Didn't that just take the cake.

He hadn't meant to hit Venom—or rather . . . take him down—quite so hard.

Wheeling above huge pines, he circled back around. Cold air blasted him, rattling his midnight-blue scales, catching at the dark webbing of his wings, pushing him sideways into an air pocket. Muscles taut, he controlled the updraft and, gaze locked on Venom, made another pass above the place he'd chosen for the beat-down. The net contracted around Venom, tightening its grip, smashing him into the turf.

Bastian shook his head. *"Fuck."*

"Christ, B." Flying in his wake, Rikar huffed. *"That's some wicked shit."*

Wasn't it, though? Maybe *too* wicked. Freaking lightning net. He really needed to practice throwing the stupid thing more often. Maybe take a stab at downgrading its intensity too.

Evidence of that fact slid to a stop on the far side of the clearing. Black wings bent at odd angles, head half-buried under a mound of dirt, Venom's interlocking dragon skin clicked as he fought to get his paws underneath him. Cursing colored the frosty air, rising over the tops of ancient trees. With a growl,

Venom thrashed, spiked tail flying, struggling to break the electric lockdown. Bastian's lips twitched as relief rushed through him. His warrior wasn't hurt. No permanent damage done.

At least, not yet.

"You gonna let him go?" Rotating into a sidewinding flip, Mac eyeballed him with shimmering aquamarine eyes. *"Or let him rot?"*

"I vote for the latter," Forge said, brogue thick, a load of pissed off in his tone. Playing fast and loose in the north current, he flew through unstable air. Turbulence rattled his purple scales, shaking the Scot like a passenger jet in unfriendly skies. *"Let him stew for a bit, B. We'll come back in an hour."*

Bastian snorted. Tempting . . . so very *tempting.* Under normal circumstances, he might've done it—angled his wings, flown in the opposite direction, set up shop a couple of miles away while his warrior stayed locked down. Venom deserved it for leaving the lair alone. The dumb-ass. Of all the idiotic things to do. Particularly right now. Bastian growled. Jesus. Like he didn't have enough problems already? He was under attack on multiple fronts, for fuck's sake—the Gage and Haider situation, the absence of rogues in the city, Rodin's obsession with killing Forge, the possibility of *Xzinile* for his pack, a pregnant female at home.

Myst. Bastian hummed. His love, his life, and now his mate.

Tucking into another turn, Bastian exhaled long and slow. Thank God for her. Thinking about Myst always had the same effect. She calmed him down, helping center him like nothing else could. Now he was ready to go. More than able to deal with Venom's insubordination and enforce the rules.

Not something he did often . . . or relished doing.

For the most part, the warriors under his command toed the line. Were respectful of protocol and followed it without question. Good thing too. The rules existed for a reason. Going it alone got a male killed. AWOL wasn't where he wanted his warriors. As commander of the Nightfury pack, it fell to him to see that everyone thrived and made it home in one piece. He loved his brothers-in-arms. Each male brought something to the table—all kinds of cunning, savagery when needed, unique skill sets, and magical aptitudes . . . the bond of brotherhood made leading the pack a pleasure. Well, at least, most nights. Right now landed nowhere near *most.* Normal no longer applied, which meant Venom was about to get more than he bargained for and everything he deserved.

Perfect timing.

Really, it was . . . completely *perfect.* Particularly since he needed a fight. A knock-down, drag-out to ease the tension and put him back in neutral territory. Maybe then he'd be able to think straight—come up with a new plan before the situation in Prague deteriorated and the Metallics ended up dead half a world away.

Wings angled, Bastian whirled above the forest. Green eyes aglow, light rushed out in front of him, coating the treetops, casting uneven shadows as he set up his approach. One clearing dead ahead. Time to tuck his wings and set down. Engage fast and hit hard. Quick and clean. The optimal strategy. Venom wasn't a lightweight. The male was a skilled tactician and, despite his affable demeanor, adored a good brawl. Which meant the faster he put paws to ground, the quicker he'd get what he wanted—a knuckle-grinder with a warrior who could handle whatever Bastian threw at him.

Clearing the edge of the pinewood, Bastian tucked his wings. Gravity took hold, dragging him out of the night sky. Stars blurred into pinpoint streaks. Fierce moon-glow wavered in his field of vision. Hundred-year-old tree trunks swayed and pine needles jumped, reacting to the blow back. Gaze locked on his warrior, Bastian thumped down in the center of the clearing . . . ten feet from his target.

Crouched like a cat, horns poking through the net, Venom glared at him through the holes. *"Goddamn it, B."*

He snarled back. *"Shift."*

All kinds of pissed off, Venom obeyed, moving from dragon to human form.

Yanking on individual lightning strands with his mind, Bastian shut down the light show. The net contracted. Magic boomeranged, blowing through the clearing, making branches creak in protest and . . . snap, crackle 'n pop. The electrical web evaporated into thin air. Both hands cranked into fists, Venom bared his teeth. The show of aggression put Bastian in motion. Toes of his combat boots digging into overturned earth, he ramped into a run. Four feet from Venom. Now three. Fighting stance set, his warrior raised his guard. Eyes riveted on his target, Bastian put his head down and—

He rammed his shoulder into Venom's stomach.

Venom grunted as his lungs emptied. The harsh exhale rang through the clearing. Bastian snarled and fisted his hand in his warrior's jacket. Shifting left, he jacked him upright. Venom's feet left the ground. Without mercy, he propelled his friend backward, using every ounce of leverage he possessed. Momentum took over. Bastian dug in and, working with gravity, drove Venom back-first, toward the turf.

Surprise sparked in his friend's eyes.

Adding a nasty spin to the body torque, Bastian held on hard and took his warrior down. With a curse, Venom slammed into the ground. A thud echoed, cracking through the quiet. Satisfaction surged as Venom sucked in a breath. Bastian shoved it aside. No time to gloat. So he'd gotten the upper hand. Big deal. The tide always turned. The most firm grip always loosened, so . . . no question. His warrior might be down, but he wasn't out. Not by a long shot. Which meant . . .

Time to make his point.

Planting his knee in the center of Venom's chest, he cranked his arm back and let loose. His fist shot forward like a piston and . . . crack! He hammered the idiot he called friend with a solid right cross. Venom's head snapped to the side. Brutal sound splintered the silence. Bastian heard the other Nightfuries land behind him. He didn't care. He hit Venom again—and then again—driving his point home.

Double damned jackass. Leave the lair without a wingman, would he?

He let his fist fly again.

His warrior countered and, with a vicious twist, blocked the next volley. Off balance, losing his grip, Bastian struggled to land another punch. Reflexes lightning quick, Venom slammed the heel of his hand into Bastian's solar plexus. Air left his lungs in a rush. His stomach pitched. Bile rushed up his throat. Bastian gagged. Jesus, a direct hit. Precise. No mistakes. In exactly the right spot.

Eyes watering, he coughed, but kept a grip on his brother-in-arms. Both hands fisted in his leather jacket, he shook Venom hard, rattling his teeth. He wanted to hit him again. Take the male apart piece by fucking piece, and then hammer him some more. For disobeying a direct order. For being an idiot. For causing him to worry.

"Okay. Okay," Venom said, dropping mind-speak. Eyes shimmering, his friend glared at him. "Enough, B."

"You asshole. What the hell do you think you're doing?" Chest pumping, Bastian leaned in. Nose-to-nose now, his gaze bore into a ruby-red one. "Give me one good reason why I shouldn't rip your head off."

"You should." Venom swiped at the blood running from a cut above his eye. He grimaced, making a face of distaste. "Hit me some more if you want. I deserve it."

The statement doused the flames of his fury. Bastian sighed. Freaking Venom. Trust the male to be reasonable while receiving a face full of *fuck you*. Retreating with a grumble, he removed his knee from the center of his friend's chest. "Jesus, Ven."

"I know. I know. Sorry, but . . ." Remorse in his eyes, Venom blew out a breath and sat up. A furrow between his brows, he dug his heels into overturned topsoil, rested both forearms on his bent knees, and shook his head. "Ah, hell."

Ass-planted in the dirt beside him, Bastian waited for an explanation. He knew Venom had one, but well . . . shit. No matter how good the excuse, it wouldn't be good enough. Nothing overrode the safety of his pack. *Nothing*. So Venom's stint outside Black Diamond without a wingman wouldn't stand.

Nor would it happen again.

He knew it. So would Venom after tonight. Or at least, he'd better. Otherwise, the male was in for another beat-down . . . while each member of the Nightfury pack stood in line, waiting to drive the importance of following the rules through his thick skull.

The image reignited his temper. Bastian threw his friend an exasperated look. "Tell me what's going on."

Venom grimaced. "It's hard for me to stay home while Wick and J. J.—"

"Ignore you and spend time together across the hall?" Rikar asked, entering the fray.

The question hung in the cold air, dragging insight into view.

Bastian blinked. Shit. He was an imbecile. A huge one who needed his head examined. He should've realized what sharing Wick with another person would do to Venom. His warrior might be strong, but he was also sensitive. Attuned to others' needs. Protective to the point of self-annihilation. So bighearted he always put others first. Which meant change, of any kind, threw him. Venom thrived on the status quo. Loads of stability too, not the strange and unusual.

Which should've clued him in.

All the upheaval the past few months—the escalation of the war with the rogues, the inclusion of four HE females and two additional warriors into the fold, the absence of Gage and Haider—had finally taken its toll. Now the male struggled with a new norm. All of which entailed sharing his best friend . . . with a female. Nowhere near easy for a male as possessive as Venom. Gaze steady on his warrior, Bastian moved past anger, accepting responsibility for his friend's slide into stupidity tonight. He should've paid better attention. Been more attentive to the needs of his pack, instead of preoccupied with the problems in Prague.

Not that he could fix his mistake now.

It was over and done. Nothing left to do now but let Venom off the hook.

Sore muscles squawking, Bastian popped off the cold ground. His boot soles touched down with a soft thump. Brushing the dirt off the seat of his jeans, he flexed his busted-up knuckles and offered Venom his hand. The second the male grabbed hold, Bastian pulled him to his feet. "It's not going to get any better, Ven. J. J. is a part of Wick's life now. You need to accept—"

"I've accepted it. And it *will* get better," Venom said, an intense look in his eyes. "It already has."

The phraseology sparked an emotional switch-up. A half smile on his face, Venom squared his shoulders. Bastian went on high alert. He recognized that expression. Half excitement, half stone cold certainty and . . . huh. Wasn't that interesting? Venom had new intel, maybe even a secret to share. Glancing sideways, he tossed Rikar a you'd-better-get-ready look.

Quick on the uptake, his XO raised a brow. "Better? How?"

"I found her," Venom said, his half smile spreading into a full grin. "It finally happened. I found her."

Forge stepped into the circle. "And who might that be, lad?"

"My mate."

"Your *mate*?" Mac frowned as he joined the party.

Bastian frowned. "You sure? You're toxic, Ven. Females can't tolerate your touch for long, so . . . be sure. Very, *very*, sure. Otherwise we'll end up with a mess on our hands."

"A dead female too," Rikar said.

"I'm sure." Excitement in his eyes, Venom cleared his throat. He rolled his shoulders, shuffled his feet, and flexed his fingers, fidgeting as though the mere thought of his mate made his skin prickle. "She's not like the others, B. She's immune. My touch doesn't hurt her."

Blowing out a pent-up breath, Bastian stared at his warrior. He needed to be sure. Was hoping like hell Venom wasn't out of control, creating a fairy-tale connection, believing he'd found his mate for no other reason than he wanted it to be true. Desperation did strange things to a male, and Venom wasn't immune. None of them were, but as he held his friend's gaze, he saw the truth in his eyes. Flat-out conviction. Perfect certitude. No fairy tale in sight. Venom believed he'd found *the one* with intensity that didn't lie. Which meant so must he.

Palming his friend's shoulder, he squeezed. "Okay, then."

"Well done." With a quick shift, Mac raised his fist and lashed out. The punch/love tap nailed Venom in the bicep.

"Ow—goddamn it." Rubbing the sore spot on his arm, Venom threw Mac a dirty look.

Mac grinned. "Congrats, man."

Rikar looked around, searching the tree line. "So—where'd you stash her?"

"I didn't." His expression wary, Venom shrugged. "I let her go."

"You *what*?" Forge's brows popped skyward. Bafflement winged across his face. "Are you mad, lad? No one in their right mind lets his mate go."

"Not without him along for the ride anyway," Bastian murmured, watching his warrior closely. Venom glanced his way, a quiet plea for understanding in his ruby-red eyes. And he got it. Bastian knew exactly what had prompted Venom to allow his mate to leave without him. Bastian's lips twitched. Freaking Venom. The male never took the easy way out. He had standards instead. An elevated sense of integrity that more often than not got him into trouble. "You didn't want to abduct her. You plan to pursue her instead."

"We have a dinner date tomorrow night."

"Well . . ." A teasing light in his eyes, Rikar grinned. "I guess that confirms what we've known all along. You're insane, brother."

"Asking for trouble as well," Forge said, sounding more pissed off than usual. "Bring her home, Ven. Given enough time, she'll accept you."

Venom shook his head. "I'm not going to force her. Evelyn deserves better and . . . hell. Might as well admit it." He blew out a long breath. "I like the idea of dating her . . . spending the time. I want to give the whole wooing thing a try."

"God save us all." Forge sighed. "You're a bloody romantic."

Rikar's lips twitched. "Try it sometime, Scot. You might like it."

"No chance of that." A shuttered look in his violet eyes, Forge glanced away. Expression set, a muscle jumped along his jaw line as he stared across the clearing, gaze fixed on the sway of thick field grass. "I've no need for that bullshite."

The harsh comment stalled the conversation.

Winter wind tousled the treetops. Pine needles lost the battle and tumbled, playing in the breeze as everyone focused on Forge. A natural reaction given the vehemence of his denial. Message sent and received. Loud and clear. No chance for misinterpretation. Bastian cleared his throat, his heart aching for the Scot. He couldn't imagine the pain Forge lived with day in and day out. Or having to deal with that kind of grief. Losing a female in childbirth never got easier. The passage of time made no difference. Horrific memories stayed with a male forever. And never faded.

So fresh. Too raw. Just months old. The loss was hardly behind Forge at all.

The fact the Scot's son had survived didn't lessen the grief. Or ease the agony. Bitterness and guilt picked Forge apart instead, sealing him up tight, driving him away from connection and the anguish that kind of vulnerability could cause. Healing would come, but until then, Bastian knew the new addition to the Nightfury pack needed to be handled with kid gloves.

And a huge amount of understanding.

"Evelyn," Mac said, breaking the rough silence, rescuing his mentor by bringing the conversation back on track. "Pretty name."

"Stupid plan." The pain Forge tried so hard to hide crept into his tone. Lifting his foot, he kicked a rock toward a boulder half-buried in the ground. Stone cracked against stone. He growled. "Pull your head out of your arse, Venom—go and get her."

Eyes narrowed, Venom opened his mouth, no doubt to shut Forge down.

"Let it go," Bastian said, tone soft, yet firm, stopping a confrontation before it began.

Neither male needed a fight right now. At least, not with each other. The Razorbacks, however? Different story. Killing the enemy would ease the tension. It always did. But with Ivar and his pack in absentia, ripping apart rogues to soothe frayed nerves seemed unlikely. Which left everyone wound too tight, and him looking for ways to keep the peace inside the Nightfury pack.

A dicey proposition.

Nowhere near easy with his warriors on edge. Toss in a handful of volatile personalities and each male's propensity for violence and . . . Bastian huffed. Hell. Forget unstable. The situation flirted with unsafe.

Giving Mac a playful shove to lighten the mood, he palmed Forge's shoulder. A quick squeeze relayed the message—don't spoil Venom's fun. Holding his gaze, the Scot exhaled and relaxed beneath his hand. Bastian nodded in approval and gave his warrior a solid slap of approval. His palm connected with Forge's leather jacket. Sharp sound rippled, cracking through the clearing as he turned toward Venom. Support. Help. New ideas . . . proven dating techniques. All the time and money Venom needed to do it up right and bring his female into the fold. Bastian wanted to provide it all, 'cause . . . yeah. No question. His brother-in-arms' happiness trumped the mess brewing in Prague. Much as it pained him, he must play a game of wait and see, and pray Gage and Haider made it out alive. Which meant he couldn't help the Metallics right now.

But that didn't mean he couldn't help Venom.

Tipping his chin, he prompted his friend. "What do you know about her?"

Dragging his attention from Forge, Venom refocused on him. "Not much, but I've got some intel. I need Sloan to source it before I meet her again."

"Home, then," Bastian said, turning toward the large trees standing sentry at the edge of the dell. "We've got shit to do."

An understatement.

A serious one given his earlier conversation with Sloan. The male was onto something. Up and running in the cyber world, chasing down a lead. *Granite Falls.* Small town up north, big trouble if what he suspected proved true. The absence of rogues in downtown Seattle coupled with Azrad's message meant Ivar was on the move. Up to no good somewhere inside the Cascade Mountain Range. The location made Bastian uneasy. It was far too isolated. Not exactly the best place to launch an assault.

But that didn't mean it wouldn't happen.

Ivar didn't do anything without forethought. He planned big, moved fast, and struck with precision inside well-defined parameters. Random strikes weren't his strength. So if Granite Falls was on his radar, the bastard had a reason for singling it out. One that leaned toward ominous and away from sane. Bastian clenched his teeth. Only one conclusion to draw—Ivar was planning something big. Something that involved humankind. Which placed those in Granite Falls in the middle of a war zone.

With a growl, Bastian stopped in the middle of the clearing. Boots planted, he glanced at the night sky and shifted into dragon form. His claws scraped through overturned topsoil. Shaking free of the dirt, he unfolded his wings and launched himself toward pinpoint stars.

His warriors took flight behind him.

Ascending fast, Bastian banked east toward Black Diamond, his mind mired in problems and the welfare of his younger brother. He blew out a steadying breath. Man, he hoped Azrad was all right. His message to Sloan skirted the boundaries of safe, putting his brother in dangerous territory. The more he risked his life to warn the Nightfuries of trouble, the easier it would be for Ivar to find him. After tonight, Azrad was officially out of pocket, vulnerable to discovery, easy pickings for Ivar inside the Razorback pack.

Worry came calling.

Fear for his sibling upped the ante, making his heart pound and unease creep into the center of his chest. Spy game central—such a lethal sport to play. Beyond dangerous for Azrad. Nowhere near easy for Bastian to watch. One false move, and it would be over. His baby brother would be caught. And Ivar would hold the upper hand in a war Bastian desperately needed to win.

Chapter Ten

Shoulder blades pressed to the wall inside Cascade Valley Hospital, Evelyn crossed her arms and stared at the deserted nurses' station. All quiet on the medical front. No one running to and fro. No file folders stacked on the high countertop. No phone ringing off the hook either. Just a wide-faced clock for company, the quiet tick-tock the only sound in a compact stretch of corridor. More than a little eerie. Usually hospitals brimmed with activity. But not here. Not where she stood, watching the second hand mock her from ten feet away.

7:31 a.m. Almost dawn. Half an hour at most and the sun would rise.

Not that she would get to see it.

Devoid of windows, the waiting room sat at the center of the hospital, across from a nurses' station, somewhere between worry central and scream-worthy frustrating. Add fear to the mix and, like it or not, she held all the ingredients for a serious scare fest. A real party for one. And no wonder. She'd been alone and waiting for hours—for news about her grandmother. For hope delivered by doctors. For the electronic locks barring the doors on both ends of the corridor to open and set her free.

Preferably in the next minute.

She counted to sixty, then sighed. Wishful thinking based in bad luck. Still no Dr. Milford at the door.

Evelyn swallowed past the lump in her throat. She hadn't expected that—to be met at the front doors by strangers and escorted into lockdown. Pushing away from the wall, she glanced one way, and then the other. Nothing new to examine. The ocean of pale walls hadn't changed. Boxy fluorescents still buzzed overhead, making the silence seem ominous as she focused on a set of double doors. The pair led into the ICU. Thick, unbreakable windows surrounded by reinforced steel. Electronic locks engaged, impossible to bypass. Twin impediments that left her trapped in a place no one seemed inclined to visit.

Framed by glass, a team of nurses rushed past. Pace quick. Movements harried. Surgical masks in place, the gaggle pushed an empty gurney down the hallway.

Unease tightened its grip.

Evelyn took flight.

Leaving her purse on the chair and her shoes on the floor, she ran toward the doors. Maybe if she yelled loud enough the nurses would hear her. Maybe one of them knew something. Maybe if she pled for news through the glass someone would take pity and tell her the truth. She upped the pace. Her bare feet beat against hard linoleum. The sharp slap-slap ricocheted in the compact space, rippling like waves as she neared the doors. Clipboards in hand, deep in discussion, two doctors walked past. She put on the brakes and, sliding to a stop, banged the heels of her hands against the window.

The duo jumped like jackrabbits. Two startled gazes swung in her direction.

She slammed her palm against the glass again. "Let me out of here."

Medical mask tucked beneath his chin, doctor number one blinked. "Miss?"

"I've been stuck in here for hours. Let me out."

"I'm sorry, but I can't," doctor number two said, stepping up to the door. Eyes full of compassion, he stared at her through the glass. "The entire hospital's on lockdown. All the codes have been changed. Only senior staff and the hospital administrator have them."

Panic clogged her throat. "But—"

"It's been crazy here tonight. We've got more patients than we can handle." Tucking his clipboard under his arm, doctor number one shook his head. "They probably forgot about you in set up."

The *set up*? More patients than the hospital could handle? A nice piece of information. Scary intel that in no way inspired confidence. Or gave her any hope at all. An image of her grandmother streamed into her head. Fear tightened its grip, making her heart gallop like a runaway horse. Breathing too fast, Evelyn looked at one doctor, and then the other. As her gaze ping-ponged, she tapped her hand on the window. Her fingers shook, bouncing against glass. Uneven sound spiraled out, reached up, rising hard in the quiet.

An announcement came over the PA, paging Dr. somebody-or-other.

"Sorry." Turning away, doctor number one threw her an apologetic look over his shoulder. "That's me."

"Listen," number two said, watching his colleague disappear down the hallway. He took a step back, widening the distance between them. "I've got to go, but—"

"Wait." Evelyn exhaled in a rush. Her breath fogged up the glass. "Will you do something for me?"

He tipped his chin. "What?"

"Find Dr. Milford. Tell him Evelyn Foxe needs to speak with him."

He nodded. "I'll try."

She murmured her thanks. And then he was gone, jogging down the corridor, clipboard in hand, leaving her locked behind closed doors. Pressing her forehead to the glass, she squeezed her eyes shut. God. Unbelievable. It was a nightmare without end. One that gave her too much time to think—to imagine the worst—and not enough to process the facts. She huffed. *The facts.* Right. What a laugh. The wrong word to use too. Particularly since she didn't have any *facts.* Just loads of supposition supported by fear.

"God help me," she said, turning to press her back to the door.

Steel against her spine, she slid down to sit on the floor. Cold seeped through her dress as she bent her knees and bowed her head. The ring she wore winked up at her. Unable to resist, she smoothed her thumb over the blood-red rubies. Touching the antique gemstones calmed her. It always did, and as her heartbeat settled into a less erratic rhythm, she spun the gold band around her middle finger. Round and round. Fiddle, spin, twist, and turn.

Tears pricked the corners of her eyes.

She shouldn't be wearing it. Should never have taken it out and risked losing it to Markov tonight. It was too precious. Represented happy memories and better times. Grounded her in history—and reminded her of the day her grandmother handed her the gilded box after her college graduation. Her degree in one hand, the ring Mema had worn for half a century in the other. Such a momentous occasion. Noteworthy. Important. A pride-filled moment wrapped in family tradition as one generation passed its birthright on to the next.

Which explained why she rarely wore it. And refused to risk it.

Well, at least, most of the time.

Tonight had been an exception to her rule. The thought of meeting Trixie—and her first client—at the hotel had made her take the ring out of its box. She'd needed the boost. Had longed for confidence and the courage to do what needed to be done. To remember whom she protected, the reason behind her actions, her decision to enter the Luxmore and meet—

Venom.

Evelyn blinked as his name streamed into her head. Her mouth curved, threatening to widen into a smile. The urge shocked her. Especially since she hadn't thought smiling was possible tonight, but . . . surprise, surprise. Thinking of him brightened her mood. Gave her a way out of mental anguish. Made her feel less afraid and more in control. An odd reaction to a near stranger. Startling too. Not her usual style at all. Caution and mistrust were more her thing, and yet, she couldn't deny how he made her feel. Safe. Secure. More in control than she'd been in ages. Now, for the first time in forever, she felt as though someone stood in her corner. A powerful someone who might be able to get her out of trouble. Such a huge surprise. He'd been incredible to her. Gentle. Patient. Protective even though he knew little about her. The one bright spot in nine months of dark days and scarier nights.

And she would see him again.

Tonight at Figorelli's. Twelve hours, give or take, and—

"Oh, crap," she whispered, more gasp than word as realization struck.

Less than twelve hours until their dinner date, and she didn't have his number. Which pushed her past trouble into completely screwed. With Mema sick, she couldn't leave the hospital.

Without Venom's phone number, she couldn't let him know. And without the money, Markov would skin her alive at nightfall.

Alarm expanded between her temples. A roar lit off, raking the inside of her skull, throbbing so hard she lost track of her surroundings. But even as worry churned her stomach, Evelyn pressed the trio of rubies into her palm and reached for calm.

Her grandmother never approved of panic.

Pragmatic and smart, Mema understood crisis. Maneuvering in difficult situations was one of her specialties, so . . .

Evelyn's eyes narrowed. Think . . . she needed to *think*. There must be a way of reaching Venom. A message left at Figorelli's for him. The yellow pages. Online directories. List upon list of phone numbers and alphabetized names. And honestly, how hard would it be to find a guy with a name like *Venom*? Her gaze snapped toward the nurses' station. A second later, she popped to her feet. All she needed was a computer. One must be hidden behind the high countertop along with a telephone. Maybe if she got lucky, a quick search would provide what she needed. After that, she'd let her fingers do the walking and—

A click echoed down the corridor.

Halfway to the countertop, Evelyn spun toward the entrance opposite the ICU. A man came into view through the glass. The door swung open. Rotund form covered in a white lab coat, bald head gleaming under bright lights, brown eyes brimming with concern, Dr. Milford stepped into the waiting room.

"Oh, thank God." She stepped toward him. "Dr. Milford, what is going on?"

"I'm so sorry," he said, his voice muffled by the surgical mask covering the bottom half of his face. Evelyn opened her mouth to ask again. The aging physician shook his head, then sighed, fatigue evident in the ragged sound. The door clicked shut behind him. “I didn’t intend to leave you here so long, but I couldn’t get away any sooner.”

“I don’t care about that, just . . .” she whispered, waving his apology aside. The delay—along with the lockdown—no longer mattered. Not anymore. She needed answers. “Please, tell me what is going on. Where’s Mema? What happened? Is she all right?”

A shadow in his eyes, Dr. Milford shook his head. “How are you feeling?”

“Stressed, worried . . . freaked out.”

His eyes crinkled at the corners. “I meant physically, Evie. Sore throat? Headache? Any chest pains or trouble breathing?”

“No.” She frowned. The question piqued more than just curiosity. It made instinct sit up and take notice. Something about the inquiry felt wrong. Especially since Dr. Milford knew her history. She never got sick. Ever. No one could remember the last time she’d had a cold, never mind the stomach flu. And truth be told, neither could Evelyn. “I feel fine.”

“Good,” he murmured, relief in his tone. “Bring your things and come with me.”

“But—”

“I’ll explain everything, Evie, but the hospital needs this space and we’ve got somewhere to put you now.” Slipping his hand inside his coat pocket, he pulled out another mask, identical to the one he wore. He held it out, inviting her to take it. “You need to put this on and come with me.”

Evelyn blinked. *Somewhere to put her.* Oh lord, that didn’t sound good. And yet, she didn’t hesitate. Not for a second. Slipping her shoes on, she grabbed her purse off the chair and hurried in his direction. Finally. At last. After hours of waiting, she’d get what she wanted—much-needed time with Mema. Enough to make sure everything was all right. The click of her high heels loud in the quiet, she stopped in front of Dr. Milford and accepted the surgical mask. Soft cotton brushed her cheeks as she put it over her nose and mouth. The second she looped the elastic bands over her ears, securing the mask in place, he turned toward the door and punched in the key code.

Electronic locks hissed.

He stepped over the threshold.

Right on his heels, Evelyn followed him out into the hallway. A left turn took them down a narrow corridor. The sound of hushed voices broke through the silence. Her eyes on Dr. Milford, she trailed him around the next corner—past a makeshift medical depot, worried-looking nurses, and doctors suiting up in hazmat gear—toward a door at the end of the hall. Evelyn sucked in a quick breath. Holy God. Talk about surreal. A sign, printed in black, read "Quarantine Area. Do Not Enter."

Disbelief widened into shock. Numbness spread in the center of her chest. She hesitated, wobbling on her heels. Dr. Milford murmured her name. Her focus bounced from the sign to the hazmat suits, then back to him. She met his gaze, a question in her own. He shook his head, opened the door into the quarantine area, and gestured her through, making Evelyn wonder when she'd stepped out of the Cascade Valley Hospital and into the twilight zone.

* * *

Massive tree trunks bowed in deference as Venom took the turn too fast. Inches away, his wing tip blasted past the treetops. Ancient beeches groaned in protest. He didn't care. Screw the forest. The rush of chilly midnight air and the whirl of leaves behind him too. The pine needles, though, were a bit of a problem.

Like tiny razor blades, the mess blew skyward, nicking his scales, chasing his tail, playing catch-the-dragon in the dark.

He snorted. Luminous green mist rose from his nostrils. *Play.* Right. Nowhere near accurate considering he wasn't playing. He needed the speed along with the mind-bend of muscle torque. The physical explosion acted like an outlet, helping to settle him down. He swallowed another snort. *Settle* wasn't the right word either. Especially since uncertainty wouldn't leave him alone. It kept hammering him, flogging him with the cruel lash of irony.

Goddamn his protective side. Playing knight-in-shining-armor sucked.

Gritting his teeth, Venom shook his head. He'd been so sure. So damn *sure* letting Evelyn go had been the right thing to do, but—

He cursed under his breath.

Maybe Forge was right. Maybe releasing her back into the wilds of human society qualified as a boneheaded move. Maybe flying home alone signaled failure instead of wisdom. He blew out a long breath. A cloud of frost shot from between his fangs, picking up the moon-glow before swirling over his horns on his head. The blow back brushed his scales, making him look more black than green in the weak light. Muscles taut, he increased his wing speed. Faster. More ball-busting velocity. Another round of muscle-stretching torque. He needed it all to stay sane—to remain on course instead of hunting down his female.

Half an hour max.

A quick about-face.

A fast fly into Seattle before he turned north.

That's all it would take. Wham-bam, no-holds-barred, and he'd have her in his arms again. Be tasting her deep. Pleasing her well. Getting what he needed while he gave Evelyn her due—everything she demanded of him. Temptation banged on his mental door. Venom held the line, refusing to open it, never mind step over the threshold. He'd made his decision. Now he must honor it, along with her right to choose. No matter how painful he found the separation.

Angling his wings, he forced himself to fly for home. The woodlands dipped beneath him. He rocketed over the next rise. A rural road cut a swath through the forest, two lanes slipping between towering oaks and one-hundred-year-old pines as though it belonged. As though humans hadn't invaded pristine wilderness and tried to make it their own. The nature of the beast, he guessed. Humans enjoyed the idea of supremacy. Conquer or be conquered, a mantra the destructive race lived by. Although, he had to admit the idiots were getting better. Well, at least in the environmental arena anyway.

Government agencies were working hard, protecting endangered species, cleaning up the groundwater, pushing for stricter pollution regulations for corporations. Lobby groups had cropped up in recent years too, putting the screws to the US Senate and Congress, expecting more from elected officials. And the global population as a whole? Getting better by the day, jumping on board to support recycling programs and reduce waste. It wasn't enough. Not yet, anyway. But it wouldn't be long before the planet felt the effects.

A good thing if it meant cleaner air to fly through when he left the lair each night.

Leaving the slither of blacktop behind, Venom spotted the twin cliffs. Eyes narrowed on the pair, he went wings vertical. The spikes along his spine rattled. Slivers of shale rumbled, tumbling down the rock face as he rocketed between the bluffs. Thick forest greeted him on the other side. The landscape launched more debris at him. He hummed. Good luck hitting him. Velocity supersonic now, the forest didn't stand a chance of grabbing hold of his tail.

Neither did his buddies.

Left to play catch-up, the Nightfury warriors flew in his wake. Fine by him. He'd taken the lead position for a reason. Namely—to keep his sanity. He didn't need to be treated to any more of Forge's sidelong glances. Or the doubt that eclipsed him every time he caught the Scot's eye. He knew what the male thought. Knew what the rest of his pack thought too . . . even if B and the others were too polite to say it out loud. Despite all the congrats and high fives in the clearing, none of them understood his need to woo Evelyn. To take her out. To treat her right. To initiate her into the Dragonkind way of life gently. Kidnapping—at least in his brothers-in-arms' opinions—was much more expedient. Safer. Smarter. More in keeping with his protective nature too, so—

He huffed. Yeah. No question. Better to leave that argument alone. Far behind and for another time. Particularly since he flew toward the demilitarized zone.

One with a name—Wick.

Venom grimaced. No way around it. He was in trouble. In for a fight the second he landed at Black Diamond. Forget Bastian. The true threat stood just outside the front door, a hop, skip, and jump away from the driveway and the aboveground lair. Waiting. For him. To land. Ah, hell, had he said trouble? Strike that and call it *screwed* instead. Again. For the, well . . . shit. He didn't know how many times he'd been neck-deep in uncharted territory tonight.

More than was wise, for sure.

With a sigh, he settled into a glide. The trees creaked, approving the downgrade from supersonic to slow and smooth. The webbing on his wings fluttered as the forest started to thin. A minute tops, and he'd be face to face with his best friend, trying to explain why he'd gone AWOL. Not that Wick would care why he'd broken the rules. The male didn't give a damn about protocol. He'd be angry for another reason. One that began and ended with Venom leaving him behind tonight.

Not a great move. But even headed into the impending showdown, Venom refused to regret it. Pulling a flash'n fly might not qualify as smart, but it had produced results, providing what he needed, so . . .

Screw it.

Wick could tune him up every night for the rest of his life. Venom didn't care. He'd found her. Goddamn, he'd *found her.* In a sea of wrong females, he'd finally met the right one.

"Evelyn," he murmured, testing the phonics.

His mouth curved. Even her name sounded perfect. Just right. The absolute best thing he'd ever heard as he pictured her face and relived her taste on his tongue. Desire clawed through him, putting a shoulder to his mental door. The thing groaned, threatening to shatter. Satisfaction spilled through the gap, warming his chest, raising his internal barometer, making him want to forget the game plan and go after her. Rocketing into the last bend, he leveled out and tapped into her bio-energy. Gorgeous and full, the thread of her life force expanded between his temples.

His sonar pinged.

His dragon half rose, riding a voracious wave of need.

With a growl, Venom fine-tuned the signal, zeroing in, chasing her bio-energy across rough terrain and . . . oh, baby. There she was: just north of Seattle, surrounded by forest, somewhere inside the Cascade Mountain Range. Without coaxing, the buzz of recognition solidified inside his head. He could track her now . . . from miles away if necessary. All right, so it wasn't perfect. No matter how strong the ping, he could only approximate her location. At least, right now. That would change soon. The second he touched her again—took another sip and fed from the source—the mating bond would strengthen. Become more powerful as it locked him into place, aligning his life force with hers. For now, though, he must accept the limitations of their first encounter and be patient.

Even though it pissed him off.

Eyes narrowed, Venom tucked his annoyance away. Tilting his head, he mined the signal instead. Forget the limitations. He couldn't curb temptation. He wanted to get a more accurate lock on her. Needed to feel her. Craved the warm buzz of her energy in his veins.

Adjusting the cosmic dial, he felt the buzz amplify and . . . hmm, yeah. Definitely. She must be home by now. Was probably slipping out of her killer stilettos. Stripping off her sexier-than-sin cocktail dress. Putting on too-big pajamas before sliding between the sheets to snuggle into bed. Maybe even thinking about him. The idea burrowed into the back of his brain. His heart pounded harder. Oh, please. God, yes. He wanted to be on her mind. Needed her to wonder. Wanted her taut with anticipation. Full of yearning as she imagined their next meeting, his plans for her, the way he would touch and taste her.

Arousal spiraled deep, making his scales tingle and—

"Venom, you asshole." The vicious growl cut through mind-speak like a knife. Venom winced. Lovely. Just frigging great. Wick had a lock on him. Was still waiting outside, a load of pissed off headed into full throttle. *"Get down here."*

Delaying the inevitable, Venom slowed his wing speed. *"Give me a minute."*

"No."

"Wick," he said, a warning in his soft tone.

"Don't start. Land or I'm coming up there."

Not a good idea. Pissed off in human form, his best friend was a handful. But an angry Wick in dragon form? Venom grimaced. Only an idiot invited that kind of trouble. *"Don't get your panties in a wad. I'm coming up over the last rise."*

Wick growled something inaudible.

Venom ignored the nasty undertone. He'd expected it. More than deserved it too for playing fast and loose with the rules. Not that he regretted leaving Wick at home. His friend needed the R & R. Had earned some serious downtime with J. J., but . . . well, hell. After getting yanked out of the sky and tuned up by Bastian? Venom swallowed the bad taste in his mouth. The last thing he needed was another reprimand.

Or a showdown with Wick.

With a sigh, he shook his head and corrected his trajectory. Almost home. Five hundred yards and closing fast. Which meant he'd better come up with an excuse. Faster than fast. A couple of creative one-liners would do it. A tactical two-step, the perfect dodge in the verbal arena. Little else would appease Wick. Then again, maybe he'd just go with the truth. Tell him about Evelyn. Ask his advice. Which . . . yeah, come to think of it . . . might be straight-up brilliant on the strategy front. A way to avoid his friend—and the nasty convo—without giving any ground.

Despite his new status as a mated male, the sharing and caring shit never went over well with Wick. He didn't embrace emotion, much less show it. Not with Venom anyway. J. J. on the other hand? Hell, she'd cornered the market—bonding with his best friend, drawing Wick out, accepting her mate without hesitation even as she got him to talk, if only behind closed doors. A good thing. Wick needed someone to talk to, but . . .

Venom bit down on a curse.

He might as well admit it. He wanted to be the one Wick confided in. Which made him a total idiot. A jealous asshole too. He should be happy for his friend—and was, at least, most of the time. Some days, though, yearning seeped through the cracks, preying on him like a pack of piranhas. Eating him alive. Stripping him to the bone. Hurting him deep. After all they'd been through together, he deserved better from Wick. Inclusion. Trust. Whole-hearted respect, the kind that bonded brothers. Particularly since Venom had done the unthinkable to save Wick's life.

Sorrow turned the screws inside his chest. It always did when he remembered that awful night. His heart reacted to the memory, aching so hard he wondered how it kept beating. Murder. He'd committed *murder.* Slain his sire to pull Wick from hell and keep him safe. Not that he'd meant to do it. He hadn't known his own strength. Hadn't understood that the *change*—and his first shift into dragon form—would bring such startling results: unholy strength, raging power, a venomous nature that was second to none. Now it didn't matter. He couldn't retrace his steps and go back. Couldn't temper brute force, find a better way, or stop the accident from happening.

Couldn't wash the blood and dragon ash from his hands either.

It was too late to make amends. Inexorable guilt wouldn't let him.

The tree line thinned, then dropped away, revealing the sprawling complex nestled in the center of a large plateau. Black Diamond. His home. The one place on earth he belonged. And yet, his mind traveled, taking him away from Washington State, back to another time, inside another place, planting him in the past. To the moment of his *change*, and his sire's decision to thrust him headfirst into the hypocrisy of Dragonkind aristocracy . . . and the twisted games played by the Archguard.

Wick had been a victim of the fallout.

So had he, but even with sixty years between then and now, Venom struggled to forget. To shake the brutality and move on. Time didn't heal all wounds. Whoever had said that was wrong. The hurt remained fresh. The rage remained untouched. And his savior complex—the need to compensate for his crime by protecting others, by beating back injustice and fighting for the underdog—never went away. His cross to bear. Penance for a legacy left by his sire and the tainted blood running through his veins.

Goddamn his father.

No matter how hard he tried, he still couldn't understand. How could his father—a general with influence among their kind and Rodin's ear—be so uncaring? So amoral? So corrupt and without conscience? How could he have—

A shiver rolled through him, rattling his scales.

He hated the memories. Didn't want to remember the past. Too bad he couldn't forget. Or leave the psychological trauma behind. Not after witnessing his sire's cruelty. Not after watching beardless boys in combat—knives raised, fighting for their lives, dying horrible deaths to entertain Dragonkind elite. Learning of the fight clubs had been terrible. Seeing the cages backstage where young males lived had been worse. Being ordered to load a dying Wick onto a truck bound for Tanzenmed, the Dragonkind prison renowned for torture, had proven to be his breaking point.

He hadn't been able to stomach it.

Not after looking Wick in the eye. Not after seeing the blistered wound and raw skin. Not after recognizing the sequence of numbers burned into Wick's forearm—all the while knowing what awaited the young male he hadn't known then, but now considered his best friend.

The savagery of it struck him. As the injustice tunneled deep, infecting his heart, his sense of right and wrong reacted. It always did, causing a chain reaction. Past. Present. It didn't matter. His feelings remained the same. Disgust. Sorrow. Incurable rage. A fury so profound, he'd lost all restraint sixty years ago, turned on his sire and—

"*Ven*," Wick growled, cutting off Venom's reunion with the past.

Folding his wings, Venom dropped out of the sky. Unleashing his magic, he released the cloaking spell. The invisibility shield flexed around him, then ripped wide open. He sighted the ground. The wind picked up, whistling in his ears, pushing the scent of cedar and clouds across the night sky. The moon disappeared behind the coniferous tumble, enfolding him in darkness. His talons thumped down in the center of the driveway. Gravel rolled, pinging off industrial-size garage doors, crunching beneath his claws, digging into the sensitive pads of his paws. Taking a deep breath, he filled his lungs and, preparing for the showdown, glanced toward the house. Porch light spilled down the walkway leading to the front door, bouncing off his dark-green scales, illuminating Wick in the low light.

Golden eyes aglow, his friend snarled at him.

Venom growled back. Probably not the best idea, but . . .

To hell with it. He refused to apologize again. Once tonight had been enough. Quota filled. Guilt assuaged. Looked like another ball-busting fight on the horizon, though, 'cause . . . yeah. Wick looked more than unhappy. The male embodied fury. Toss lethal into the mix. Add a dash of holy hell and get ready for the explosion. His friend was cranked to full throttle. Foot to the floor going two hundred miles an hour, wearing an expression that said, "I'm gonna rip your face off."

Now nothing but a fight would alleviate the tension.

But as Venom shifted into human form and prepared for the fallout, he knew he shouldn't let it happen. It was his fault, not Wick's. A few well-placed words would slow his brother down. Long enough for Venom to explain and tell him about Evelyn. Too bad he couldn't find a single thing to say. Didn't want to either. After getting nailed by Bastian, he needed the brawl almost as much as his friend. So instead of calling it off, he waited, fists raised, fighting stance set, and watched Wick ramp into a run, coming down the flagstone path like a runaway locomotive. Which meant . . . screw placation. Set up the party parade instead. He was headed into a knuckle-grinding brawl with his best friend. Collision not only inevitable, but assured.

Chapter Eleven

Dragon senses run amok, Gage stumbled on an uneven patch of stone floor. Righting his balance, he swallowed his growl of disgust. The underground passageway smelled the same way it looked—dark and dank with a nasty hit of eau de grunge. He grimaced as his shoulder brushed the wall. The wet chill registered, sliming his skin with . . . fuck. He didn't know what the hell he'd just touched. Something cold. Something long past putrid. Something he didn't want to think about, never mind identify.

Slick stone walls funneled into another intersection.

The kid paused on the lip a second, then turned right. Gage followed, keeping a firm hold on Osgard. His muscles squawked, spotlighting his injuries, setting fatigue center stage.

One hallway slid into the next. This one narrower than the last.

Another round of revulsion punched through, competing for airtime inside his head. Fighting the pain, Gage beat back his aversion. He flexed his hand, bunching the back of Osgard's T-shirt against his palm. He needed the handhold along with the stability. The kid might not be full grown yet, but he was strong. An excellent hitching post. Or trailer hitch. Whatever. Gage wasn't sure right now. All he felt was grateful. The youngling was leading the charge, head up, feet moving without making a sound, towing him through the enemy labyrinth with stark efficiency.

Another round of thankfulness washed through him.

Go figure. Osgard was a godsend. An excellent find considering Gage didn't know how much longer he could hold out. Agony amplified by the moment, draining his already-low energy reserves. The sharp dip sent him into uncharted territory—energy-greed. A state most males feared. And like it or not, he wasn't an exception to the rule. Which meant he needed to feed . . . and soon. Otherwise he'd spiral out of control, tumble down a rabbit hole, and hurt the first female he encountered. His stomach pitched. Lightheadedness hit, making him sway on his feet as he reached another perilous conclusion.

Haider would be in the same state. Maybe even worse than him.

Gage gritted his teeth. Talk about hazardous. Two males in the throes of ravenous hunger headed into the light of day. Nowhere near advisable. He huffed. The situation couldn't get any worse.

Osgard took a sharp turn.

Angling his shoulders, the kid dipped his head to avoid the low ceiling and drew Gage into a triangle-shaped corridor. The torque and twist jarred his arm. Bone-piercing pain spread across his chest, then spiraled into his abdomen. Gage winced. Holy fuck, that hurt. His body wanted him to stop. Was begging for rest, a moment or two to regroup, sending out agony like warning shots. He tightened his grip on Osgard and kept his feet moving. Forget the discomfort. Shove it into a dusty corner somewhere. With time running out, he couldn't afford to stop. So instead of asking Osgard for a second to catch his breath, he stared straight ahead, ignoring his injuries while trying to pretend the tight space didn't make his skin crawl.

His reaction bordered on idiotic.

The narrow passageway shouldn't bother him. He'd been in worse places. Locked up for months before Haider busted him out of solitary confinement. The memory jabbed at him. Sweat dripped into his eyes as he shook his head. It had been years. Eons since his stay inside an eight-by-eight-foot holding cell. And yet, contrary to his nature—and a heavy dose of dragon DNA—the labyrinth gave him a bad case of the heebie-jeebies.

He preferred the great outdoors. Fresh air and sunlight. The scent of pine trees and rushing river water through forests and fields. But mostly, the sound of birds singing in the morning. Not the subterranean hovels most dragons took refuge in. Given a choice, he would've spent all day, every day, outside. Under the golden glow of a warm afternoon, deadly UV rays be damned. Unlike the rest of his kind, he could tolerate sunlight in small doses. Haider believed Gage's ability stemmed from his subset's communion with the sun in ancient times. When the Greeks had ruled the world, before the birth of the Roman Empire.

Born of a long line of bronze dragons, Gage knew his history. His forefathers had believed in the Sun Queen and taken pains to honor her. Had observed the rituals and performed ancient rites, paying homage to Silfer the dragon god and the deity's love of the sun. He'd only seen it a handful of times, basking beneath the glory of the midday sun just as his ancestors had done. His tolerance levels wavered, depending on the day and his energy reserves. Topped up, he could endure half an hour. Hungry, in need of a good feeding, the time frame dwindled to less than fifteen minutes. Missed opportunity. A lost calling. A terrible shame all the way around. He would've been good at it. An absolute pro at welcoming the dawn and serving the Sun

Queen, better known as the Goddess of All Things—the touchy deity who continued to curse his kind.

Gage ground his teeth together.

The stupid prick. The dragon god's greed had ruined them all. Cursed Dragonkind so well the connection between his kind and the Meridian lay shattered. Which elevated FUBAR to whole new levels. A state he should be accustomed to by now as hunger gnawed on him, blooming into a full-blown ache. He swallowed a mouthful of saliva. Fucking hell. Just what he didn't need—more energy-depleting fatigue. He could feel it slithering through his body, tugging at his muscles, eroding his mind, making his vision blur.

Gage wiped the sweat out of his eyes.

"Where are we?" he asked, sounding rough, more like a train wreck than a flesh-and-blood male. Gage grimaced. God. His voice was shot. Too raspy. Far too thin. No authority in the words at all. Hating the weakness, he forced himself to focus. His night vision sparked, magnifying the chisel marks filled with slimy residue on massive stone blocks, making the walls contract around him. Breathing in through his nose, he exhaled out his mouth and tightened his grip on Osgard. The kid flinched, but didn't stop. The youngling continued to walk, pulling him in his wake. "How much farther?"

Osgard glanced over his shoulder. Pale eyes met his. "End of the hall. See the door?"

Gage squinted, trying to see that far, making out a glimmer in the dark. A metal handle, maybe. Some ancient hinges too. Yeah, definitely. *Something* dead ahead. All right, so he couldn't focus well enough to see the whole of it, but—

"How bad is it?" Osgard asked, voice hushed.

"What?"

"The pain?"

"Manageable," he said, lying like a pro. Leaning harder on Osgard, he pushed him forward, his gaze on the blurry outline of the door. "Just get me to Haider."

The kid nodded. Footfalls nothing but a rasp on uneven stone, Osgard stopped in front of the narrow door. Faded by time, the graying oak screamed of neglect. Pock marks marred the face, matching a set of beat-up hinges and the rusty metal studs holding individual planks together. Even the bottom of the wood took up the cause, the plank ends eaten away by the damp, looking like jagged teeth snarling at the floor they no longer touched. A soft glow slipped through the gap, tumbling out of the chamber beyond to surround his feet.

Osgard reached for the ancient handle.

"Don't." With a firm tug, Gage drew his new charge backward. Away from the door. Out of range. Out of the line of fire and the possibility of hidden dangers. He didn't want the male in the thick of it. Hadn't agreed to take the youngling with him—to protect him—only to thrust him into the middle of a fight. Maneuvering in the tight space, he planted his palm in the center of the kid's chest and shoved him back another foot. "Any guards?"

"No, but—"

"Stay behind me. If shit gets critical, you run. Understood?"

Shoulder blades pressed to the wall, Osgard frowned. "I can fight."

"I know you can," he murmured, lying again to assuage Osgard's pride. Young males were an interesting breed. A delusional bunch. Each liked to believe he was invincible—all balls, no brains in high-octane situations. Gage understood, but knew better. He'd been just like Osgard long ago. Full of piss and vinegar, willing to throw himself into the fray without thought to the consequences. "Hold the line, kid, but stay out of my way."

"As you wish." Pushing away from the wall, Osgard shifted behind him. Gage shook his head. Fucking male. The move was all about watching his back, positioning himself as a warrior would in preparation for combat. "But I'm not running."

He stifled a snort. Mouthy little whelp. Too tough for his own good, which . . . well, just made him like the kid even more.

Gaze pinned to the door, Gage rolled his shoulders. Agony murmured. He ignored the sting. Distraction wasn't a good idea. Neither was stalling. The situation required stealth and speed. Not something he had much of right now. He pushed past the pain anyway, forcing focus, calling on aggression and muscle memory. His body knew what to do. His nature picked up the slack, unleashing the rage buried deep inside him as he reached for the door.

Icy metal touched his palm.

Steel clicked against steel.

Rusty hinges squeaked as the door swung inward on a slow glide. Light slipped through the widening gap, illuminating stone and wood. Not waiting a second, he stayed low and slipped over the threshold. Quick. Smooth. Fury filled. His body language spoke volumes—bring-it-on peppered with a don't-fuck-with-me vibe. His gaze started to glow as he bared his teeth and raised his fists. The hum of electricity crackled in the quiet. With a low snarl, he searched the shadows. His gaze swept left to right. Stone walls. Slimy rock. A single bare lightbulb hanging from a timber-beam ceiling.

Not much else so far.

No soldiers hiding in the dark corners. Not a guard dog in sight. Nary a whisper of sound or—

"About time you showed up," a deep voice rasped, drifting on stale air.

His attention snapped left.

Shimmering silver eyes met his.

Gage exhaled in relief. "Alive and well, I see."

Haider shrugged. "More or less."

No kidding. His friend looked more than just a little worse for wear. He looked wrecked. Clothes ripped ragged. Pale skin smeared with dirt and blood. Back propped up against the back wall. Legs stretched out in front of him. Trapped inside a steel cage charged with electricity. High voltage snapped around the vertical struts, forming an impenetrable maze around his friend, warning him away.

Dragging his gaze from Haider's, he examined the cage. "Been waiting long?"

"Didn't I say it was about time?"

He huffed and, eyes on the prison cell, moved farther into the chamber. Uneven stone scraped the bottom of his bare feet. He ignored Haider's pissy tone in favor of finding the cage's weakness. From six feet away. Despite the urgency, it was safer that way. At least, for the moment . . . until he figured out how to get his friend out from behind bars charged with electricity. He focused on the single door. Thin bands of lightning arced off the steel, protecting the hinges, handle, and lock, lying in wait, daring him to come closer.

Heart thumping, he studied the setup more closely. "Better late than never."

"True." Haider coughed, the harsh sound full of pain. "Expected you sooner, though."

"Like a princess waiting for rescue?" The old tease and taunt. The usual thing with him and Haider—even now, with the stakes high and possibility of death looming. Strange as it sounded, the return of routine—the bitchy exchange—reassured him. His friend might be banged up, but nothing had changed. Haider was all right. So was he. The realization focused him further, clamped down on worry, settling him like nothing else could. "Aww, how sweet, Haider. I had no idea I'm your Prince Charming. Should've told me sooner."

"Go fuck yourself."

Gage grinned.

Haider smiled back. Not a lot, a slight curve at the corners of his mouth. But Gage got the message, and it was enough. A silver dragon with unequaled negotiating skills, Haider liked to talk, the more words the better, and telling Gage off? His lips twitched. Razzing him qualified as his friend's favorite pastime. Eyeing a bundle of cables, Gage stopped a few feet from the door. He followed the wires across the top bar. Clamped together, strung across steel, a thick power line made the jump from cage edge to stone wall. Pivoting, he turned full circle, going where the mess led him and . . .

Eureka. *X* marked the spot.

A junction box next to an electrical panel. State-of-the-art circuitry. A complicated setup mounted to the wall behind the door. Turning his back on Haider, he ignored Osgard hovering on the threshold and limped toward the steel-gray box. Time to pray. With the panel door shut tight, he couldn't see the breakers, but knew it contained complicated electrical circuits. As in multiple. The heavy cable running into the top of the panel box gave the game away. Which meant the bastards might have armed the thing with a security system. One set to go off the instant he started tampering with the circuitry. Stranger things had happened. Zidane might be an asshole, but he wasn't stupid. More's the pity, so . . . yeah. Mucking around inside the box might trip an alarm and bring the Archguard death squad running.

"Hang tight a second." Facing off with the electrical panel, Gage studied the framework, then raised his hands. Cold metal slid against his palms as he gripped the sides of the large, metal box. Nothing happened. No alarms. No laser sensors protecting the thing. He exhaled long and smooth and, fingering the latch on the side, swung the door open and . . .

He blinked. Holy shit. Talk about complicated.

Trained as a structural engineer, good with his hands, he understood how individual components of complex projects fit together to ensure the whole served its purpose. Hell, he could visualize, design, and implement any structure he wanted. Toss in his passion for auto mechanics—and the fact he loved taking engines apart just to see how they worked—and his know-how rivaled genius in most circles. But as he faced off with a panel packed full of circuits, unease came calling. So many cables of varying thickness, candy-coated every color of the rainbow, jammed into a very small space.

No easy fix.

Gage cursed under his breath. "Give me a second to figure this mess out."

"By all means," Haider said, sarcasm out in full force. "It's not as though we're pressed for time or anything."

"Guess it's my turn to tell you to fuck off."

"No different than any other day."

"Comforting to know nothing's changed, isn't it?"

"Hey, Gage?"

"Yeah." Fingering a green and blue wire, he glanced over his shoulder.

Haider met his gaze. "I'm having some trouble. I can't see anything out of my right eye."

"Can you walk?"

"Yeah." Pressing a palm on the concrete floor, Haider struggled to his feet. He swayed, then stumbled sideways inside the cell. Electricity crackled, reacting to the shift. With a curse, his friend doubled over and, fighting to stay upright, gasped. With a growl, Gage turned back to the electrical panel. Fingers flying now, he sorted through each wire, looking for the magic bullet . . . the one pairing that would cut power to the cage. "Might need some help, though."

"I can help," Osgard said, stepping over the threshold and into the room.

Haider sucked in a breath. "What the—"

"Picked up a tagalong," he said, cutting off his friend's question.

"I can see that," Haider murmured. "Probably should tell you I picked up one of my own."

"A tagalong?"

"More like a brother-in-arms." The sound of uneven footfalls echoed. Focus still on the wires, Gage multitasked, playing electrician, testing cables, listening as Haider made his way to the other side of the cage. "Nian, man—I know you're hurting, but you need to get up."

"What?" Dulled by pain, thickened by sleep, the male's voice rose in the quiet. "W-where—"

"Still with me. You're safe," Haider said. "But not for long if you don't move your ass. Come on, Nian. Get up. We're getting out of here."

A scraping sound slithered on damp air. "How?"

"Prince Charming's arrived."

The comment might've been funny had Gage been in the mood. Being near members of the Archguard, however, never put him in a joking frame of mind. Under any circumstances. And Nian didn't qualify as a laugh a minute. As the youngest member of the high council, the male was not only dangerous, but untrustworthy.

"Damn it, Haider," he said, sounding pissed off, unable to help it. "We're not taking that prick with us."

"Yes, we are. He's solid, Gage. He's been targeted by Rodin for helping us."

Examining another wire, he scowled. "So?"

Haider sighed. "Gage . . ."

"I don't like it."

"You don't have to. Bastian's given his support. Our pack is backing Nian." His friend paused, letting the nasty tidbit sink in. "He's coming with us."

Gage grimaced. Talk about bad news. He'd been dying to kill Nian for weeks. Ever since he'd first laid eyes on the namby-pamby aristocrat. Now his pack was supporting the prick and his screwed up agenda? It was worse than *bad news*. The turnabout equaled catastrophe. Fucked up on a grand scale.

"All right," he said, refusing to go against his commander. Bastian was solid. The male always knew what he was doing. Although, this time Gage wanted to bet against the bank. Forget protocol and flout B's authority, 'cause . . . Nian inside the Nightfury pack? Just the thought gave him a raging case of indigestion. Isolating the junction he needed, Gage yanked on the green and orange cable. The tug gutted the breaker. Copper wiring shrieked against metal, coming away in his hand. Electricity buzzed around the cage an instant before it powered down. Spinning around, he nailed Haider with a warning look. "But don't expect me to be nice to him. One wrong move, and I rip his head off."

"Fair enough," Haider said, amusement in his tone. "Better behave, Nian."

"No kidding." Battered and bruised, in no better shape than Haider, Nian hugged his rib cage and shuffled forward. Gage sighed. Well, hell. Would you look at that? Zidane had done a number on Nian too, beating him so badly both the male's eyes were swollen shut. "And not a problem. I can hardly move at the moment."

Crossing the chamber, Gage met his friend at the cell. With a flick, he lifted the steel bar locking the door in place and swung it open. Haider sighed as he stepped out of the cage. Running his gaze over him, Gage reached out and cupped his brother's nape. "You sure you're okay?"

"Yeah." Still pale, but steadier on his feet, Haider nodded. Relief in his eyes, he palmed Gage's forearm. The warm weight of his hand spoke volumes—of relief and urgency, but mostly gratitude. "Let's move."

Returning the gentle squeeze, Gage dropped his hand. "Osgard."

"Yeah."

"Best way out?"

"Underground garage," Osgard said, reaching out to steady Nian as the male stumbled across the chamber. Without missing a beat, the kid slung Nian's arm over his shoulder, then turned and half carried, half walked him toward the door. "Rodin keeps a car there. Blacked-out windows so he can travel from place to place in daylight."

"He's handy," Haider said, gaze glued to Osgard's back.

Gage's mouth curved. "Isn't he, though?"

Best split-second decision he'd ever made. No question. He had a feeling the kid would more than earn his stripes. Now and in the future. First things first, though. He needed to slip past Rodin's sentries. Get the hell out of hostile territory with everyone's arms and legs still attached. A tricky proposition with three injured. Toss in a sketchy, underground escape route inside a lair full of enemy soldiers. Compound the problem with a member of the Archguard high council, aka potential traitor material, playing tagalong and . . .

His gaze narrowed on the back of Nian's head.

The namby-pamby prick. The male was slowing them down. Gage frowned. All right, that wasn't quite true. Not really. Nian was moving—not well, granted, leaning on Osgard, struggling to keep his feet under him—but . . .

Gage sighed. He might as well accept it. Haider was right. Nian couldn't be left behind. Much as he disliked the male, he deserved better than rotting inside a slimy excuse for a hellhole.

Avoiding the petri dish doubling as a stone wall, Gage shuffled sideways along the narrow corridor, his eyes glued to the pair in front of him. Silence reigned in the passageway, the dank, musty odor taking over where sound left off. The slash of bare soles across wet stone pushed at the chilly air. The kid took a left, leading the way, forcing him and Haider to follow. But as one hallway bled into the next—and one turn spun into more—worry got the better of him. Gage blew out a long breath and, battling fatigue, tried to ignore the stitch in his side as the truth struck home.

Navigating the labyrinth was taking too long.

Too bad he couldn't slow time. Or shorten the distance from here to there. A pity in more ways than one. Time wasn't on their side. New guards would come back from the morning meal any minute. The second the enemy discovered the empty kill room and prison cell, a call to arms would go up, and he'd lose the only advantage he possessed—the element of surprise. So only two things left to do, keeping moving and start praying. Hope like hell his merry band of four reached the garage before Rodin's death squad pulled up stakes and closed in for the kill.

Chapter Twelve

Boot treads skimming over stone, Venom shifted away from the front of the house. He stepped off the flagstone path onto the driveway. Gravel crunched beneath his feet. He barely noticed. Eyes locked on Wick's face, he assessed the threat level. Clockwork Orange territory. Cuckoo-crazy with a nasty hit of temper. He cringed and, raising both fists, prepared for the main event—or rather, the assault—even as he searched for a way out.

A lovely thought. An even better plan. One big problem with both.

No way in hell a ceasefire was going happen.

Not with Wick out for blood and headed straight toward him.

Gritting his teeth, Venom shifted mid-stride. He dodged right. Not fooled, Wick moved with him and, timing it to perfection, lunged. Big hands grabbed hold, sinking into Venom's leather jacket. With a snarl, his friend jacked him upright. A savage shove sent him backward. A forearm to the throat did the rest, cutting off his air supply. Trying to break his friend's grip, he struggled to breathe. Hard bone pressed against his windpipe, Venom coughed. Wick didn't relent. He jammed his fist beneath Venom's chin instead.

Sharp knuckles jabbed his jawbone.

Venom growled. Such a dirty move. Nowhere near surprising. Wick didn't know the first thing about fighting fair. Didn't know the meaning of restraint either. Toss in his need to maim a male while making a point, and . . . yeah. Score one for the other side. They had a ball game. Not that he had time to worry about his friend's lack of finesse. Wick was too busy trying to kick his ass. Another fist thrust. More shoving. A snarl echoed through the quiet. His? Wick's? Venom didn't know. Not that it mattered. Blocking another punch, Venom lost his footing. Wick took advantage and pushed harder, propelling him across the driveway, toward the garage and away from the aboveground lair.

Frozen grass crackled underfoot, scrambling the silence.

Off balance, feet moving in the wrong direction, Venom glanced over his shoulder and . . . oh, shit. Not good. He knew exactly where Wick was taking him—on a carnival ride called Big Trouble. Or Holy Hell. Whatever. Naming the situation wasn't a priority. Dialing down the death factor, however? No question, that qualified as job one. Otherwise, he'd end up two front teeth shy of a mouthful.

"Wick—stop. Hang on a second."

Wick brought his elbow up in answer.

The quick jab clipped Venom's cheekbone. His head snapped to the side. The sharp *crack!* echoed inside his skull, killing more brain cells than he could afford to lose. Venom clenched his teeth. Goddamn it. He should've heeded his own advice. Said forget it. Gone with gut instinct and thrown the first punch, along with the urge to be sensible out the nearest window. It would've been easier. More expedient, for sure.

A helluva lot more satisfying as well.

Too pissed off to care, Wick wasn't fooling around. Out for blood. Murder on his mind. Pick one. Pile it all on. Neither mattered when both possibilities summed up the situation. Feet sliding on ice, Venom blocked another punch. The move left Wick open to attack. With a quick shift, he launched his offensive. His fist grazed Wick's jaw.

His friend snarled.

"Just hear me out," he said, more growl than plea. "I can expl—"

Grabbing his jacket, Wick thrust him backward. The garage loomed behind him. Thick corrugated side panels gleamed in the low light and—

Wick slammed him into the wall.

Air left his lungs in a rush. Venom wheezed. Steel groaned as the industrial-size doors rattled in protest. The metal rivets beside his head strained, threatening to pop from the pressure. His spine echoed the sentiment, murmuring in discomfort, making him aware of the cuts and bruises. All the aches and pains. The ones he'd received from Bastian in the clearing. He grimaced. Goddamn B and his stupid lightning net. He had the worst luck. Could never seem to fly under the radar. Or get away with anything.

Resetting his balance, he thrust his arms between Wick's. Quick. Decisive. A skilled move with one purpose—freedom, separation, and distance from his friend. Without mercy, Venom brought his forearms around, pinwheeling to break the hold. Wick cursed as he lost his grip. Not wasting a second, he planted both palms in the center of his friend's chest and shoved. Wick stumbled backward. Closing the distance, Venom pushed him again. And then again, refusing to unleash his fist a second time.

Hitting Wick never felt good. He loved the male too much to inflict serious damage. No matter how much the stubborn SOB deserved it.

His eyes started to shimmer. Red light washed out in front of him, painting Wick in ruby glow as Venom glared at him. "I don't want to fight anymore."

"Too bad," Wick said, a lethal cocktail in his tone. Worry. Disappointment. Betrayal. All took a turn in the undertones. Rage, however, led the parade, dropping his voice into guttural. "Should've thought of that before you went AWOL."

"What would you have done in my place?" Just as angry now, Venom stepped into Wick's wrath. Hands cranked into fists, he moved away from the wall, forcing his friend to back up. "Banged on your door and dragged you away? Forced you to leave J. J. and—"

"No." Gaze fierce, dial still set to deadly, Wick drilled him with a look.

Venom stood his ground, refusing to give an inch. All right, so it was his fault—the entire mess along with the upheaval. The upset he caused the Nightfury pack too. But that didn't mean he needed to be flogged. Again. For the fifth time tonight. Nor did it mean he'd walk away from making his point.

He'd been restless.

He'd needed out of the lair. To stretch his wings and banish the shadows growing inside him.

Wick ought to understand that. Hell, the male lived in the shadows, in dark places not many survived. But as silence descended, raging between them, Venom grew so tense he feared he might break. Just snap under the strain and say something stupid. Something hurtful. Something Wick might not forgive. So instead of opening his mouth, he held his friend's gaze, asking without words for understanding.

One intense moment slid into the next.

"Fuck." His friend exhaled hard. The harsh sound ricocheted as he dropped his fists. "I don't know what I would've done. Same as you, maybe. But if you'd asked, I would've gone with you."

"I didn't want—"

"*Want* has nothing to do with it," Wick said, the voice of reason for a change. "I'm your best friend, Ven. I watch your six. You don't leave the lair without me—ever."

Venom's mouth fell open. Well, would you look at that? More than four words in a row. More than one full sentence . . . from Wick. A male who never said much of anything. Talk about a huge kick in the pants. Surprising in the extreme. His throat went tight. Over sixty years together, and his friend was finally coming around. Starting to come out of his shell. To voice his opinions while making his wishes known.

The realization turned Venom inside out, then cracked him open.

Guilt sped through the fissure. His conscience squawked. Venom swallowed past the lump in his throat. He'd turned the tables tonight. Done what Wick often did to him, put himself at risk and his best friend on edge by being selfish. Which meant, like it or not, he owed Wick an apology. His reason for breaking the rules no longer mattered. Nor did the success of his mission or the exquisite nature of his find—Evelyn in all her high-energy glory. He'd scared the hell out of the male he considered his brother. Had made him worry. He could see the truth of it in Wick's eyes and understood the feeling. The absolute panic at the thought of losing his friend. Of not being there when the male got into trouble.

He'd lived with the fear for years. So yeah. Tonight signaled a total role reversal. One that left him on the wrong side of the equation, apologizing instead of on the receiving end of contrition.

"Sorry. I should've stayed put, but . . ." He shrugged, not knowing what else to say. Or how to explain without sounding needy. He needed Wick to be happy. Wanted him to spend as much time with his female as he liked, but well . . . hell. He felt neglected. As though J. J. took so much of Wick's time, there wasn't any left for him. And honestly, as much as he hated to admit it, he missed his best friend. "I just . . ." He sighed, lamenting the weakness and his new pansy-ass status. "Couldn't stay home."

Wick frowned. "What the fuck is going on, Ven?"

Raising his hand, he ran it through his hair. The long strands clung, knotting around his fingers, pulling at his scalp. "Guess I'm just restless."

"J. J. thinks I'm neglecting you."

"What?"

"She's worried about you. Says you're lonely or some shit."

Venom choked on surprise.

Wick raised a brow. "Is that true?"

"Not anymore."

Taking a step closer, Wick inhaled through his nose, using keen dragon senses to scent the air. Golden eyes narrowed on him. "Something's different. What's changed?"

"I found her."

"Who?"

"My female."

Wick blinked. "Where?"

"At the Luxmore, Sloan's spot." A frisson of excitement skittered down his spine. Venom rolled his shoulders, trying to tame the shiver. It didn't work. Not surprising. Just thinking about her put him on edge. "Her name's Evelyn."

"Dark skinned?"

Venom nodded. "Dark curly hair too."

Wick's mouth curved. "Your favorite."

"Yeah. She's incredible. Beautiful. Pushes every one of my buttons."

"Good." Relief in his eyes, Wick slapped him on the shoulder. Skin slapped against leather. The love tap rocked Venom sideways as Wick scanned the driveway. Ancient pine trees waved from the opposite side of the open expanse. He searched a second longer, then glanced toward the front of the house. Finding nothing, Wick frowned. "Where is she?"

Searching for the right words, Venom drew a deep breath, preparing to spill all and—

The flap of wings blew in, beating against the frosty air.

The clamor expanded. Stone dust swirled. Venom huffed, but waited out the flap fest. No sense trying to talk over all the noise. Or compete with a Nightfury landing party. He'd explain everything to Wick once inside the lair. He needed the privacy. Waiting until the others were out of earshot qualified as a good idea. No way he wanted to go another round with Bastian and the boys. His brothers-in-arms were already skeptical of his plan to date Evelyn. And all right, so maybe the concept was a touch left of center. At least, in Dragonkind circles. Still he couldn't deny the allure. Or resist the need to do right by her. To give her a taste of normalcy. To ensure her acceptance of him before he tugged her off balance by introducing her to the complexities of his world.

The first to arrive, Forge uncloaked.

The invisibility shield fell away, shredding like old fabric. Purple scales flashed in the low light, picking up the glow of porch lights. Wings spread wide, the male set down. Razor-sharp claws clicking, the Scot nailed Wick with shimmering violet eyes. "Did Venom tell you yet?"

"Tell me what?" Wick asked.

Venom opened his mouth to tell Forge to zip it.

The Scot beat him to the punch. "Stubborn arse let her go."

Bafflement winged across Wick's face. "What the fuck?"

Venom growled. Super. Just great. Nothing like having the moment ruined. And the rug pulled out from under him . . . by an idiot Scot with a big mouth.

"Asshole." Stepping off the grass, Venom rolled his shoulders. Eyeballing Forge, he flexed his hands, making twin fists. He might not like the idea of hitting Wick, but the Scot? The male was fair game. Especially right now. The jerk had just landed himself on the endangered species list. "Nothing like giving me a chance to explain."

"What's tae explain?" With a snort, Forge shifted into human form. Conjuring his clothes, he stomped his feet into his boots. Gravel ricocheted, rolling into the raised lip of the flower bed flanking the front walkway. "You made a bad call. Letting yer mate go in hopes of wooing her. Bloody hell, lad—whoever heard of such a thing?"

Staring at him as if he'd grown two heads, Wick scowled. "You let her *go*?"

"Bull's-eye. Middle-of-the-rings accurate." Dragging a thundercloud in his wake, Mac touched down.

Water droplets flew, then fell, sliding along the razor blade following the curve of the male's spine. Venom frowned at him, even as he looked Mac over. He still couldn't get used to the differences and well . . . wow. Just wow. No other word worked when his new comrade arrived in all his water dragon glory. A rare breed, Mac deviated from the whole of Dragonkind. Smooth interlocking dragon skin instead of ridged scales. Webbed paws in the place of regular talons. Bladed spine instead of spiked. The power to control one of the most destructive elements on earth.

Venom stifled a shiver. Man, he hated water. He really did.

Scaly brows furrowed, Mac shook his head. "Still can't believe you sent her home, Ven."

"It's no big deal." Wiping a rogue raindrop from his cheek, Venom tried to downplay his decision. Not that he enjoyed being stuck on defense. Offense, knocking heads together, was much more his style. "Humans woo their females all the time."

"One problem with that argument," Rikar said, landing behind Forge without making a sound. Snow blew in, camouflaging the white weave of scales before swirling over his XO's horned head. "You're not human."

True enough.

Pretty good argument all the way around.

Which pushed Venom back into uncertainty. As insecurity poked at him, he started to second-guess himself. Goddamn it. Forge might be right. And judging by everyone else's reaction, Wick's included, everyone agreed with Forge. Venom sighed, accepting the truth. Frigging hell. No question. He sat on a limb. A thin one that threatened to snap any second.

"Look." Blowing out a breath, Venom shook his head, bowing beneath the weight of a good argument. "I'm meeting her tomorrow evening. If it'll make you all feel better, I'll kidnap her then."

"No one's asking you to kidnap her." Coming in on a fast glide over tall treetops, Bastian folded his wings. Midnight-blue scales rattled as gravity yanked his commander out of the sky. Huge paws thumped down behind him, flattening frozen blades of grass, making the garage doors jump a second time in one night. "We just don't want you to lose her, that's all."

"Fair enough." Glancing over his shoulder, he stared at Bastian, then gave in and nodded. "But I do it my way, B. Bring her here by car instead of in flight. I don't want her to freak out and . . ." He trailed off, meeting each warrior's gaze in turn, putting a warning in his own. "No one touches her but me or I'll—"

A creak rippled through the quiet.

Venom's gaze cut toward the house.

The front door banged open.

Heavy footfalls paused as Sloan stuck his head outside. "Thank Christ. About time you guys got home."

Magic murmured as Bastian shifted into human form behind him. "Any news?"

"Tons," Sloan said. "Granite Falls is on somebody's shit list. Better come inside."

Already on the move, Venom led the charge and, stepping onto the flagstone path, jogged toward the lair's main entrance. Six steps up and he crested the top tread. Pace steady, he strode across the porch, pushed the door wider, then followed Sloan over the threshold and into the aboveground lair. The smell of homemade bread drifted down the main corridor. His mouth started to water, but Venom didn't stop. Or head toward the kitchen and the culinary wizard wielding a baking pan inside it. He took a left instead, moving away from the decadent aroma and what it signaled. The morning meal. Relief for his empty insides. Fuel for mind and body.

His stomach rumbled again.

Temptation tugged, urging him down the opposite hallway, toward Daimler and the promise of extraordinary eats. It would just take a second. A slight correction in his trajectory. No big deal. A minute tops, and he'd grab a slice, slather it with butter and—

Shaking his head, Venom forced his feet to remain on course. Another round of mmm-mmm-good floated down the hallway. His insides tightened on a pang. Venom sighed in resignation. No matter how hungry, he didn't have time to make a pit stop in Daimler's domain. Not right now. Not with the boys at his back and Sloan in a tizzy about whatever intel he'd picked up about Granite Falls.

Tragic, really. A shame in more ways than one.

He could already taste the hot cross buns. Smell the cinnamon goodness. Imagine the sugary perfection. Feel the melt-in-your-mouth decadence. Just the thing every male wanted to come home to after a night spent hunting Razorbacks. His sweet tooth whined. Venom stifled a groan of longing and crossed under an archway. Boots thumping on the hardwood floor, he jogged down the stairs and into the living room.

Familiar décor greeted him. Huge double-faced fireplace rising beyond a leather sectional dead ahead. Entertainment center with fifteen comfy chairs and an enormous flat screen to his right. Twin billiard tables to his left. Standing behind the second one, laptop set up and sitting on green felt, Sloan didn't look up. Absorbed in cyberspace, his fingers flew over the computer keyboard. A wall of windows rose behind him. Clear glass rippled with magic, becoming darker by the moment as Washington State woke under the influence of the rising sun.

An orange line appeared on the horizon.

Covered in frost, the winter landscape sparkled under the warm glow.

Alive with movement now, the windows darkened even further.

A necessary thing. A great protective measure. The magic that protected Black Diamond—and hid the lair from outsiders, human and Dragonkind alike—always reacted at dawn. Tightening its grip. Shutting the house down. Blocking out the sun to prevent deadly UV rays from spilling into the aboveground lair. Excellent all the way around. The spell surrounding the Nightfury lair shielded them all, allowing each warrior to move around during the day without threat of getting fried.

Or suffering the inevitable blindness that would follow.

"Sloan, man," Venom said, halting opposite his friend. Billiards table acting like a barricade between them, he listened to the clickety-click of computer keys. "Whatcha got?"

"Some kind of epidemic in Granite Falls," Sloan said, more mumble than words. Fingers still flying over the keyboard, he shook his head. "Nothing on the news yet, but the Cascade Valley Hospital in Arlington is taking all the cases. I'm mining the system, looking for medical data to run by Myst, but so far, there's not much. What I do have doesn't look good."

Venom tipped his chin. "Nasty flu bug?"

"Or suspicious circumstances?" Wick asked, rolling in behind him.

Planting both palms on the felt beneath his computer, Sloan looked up from the screen. Mocha skin looking dark in the dimness, worried brown eyes met his. "The CDC has been called in."

"Motherfuck." Footfalls silent, Mac skirted the table edge and stopped beside Sloan. Aquamarine eyes on the screen, he shook his head. "Not good. Center for Disease Control—they've called in the big boys."

Forge joined the party, setting up shop opposite Mac. "Which means the doctors donnae know what it is."

Flanked by the wonder twins, Sloan blew out a breath. "Fifteen cases so far. All in the hospital now. But if the humans don't know the cause of the outbreak—"

Bastian growled. "Myst won't know what it is either."

"Bad news." Arms crossed over his chest, Rikar leaned his hip against the end of the table and threw B a worried look. "Ivar's doing?"

"Could be. Good guess." Palming the back of his neck, Bastian bowed his head and pressed down. Classic move. No mercy either. Hell, Venom could practically hear the muscles bracketing Bastian's spine squawking from five feet away. Typical of B. Pain focused him. So a nasty stretch with a healthy dose of discomfort? Always an effective stress reliever. "The bastard's a microbiologist. He knows how to put lethal viral loads together and—"

"The best way to infect a human's immune system. How to ensure maximum infection rates to inflect major damage," Rikar said, finishing B's thought.

"Might go worldwide," Forge said. "Result in a big death toll."

"Christ." Skimming both hands over his skull-trim, Rikar pushed away from the table and pivoted full circle. He looked straight at Venom. "We need to get into this."

A simple sentence. Harmless on its own. Huge when put together with a biological weapon released into the wilds of human society. Which meant . . .

Message sent.

Venom received it just fine. "*We* aren't doing anything. Not until I check it out first."

Wariness sparked in B's gaze. Green eyes glittering in the low light, his commander eyeballed him.

Venom met the perusal head-on, refusing to back down.

"Okay, Ven. You're on," B said, relenting, giving him the go-ahead even though it meant sending him into a human town alone. First in. Last out. Kind of like the US Marines. "We'll take the day. Rest up, take a look at any new data Sloan collects before sunset, then fly to Granite Falls."

On board with the plan, Wick murmured his assent.

"Good." Expression thoughtful, Rikar scrubbed his hand over his jaw. Stubble rasped against his fingernails. "We'll set up a perimeter—seven, maybe ten miles outside of town. Wait for Venom to clear the scene. Once he green-lights it, we'll—"

"Wait a second." Brows drawn tight, Mac stared at him. He frowned. Venom smoothed his expression. No sense giving the game away. Smart with an extra helping of curious, the ex-cop would figure it out soon enough. But as Mac shifted focus to drill Rikar with a serious look, then turned to glare at Wick, Venom struggled to keep amusement at bay. His usual silent self, no help on the find-a-clue front, Wick didn't say a word. Silence swelled. Playing another round of visual merry-go-round, Mac's gaze bounced over the group, nailing each warrior before he gave up and scowled at Bastian. "No way we're sending him in there, B. Humans are dropping like flies. Whatever bug Ivar's cooked up could be contagious to Dragonkind."

Wick snorted.

Rikar grinned.

Mac frowned harder. "What the hell am I missing?"

"Ven's a venomous dragon, Mac. One of the most powerful of his kind," Sloan said, as though the tidbit of information explained everything.

It did . . . in a way.

Not that Mac knew it. At least, not yet.

New to Dragonkind, the new boy still had a lot learn. Raised in the human world and outside a pack, Mac lacked the fundamentals—a lifetime of education, all the information needed to understand their kind. All right, so Mac excelled in combat. Was more than kick-ass when it counted, but knowledge required more than know-how. It required classroom time too. As the male's mentor, Forge would ensure Mac completed the handbook—thick-paged monstrosity that it was—but until then, he'd remain a few pallets shy of a full load on the information front.

So today's lesson? A rundown on the unique subsets of Dragonkind.

Each subset carried different DNA markers that ensured a myriad of talents. As a frost dragon, Rikar commanded ice and snow, the wind and weather too. Mac, freak show that he was, controlled water. Wick and Forge shared an element—fire, although each warrior wielded it in different ways. Forge's exhale combined fire and scale-eating acid. Wick, on the other hand, was a lava dragon—his weapon of choice a fireball with three layers of lethal that sent Razorbacks running. Sloan, however, broke the mold, spinning talent in new and interesting directions. An earth dragon with scorpion venom in his exhale, the Nightfury IT genius harnessed the energy of the earth, controlling plant life, whipping sand into raging storms, controlling animals when necessary. And Bastian? His commander outdid them all. A lightning dragon, B unleashed his freaky, neurotoxic exhale on a regular basis, zapping enemy soldiers and . . . ahem, frying urban electrical grids on more than one occasion.

Last but not least—him.

A venomous dragon, he was so poisonous anything he came into direct contact with died. Sometimes slowly. Other times within seconds. Zip. Bang. Gone. Toxicity without limitation or end—skin and bone, muscles and blood, every cell in his body venomous from the inside out. Which explained the short timeframe he adhered to with the fairer sex. Too much of him and a female would become ill. Prolonged contact meant certain death for her and a truckload of guilt for him. All in the past. Enter the future. With Evelyn in the picture, he could touch and taste—spend as much time as he wanted—without fear of hurting her, even a little bit.

Thank God.

Finally. Someone to call his own. Someone to spoil. Someone to hold, lounge in bed with after bone-melting sex instead of making a fast exit in the aftermath.

Clearing his throat, Venom broke the stalemate. "Probably should know something about me, Mac."

"What's that?"

"I'm toxic," he murmured, surprised when the admission didn't bother him. It had for as long as he could remember. Then again, he hadn't had hope then. No faith either. With a single encounter, Evelyn had restored both without even knowing it. Walking around to join Sloan on the other side of the table, he palmed Mac's shoulder. The move was all about reassurance. And surprise, surprise? Mac accepted it without hesitation. "So poisonous, there isn't a biohazard, pathogen, contagion . . . whatever . . . that can infect me. Safest bet is to send me into Granite Falls first. If I can locate the source of the virus, I can kill it."

Mac raised a brow. "Preventing any more humans from becoming infected."

"Exactly," Forge murmured, giving Mac a playful shove.

As the new boy cursed, Bastian smiled. "Sun's up, boys. Daimler's waiting for us. Grab some grub, then get some shuteye. We've got a lot of work ahead of us."

Good plan.

But as the boys bugged out, heading toward the dining room and the promise of the Numbai's cooking like a pack of wild dogs, Venom grabbed Sloan's shirtsleeve. In the process of shutting down his computer, his buddy paused. Dark eyes met his a second before Sloan raised a brow.

"Got a minute?" he asked, watching the last Nightfury disappear into the dining room.

One hand curved over the top of his laptop, Sloan tipped his chin. "What do you need?"

"Info."

"About what?"

"A female."

"On the hunt, are you?" When he shrugged, Sloan's mouth curved. With a flick of his fingers, he powered the MacBook Air back up and opened a search window. "Name?"

"Evelyn Victoria Foxe," he said, feeling self-conscious. All kinds of guilty too. Venom grimaced. Shit. He shouldn't be digging into her life. It felt too much like spying. Like an invasion of her privacy, but well . . . hell. Compulsion kept yanking his chain. Worry and suspicion too. Something was off. Very, very *wrong*. Nothing else explained her presence inside the Luxmore tonight—never mind her reason for being there. She was in trouble. Was afraid of something or maybe—Venom frowned—being threatened by someone. "Foxe with an *e*."

"You looking for anything in particular?"

"How about everything you can find."

Sloan nodded. "Give me a minute."

"Sure. No problem."

Indulging in a shoulder roll, Venom attacked his tension. Tired muscles sighed, enjoying the stretch as he fiddled with blue chalk sitting on the narrow lip of the billiard table. Turning the cube over in his hand, he glanced toward the wall of windows. Alive with magic, the glass rippled like black water, washing against steel frames, reminding him Evelyn was out there. Somewhere. Alone in daylight. Clenching his teeth, he reached for patience. Dragon sense pinpoint sharp, he listened to the quick click of computer keys and—

"Twenty-eight years old. Of African-American descent. Entered college early, graduated summa cum laude at twenty-one." His focus locked on the screen, Sloan scrolled through a page of information. "A forensic accountant. A skilled one too, by the look of this and . . . ah, man. She lost her job three months ago."

"I know." Dragging his gaze from the shifting glass, Venom turned toward his friend. A quick side step, and he set up shop next to his buddy. His eyes landed on a screen full of information. "She told me."

"Did you know her firm was part of the Amsted scandal? The company filed for bankruptcy. Top-level executives are under investigation . . . legal action pending."

Well now, that explained a lot, didn't it? Like why Evelyn hadn't found another job. With her qualifications, finding new employment should've been a snap. Instead, she remained unemployed three months out. "What else?"

Index finger poised over the trackpad, Sloan frowned. "Huh, that's weird."

"Show me."

His friend pointed to the screen of financial information. "She liquidated everything. And I mean *everything*, Ven. Sold her condo downtown. Her Audi A6 too. All kinds of stuff on eBay as well . . . clothes, handbags, sunglasses. You name it, she unloaded it. I'm surprised there's anything left in her closet."

"Bank accounts?"

"Empty. She withdrew all her savings—$38,000 dollars' worth—five months ago."

"Goddamn it." Unease hit Venom like a runaway train. "I figured she was in trouble but . . ."

As he trailed off, Sloan glanced at him. "Looks like it could be the serious kind."

"Yeah, the owe-someone-scary-a-lot-of-money kind." Venom cursed under his breath. The three grand he'd given her tonight pretty much assured it. "Got a current address on her?"

"Let's see where she forwarded her mail." Within seconds, Sloan hacked the US Postal Service firewall. He typed Evelyn's full name into the system's search engine. "Oh, shit."

"What?"

"Not good," Sloan murmured. "She lives in Granite Falls . . . 2301 Church Street."

Venom's heart stalled mid-beat, then dropped into his stomach. "No—no way. Check again. Run it again, Sloan."

Muttering a curse, Sloan retraced his cyber steps. The same address popped onto the screen. Venom stared at it, then shook his head. His throat went tight. Pressure expanded between his temples, rising like a tsunami inside his head. Alarm for her rode the wave, making his mind race and his heart sink as Sloan ran the info again. But double- and triple-checking wouldn't change a thing, much less cure his unease.

If Sloan was right, something nasty was unfolding in Granite Falls. A potentially life-threatening event. One he'd let Evelyn return to tonight. It didn't matter that he hadn't known. What mattered now was his ability to keep her safe. The kicker, though? The absolute hell of it all? He couldn't do that now. Or go after her.

Not while the sun rose and deadly UV rays ruled.

"Call her." Gaze glued to the phone number listed below her address, he grabbed Sloan's shoulder. "Call her, Sloan. Text her . . . whatever. Just reach her—right now."

"Hang on," his friend said, pulling up an Internet call service.

The computer speaker crackled. A dial tone sounded a second before Evelyn's phone rang. Six rings in and—

Her voice mail kicked in.

Sloan tried again.

Same result. No answer. Just an automated message on the other end of the line.

Concern pounded through him. Fear picked up the thread, slamming his heart against the inside of his breastbone. Venom shook his head. Okay. Stay calm. No need to freak out. At least, not yet. She could be sleeping. Her ringer could be turned off. Maybe she was simply ignoring her phone. Any number of possibilities fit the scenario. But as his throat went tight, and Venom backed away from the billiard table, he forced himself to face the truth.

Forge had been right.

And he'd been wrong. He never should have let her go.

Chapter Thirteen

On-point and ahead of the pack, Gage slipped around a blind corner. Dragon senses sharp, he settled into a crouch and listened hard. Nothing. No faint noises at either end of the subterranean corridor. No enemy soldiers hiding in shadowed alcoves. No sound at all. Just the chaotic beat of his own heart. Taking a deep breath, he forced the blood rush to slow. Calm. Even. Ever-steady. The ultimate trifecta, pillars of a solid plan as he moved into the teeth of the unknown.

Danger around every corner. Outnumbered inside an enemy lair. Trapped underground. Still no exit in sight.

Gage clenched his teeth. *Screwed* seemed like a better word to use right now. Unlucky might be worth his vote too, but well—fuck it. He couldn't change the circumstances and erase the last six days. His colossal screwup aside—the fact he hadn't seen the ambush coming—wasn't worth the brain power.

Neither was second-guessing himself.

Not if he wanted to stay alive long enough to get out of enemy territory.

Scanning the short corridor, he hunted for pitfalls, then shuffled along its length. Cold stone chilling his bare feet, he slipped around the next corner. Illumination bloomed at the end of the hallway. The swath sliced through the darkness, drawing straight lines across slimy stone walls. The light blinded him for a moment. His eyes adjusted, downgrading the glow, giving him the lay of the land and—

About fucking time.

Just what he'd been searching for—a way out of the labyrinth. The end of the line. His escape route in the shape of a small open-ended foyer. Narrow on his end, the entryway flared out at the other, opening into a much larger space. Staying low, Gage crept toward the open expanse. His back to the wall, he paused on the lip of the vestibule.

A loading dock stretched out in front of him.

His mouth curved. Jackpot. God bless good luck. An island of concrete, at least sixteen feet of cover. But even better? The barricade created by a pile of supplies. Stacked like Lego blocks, wooden crates sat in a straight line, rising as visual impediments from the edge of the platform. The huge pile of canvas bags marked "Laundry" helped too, looking more like sandbags in a bunker than reams of clean sheets on the other side of the dock. And beyond the supply-the-manor stack? An enormous garage, complete with a lineup of vehicles. He scanned the space again. Hmm, lovely: Maseratis, Lamborghinis, Audis, and BMWs parked in neat rows, high-gloss paint sparkling beneath the watchful eye of industrial-grade lights.

Gage growled in satisfaction.

Come one. Come all. He had his pick of the litter.

Moving as fast as his injuries allowed, Gage slipped across the loading dock. He studied the fancy sports cars, then shook his head. None of the two-seaters fit Osgard's description. He assessed the collection again. Shit. Not good. He couldn't see a—

His gaze skipped over a Bentley, then came right back.

Bingo. Just what the escapee ordered. Vehicular perfection dressed up in shiny black paint. Yeah. No doubt about it. The Bentley sitting in the ninth row was the one Rodin used during the day. Blacked-out rear windows. Reinforced steel body designed for protection. A big V-8 engineered for speed under the hood. Eyes narrowed, Gage studied the setup. Three industrial-size garage doors occupied the opposite side of the building. No impediments between the Bentley and the middle door.

Perfect. Absolutely brilliant. One exit point dead ahead. One escape now in full swing. Time to see if he had any company inside the garage.

Hitting his haunches beside the first crate, he raised his hand and made a fist. Halfway across the foyer, Haider took the cue. His friend relayed the message, clenching his own hand, warning Osgard and Nian to stop. The shuffle of footfalls quieted behind him. Another hand signal told the males to stay put.

Without making a sound, Gage shifted right and peered around the corner of the crate. His skin brushed against rough plywood. Pain punched through. The burn marks on his chest squawked, causing a chain reaction. He flinched, fighting the backlash as anguish pushed him one step closer to weakness. He shoved back, refusing to stop, ignoring the slide into exhaustion in favor of looking on the bright side.

So far, so good.

Nothing to worry about yet. No movement inside the large bay beyond the loading dock. Mathematical mind churning, he searched the space and made some quick calculations. A grid flared inside his head, drawing lines, charting a course, giving him approximate dimensions of the garage. One hundred and twenty feet wide, sixty feet deep . . . ceiling height, thirty feet, give or take. Giving up his vantage point, he crab-crawled to the other end of the crates. Poised at the corner, he looked both ways and, ignoring the pain, hobbled behind the pile of canvas bags.

Nothing moved. No one shouted. No alarm bells went off either.

He released a pent-up breath and got ready to—

Heavy footfalls sounded, pinging off steel to reach the high ceiling. A door slammed somewhere to his right. Male voices followed. Gage tensed. Ah, hell. Too little, too late. Archguard watchdogs, returning from the morning meal.

Gage slid lower, using the laundry bags for cover.

"I'll make the rounds," one of the guards said. "Put on a fresh pot, would you?"

"Got some whiskey," guard two said, from the other side of the garage. Keys rattled. Metal rasped against metal. Hinges squeaked as a door opened. "Want a splash in your coffee?"

"Sure," the first male murmured, stopping beside the loading dock. Gage bit down on a curse. No more than five feet away. The bastard had just set up camp on his doorstep. A lighter flicked. Once. Twice. A third time before the male inhaled hard. Cigarette smoke drifted up from the other side of the canvas barricade, making his nose twitch. "Make mine a double."

A third male chimed in. "Game's on."

"Sounds good," another said, stopping next to the male sucking on a cancer stick. "Can I bum one of those?"

The lighter flicked again. More smoke wafted up from the other side of the laundry bags as the enemy exhaled at the same time.

"Where's the fucking remote?" a fifth guy asked, voice full of pissed off.

"Right here." A thump echoed as another entered the conversation. "Jesus. What are you—blind?"

Gage swallowed a curse. That made six. *Six* enemy soldiers, two camped on his doorstep, less than three feet away, another four somewhere across the garage. Pivoting on the balls of his feet, he glanced over his shoulder.

Haider drilled him with intense silver eyes.

"Get ready," Gage murmured, holding his friend's gaze, listening to enemy chatter. *"We're fighting our way out."*

"Say when."

"Give it a minute. I want the others inside the office before I make a move," he said, glancing over the top of the pile. Leaning against the loading dock, the guards stood shoulder to shoulder, each busy filling his lungs with carcinogens. *"Killing two guards quietly I can do. Six at once, on the other hand?"*

"Yeah." Flexing his fists, Haider inched forward, trying to get a better look. *"Too much noise."*

Gage nodded. *"At least one will get to the alarm before I get to him."*

"Shit."

No kidding. The perfect word to use. *Shitty* about summed it up, considering the situation. Six healthy males against three injured ones and a youngling.

Not great odds.

Gage didn't care. He moved instead.

Pace quick, feet quiet, he shifted toward the lip of the loading dock. His gaze ran the gauntlet, roaming the walls, searching for more pitfalls. Anything that might trip him up before he leapt into the open. Motion detectors? Trip wires? An alarm system complete with laser sensors? He needed to know before he took out the guards . . . without making a sound. The skill always came in handy. His brothers-in-arms loved him for it. The enemy? Not so much. Then again, the bastards never heard him coming, so . . .

He never heard any complain.

The thought made him smile. His bloodthirsty nature urged him to unleash. Let loose. Deliver hell to those standing between him and freedom. Bowing his head, Gage closed his eyes and visualized the kill. Each move. Every detail. The sight, sound, and smell as he became a predator and protected the males at his back.

His nostrils flared. He cranked both fists in tight.

"On the count of three," he murmured, giving Haider a heads-up. *"I'll take out both guards, then we make a run for—"*

"No need," Nian rasped, inching onto the loading dock. *"The bastards won't see us."*

Gage blinked in surprise. *"They'll sense us the second I move."*

"No, they won't. I'm an illusionist. Once I set the spell, no Dragonkind male can detect me." Gritting his teeth, Nian belly crawled behind the wooden crates. Osgard picked up the slack, helping the male to cross the open space. One eye on the guards, Gage waved the duo forward. The pair came in for a smooth landing next to him. Nian grunted as the kid let him go, but managed to stay upright. *"I'll create an invisibility bubble. Stay close to me and you're covered."*

Crouched behind the pair, Haider studied Nian a moment, then met Gage's gaze over the top of the male's head. The look spoke volumes. Gage picked up the thread along with its meaning. His friend was right. Zidane had done a number on Nian: blackened both his eyes, broken five of his fingers, driven spikes through chest and thigh muscles, taken a blowtorch to his spine, burning his skin to a crisp. Now the male suffered. Was in so much pain, he could hardly move, never mind think straight.

"You're in bad shape, Nian," Gage said, tone soft as he assessed the male again. Fuck. It was worse than he'd thought. Nian's

bio-energy dipped low, moving into single digits. Which meant Nian needed to feed . . . and soon. *"You're not strong enough to—"*

"My magic will hold long enough to get us to the car."

Looking for a second opinion, he glanced at Haider.

His friend nodded, confirming the play.

"Move on my signal." Turning toward the staircase, Gage rechecked his position. Steps off the loading dock to his left, Rodin's lackeys to his right. Less than five feet away now, one of the guards drew another cigarette from the pack in his hand. The lighter clicked. Flame rose. Smoke followed in a gray curl, drifting over the guard's head toward the ceiling. *"Good to go. Fire it up, Nian."*

"Keep ahold of me, Osgard," Nian whispered, dropping mind-speak to include the youngling in the conversation. "Whatever happens, don't let go."

Osgard nodded.

Calling on his talent, Nian inhaled slow, then exhaled smooth. Multicolored eyes the color of opals started to glow. Magic flared in the center of Nian's palms. Power bled into the open air. One second flowed into the next. A bitter chill slithered in to surround the group. The male murmured. The spell rose, sucking at Gage's skin, rubbing his nerve endings raw as the invisibility bubble expanded. Warm air warped around him. Displacement rippled, then smoothed out, wrapping each male in a spell so strong it obliterated all trace of life. His heart stalled, pausing inside his chest as he and the others disappeared into thin air.

Cold clawed at him. Gage stifled a shiver. *"Holy fuck."*

"Told you." Satisfaction winged across Nian's battered face.

Gage snorted. *"Gloat later—move now."*

Testing the invisibility spell, Gage pushed to his feet. He took a step toward the staircase. Neither guard looked his way. He took another, and then a third. No shift at all. Hell, the bastards didn't even twitch. No movement from inside the small office across the garage either. Clear windows revealed four males sitting around a beat-up table. Eyes glued to a TV, the clueless quadruplets watched a soccer match. Orange and green uniforms flashed across the flat screen. Gage frowned.

Germany versus the Netherlands, maybe.

Not that he cared. The game didn't matter.

He was too busy navigating the stairs, descending on silent feet, stepping onto the garage floor, hoping like hell Nian held it together. Sparing a second, he glanced over his shoulder.

Osgard met his gaze.

Gage tipped his chin, asking without words for an update. Arm muscles straining, the kid readjusted his grip on Nian, but nodded, reassuring him. Gage blew out a measured breath. Fantastic. Everybody was on track. So was his trajectory. A few more car bumpers to bypass—ten, fifteen feet tops—and he'd be home free. Next to the Bentley. Seconds from firing up the engine. Mere moments from slipping inside and putting the pedal to the floor.

Focus split, he kept one eye on the assholes in the office, and the other on the males blowing smoke rings. Skirting a bright-orange Ferrari, Gage turned into the fifth row and slipped down the aisle. Muscle cars sat beside expensive European models. Every color of the rainbow. Waxed steel. Curved lines. Shiny chrome. A mechanic's wet dream, which, naturally, made him yearn for home. For the comfort of Black Diamond and the two thousand square feet of heaven the Nightfury warriors called "the garage" . . . and he called his bedroom. One hundred percent his domain. Every tool known to mankind under one roof.

The Corvette he rebuilt last summer sprang to mind.

He shoved the mental image aside, stuffing it into the back corner of his brain. Later. He'd think about the gorgeous ZR1 *later.* Think about driving her again too, but only after he'd gotten everyone to safety.

The guard took another drag from his cigarette.

The cloaking spell flexed. Magic wavered. Chilly air rippled, flickering around him. Nian gasped. The invisibility shield shattered, making him visible to enemy eyes. He ducked between two muscle cars. With a curse, Osgard shoved Nian to the floor behind him. Belly down beside a tire, Gage glanced over his shoulder. Nian crumpled, the shimmer in his eyes dying along with the spell as Haider dove for cover. His friend landed with a thump. Palms slapped against concrete.

Sharp sound ricocheted, cracking through the quiet.

One of the guards shifted. He dropped his cigarette, then ground it out beneath his boot sole. "Did you hear that?"

"Yeah," the other answered. "You go that way. I'll check the doors."

Bleeding from a cut above his eye, Nian shook his head. *"I'm too weak. I can't get it back. I can't—"*

"Shit." So much for trusting the namby-pamby.

He should've gone with his gut and killed the guards. Quickly. Quietly. Like he'd wanted to when he'd had the chance. Now, he was out of time. Hemmed in between two cars, little room to maneuver, listening to enemy males make the rounds. Boots thumped in the quiet. Each stride brought both guards closer by the second. Staying low, Gage army crawled down the aisle. Parked on his right, the Bentley acted like a mirror, shiny black body reflecting guard number one. Seven rows away. The enemy male kept coming, striding in front of the car bumpers, checking each row. Shifting into a crouch beside the Bentley, Gage popped up to glance through the driver's side window.

Unlocked. Keys lying like a gift in the center console.

"Haider."

"Yeah?"

"Got any juice left?"

Haider hummed, more growl than purr. *"Enough to start some trouble."*

"Get ready. On my mark . . ." Trailing off, Gage rechecked the guard's position, then cupped the Bentley's rear door handle. With a gentle tug, he popped the latch. The door eased open on well-oiled hinges. He listened to the guard approach his hiding spot. Twenty feet away. Four rows to go. He met the kid's gaze, dropped mind-speak, and whispered, "Osgard—the second I move, get Nian into the backseat."

"Can you drive?" the kid asked, mouthing the question.

"Excellent question," Haider said.

"With my eyes closed," Gage said, ignoring Haider, hoping he wasn't lying. Hurting almost as much as Nian, his bio-energy ebbed, flirting with critical. *"I can handle sunlight."*

"How much?" Nian asked, looking more dead than alive. *"And for how long?"*

"Twenty minutes." Gage tensed as the guard paused two rows away. *"Half an hour tops before I—"*

"Go blind." Haider snarled. The nasty sound spiraled, raking the inside of his temples. *"It's too risky, Gage. Let Osgard drive. Sunlight won't hurt him."*

A load of *fuck you* locked in his throat, Gage didn't answer. He popped the driver's side door without making a sound instead. Haider cursed. Footfalls echoed, pinging off garage walls, bringing both guards closer. One eye on the male's reflection in black paint, Gage counted off the seconds, waiting for the enemy to come within range, turning Haider's concern over in his head.

He clenched his teeth.

Screw his friend's bright idea. Sure, letting Osgard drive might be safer, but . . . no way could he do it. Putting Osgard in the hot seat amounted to a bad idea. For better or worse, he'd vowed to protect the kid. Not get him killed right out of the gate.

The thud of footfalls quieted.

Back pressed to the Bentley's front door, Gage watched the enemy stop on the other side of the car through the windshield. Kitty-corner to him. Less than a car length away. In range, well within striking distance. Gage drew a deep breath. Brows tight, the guard glanced over his shoulder. He called to his buddy. With a snarl, Gage launched his attack. Legs acting like pistons, he exploded from behind the Bentley. Planting his palm on the roof, he leapt over the hood to reach the guard.

His jeans scraped over steel.

Enemy eyes widened in surprise.

He struck, closing the distance in seconds. His fist connected. Bone cracked against bone, snapping the male's head to one side. The bastard stumbled backward. Gage didn't hesitate. He hammered the asshole again. Blood arced, splashing across the windshield. Magic hummed, streaming through his veins as Haider unleashed. Silver bullets whistled through the air, ripping through the second guard's chest. His body hit the floor behind a muscle car. Gage tightened his grip on the asshole under his control and—

Crack!

He snapped the bastard's neck.

Violent sound ricocheted. Time lengthened. The enemy ashed out in his hands. As gray flakes exploded around him, he pivoted toward the Bentley. On the move, Osgard shoved Nian into the backseat. A shout of alarm went up. Movement flashed in his periphery. The soldiers inside the office scrambled to their feet. Chairs flew backward. Metal screeched as wooden seat backs tipped and slammed into the concrete floor.

An unearthly snarl exploded through the garage.

Gaze locked on the head guard, Gage leapt over the hood. He landed with a bang beside the driver's side door. The male transformed, shifting into the dragon form inside the office. Glass shattered. Wood splintered. Magic blasted through the garage. Red scales glittered as the enemy roared. Huge fangs gleamed in the bright light. An orange glow grew in the back of the dragon's throat, forming into a fireball.

"Haider—" With a mental command, Gage started the engine. The big V-8 snarled, coming to life with a vicious rumble. "Get in the fucking car!"

Leaping over a Lamborghini, Haider jumped into the backseat. "Go. Go. Go!"

Gage slammed the driver's side door with a bang. "Force field."

"Up and running," Haider said.

Thank fuck. Out of time. Almost out of luck. About to be fried by the enemy with a nasty-ass fireball. Not great in the largest scheme of things. Gage didn't care. Gripping the steering wheel with both hands, he hit the gas, pressing the pedal to the floor. The Bentley screamed and shot forward.

Tires squealed. The smell of burning rubber infused the air.

The enemy dragon exhaled.

A stream of fire rocketed toward the back of the car.

Haider muttered something obscene. The force field flared, curving around the back of the Bentley. Flames roared toward the back bumper. The fireball slammed into the shield, thrusting the car forward. The rear end fishtailed. The heavy steel frame groaned. Haider held the line, bearing down, shaping the shield, fighting to keep the inferno at bay.

The enemy dragon inhaled again.

Digging deep, driving like a demon, Gage called on his own power. Tires screaming against concrete, he opened his mind. Magic crackled, howling inside his head. Magnetic force traveled through his veins, vibrating in warning. He hung on to it a moment, bending his ability, allowing the energy to build inside him. As it reached the pinnacle, he thrust it in all directions. The powerful stream raged around the Bentley. Expensive sports cars blew sky-high. Metal groaned. Enemy males cursed. The dragon dodged to avoid getting a face full of Mercedes Benz.

The smell of gas infused the air.

A spark lit off, igniting the fuel source. A firestorm erupted, blasting through the garage. With a snarl, Gage launched more vehicles into the air. Steel screamed, twisting beneath the force of his magic. Foot to the floor, he asked for more speed. Engine whining, the Bentley shot toward the exit. Cars cartwheeled, flipping in mid-air, flashing in the rearview mirror, sending the guards running for cover.

In control of the devastation, Gage set his sights on the garage doors. Superconductor inside his mind raging, he sent out a shock wave. Reinforced steel resisted. He struck the barrier again. The bottom of all three doors twisted. Steel ripped up the middle. Sunlight bled through jagged cracks. Gage bared his teeth and accelerated. Almost there. Ten feet away. Now five . . . four . . . three . . . two . . .

He hammered the doors one more time.

Heavy metal folded in half, peeling away from the rails. Each panel blew out and up, rocketing toward the bright-blue sky. Deadly UV rays flooded the garage. The enemy screamed in agony. Gage didn't look back. Didn't slow down either. Double-fisting the wheel, he hammered a button on the center console—raising dark glass to protect the backseat—and drove through the hole into the light of day.

Heat burned across the backs of his hands.

Pain prickled across his skin, ghosting up his forearms a second before his eyes started to sting. Squinting against the glare, he conjured a pair of sunglasses. He slipped the protective gear on, shielding his eyes from the sun. It wasn't much—hardly anything at all, but at least it helped. The Ray-Bans would get him farther down the road. An excellent strategy considering the damage he'd left in his wake. Satisfaction sank deep. It didn't last long. Sure, he might be free for the moment, but things changed fast. Rodin's death squad was now on full alert. The bastards were no doubt already on a computer. Hooked in and monitoring the state-of-the-art GPS system built into the Bentley. Which meant . . .

No time to lose. Even less to waste.

"Shit."

"You okay?" Haider asked, voice muffled by the partition.

"Fine," he said, trying to sound normal. How he managed it, Gage didn't know. Thirty minutes in the sun, his ass. Make it fifteen, 'cause . . . man. It hurt more than he expected.

Normally, he tolerated the sun better. Could stand outside for a while in human form, soak up a little, and enjoy the warmth. Not today. Little wonder. Less than full strength equaled nowhere near capable. A pity. More than disappointing too. Of all the times for his tolerance level to crap out on him, here . . . right now . . . amounted to the worst. Biting down on a curse, Gage sped past the end of the driveway. He cranked the wheel and swung into a tight turn. The Bentley fishtailed. Controlling the skid, he shot onto the main road. He scanned the terrain on either side of the two-lane highway. Nothing but forest and fields for miles around. Not surprising. An Archguard death squad liked privacy and rarely operated inside city limits.

Too much chance of discovery. Not enough time to play with their prey.

Glancing at the center console, he searched for the intercom. Flipping a switch, he powered up the first-class com system. "Nian, give me a place to go—somewhere we can lie low until sundown. I'm not going to make it far."

Nian groaned as he shifted in the backseat. "Head for the airstrip."

Gage frowned. "Where?"

"Fifteen minutes from here. Take the east road. I have a private jet waiting."

"In your name?" Eyes locked on the road, Gage scanned the horizon. Nothing and nobody. Not a single car in sight. With a jerk, he swerved into the oncoming lane, into the shade of the ancient oaks standing alongside the road. Massive tree limbs blocked out the sun. Gage sighed in relief. "If it is, Zidane already knows about it. No way it's still there."

"Give me some credit, Nightfury," Nian said, a grumble in his voice. "The plane isn't mine. Neither is the airstrip. I borrow both from a human whenever I fly by day."

Haider snorted. "Borrow?"

Nian huffed. "All right, then—steal temporarily. Happy now?"

Not even close. *Happy* didn't begin to describe the situation.

Or him at the moment.

Not with the sun burning bright and agony taking a sledgehammer to his skull. Thick branches parted above him. Sunlight spilled through the gap, zapping him with another round of UV rays. Gage gasped in pain, but kept the car on the road. Taking a sharp right, he turned down a gravel lane. Stones kicked up, pinging against the undercarriage, leaving a trail of dust in his wake.

Due east. A straight shot to freedom.

Now all he needed to do was hang on and hope like hell he made it in time. Before the sun took his vision. Before he left them all stranded in the middle of nowhere. Before dusk arrived and the Archguard went on the offensive, sending its death squad to hunt them down.

Chapter Fourteen

Personal guard flying in his wake, Ivar rocketed out of the mountain pass. Sheer cliffs gave way to thick forest as rough terrain smoothed out. His night vision sparked. He banked into a tight turn, then leveled out over a deserted two-lane highway. Night chill slipped over his scales. Ivar grimaced, but increased his wing speed anyway. His aversion to the cold didn't matter. His fire dragon tendencies needed to take a backseat. Or at least, get on board.

He didn't have time to fuck around.

The promise of catastrophe awaited . . . along with his superbug.

Ivar hummed. Superbug number three had taken hold. Now the virus wreaked havoc, infecting more humans by the hour. Nothing left to do now but pop in, take a look-see, and record the damage.

Descending through low-lying clouds, Ivar came up over the next rise. His warriors shifted in mid-flight, following his lead across the frozen landscape. Porch lights winked in the distance, then multiplied like brilliant dots on a map, drawing him toward the center of town. His night vision sharpened another notch, then settled, adjusting in urban glow. Cold mist dotting his scales, Ivar swung into a lazy turn and flew in on a slow glide.

Heavy clouds parted. Moonlight joined the glow of electric luminescence.

The gentle wash lit up shingled rooftops, drawing his attention to dark windows. Sleepy little hollow nestled at the base of the Cascades. Humans snug in their beds, behind closed doors, covers drawn up, eyes closed while each dreamed of—Ivar frowned. Hell, he didn't know what humans dreamed about. Getting out of Boring-town USA, maybe?

Amused by the thought, he shook his head. Chilly air spiraled off the tips of horns, leaving a white contrail behind him. He descended another two hundred feet. Street lamps welcomed him, spilling illumination across sidewalks, acting like a runway rushing him toward the medical complex at the end of the avenue.

Cascade Valley Hospital. Arlington's answer to essential services.

His eyes narrowed on the collection of buildings floating in a sea of asphalt. Lots of parking spaces up front, a strip of forest out back. Not much to look at from a distance. Even less to write home about. Kind of disappointing, actually. Not the sexiest place to unleash a supervirus, much less harvest the results, but . . .

Ivar sighed. What the hell. The location didn't matter. He wasn't looking for *sexy*. What he wanted was efficient. Deadly would work too.

Cloaked in an invisibility spell, he angled his wings and circled into a holding pattern above the facility. One rotation turned into another. His eyes narrowed, he made a third pass just to make sure. Yup. Satellite imaging hadn't lied. Everything sat where it belonged—medical clinic to his right, new wing of the hospital to his left. Splitting the difference, he landed in the parking lot between the two. His talons clicked against pavement. Poised on his back paws, he wing flapped, stretching taut muscles. Wind rushed across the lot, whispering against steel. Parked cars rocked on tires as stone dust swirled onto the street.

Young maple trees sitting curbside swayed in protest.

Ivar ignored the dust cloud and shifted from dragon to human form. The street light buzzed, throwing bright light, making his eyes sting. He squinted to protect his vision from the LEDs and conjured his clothes. Not his usual fare either. He played a character tonight, one of his own making—human doctor extraordinaire. Soft cotton settled against his skin. He topped the green hospital scrubs with a white lab coat, then added a name tag.

Dr. Ivar, his cover emblazoned on plastic.

He huffed in amusement. Too funny. Total make-believe, and yet, somehow the surgical scrubs fit. Felt good. Better than anything he'd worn in a while.

Fighting an eye roll, he pivoted toward the building. The lab coat flapped, brushing the back of his thighs as he crossed the parking lot. Looking both ways, he jogged across the street, ducked beneath a few low-lying branches, and stopped on a strip of lawn. Frostbitten grass crunched beneath his Nikes. Ivar didn't notice. He studied the main entrance instead. Huge timber beam pillars rose from concrete foundations. A glass facade stood just behind, rising two stories to touch the roofline. Set off by interior lights, the wall of windows glowed, showcasing a collection of chairs to the right of the front doors. A reception area lay just beyond, a pretty brunette behind the counter, ready to play greeter to those who came through the main entrance.

Ivar pursed his lips. Huh. Nice looking place, actually. Much bigger than he'd thought too. Well designed. Airy vibe. Rustic touches married with modern sensibility.

Focus fixed on the receptionist, he strode across the access road and stepped onto the curb. Stone pavers whispered underfoot. The rasp of his running shoes echoed in the quiet, sliding around timber beams to reach the overhang protecting the entrance. Each sound cranked him tighter. Excitement did the rest, making muscles tighten over bone. He felt the strain as anticipation struck. Impatience joined the parade, urging him to hurry. Ivar shoved both aside and, pace even, kept walking.

No need to hurry. No reason to ruin the moment either.

Delayed gratification intensified an experience. Heightened awareness. Elevated sensation, sculpting the anticipation of an "I can't wait" moment until physical feeling melded with emotional. Now he felt everything—his heart pump, his fingertips tingle, the blood rush that made the fine hairs on his nape stand straight up. Flexing his hands, Ivar growled. Glory, glory, hallelujah. This was it—here, now. After months of work. After a week of waiting. The day of reckoning had finally arrived.

Now he stood at the gates, triumphant.

Moments from seeing his superbug in action. Seconds from viewing the damage caused by the progression of his scientific experimentation. Minutes from recording symptoms and pulling blood samples to take back to his lab. Testing would take weeks. And, hmm, he couldn't wait to get started.

Rolling his shoulders, Ivar paused beneath the timber beams and glanced over his shoulder. Searching the sky, he fired up mind-speak. "*You coming?*"

"*Do I have to?*" Hamersveld asked, a grumble in his voice. Wintry air warped over the crosswalk. A wormhole opened a second before the male uncloaked. Smooth shark-gray scales winked in the low light. Mist swirling from his nostrils, he dropped out of the sky. Webbed paws thumped down on asphalt, making window glass rattle. *"I hate hospitals."*

Ivar raised a brow. *"Been in many, have you?"*

"None, actually." His friend made a sound of distaste. *"I dislike them on principle. Too many sick humans."*

"There's a pretty brunette inside," he said, tone all about temptation.

"Where?"

"Behind the reception desk."

Rapt interest in his expression, Hamersveld shifted sideways. Craning his neck, the Norwegian peered around one of the square pillars. Black eyes rimmed by pale blue widened as he spotted the female in the waiting room. *"Silfer's balls—look at her. How much time do you need in there?"*

"Half an hour," he murmured, swallowing his amusement. But it was hard. He wanted to laugh at his new XO. The male fit the mold. Was way too predictable. At least, on the female front. No matter what happened, Hamersveld never passed up an opportunity to lay out a female. *"Forty-five minutes, tops, to check it out and collect blood samples."*

"No need to hurry." Shifting into human form, Hamersveld stomped his feet into his combat boots. The quiet thud echoed, drifting on night air. Focus still riveted on the brunette, his friend crossed to meet him. As Hamersveld stopped next to him, he grinned, all mercenary, no mercy. *"Take all the time you want. I'll try her on for size while I wait."*

Ivar snorted.

Hamersveld growled. *"Wonder if she's got a friend nearby."*

"Greedy bastard."

"I take it where I can get it."

"Which is everywhere," Ivar said, putting his feet in gear, leading the way to the front door.

"You're no different, Ivar."

"True enough."

A complete lie. Ivar knew it the second the words left his mouth, but well . . . whatever. Let Hamersveld believe he craved a hot threesome as much as other males. No skin off his nose. A terrific misconception. One that worked in his favor, elevating his status inside the Razorback nation. As leader of a large pack, he needed to foster the illusion. Liked that his warriors looked at him with awe and respect. The truth of his preferences, after all, was no one's business. Least of all Hamersveld's.

No one needed to know he didn't enjoy gluttony.

Or that he preferred one-on-one action, not multiple females at once. Sharing with another male wasn't his favorite thing either. Given a choice, he'd have one. Just *one* female on tap. A go-to girl for when he needed to scratch an itch . . . and feed. The perfect arrangement, really. He'd get what he needed, then go back to doing what he did best—being alone.

Too bad that rarely happened.

Finding alone time seemed an impossible endeavor. At least, for him. Which left him playing catch-up. Keeping up appearances too—feeding and fucking in front of his personal guards. Stuck sharing females with Hamersveld, only to pretend it didn't bother him. Walking beneath the hospital portico, Ivar grimaced. More orgy-ish than intimate. No wonder he only fed when forced. When ravenous hunger took hold and his body demanded sustenance.

Not a great idea. Bad headspace for a Dragonkind male.

Being blinded by hunger—falling into energy-greed—wasn't fun. And yet, he flirted with danger on a regular basis, shying away from physical contact, breaking the cardinal rule more than once. Embarrassing, but true. Especially since he'd lost control and killed females by accident . . . on more than one occasion. He might've done the same to Sasha . . .

If she'd allowed it.

The blond beauty had turned the tables instead. Linked in and taken his energy before he'd stolen hers. An image of her rose in his mind's eye. Messy long hair. Sleepy bedroom eyes. Sex kitten smile in place. Ivar shivered in appreciation, then shook his head, trying to shove her from his mind. She pushed back, refusing to go, entrenching herself, making him acknowledge her odd effect on him. She was a puzzle. Baffling. Intriguing. Beyond disturbing too. Particularly since her strength highlighted a weakness in him. One he didn't understand and couldn't begin to unravel. Her ability to connect to his life force defied logic. It should never have happened.

His gaze riveted to the front doors, Ivar swallowed a snarl.

Another sin to lay at the Goddess of All Things' feet.

Damned curse. Totally unfair.

What the hell did the deity know about suffering anyway? About pain and loss? How dare she damn an entire race for the sins of one male? For infidelity, a crime no one ever went to jail for, and yet, his kind had been imprisoned for years. Bound to humankind. Cut off from the direct source that nurtured his species' dragon half—and the magical abilities each male possessed. His brows collided. No doubt in his mind. Dragonkind had suffered enough. The goddess must realize her mistake by now—the outright selfishness of her actions . . . temper tantrum . . . or whatever she labeled it.

Yet, nothing changed.

Everything stayed the same. And his race remained cursed. Tied to humans in irrevocable ways. Forced to procreate with an inferior race. One hundred percent dependent on someone else to survive.

Gritting his teeth, Ivar reached the entryway. With a mental tug, he tightened the cloaking spell, then grabbed one of the door handles. Cold metal slid against his palm. He yanked. The door flew open. Glass rattled in the steel frame. Hinges hissed. Ignoring the squawk fest, he strode over the threshold, into an open space with thirty-foot ceilings.

Hamersveld veered right, heading toward the reception desk. *"Call if you need me."*

"Uh-huh," he said, turning toward the staircase.

Tucked behind the sweep of open treads, a hallway snaked off the main entrance. His gaze bounced to the corner wall. A sign with block letters and red arrows pointed the way, giving him the lay of the land. A quick left turn took him down a short corridor and—

Bingo. Emergency Room, dead ahead.

Pace steady, Ivar entered the main lobby. Wide sliding glass doors led outside. An island of chairs occupied the middle ground, each one empty. Pale walls. Ugly picture frames. Nary a human in sight. Made sense. Humans might be annoying, but they were efficient. Particularly in medical emergencies. Shutdown protocol explained the non-action inside the ER. With his superbug in full swing, the hospital had done what he expected—raised the threat level, cleared the hospital of all nonessential personnel, diverted incoming patients to other medical facilities.

Perfect. Fewer humans to avoid while he went about his work.

The click of computer keys sounded to his right.

His gaze snapped in that direction. A nurses' station. Three females, surgical masks in place, worked behind the high counter. Movements frantic, one entered data into the computer. The other two shuffled paperwork, stuffing file folders, looking harried and . . . yeah. His mouth curved. More than a touch afraid. Excellent. Right on time. He'd come to the right spot. Now all he needed to do was locate the infected patients.

Gathering a stack of files, a nurse stepped out from behind the counter. "I'll get these to the second floor."

Computer nurse glanced away from the screen. "Don't go into the quarantine area, Becky. Hand them off to a hazmat suit and get back here."

"Will do." Rubber soles squeaking, she pivoted and high-tailed it down the hall.

Gaze glued to her back, Ivar followed. No sense wasting a golden opportunity. The female knew the layout, the fastest way into the quarantine area too. Hugging the files to her chest, she turned down another corridor and stopped in front of a bank of elevators. Hidden by magic, he set up shop at her back. He ran his gaze over her curves from behind. Kind of petite, a whole lot nervous. He smelled her fear. It permeated the air around her, rising to tease his senses. And yet she hit the "Up" button anyway, moving toward danger instead of away.

Curious in many ways. Brave in others.

Most humans would've run. Been long gone by now in the hopes of saving their own skin. Not that it mattered now.

She was already infected.

Dragon senses up and running, he registered the sickness in her blood. Twelve hours at most, and the nurse would succumb, become ill . . . be in need of the same kind of medical attention she gave others every day. She fidgeted in front of him. A small cough emerged from her throat. Compassion for her eventual suffering tightened his chest. Ivar smothered a grimace. Well, hell. That wasn't a good sign. He shouldn't be feeling anything but triumph. But as she coughed again and pressed the button a second time, trying to hurry the elevator along, his conviction wavered. He sighed. Poor human. She'd been caught in the crossfire tonight. And honestly, he felt bad for her. More than a little guilty too. It wasn't her fault humankind couldn't get its act together.

Or that her race killed the planet bit by bit every day.

The elevator pinged. Double doors slid open. The nurse stepped inside.

Ivar hesitated. Shit. He couldn't do it. Couldn't share space with a female dying from a superbug he'd created. It seemed disrespectful somehow. So instead of getting in with her, he let the doors close and turned toward a door labeled "Stairs." A hard shove opened it. He entered the stairwell. Cinder-block walls rose on his left as he took the concrete treads two at a time. Within seconds, he stood on the landing to the second floor. Cranking the door open, he crossed the threshold into a corridor.

A man in a hazmat suit walked toward the end of the hall. Toward a door with a sign that read "Quarantine Area. Do Not Enter."

Ivar jogged past the dummy dressed in plastic. Powering up his magic, he bypassed the security and strode into the restricted area. The scent of antiseptic hand soap nailed him first. The smell of blood registered next. His nose twitched an instant before his other senses came online. Medical machines beeped. Paper rustled, IV bags crackled in nurses' hands, and shoe soles squeaked on the industrial-grade floor. Humans moaned, pleading for mercy, as medical staff—suited up in protective gear—tried to help. Desolation hung in the air. Organized chaos too, the kind that hinted at panic.

And no relief.

Jesus. What a mess. The kind he'd hoped to create, but hadn't really expected.

Moving farther down the hall, Ivar peeked into the room on his right. Four beds lined the back wall, all occupied by sick humans. Curtains drawn. Blue blankets pulled up beneath each chin. IV bags hung from metal poles, delivering fluids, maybe even antibiotics, to each patient. Taking a fortifying breath, he walked into the devastation. No time like the present. He had work to do. Forty minutes and counting before Hamersveld got his fill and came up for air.

Centering himself, Ivar settled into the cradle of discovery—where the scientist in him lived and compassion failed to exist. Ignoring requests for help, he pushed the sight of suffering from his mind. *Stay calm. Remain aloof. Forget the pain.* He repeated each phrase over and over as he made the rounds and collected samples from each patient. Magic rising, he stored each blood-filled test tube inside his mental vault to pull from later . . . when he returned to his lab. Room after room. Patient after patient. Infection rate consistent, symptoms all the same.

High fever. Pustules full of poison. Eventual respiratory failure.

Effective killers, but as he stepped into the fourth room, Ivar started to worry. Something was wrong. Very, very *wrong.* Halfway through the sample pool, and he hadn't encountered an infected male. Not a single one. Every patient he sampled was female.

Sixteen for sixteen. All *females*, for fuck's sake.

Unease ghosted down his spine.

Alarm arrived next, throbbing inside his head. Feet planted beside a hospital bed, Ivar stared down at the middle-aged female occupying it. Hooked up to oxygen, hours from death, she struggled to breathe. He frowned. The results didn't make sense. No way could his findings be right. Disease didn't discriminate. Viruses attacked in even ratios. Gender was never a deciding factor in infection. And yet, the quarantine area didn't lie. Neither did the samples.

Somehow . . . some way . . . he'd miscalculated.

Ivar shook his head. Perhaps he'd added the wrong biotoxin to the viral load. Maybe he'd oversynthesized the superbug. Could be a problem with the delivery system too. Maybe infecting humans via water hadn't been the best idea. So many possibilities. Too many to run down. The facts, however, couldn't be disputed. His experiment had gone wrong. Now females bore the brunt, dying, while human males remained untouched.

"Fuck," he murmured as the ramifications hit him.

If allowed to incubate, his superbug would kill females the world over—and eliminate Dragonkind's only way of connecting to the Meridian. His chest went tight. Fear slithered in as he imagined the worst. Ivar shook his head. Only one conclusion to draw. He needed to kill his bug. Right now. Before it spread to larger populations and became unstoppable. The second it jumped from Granite Falls and Arlington to other communities, it would be too late.

Forget the eventual extinction of the human race.

It was much more serious than that.

Dragonkind needed human females. Without the fairer sex, none would be able to connect to the Meridian—to feed and draw the life-sustaining nourishment his kind required to stay strong and healthy. Starvation would follow. Suffering on a grand scale. A horrible withering of mind and body that would ensure Dragonkind perished alongside the human race.

Heart thumping, Ivar spun away from the bed and headed for the door. He needed to yank Hamersveld's chain and get back to his lab. Sooner than soon. The faster he synthesized the blood samples, the quicker he could create a targeted antivirus. The human doctors would need it. No way any of the idiots would figure out the correct sequencing on their own—one capable of killing his superbug in time.

The thought cranked him tight.

Panic turned the screw.

Footfalls echoing, Ivar ran into the corridor. The door to the stairs loomed at the end of the hall. He pivoted toward the exit and upped the pace. Dodging a cart full of medical supplies, he slipped past a nurse, avoided another walking hazmat suit and—

Soft green light bled into the hallway.

An unfamiliar buzz tweaked his temples, making him pause mid-stride. He frowned and, skirting a male pushing a gurney, slid to a stop in front of an open doorway. His sonar pinged. His gaze narrowed on the pair of humans standing beside a lone hospital bed. One male, short, balding, rotund form wrapped in a doctor's coat. He frowned. No threat there. His attention snapped to the other occupant in the room and . . .

His breath caught, stalling in the back of his throat.

Fucking hell. A high-energy female, bright-green aura glowing like a halo around her. Shock grabbed him by the balls. Incomprehension circled a moment before his brain slammed back into his skull. Unbelievable. After months of searching for another HE to help get his breeding program off the ground, here she stood. Right out in the open. No more than fifteen feet away.

He ran his gaze over her again.

Tall and leggy. Flawless skin the color of milk chocolate. Curly black hair brushing her shoulders. A lovely specimen. A rare find. One hundred percent healthy as well. Attention locked on her, Ivar took a step toward her. And then another. Letting his magic roll, he halted just outside the door, dragon senses writhing as he analyzed her bio-energy. He needed to be sure. Wanted to be right and . . . he sucked in a quick breath. Bang on. No doubt at all. She wasn't infected. The virus hadn't touched her despite the superbug running rampant inside the quarantine area.

Something in her blood made her immune.

Warrior antibodies, maybe. A talent for fighting off infection. An enzyme manufactured by her high energy, perhaps. One that killed any toxin it encountered. Whatever the reason, she was a gift—an excellent reference point for his lab, the perfect addition to his breeding program too. Two birds with one stone. A live specimen with the right antibodies flowing in her veins. Another female for his warriors to compete for when the Meridian realigned in a couple of months.

A win-win all the way around.

A sheen of sweat on his bald head, the doctor murmured something.

Snapping back to attention, Ivar stared at the pair and listened in.

Brown eyes wide with upset, the female shook her head. "It can't be true, Dr. Milford."

"I'm so sorry, Evelyn," Milford said, trying to soothe her. "We did everything we could, but she's gone. She's gone, sweetheart."

"No." A sob made her voice hitch. "Not Mema, Dr. Milford. She's all I have left, I can't . . . I don't understand." Tears pooled in her eyes. She breathed in, the inhalation choppy as she wrung her hands. "She was fine. I had supper with her before heading into the city, and she was fine!"

"I know." Taking a step toward her, Milford reached out. His gloved hands cupped hers. "I know, Evelyn, but she's gone. The virus put her into respiratory failure fifteen minutes ago. I tried, but I just . . . I couldn't revive—"

"Oh God," she rasped, looking so lost Ivar's heart clenched.

He huffed in annoyance. Hell. There he went again—sympathizing when he shouldn't. But then—Ivar frowned—maybe his reaction wasn't all that strange. He understood loss. Still lived with the pain of losing Lothair, a male he'd valued above all others.

"I want to see her, Dr. Milford." Blinking away tears, Evelyn leveled her chin. "Can I see her?"

"Not yet. An epidemiologist from the CDC is en route from Atlanta. As soon as she releases the body, I'll take you to see your grandmother."

"I need some air." Looking stricken, Evelyn cupped her mouth and looked toward the door. Her gaze swept over Ivar. The invisibility shield he held with his mind rippled, but stayed strong, preventing her from registering his presence. "I need to get out of—"

"You can't leave the quarantine area, Evelyn. You need to stay here until your blood tests come back. Until the doctors clear you."

Entirely unnecessary. Screw the rules along with human protocol.

Evelyn didn't need to wait for anyone. She'd be leaving now . . . with him. Would be providing a valuable service as an antivirus guinea pig inside his lab. Not that she knew it yet. But as he stepped out of the corridor and into the room, prepared to perform a fast snatch-and-grab, Ivar knew she would catch on quick.

HE females always did.

Chapter Fifteen

Speed supersonic, Venom rocketed out of storm clouds. Moonlight disappeared behind a load of thick-dark-and-nasty. Thunder rumbled in the distance. Street lights flashed, blurring into streaks below him. Frigid air rattled over his scales, then jetted from the jagged horns on his head. Nothing surprising there. His bone-bending flight broke through boundaries, pushing past safe to reach insane.

Not that he cared.

Fast equaled better right now, even if the velocity stretched his muscles in uncomfortable ways. Flipping into another death-defying spiral, Venom increased his wing speed. Pain clawed over his shoulders and down his sides. He shoved the discomfort away. He could handle the body torque along with the pain. What he couldn't do was fail. He needed to reach Arlington. Now. This instant. Before Evelyn ended up hurt.

Night vision dialed to precise, he banked into a tight turn. Ruby eyes aglow, he searched the landscape below. Dense forest gave way to small houses and squat apartment buildings. The road funneled into the downtown core. Venom growled as he caught sight of his chosen landing pad. Folding his wings, he dropped out of the sky. *X* marked the spot. Front and center, smack-dab in the middle of the Cascade Valley medical complex.

Two hundred yards below him. Now fifty.

He bared his fangs. Gravity responded with a vicious yank. His talons slammed down on the hospital rooftop. Steel groaned. Muscle-wrenching momentum threw him sideways, ruffling his scales. As the hiss and clank got going, friction scorched the pads of his paws. With a snarl, Venom dug in. Metal sheeting shrieked, protesting the sharp stab of claws.

He ignored the racket. Gaze riveted to the door one hundred and fifty feet away, he shifted into human form mid-skid. Leather settled against his skin. His feet slid across the rigid tiles of the helipad. The slip 'n slide didn't register. Magic exploded instead, heating the air around him. Snow melted and mist blew toward thunderclouds. Not that the icy blow back mattered. Neither did the damage he left in his wake. Only one thing held sway—his female. He needed to reach her before time ran out. The thought made his heart pound harder. Blood rushed in his veins. Adrenaline did the rest, propelling him toward the rooftop door. Leaping over a ventilation shaft, Venom sprinted across the open expanse.

So close.

Goddamn, he could feel her. She was so very *close*. Two floors down. A few corridors over. Somewhere inside the human facility overrun by an infectious disease.

Locked onto her, needing to be sure, Venom mined her bioenergy. The sizzle of her life force grazed the inside of his skull. He fine-tuned the connection. The beacon throbbed like a heartbeat, keeping time with the slam-bang of his own, pointing him in the right direction. Grinding to a halt beside the entrance, he yanked the door open and roared over the threshold. Three strides in, he paused on the shallow landing. His night vision adjusted. As the red glow washed out in front of him, he saw everything in stark contrast. Grainy cinder-block walls painted beige. Narrow staircase with steel treads leading down. Exit sign hemorrhaging white light above his head. A straight shot down into hospital corridors full of medical professionals.

Feet working double time, Venom raced down the stairs. *"I'm in."*

"Motherfuck, Ven," Mac growled through mind-speak. *"Wait for Forge and me to land before you—"*

"No time."

"Bloody hell, lad." Wind whistled through the cosmic connection, muffling Forge's voice. *"Give us a chance tae get there before you go off half-cocked."*

Half-cocked, his ass. Call it fully loaded instead.

Venom couldn't wait. He needed to see Evelyn now and ensure she was all right. Her bio-energy told him she wasn't hurt, but . . . goddamn it. Screw the consequences along with the Scot's instructions. He refused to leave anything to chance.

Or play a game of wait-and-see and hope for the best.

Boot soles banging on steel treads, Venom tightened his hold on the beacon Evelyn threw off like pheromones. Witchy connection. Fantastic barometer too. It relayed her emotional state, preparing him for what lay ahead and—

Her tension came through, lighting him up from the inside out. His stomach dipped. Ah, hell. Nowhere near good. She was upset about something: in tears, mind churning, disbelief rising as she struggled to accept bad news. Far-fetched? No chance in hell. Energy-fuse allowed him to take her mental temperature. Evelyn's was about to boil over. Which meant fast wasn't going to be fast enough. She needed him now. And he was still minutes away from reaching her.

The thought ratcheted his tension up another notch.

Reality settled him down. He couldn't change what had happened to her tonight. All he could do was try to make it right. Listen if she needed to talk. Hold her if she wanted him to, strengthen the bond, encourage her trust, soothe her the way a male did his mate.

Liking the plan, Venom rounded the first landing. Halfway down the next set of treads, a buzz expanded between his temples. Sensation turned into spikes. The warning twisted his mental screws. His dragon half reacted. Instinct narrowed into perception. Experience honed both, making unease rise and his heart throb.

No mistaking the nasty vibration. Or what it signified.

"Rogues. We've got a pack in the area and . . ." Venom trailed off, trying to get a better read. The signal hammered his temples. He narrowed the scope, pinpointing the source. Two competing beacons morphed inside his head. The first belonged to Evelyn. The other attached itself to a Razorback—to a powerful male planted somewhere inside the hospital. *"Goddamn it. Evelyn's in trouble."*

"Shite," Forge muttered, Scottish accent thicker than usual. *"Move yer arse, lad. Keep a sharp eye and retrieve her. Mac and I are in the pipe, thirty seconds behind you."*

"Bastian—light it up," Venom said, boots banging against steel. He needed the lay of the land. Right now. Nothing could be left to chance. Not with Evelyn in danger. Which meant Bastian's skill at picking apart rogues from a distance would come in handy. Again, for the thousandth time in . . . well, hell. Venom didn't know. Didn't care either. All he wanted was the rundown—how many rogues, age, level of talent, and exhale. The precise location of the bastard sitting inside the facility. *"Fill me in."*

"Fifteen rogues of varying talents. Eight fire dragons, two acid breathers, one who exhales Scald, *and . . . fuck,"* Bastian said, sounding pissed off. *"Mac, we've got another water dragon in the mix."*

"Hamersveld." Mac snarled. *"About time the bastard poked his head out. Tell me where he is, B."*

"No. Ven's female comes first." Deep voice rolling, Rikar pulled rank, shutting down Mac's personal vendetta against the male who'd sired him. No doubt a good idea. The new boy might be powerful, but the rogue water dragon was older, wiser, and far more experienced. No way his brother-in-arms should be tangling with the asshole on his own just yet. *"You and Forge circle back around. Come in from the north with Sloan. Let's see where the bastards are holed up."*

"Smoke 'em out." Sloan hummed in anticipation. *"Good plan. I'm three miles out."*

"And Wick?"

Wick growled. *"Inbound. West side."*

"Good," Bastian said, electricity sizzling in the background. A lightning shield, maybe? Good guess. Venom knew the sound well and almost smiled in reaction. *Almost*, but not quite. No matter how much he enjoyed his commander's ability to fry rogues on contact, the setup bothered him. Outnumbered with his mate to protect—not good odds. *"Stay on Ven's six. If shit goes south, back him up."*

"On it," Wick murmured.

"Keep it tight. Stay on script, boys." Frost crackled, rolling with Rikar's voice through mind-speak. *"We'll keep the assholes busy long enough for Venom to break free, then hit 'em hard."*

Mac grumbled something about missed opportunities.

Forge grunted in agreement.

Claws scraped against steel as Wick landed on the rooftop.

"Stay on the roof, Wick." Reaching the next landing, Venom vaulted off the last step. Evelyn's bio-energy whiplashed inside his head. He cranked the dial, tuning in to her mood. She was upset, but . . . he frowned . . . not frightened. Which meant the rogue hadn't discovered her yet. Relief opened his lungs, allowing him to take a deep breath. *"I'll bring her out."*

Wick snarled his assent.

Venom grabbed the handle. He yanked. The door flew open and slammed into the back wall. The bang echoed up the stairwell as he ran into a wide corridor. Sliding to a stop, he glanced both ways. Empty. No nurses. Not a doctor in sight. Nothing but bright lights, pale hospital floors and—

A row of biohazard suits hanging from hooks farther down the hall.

Jackpot. Infestation central. Just what he needed to find.

His gaze narrowed on a set of doors at the end of the hallway. He read the sign warning people to keep out. His muscles bunched in preparation. Venom pulled the rip cord and unleashed his speed, racing past an abandoned gurney. Footfalls raging in the quiet, he punched through the double doors. Hinges hissed as dual panels swung inward. Radar tuned to maximum, he jogged into the quarantine area.

A long hallway stretched out in front of him.

The stench of sickness slithered on warm air, assaulting his senses. Rolling his shoulders to release the tension, he listened to the low murmur of female voices. He sidestepped a bunch of nurses in the corridor and sifted through noise, hunting for the right vibration. Evelyn's bio-energy cut through the human hum and—

A low growl rose above the quiet chatter.

The fine hairs on Venom's neck stood on end. Holy shit. He recognized that sound. Sensed the danger even before he laid eyes on it. Cranking his hands into fists, he tracked the unearthly snarl. It came again. His focus snapped to the left. Venom bared his teeth. There . . . right there—half-hidden by a screen, dressed in a white lab coat, the rogue stood on the threshold, fixated on something inside one of the hospital rooms. The glow of Evelyn's bright-green aura ghosted around the makeshift barricade and into the hallway. Venom's protective instinct came alive, moving him from half to full throttle.

He snarled in reaction.

The Razorback glanced his way. Pink irises shimmering, Ivar's eyes widened in surprise, then narrowed in challenge. Shifting into a fighting stance, the bastard put his back to the room, blocking the doorway. "Venom . . . long time, no see. Come to protect the humans, have you?"

"Move away from the door."

"And if I don't?"

"You'll die faster," Venom said, erring on the side of caution instead of starting a fight. A difficult urge to deny when he longed to attack. Just let loose and rip Ivar to shreds. Killing the asshole would solve so many problems. Right so many wrongs. Avenge so many deaths. Lovely inspiration that, like it or not, amounted to a terrible plan. The bastard had ten feet on him. Stood much closer to Evelyn than he did and wouldn't hesitate. Even if he unleashed his magic, Ivar would reach his female first and snap her neck . . . just to slow his pursuit.

Aggression yanked his chain.

Venom smoothed his expression. He mustn't react. The second Ivar realized Evelyn's importance to him, she was dead.

Dancing the dance, Venom shifted toward his prey. "You responsible for all this?"

"Science is my forte." With a wink, Ivar countered each step Venom made, moving with him, refusing to give ground. "Playing with human lives too."

The comment threatened his control. Venom reeled it in, refusing to give the game away. "Leave now, Ivar—live longer."

"Willing to let me go? Strange, unless . . ." Intelligence gleaming in his eyes, Ivar grinned. "Ah, I get it. You're here for the female. Such a lovely HE . . . nice piece of ass."

Venom bared his teeth.

"Temper, temper, Nightfury." Staring at him beneath his brows, Ivar took a step back. Magic writhed around him, hiding him from human eyes. But not from Venom. He saw everything in startling detail. The bastard's intent too as Ivar planted himself between the doorjambs, trapping Evelyn inside the room, denying Venom a clear path. "One wrong move, and she gets hurt."

"I'm going to enjoy killing you," Venom said, shifting onto the balls of his feet.

Almost there. Seven feet, and he'd close the gap. Come within striking distance. Close enough to unbalance the bastard. Venom moved right, inched forward, setting up the takedown like a master chess player. His palms itched. His fingers twitched. God, how he wanted to wrap his hands around Ivar's throat. A quick yank. One brutal snap, and . . . bam! Game over. One dead rogue leader.

Peace on earth, goodwill to all Dragonkind males.

Tension rolled, tightening muscles over bone. Gauging the distance, Venom started the countdown. Five . . . four . . . three . . . two . . .

One!

He leapt toward his enemy.

Ivar cursed and spun, retreating into the hospital room. Venom swiped at him. His fingertips brushed the shoulder of the asshole's lab coat. Cotton ripped, coming away in his hand. A pop-pop-pop sounded. The spell keeping Ivar hidden from human eyes tore open.

"What the hell?" a human doctor muttered from inside the room.

"Holy crap!" Evelyn gasped, alarm in her voice.

With a snarl, Venom tossed the jacket and went after the bastard. Evelyn's profile flashed in his periphery. She looked away from Ivar toward him. Time slowed. Perception twisted. His chest heaved. Eyes aglow, Venom painted the room red with his gaze. Her eyes widened as she met his and . . . Goddamn it. He wasn't going to make it. Wasn't going to reach her in time. Ivar was too fast and—

Venom lunged at him.

The bastard threw out his hand.

Powerful magic poured out of Ivar's palm. The smell of brimstone rushed into the room. Poison slammed into Venom, then clawed at this throat, trying to steal his air. His venomous half rose to counteract the toxin. Fisting his hand, Venom unleashed his magic and sucked the noxious fumes from the room. Evelyn coughed as the oxygen level thinned. Without thought, he enclosed her in an air bubble, protecting her from suffocating in the toxic swill.

Ivar hit him with another dose.

He fired back, blasting the bastard with neurotoxins. Hauling ass toward the window, Ivar smiled. And Venom realized his mistake.

He sucked in a quick breath.

Fire dragon side out in full force, Ivar lit the match.

Noxious vapor fed by Venom's magic exploded into a flamethrower. Heat went cataclysmic. Curtains caught fire. Flames blew into the hallway. The bed flipped, rolling end over end. Glass shattered across the room as smoke billowed, limiting his ability to see. Ignoring the lick of open flames, Venom jumped through a wall of fire. Red scales flashing in the firestorm, Ivar escaped out the window, into the open air. Venom snarled, wanting to go after him. But he couldn't. Not now. He needed to find Evelyn and become her shield. Before the oxygen tank across the room blew sky-high. Before the fire reached her and she burned alive.

Hunting for her in the chaos, Venom turned away from the window. Thick smoke rolled, stinging his eyes, clogging his lungs, setting off the alarm. The sprinkler system went active. Water sprayed in all directions. Humans shouted in terror. Venom leapt the overturned hospital bed. His boots thumped down on the other side and slid on wet linoleum. Fire snarled overhead. Ceiling tiles melted like wax, dripping into a toxic mess above his head.

His senses contracted. Opening the valve to feed sensory perception, he clung to the cosmic tether and widened the scope, pushing the limits of his control. The signal—her *signal*—he needed to find it. To reconnect with her life force. Static hissed between his temples, then died. He tried again, clinging to the magical anchor in the firestorm.

Choking on the fumes, Venom shoved a cart out of his way. "Evelyn!"

No answer. No movement. Not a whisper in the smoky air.

Fear stripped him of reason.

Panic compressed his rib cage. He yelled her name again. And then again. Nothing but silence and the hiss of ravenous flames rose to greet him.

Thrown clear by the explosion, Evelyn struggled to get her bearings. Somewhere near the back of the room, maybe? To the left of the window? She shook her head. God, she didn't know. The shockwave had done a number on her. Picked her up. Tossed her to one side. Rattled her cage, bashing her head into the wall. Now she could only be sure of one thing—her ears were ringing. But oh, wait. That wasn't true. She knew something else too—that she couldn't see a damned thing. Not with the twisted vinyl seat back and hospital bed blocking her view.

Forcing her arms to work, Evelyn shoved at the chair pinning her to the floor. Pain spiraled up her forearm. She grimaced. The smell of smoke slithered in, teasing her senses. Awareness and panic hit her as the gray coil thickened, rolling on a wave of hot air. Alarm thrust shock out of the way. She pushed harder, trying to wiggle from beneath the wreckage. Bent in the blast, the heavy frame refused to budge. She tried again. Sharp metal grazed her palms. Blood welled on her skin. She didn't care. The shallow scrapes barely registered. Only one thing mattered. She needed to get out from under the damn chair. Right now, before . . .

She glanced to her right.

Undulating like a wave, fire crept across the ceiling. Eyes riveted to the flames, she watched them lick down the walls and reach through the broken window, curling over the twisted steel frame like long, witchy fingers. Smoke followed, billowing into the night, sucking air into the room, providing plenty of oxygen . . . fueling the firestorm.

With a cry, she thrashed, bucking beneath the debris.

The fire inched closer. Smoky froth rolled in like ocean surf. Helpless in the onslaught, Evelyn inhaled deep, filling her lungs to capacity. She needed oxygen. Enough to give her the strength—and time—to wriggle free. Otherwise, the smoke would suffocate her.

The wall of gray tendrils reached out to surround her.

Evelyn counted off the seconds. She prayed for a miracle. A change in direction. A shift toward good luck. Something. Anything. Another minute to figure a way out and—

The oncoming smoke shifted away from her.

Evelyn blinked. No, that wasn't quite right. The smoke had hit something. Inches from her nose, she watched the thick cloud slide over smooth contours—up and over without touching her. Her mouth fell open. Another round of ash puffed against the side wall. The strange barricade held, keeping the toxic swill at bay. Not understanding, she reached out. Blood smeared across the inside of the barricade as she brushed it with her fingertips. Transparent walls sucked at her skin, rippled like water, then went still as glass. She frowned and pulled her hand back. The curved sides reacted again, contracting into a multicolored wave. Red, green, and blue brushed shoulders, revealing the shape of the structure surrounding her.

Smooth walls. Shaped like a sphere. Thin as paper.

Another rolling puff kissed the strange barrier. An orange glow followed, approaching with frightening speed. High flames flicked the side of the bubble. The smooth wall warped. Panic set in. She lost the lungful of air she'd been holding and—

"Evelyn!"

The shout turned her head. Recognition struck. Evelyn sucked in a much-needed breath. Deep voice. Eastern European accent. Venom. No one else sounded like that and . . . Lord love her. Was she really hearing him? Or was her mind playing tricks, searching for help where none existed?

He shouted her name again.

Reality spun her toward belief. Oh, thank God—Venom. He was here. Really *here.* Not a figment of her overwrought imagination, but flesh-and-blood real. How? Why? Her analytical side wanted her to ask. Evelyn killed the questions. Her need to know—to solve the puzzle—could wait until later. Until after he pulled her free and helped her get away.

"Venom!" she yelled, struggling beneath the weight of the chair. Oh please, let him hear her over the roar of flames. "Over here—I'm here!"

Backlit by fire, a dark silhouette came through the smoke.

"Venom." Reaching out, she stretched her hand toward him.

Shoving an overturned table out of his way, he slid to a stop beside her. "Turn your face away."

Evelyn obeyed without question. The second she tucked her cheek against her shoulder, he grabbed the chair. He tossed the heavy piece of furniture aside with one hand. Twisted steel and broken wood went flying, flipped up and over, hurtling toward the other side of the room. A crash sounded next to the window. The bubble surrounding her evaporated. Smoke hit her in the face. She coughed, fighting to breathe. Venom's arms came around her. He lifted her off the floor. Relief collided with gratefulness, and Evelyn didn't hesitate. She curled her arms around his neck and held on hard.

"Go," she rasped as ash coated her skin.

"Hold on tight," he said, mouth against her ear.

She nodded.

With a quick move, he spun and leapt through the wall of flames. Heat rushed over her bare feet. Climbing Venom like a jungle gym, she tightened her grip and, bending her knees, wrapped her legs around his waist. His feet thumped down on the other side of the flames. Face pressed to his throat, she felt him shift against her. Hard muscle flexed. He changed direction, then dipped his head beneath something. Strong thighs brushing her bottom, he started to run.

The snarl of fire receded.

Heat downgraded from punishing to unpleasant.

The air cleared a little at a time.

Gasping, the smell of sulfur in the air, Evelyn raised her chin and looked over his shoulder. Fluorescent lights flickered overhead, hurting her eyes. She squinted, forcing her vision into focus. Men shouted instructions. Water fell like rain from sprinkler heads. Steel banged against walls and door frames. A group of firemen dressed in full garb sprinted past. Panicked nurses rushed to help doctors treat patients in the wide corridor. White coats smeared with soot. Faces pale with shock. Chaos squared.

The sight jump-started her brain.

"Wait—Venom, slow down."

Scanning the hallway, he shook his head.

Both hands fisted in the back of his leather jacket, she stared at his profile. "Dr. Milford was in there. We have to help—"

"He's fine. The humans already have him."

Evelyn blinked. "Humans?"

He glanced at her from the corner of his eye. "I'll explain later."

The brief moment of eye contact set her on edge. Something wasn't right. She frowned. Well, okay, besides the obvious. Someone had started a fire. Inside a hospital room. With her in it, damn it to hell and back. But with Venom's arms around her, his fast pace and her fear fading, a more immediate problem sprang into view. His gaze was shimmering. In the hotel room, she'd been sure he had brown eyes. But now? Releasing her death grip on his jacket, Evelyn grasped his chin. Day-old stubble pricked her fingertips. She applied gentle pressure to turn his head. He resisted a moment, then gave in, taking his focus off the hallway to look at her.

She lost her ability to breathe. Holy crap. Not dark brown at all, but a deep ruby red. Pretty color. Completely unnatural considering the soft glow of his irises. He held her gaze a moment. The shimmer intensified an instant before he returned his attention to the double doors at the end of the hall. She tried to rationalize her discovery. Seconds ticked past. Evelyn forced her mind to sift through the facts.

It could be a trick of the light. Could be she'd suffered a concussion and was now seeing things. Imagining the worst. Creating problems where none existed. Or it could be that her mind was working just fine and there was something odd about him.

The last thought resonated, gaining speed inside her head.

She rubbed her eyes, mashing her lashes together, then looked again. Yup. No question. Definitely dark red—a shimmering, unearthly *red*. Self-preservation sounded the alarm. The fine hairs on her nape rose in warning as unease prickled along her spine.

Unhooking her ankles from the small of his back, she inched away. "Ah, Venom?"

His grip on her tightened. "Don't let go, Evie."

"I think you should put me down."

"Not going to happen."

"But—"

"We're getting the hell out of here. I'm not letting you go again."

Again? Evelyn frowned. What the hell did that mean? Excellent question. One in need of a quick answer. The problem? Venom didn't appear to be in an indulging frame of mind. Expression set, boots splashing through puddles on the floor, he jogged toward the exit. More alarm bells went off inside her head. Evelyn reared and, pushing against his chest, tried to break free. Grasping the back of her thighs, he kept her snug against him. Calloused palms slid beneath the hem of her raised skirt. Shivers erupted, exploding over her skin, making her tingle, muting her objections as he cupped her bottom with both hands.

Planting her hands, she shoved at his shoulders.

"Relax, *mazleiha*." Skirting a wheelchair, he adjusted his grip. His fingers slid beneath the edge of her panties. She gasped in surprise. He lowered his head and rubbed his cheek against hers. His stubble rasped against her skin. Pinpricks of pleasure raced to places she wanted to ignore. Evelyn drew in a quick breath. Good lord. There was something wrong with her. Arousal was not a normal reaction. At least, not right now. She should be scared, freaked out about all the craziness, not remembering the way he'd tasted in the hotel room. "Almost there."

Turning his head, he nipped her earlobe.

Delight trickled down her spine. Evelyn clenched her teeth to stifle a sigh. "Stop it."

"I'm not doing anything."

"Yes, you are," she said with a growl. "You're trying to distract me."

His lips twitched. "Is it working?"

Too well. Better than it should be. Not that she would admit it. "Let me go—right now."

"No."

His denial lit the fuse on her temper. Evelyn tamped it back down, banking it in favor of going the reasonable route. Antagonizing him wasn't the best idea. Guys like Venom didn't respond well to threats. All the hours she'd spent sitting around boardroom tables with bigwigs told her that much. Venom possessed that kind of stubborn streak. She could tell just by looking at him. And honestly, he held all the cards—along with her ass—in the palm of his hand at the moment. Needing the lay of the land, searching for a way to reason with him, Evelyn glanced over her shoulder.

Ah, crap. She'd just run out of time.

Exit door at twelve o'clock and coming up fast.

"Venom, listen to me," she said. "I can't leave here."

"Sure you can."

God help her, he didn't understand. No way she could leave the quarantine area. Not without confirming the results of her blood tests first. It didn't matter that she felt fine. Asymptomatic didn't mean uninfected. It simply meant the virus hadn't struck yet. Dr. Milford had warned her about the possibility of delayed onset. She was young. She was healthy. She'd never been ill a day in her life, so . . . yeah. Being the last one to get sick made a certain amount of sense.

"Don't worry about it," Venom murmured, breaking into her line of thought.

"What?"

"You're not sick."

"You can't know that."

"I already do," he said, reaching the end of the corridor. Without breaking stride, he leaned in, used his shoulder, and slammed into the twin panels. The doors flew open, then closed with a violent hiss behind them. "If you were, I'd have detected the sickness in your blood. You're free and clear, Evie."

His assurance made her heart skip a beat. She blew out a shaky breath. *Free and clear.* Both sounded wonderful right now. Like great news after a terrible scare, but . . .

It didn't make any sense.

Venom couldn't know. Couldn't be sure of her health any more than she could be sure of his motives. Everything about the situation pointed to crazy. Venom's arrival inside the hospital. The unusual color of his eyes. Her reaction to him. Despite all the chaos, she didn't feel threatened by him. Worried by the situation? Yes. Frightened by all the chaos? Sure. Off balance and headed into foreign territory? Absolutely. Even so, something about him settled her nerves. Made her feel safe and put her on solid ground.

She could trust him.

He wouldn't hurt her.

Staring at his profile, Evelyn tested the theory, questioning its validity. Certainty rose up, then drilled down, giving credence to the idea. No rhyme. No reason. Not a shred of proof. And yet, in that moment, she picked up his vibe and read his intentions.

He had one objective—her protection.

"What's going on?" she asked, her face close to his, her voice nothing more than a strained whisper. "Why are you here?"

Venom didn't answer. Didn't look at her either.

He pivoted toward a closed door instead. With a swift kick, he hammered the handle. A bang rang out against his boot sole. Reinforced steel groaned, then obeyed, flying open, allowing him to step over the threshold and into the stairwell. Releasing her bottom, he swung her legs around. One arm caught behind her knees, the other settled against her back. Cradled in his arms now, she expected him to go down, toward the main floor and the parking lot. He went up instead. Muscles bunching, handling her as though she weighed nothing, he took the stairs two at a time. Cinder-block walls sped past. A metal railing spun them around a landing and onto another set of treads.

"Venom, please tell me what is happening." A death grip on his jacket, she jostled him.

Not that her attempt moved him. Tall, strong, built for endurance, he barely noticed the shove.

And didn't slow a bit.

Worrisome, but for one thing. She'd already determined he was on her side. The why of it, though, still bothered her. She liked neat. Enjoyed tidy. Everything stacked in perfect piles on her desk. Logic equaled sanity, and knowledge precipitated power. He must have a reason for helping her. His appearance in the hotel, and now here, couldn't be a coincidence . . . she pursed her lips . . . could it?

Chewing on the question, Evelyn frowned.

Venom vaulted over the top step. As his boots thumped down, a new idea took form. Suspicion rose in its wake. She inhaled in sharp surprise. "Are you a cop? Have you been following me? Is this about Markov?"

The Exit sign to the roof flashed in her periphery.

His gaze sharpened on her. "Is he the one who put the marks on your arm?"

Evelyn opened her mouth to answer.

Venom cut her off. "You'll tell me about him later."

His harsh tone pushed a shiver down her spine. Not a question. A statement of fact. One he backed up with his eyes. The intense look gave Evelyn pause. Again. For the hundredth time since she'd met him. It seemed to be a running theme with Venom—gentle one moment, full of warning the next.

She swallowed past the lump in her throat. "I don't understand."

"I know you don't," he said, understanding in his voice. "I didn't want it to be this way. I don't want to frighten you, but . . ." Pausing on the top landing, Venom dropped her feet to the floor. Rough concrete chilled the bottom of her bare soles. Her dress fell back into place, flirting with the tops of her kneecaps. He shrugged out of his jacket. Heavy leather settled around her shoulders, pushing Venom's heat into her skin as he raised his hands and cupped her face. "I'll answer all your questions, Evie,

I promise. For now, trust me a little further. We need to go. It isn't safe here."

He sounded so sincere. Beyond solid. More than trustworthy too.

It took her a split second to decide. Her life had seen better days. And crazier things than trusting Venom had happened. After the endless strife over the last year. After all the uncertainty. After being stuck in quarantine and caught in a firestorm. All she wanted was out—away from the chaos, far from the pain and the memory of Mema's passing. Sorrow tightened her throat. She swallowed hard and buried it deep down, refusing to cry.

He said it wasn't safe.

She believed him.

So no, now wasn't the right time. Giving voice to her grief would have to wait. For a little while longer.

"Okay." Fighting to control her fear, she held his gaze, then nodded. "Let's go."

Pride sparked in his eyes an instant before he dipped his head. His mouth brushed hers. A quick kiss. A fast taste. A gentle nip. Intimacy in under a second flat. Efficiency at its worst. Deprivation at its best, and then he was gone. Back to business, ushering her out through the open door and onto the rooftop. Chilly air made her shiver. Evelyn snuggled deeper into the folds of Venom's jacket as sharp stones bit underfoot. Thunder boomed overhead. Lightning struck, lighting up the night sky and—

Something moved in the storm flash.

Evelyn's focus snapped left. Her gaze collided with a—with a . . . incomprehension struck. Her mind went blank. Her eyes filled in the gaps. Black amber-tipped scales. Huge paws with razor-sharp claws. Golden eyes set in a horned head. A dragon . . . sitting less than one hundred feet away. Frozen in shock, Evelyn stared. The beast raised a scaly brow. Disbelief hovered. Terror shoved it out of the way. Adrenaline hit her like rocket fuel. With a yelp, Evelyn whipped around and fled toward the stairwell. Positioned like a linebacker behind her, Venom reached out. Using his arm like a bar, he curled it around her middle and lifted her feet off the ground.

"No!" Arms and legs churning, eyes riveted to the monster, she fought the lockdown. "Oh my God, are you crazy? Let go!"

"Easy, Evie. It's just Wick." The picture of calm, Venom carried her forward. She scrambled in full retreat, climbing him like a tree. Applying gentle pressure, he wrapped her up to keep her from wiggling free. "Sorry, love, but it's about to get a whole lot weirder for you. It's gonna be all right. Please remember I will never hurt you."

She heard the regret in his voice. Saw the remorse in his eyes, but didn't care as the air warped and Venom changed. As she watched in horror, he turned into a dragon. Dark-green scales replaced his golden skin. Hands and feet became huge paws with hooked claws. Massive wings with black webbing grew out of his shoulders. Ruby eyes aglow, he met her gaze as the spikes along his spine rattled in the rush of winter wind. His talons unfurled, then contracted around her. Ridged dragon skin brushed the nape of her neck. Evelyn screamed. Venom murmured her name, tone soothing, trying to reassure her.

But it was too late.

She'd trusted too quickly. Believed in him too fast. Put herself in his care without thinking through the consequences. Or demanding proof of what he intended. Now she would pay a steep price for her folly—no doubt with her life as Venom unfolded his wings and leapt skyward, away from the world she knew, into the bitter rush of danger she had yet to comprehend.

Chapter Sixteen

Clearing the top of a hospital smoke stack, Venom ascended into the sky. His night vision sparked. Prickles exploded over his horns. He angled his head and adjusted the pitch of his sonar, hunting for Razorbacks in storm clouds. Thunder rumbled above him. Humidity gathered on chilly air, preparing for Mother Nature's hissy fit as he searched the horizon. Nothing yet. No flash of scales. No snarls of warning. Not even the flap of approaching wings in the dark. Just the soft buzz of awareness that told him he wasn't home free yet.

A large pack was still in the area, playing hide-and-seek in the forest—between thick limbs of the dense foliage surrounding the town of Arlington. It wouldn't be long before he caught sight of the enemy, though. Any second now, Bastian would pull the trigger. Smoke the assholes out of their hidey-holes. Go to town and unleash hell, killing multiple males in the process.

The thought should've made him happy. Hunting rogues always did.

But not tonight.

The higher Venom climbed, the worse he felt.

With a sharp shift, he banked hard and glanced down at his left paw. Tucked into a ball in the center of his palm, Evelyn shivered in the wind rush. The narrow gap between his black claws framed her face, making her look small, putting her on display and . . . shit. No wonder she was scared. His conscience panged, kicking remorse into high gear. God. He hadn't wanted it to go this way. Too bad circumstance didn't care what he wanted. It threw up obstacles. Made him change tack. Frightened his female half to death. Now he didn't know what to do, or how to help her get past her fear.

Another tremor rolled through her.

Desperate to keep her warm, he cupped one talon over the other, creating a pocket for her between his palms, and conjured a heat shield. The warm bubble settled around her. She blew out a choppy breath. He shook his head. Goddamn it. So much for doing it right and letting her acclimatize. Wooing her human-style was no longer an option. Neither was ignoring the fallout. No way around it now. He was in deep and sinking fast, stuck in iffy territory with a female who'd sooner leave him than look at him. So only one thing left to do . . .

Make it right for her. Fix it. Mend it. Glue it back together . . . whatever. The method didn't matter as long as Evelyn ceased to be afraid of him.

"Evelyn," he murmured, hoping to calm her.

His voice reached her. Turning her face away, she compressed into a tighter ball.

"Come on, *mazleiha*." Wind rattled over his scales as the street swung into a ninety-degree turn below him. Lamplight spilled onto the main drag. Taking his gaze off the human town, Venom tucked his head under to look at her. Eyes squeezed shut. Knees pressed to her chest and, yup, still looking petrified. Vice-like pressure squeezed his rib cage. What to do . . . what to do? He wanted to soothe her. To reach out and somehow wipe away the last few minutes. To help the shock of seeing him in dragon form fade. He knew it was possible. His brothers-in-arms provided more than enough proof. Hell, the mated Nightfuries took their females on midnight flights all the time and, well . . . he'd yet to hear any of them complain. "It's all right. You're safe with me."

"You're not allowed to talk to me anymore."

Her tart tone startled him. So prim and proper. Far too ladylike. He swallowed a snort of amusement. "I'm not?"

"No."

"Well then, what do you want me to do?"

"I want you to turn this dragon around and take me back."

This dragon. Venom frowned. Seriously? "Evie . . . I am *this* dragon."

"Do I look like I care?" she asked, sounding on the verge of hysteria.

"Actually, yeah." Reevaluating his flight path, Venom turned south. City lights flashed below him. He gave her another once-over. "You kind of do."

"Shut up! Just . . . Oh God, I'm freaking out." A hitch in her breath, she covered her face with both hands. "I'm talking to a dragon. A *dragon*! I'm losing it. I've totally lost it."

Flying off his left wing tip, Wick snickered.

Venom threw him a dirty look.

"*What?*" His friend shrugged, voice coming through mind-speak. "*You laughed at me when I found Jamison.*"

"*Did not.*"

"*Did so.*"

Venom huffed in disgust. "*So what—you're returning the favor?*"

"*Payback's a bitch,*" Wick said, baring his fangs in a grin.

"*You're a pain in the ass.*"

Wick smirked.

The sudden urge to beat the hell out of his best friend nearly overwhelmed him. He wavered a moment, debating the pros and cons. Pro—he'd get to put a dent in Wick's face. Con—Evelyn would freak out even more. Venom growled. No way would he risk it. He refused to put her in the crossfire. Which meant tuning Wick up—having some fun—would have to wait.

With a sigh, he reached out with his mind and pinged his commander. *"B—we're clear. Pull the trigger, but watch your six. Ivar's in the mix."*

"Confirmed?" Rikar asked.

"Yeah." Venom nodded, even though his XO couldn't see him. *"Went head-to-head with him inside."*

Bastian cursed. *"You okay?"*

"All good."

Scales clicked as Mac moved. *"Smoke's pouring out of the building."*

Venom grimaced. All right, so maybe *all good* wasn't quite accurate.

A picture of the damage morphed in his mind's eye. Venom clenched his teeth as he relived the heat, tasted the burn . . . saw Evelyn pinned under a goddamn chair. Rage opened the valve on worry. Frigging Ivar. The bastard would pay for putting her in the line of fire. *"Ivar blew the shit out of a hospital room to evade me."*

"Fire's out now," Wick murmured, his fire dragon half on-point, monitoring the situation inside Cascade Valley Hospital. *"The humans have it under control."*

"Good." The crackle of electricity sizzled through mind-speak. Bastian turned the dial, cranking the wattage, making Venom's scales twitch from three miles away. *"Mac—you're the bait. Forge—get ready. And Sloan—"*

"All set," Sloan said, entering the conversation. *"South side."*

"Venom . . . Wick." Setting up the play, Rikar finished delivering instructions. *"Stay clear of the east side. Get the female to safety. We'll do the—"*

A fireball exploded across the night sky.

Flames roared, streaking into an inferno-fueled tail over the forest east of town. Fire licked the treetops. Damp air crackled. A boom echoed. Ancient trees twisted in the blow back, then became tinder, flickering orange in the distance.

"Bloody hell." Wood groaned as Forge took flight.

Mac growled. *"Seven rogues inbound."*

"Make that twelve," Bastian said.

"Lovely," Sloan said, sarcasm out in full force. *"On my way."*

"Christ," Rikar muttered, joining the fray. Snarls rose. Cursing ensued, beating against Venom's temples. Flipping into a sidewinding spiral, he glanced over his shoulder. Another stream of fire lit up the sky as Nightfury went claw-to-claw with Razorback. *"Ven, watch your six. We're three rogues short over here."*

"Shit."

Flipping up and over, Wick switched sides, setting up shop on Venom's right. *"You feel that?"*

Did he ever. The buzz clawed at his temples. His hackles rose. Evelyn flinched, squirming in his palm as his vibe went from calm to vicious. As she gasped his name, he murmured hers, but didn't pause to reassure her. No time. Unwise too. He needed to concentrate—stay sharp, act fast, and be deadly. Otherwise, Evelyn wouldn't make it out alive. And he'd never forgive himself.

Increasing his wing speed, Venom rocketed out of town. Not long now. Just around the corner. The bastards were setting up an ambush, looking for the best spot to inflict maximum damage. Big mistake. Time equaled distance. And space? He had more than enough now to make the bastards pay. The landscape rolled, moving from urban to rural. High cliffs rose on his right, funneling him into uneven terrain.

The buzz intensified inside his head.

Venom fine-tuned the signal. Three rogues lying in wait. Two hundred yards out and closing fast. He bared his fangs and flexed his talons. *"Wick?"*

"Locked on."

With a snarl, Venom spun into a sidewinding spiral. The quick change in trajectory put him on course. The rogues uncloaked. Wings spread wide, the trio left their hiding spots. Orange, yellow, and blue scales flashed in the gloom. Three targets, three different colors.

"Divide and conquer."

Wick hummed. *"I'll take the two on the right."*

"Perfect."

And it was. Particularly since one rogue offered little challenge. Three against one usually made for better odds. At least, for them. Given a choice, Venom liked to take on four rogues at once. More of a workout that way. Tonight, though, it wasn't about him. It was about his female. About keeping her safe. About treating her to his protective side—and showing her the difference between good and bad. And that he always landed on the right side of the equation.

Which put him in her corner. Every. Single. Time.

Speed supersonic, Venom rocketed into the valley of a deep gorge. Wick engaged with a snarl, cutting off boneheads number one and two behind him. Rogues shrieked in his wake. Venom snarled over his shoulder, baiting asshole number three. The enemy dragon hesitated, hanging in mid-air, trying to decide. Yellow scales blurred into a streak behind him. *Come on. Come on.* He needed the last of the trio to leave his friends and follow.

Divide and conquer. Separate and kill. Always the best strategy and—

The rogue banked in his direction.

Fantastic. He had liftoff. One asshole giving chase. Idiots two and three busy with Wick—fighting to stay alive as his friend went to work, taking them apart scale by scale.

One eye on the male chasing him, the other on mountainous terrain, Venom slowed, allowing the rogue to close the distance. White jets streamed from his horn tips. Evelyn gagged as velocity yanked on her stomach. He wanted to apologize—for so many things. Causing her discomfort. Scaring her into emotional meltdown. Making her shiver in his grasp. But well . . . hell, no chance that would happen. Not right now. Distraction wasn't a good idea. He needed to stay alert and on-task. Otherwise he'd make a mistake, and Evelyn would end up hurt.

The thought focused him.

Eyes narrowed, vicious nature rising, Venom drew her closer. She trembled, but tucked in, pressing her hands to the wall of his chest. *Atta girl*, he wanted to say. He rocketed around a blind corner instead. Banking hard, he dropped over a steep embankment. Jagged cliffs rose on his right. He dove toward the ground. The rogue followed him over the edge. Venom slowed more and waited. Timing was everything. He must drift in the moment. Allow the enemy dragon the illusion of victory while he rode the razor's edge and held the angle. Yellow scales flashed as the idiot closed rank behind him. Venom counted off the seconds. One Mississippi. Two Mississippi. Three Mississippi . . .

The male took a swipe at him.

Sharp claws brushed the tip of his tail and—

Four!

He torqued into a brutal backflip. The move spun him up and pushed him over. Horned head an inch from the enemy's spine, he lashed out. His claws caught scales, biting into the dragon's tail. Warm blood splashed up his forearm. The male squawked in surprise. Without mercy, Venom dug in and whirled full circle. Using his wings, he rotated into a brain-melting spin in mid-air. Wind howled, rushing into the cliff face. Shale took a violent tumble. The mountain rumbled as large sheets of stone slammed into the ground. Idiot number three's head whiplashed. Evelyn cried out, the sound so terror-filled it knocked against his heart, making it slam into his breastbone.

Venom spun around again, refusing to relent. He had one chance at a clear shot. A single opportunity to keep her safe. And like it or not, here, right now—this moment—was it.

Baring his fangs, he spun the enemy again. And again, gaining speed, increasing the mind-twist with each rotation. The male roared in pain, flailing to break free. Whipping around one last time, Venom unfurled his talon. His claws pulled out of flesh, dragged against scales, and . . .

He let go, throwing the male like a shot put.

Still spinning, the rogue sped toward the stone wall. Venom saw the whites of his eyes a second before the bastard slammed into the jagged wall. Shaped like a spear, sharp stone cut through the rogue's back and came out the front. Impaled on rock, hanging from the cliff face, blood gurgled up the male's throat, then slid down the yellow scales covering his chest.

Focus locked on the rogue, Venom spread his wings and, slowing, floated in mid-air. The male gasped once, then stopped breathing. An instant later, his enemy disintegrated in an explosion of dragon ash.

Gray flakes swirled on an updraft of winter wind, sending each one in a different direction. Muscle bunching, Venom gained altitude and flew out of the canyon. His sonar pinged. A familiar signal rose inside his head. His mouth curved. Wick.

Right on time. His friend's unique energy signal throbbed against his temples, reassuring him as he—

"Venom."

"All in one piece. You?"

"A few scratches. Two dead rogues." Still a mile away, Wick grunted. *"Your female?"*

Venom glanced down and grimaced. God, she was pale. So scared she was a breath away from hyperventilating. *"In a tailspin."*

"Get her home."

Good idea. Except for one thing.

He couldn't fly toward Black Diamond and stay out of the fray. Not with his brothers engaged in claw-to-claw combat east of Arlington. Radar up and running, he tracked the battle, hooking in to each Nightfury's life force. Thank God. No one seriously hurt, but his sonar didn't lie. His pack was still outnumbered three to one. Not bad odds, but with Ivar and Hamersveld in the mix—along with the nasty little wren—the tide could turn quickly.

"Wick—turn around. Go help B and the others."

"You sure?"

"No sweat," he said, knowing he was out of danger. No Razorbacks in the vicinity. No reason to worry. *"I'll fly west, then follow the coastline into Seattle."*

"You'll stay at the safe house?"

"Yeah." It was the better bet. An easier fly too considering the battle in progress between him and home.

Located in a swanky Seattle neighborhood, the safe house served a serious purpose. Daimler had bought the waterfront property a month ago, spending millions—at Rikar's behest. A necessary expediture. The house provided a haven of last resort, a place for Angela, Rikar's mate, to crash when she lost track of time while in investigation mode and couldn't make it home before nightfall. It had happened more than once. And when it did? Rikar lost his mind, freaking out so fast anyone with half a brain would conclude the world had just ended. Not that he blamed his XO. An HE female out after dark—especially one mated to a Nightfury—spelled big trouble. The kind that arrived with Razorbacks in tow.

And yet, Venom didn't blame her for the lapses.

Hell, he admired Angela for it.

An ex-SPD detective, she loved her work and was good at it. So skilled at unearthing facts, she now served as the Nightfury chief investigator, helping Sloan monitor the cyber highways, often digging up information that led to great intel and big leads. The biggest of all, though—her white whale . . . the location of Ivar's new lair—still eluded her. But Venom had faith. Angela would find it eventually—along with the HE females imprisoned in the bastard's subterranean complex.

"Twenty minutes max, Wick, and I'll land in our new backyard."

His friend hesitated, staying on course, rocketing toward him. *"Ven—"*

"Go." Wheeling over the thick forest, Venom recalibrated his internal compass and set a course for Seattle. With a murmur, he conjured a cloaking spell and settled into a smooth glide, flying toward the coast and more populated places. *"No rogues around. I'll be fine."*

"Later, then," Wick said, raw anticipation in his tone.

"Be safe."

"Aren't I always?"

Venom snorted. Right. Sure. The word *safe* didn't belong anywhere near his friend. Vicious? Unpredictable? Lethal in a fight with his lava-infused exhale and bad attitude? Without a doubt.

Throw all three into the pot, give it a good stir, and slap Wick's name on it, 'cause . . . yeah. The trifecta of nastiness fit the male to perfection. But as he sensed his friend shift direction mid-flight, Venom almost changed his mind and called him back.

Almost, but not quite.

He wasn't a coward. He was a warrior. A powerful one gifted with keen intelligence and the brute strength to back it up. Hell, he'd just KO'd a rogue against a cliff face, for God's sake. No reason to run scared—or dread Evelyn's reaction when he set her back on solid ground. Still . . .

Worry tweaked his tail.

Venom glanced down at his female.

Breathing easier now, Evelyn lay prone in his paw. He met her gaze. Brown eyes narrowed on him. The prickle of unease intensified, crawling under his skin. Venom bit down on a curse. Ah, hell. Not good. She was alert, fear fading fast, intellect surfacing hard. Nowhere near her happy place either. She took another deep breath, calming under the influence of his smooth glide. She pursed her lips. Venom smoothed his expression, determined to give nothing away in the face of her rising fury.

But God, it was hard.

She hardly knew him. And yet, her no-nonsense stick-it-up-your-craw look cut through all the crap, making him want to squirm. He shut down the urge, but knew her silence wouldn't last long. Her vibe said it all. The second he landed at the safe house and shifted back into human form, Evelyn would throw down. Ass-plant him like a head of lettuce or something.

He knew just by looking at her. Guaranteed. No doubt in his mind. Which left him with nowhere to run, a giant bull's-eye on his back, and an angry female he wanted to placate more than he needed his next breath.

* * *

Shifting fast in flight, Bastian rocketed toward the enemy. Engaged in aerial combat, dragons roared around him. The deafening howls blasted over treetops, giving voice to pain. Adding to the ambiance, he hammered a rogue on the flyby. His claws shrieked against scales. The Razorback snarled at him. Bastian grinned back and, vaulting into a flip, hit him again, pushing the male toward the high bluffs. Dragon blood arced in the moonglow. The metallic scent met frigid air, joining the smell of fire and brimstone.

Bastian dug in, sinking his claws deep.

The rogue spun full circle, desperate to break his hold.

Good strategy. Fat lot of good it would do the pale-scaled male. Freedom wasn't an option for the Razorback. Not anymore. The rogue was already trouble. In his sights. Tethered by his talons. Wings now immobilized by his claws. Cut off from help and the greater pack . . . about to lose his life.

One thing stayed Bastian's hand—the need for information.

On board with his plan, Mac and Forge played keep-away, protecting his right flank. Sloan and Rikar fought on the left, holding the line. Bastian bared his fangs. Lovely. Excellent. Perfect in every way. All the time and space he needed to work without interruption. To crack Razorback heads and interrogate each while in mid-air.

Great in theory. Too bad he had next to nothing to show for it.

Three rogues down. Not an iota of information.

And the Razorback in his grasp? No luck yet. He might as well start pulling teeth. Prying scales loose too, 'cause lord knew, the fourth victim wasn't the charm. No matter how much pain he inflicted, the male refused to talk—or tell him where Ivar had gone. Bastian growled in frustration. Bad timing. Even worse luck. The rogue leader had gotten away—again. For the . . . well, shit. He didn't know many times. A hundred? A thousand? He gritted his teeth. It felt like millions right now.

Night after night. Week after week. Year after fucking year.

Ivar always managed to slip through his net.

Applying ruthless pressure, he twisted his enemy's wings. "Where is he?"

A gasp. A cry of pain. Nothing more. The rogue still refused to answer.

Bastian folded the male's wings back another foot. "Tell me."

"Fuck you."

"Fine. Have it your way."

With a snarl, Bastian adjusted his hold and spun in mid-air. Talons around the back of the male's skull, he twisted. The rogue thrashed, fighting the lockdown. A brutal wrench of his claws. A single snap, and he broke his neck. The vicious crack echoed. The rogue went limp in his grasp a second before he exploded into dragon ash.

Gray flakes swirled, blowing in his face.

Ignoring the blow back, Bastian banked hard, searching for his next target. A white streak rocketed into view. Dialed in, he pinged his best friend. *"Rikar, what you got?"*

"Dick-all. No one's talking. The assholes are loyal, I'll give 'em that." Nothing but blur, Rikar blasted past him. Arctic air swirled, dragging snow in his wake. *"Any luck on your end?"*

"None. Ivar's gone. Hamersveld with him."

Rotating into a spiral, Rikar settled on his right side. *"Fucking hell. We can't catch a break."*

No kidding. Bastian cursed under his breath. Same story, different night. *"The bastard must have a lucky rabbit's foot up his ass."*

His best friend snorted in amusement.

Gaze locked on Mac and Forge, Bastian shook his head. His mouth curved. Wow. The wonder twins were tearing it up, taking on five rogues at once. And Sloan? Bastian glanced to his left. Nothing but a pinprick against the sky, his warrior flew away from the battle. Frowning, he tracked his friend. His sonar pinged and . . . huh. Strange. Not at all Sloan's style. The male never left a battle unless forced to break rank.

Which meant something was off.

Beyond wrong and headed into dangerous territory.

Bastian scanned the horizon again, looking for the telltale flash of Sloan's snow-white paws. A glint drew his eye. The flash of white, dead ahead. Wings spread wide, Bastian put on the brakes. Stretched to capacity, his muscles squawked, protesting the pull.

Rikar blew by him.

With a quick shift, Bastian changed direction. *"I'm going after Sloan."*

"I've got the wonder twins." Velocity supersonic, Rikar circled around, looking for an opening between Mac and Forge. Pale gaze narrowed on the Razorback off Mac's left wing. *"Mac—shove over. I'm coming in hot."*

"Isnae that supposed tae be 'coming in cold,' Frosty?" Forge asked, smart-ass attitude reigning supreme. With a grunt, he broadsided a Razorback. Scales rattled. A scream rippled across the night sky, streaming over treetops. *"Would hate tae confuse you with—"*

"Asshole Scot," Rikar said, getting in on the trash talking. *"Shut up and get out of my way."*

Forge huffed, the sound full of enjoyment.

Mac laughed as he fed a rogue a face full of water spear.

Leaving the trio behind, Bastian fine-tuned his radar. Unease pricked across scales. He followed Sloan anyway, swinging behind a sheer rock face. Eyes on the rough terrain, he traced jagged hollows and rocky outcroppings. His night vision sparked, allowing him to see everything. Each dip. Every spike. All the nuances. Ancient and deep, thick forest stretched to his left. Huge pines stood beside old oaks, competing for shoulder room along snaking blacktop. Under construction, the highway cut through the wilderness, playing peekaboo between heavy tree limbs and pine cones. Heavy machinery sat alongside patches of ripped-up road, faded pylons glinting orange in the moonlight.

Bastian clenched his teeth.

Wonderful. Just terrific. The perfect place to set up an attack—high cliffs on both sides, narrow valley between, little room to maneuver. His brows collided. Freaking Sloan. What the hell was he thinking? No way should the male be sailing into ambush central without someone at his back. Increasing his wing speed, Bastian sent out the call, requesting backup.

"Still busy." A grunt echoed through mind-speak. The shriek of claws on scales followed. Rikar hummed a second before bone snapped with a crack. *"We'll finish up and—"*

"Inbound," Wick said, more snarl than an actual word.

Bastian's mouth curved. Well, well, well . . . wouldn't you know it? Right on time. God love the male. Wick possessed the most impeccable timing. *"Venom?"*

"Free and clear."

White jets streaming off his wing tips, Wick shot over the top of the bluff. With an acrobatic flip, he dove over the cliff edge, the move pure kamikaze. Bastian ducked to avoid a collision. The crazy SOB changed course, missing him by inches, rattling the spikes along his spine, pissing him off in the process.

Bastian scowled at him.

"Nice to see you too." Wick grinned, all wolf, no apology. *"Where's Sloan?"*

"Right here."

Dark-brown scales tinted green and gold glinted up ahead. The flash of Sloan's pure white paws followed in the gloom. Bastian's gaze narrowed. Bingo. Target acquired. One earth dragon, dead ahead.

"What the fuck, Sloan?" Coming within range, he threw his warrior a sidelong look. Sloan didn't return the favor. Expression intent, dark eyes moving over ragged terrain, the male cursed under his breath. And Bastian went on high alert. Less volatile than most, Sloan never overreacted. He thought things through, using his off-the-charts IQ and wicked IT skills to puzzle things out. Which meant whatever had the male so focused required his undivided attention. *"Lay it out."*

"Three rogues playing hide-and-seek," Sloan said, giving him the lay of the land. *"Weirdest thing, though."*

"What?" Bastian asked.

"Seems to me they don't want to fight." Sloan glanced over his shoulder and met his gaze. *"Hell, tangling with them was more dance than combat. All theatrics, no bite."* Worry in his eyes, he shook his head. *"I can't even sense them anymore. It's as though they—"*

"Up and disappeared?" Firing up his gift, Bastian unleashed his magic.

The powerful wave rose, then unfurled, rushing over the landscape. His heightened sense of perception twitched. Sonar dialed to maximum, he hunted for the unique signature every male left in his wake. A glimmer came through, giving him a vague sense of the trio, but . . . hmm, odd. More than strange. The signal was muffled by something, preventing him from getting an accurate read. Normally, he could track males for miles. No such luck tonight. With the beacon muted, his senses blurred, running together, folding over, smothering his ability to connect.

Winter wind picked up.

Dead leaves rustled as tall trees swayed.

A hum teased his temples, urging him farther north.

Changing tack, he zigzagged in the cold air and tried again. A throb came through. Same result, except . . . his eyes narrowed. Wait a second. His internal antennae twitched, grabbing hold of a faint signal—

Bastian sucked in a breath. Holy God. He recognized the sizzle of sensation now. It had been years. Ages. Far too long. Something he'd only felt once before—when his sire had been alive.

Locked on to the vibration, Bastian flew toward the highway. *"Follow me."*

His warriors fell in beside him, taking up wingman positions as he tracked the buzz. North-northwest. Up over smooth bluffs. Around the tops of huge pine trees. Half a mile of asphalt and gravel to reach the construction site. Parked to one side, excavators sat beside graders and pavement rollers. Dropping in from above, Bastian rolled in on a slow glide, then wheeled in behind a row of dump trucks.

Black tires shone in the moonlight. North wind tumbled, blowing dust across the narrow roadway as the sizzle intensified, gouging his temples and . . . ah, yes. *X* marked the spot—a dead zone just ahead. An artificial one created by a Dragonkind male, more cone of silence than Bermuda Triangle. But just as effective. Fifty yards wide and just as deep, the enclosed area muffled signals and killed electronics, creating a force field around the user. One most males would never detect.

Nifty trick. Clever ploy. A very effective maneuver.

Without slowing, Bastian flew through the clear barrier. The side wall rippled, flowing over him like water, coating his wings. Energy shards nicked his scales. The uncomfortable prickle raced the length of his spine. Wick cursed behind him. Bastian refused to slow. He wheeled right instead, circled into a holding pattern, and scanned the terrain inside the energy shield. A whole lot of nothing special. Tall cedars standing at the edge of the dead zone. Huge boulders heaped in a haphazard pile next to an abandoned backhoe. A single pickup truck parked on the shoulder of the gravel road.

Movement flashed in his periphery.

The F-150's headlights flipped on.

Twin beams lit up the surface of the highway. The pickup swayed, rusty side panels creaking as a male uncloaked near the front bumper. Pure black scales glinted in the light, framing the blood-red spikes along the warrior's spine. So familiar. Beyond strange to see a male made in the image of his sire. But the true giveaway to his identity? The scarlet spider inked on the side of the warrior's throat.

"Holy shit," Sloan murmured.

Wick hummed, the sound full of welcome.

Bastian's mouth curved. "Azrad."

"Brother." Head tipped back, blue eyes narrowed, Azrad watched him glide overhead. "You gonna land or what?"

Folding in his wings, Bastian dropped out of the sky. The magical barrier warped. His paws thumped down a few feet away. Gravel rolled, pinging against the side of the pickup truck. Wick and Sloan landed behind him. Huge talons scraping over hard ground, Azrad sat up straighter. The slight flinch spoke volumes. Bastian got the message. His brother was uncertain of his acceptance. To be expected. Until two weeks ago, he hadn't known his father had sired another son.

Or that Azrad existed.

And yet, Bastian welcomed the news. No rhyme. No reason. Just faith wrapped up in the need for family. He huffed. God, he could hardly believe it. A baby brother who shared his bloodline. Same father. Different mother. A chance at forging a bond the same way other brothers did. Too bad familial DNA didn't mean immediate closeness. Trust and strong relationships took time to build. Lots of hard work and commitment too, so . . . yeah. He understood Azrad's hesitation. He felt it too—the need to insulate himself just in case things took a turn for the worst. Still, despite his reservations, he refused to turn away.

Too much hung in the balance.

His brother's future. Bastian's need to support him. A chance at true connection with the only male who shared his blood. All of it lay on the line.

Holding Azrad's gaze, he shifted into human form. A bold move, one that left him vulnerable. Probably not the smartest thing to do. His scales acted like armor, providing protection from attack. Human skin left him open to injury. Bastian didn't care. He needed to start somewhere. Here . . . tonight . . . seemed as good a place as any to begin building bridges that would stand the test of time. Stomping his feet into his boots, Bastian rolled his shoulders, adjusting the fit of his leather trench coat.

His gaze traveled over Azrad again. He tipped his chin. "You look a lot like Father in dragon form."

Surprise sparked in his brother's eyes. Azrad looked down at his scale-covered chest. "Really?"

"Same coloring . . . minus the spider."

Interest sharpened in Azrad's eyes. "Will you tell me of him sometime?"

Bastian nodded. "If you like."

His brother rewarded the response and returned the trust, transforming to human form. Crew-cut short on the sides, a dark Mohawk rose in the center of Azrad's head. Dark-blue eyes met his a second before the hardware arrived. Two black metal studs appeared on the male's face—one in his eyebrow, the other piercing a nostril. Bastian blinked. Well, all right then. He'd almost forgotten about all the steel. Kind of strange, but—

He swallowed his amusement. Crazy. Completely bent. Who would've thought he'd end up with a Gothed-up male for a sibling?

Shrugging into a beat-up army jacket, Azrad glanced toward Sloan, then back at Bastian. "Sorry for the theatrics. I had to make it look good for the rogues, and short of killing your warrior—"

Wick snorted in derision, interrupting the explanation.

"No chance of that," Sloan said, a hard gleam in his eyes.

"Surrounded by the enemy, warrior. I had you outnumbered," Azrad murmured, staring at Sloan as he snapped his fingers.

The cone of silence warped.

Two warriors stepped through the disturbance, becoming visible in twin tracks thrown by cracked headlights. Black hair cropped short, a leather patch over one eye, the larger warrior walked forward. Leaner of frame, but just as tall, the blond crisscrossed, moving behind his comrade. Feet crunching over crushed gravel, both warriors stopped behind Azrad. Eye Patch set up on his right. Pretty-boy blond took the left. Bastian's lips twitched. Would you look at that? Pyramid position, a formation designed for one purpose—guarding a leader's back. Heavy muscle ruffled as Wick and Sloan did the same, moving in tight to protect him.

Gaze narrowed on the newcomers, Sloan shrugged. "Three to one in a fight. Pretty good odds—in my favor."

"Arrogance is a precursor to death." Flexing his hands, Eye Patch smiled in challenge.

Unimpressed, Wick rolled his eyes. "Fuck off."

With a laugh, the big male dropped the tough-guy act. "I am Terranon. First in command to Azrad."

"Kilmar," the blond said, settling into a more relaxed stance.

Unfurling his fists, Sloan introduced himself.

The trio nodded, then looked past him, to a spot over his right shoulder. A tense moment passed. Wick remained silent. Bastian stifled a laugh. Stubborn to the point of fatalistic. Quiet per usual. Trust Wick to be the lone holdout.

"Meet Wick." Bastian hitched his thumb, indicating a spot over his shoulder. "So, now that we all know each other . . ." Pausing, he closed the distance. He stopped in front of his brother and raised his hand. Azrad flinched, but stayed true, allowing him to cup the side of his neck. "You all right? Surviving the Razorback camp okay?"

Azrad exhaled, relaxing in his grip. "I'm good. Tough going, though."

"Much infighting?"

"Some," Azrad said, shrugging his hand away. Pivoting toward the truck, he tipped his head back and looked up at the night sky. Stars blurred, pinpoint brilliance interrupted by the energy shield. "It's hard to get messages out."

"I got the one about Granite Falls," Sloan said. "Short, sweet . . . to the point."

"Best I could do." With a sigh, his brother stretched, attacking tense muscle. "Security is tight. Warriors are watched. And now that Hamersveld is the new XO?" Azrad blew out another breath. "It'll only get worse."

Hearing the frustration in his voice, Bastian stayed silent. His brother needed to talk. He could see it in Azrad's eyes. In the way he held himself and the raw undertone in his words. Not the least bit surprising. Being undercover wasn't easy, and Azrad had put himself in the middle of a mess. Toss in the fact his brother had spent years alone inside a Dragonkind prison. No one to talk to. No one to listen to. Total isolation with little noise and . . .

yeah, no question. Returning to the real world, only to be thrust into a war, couldn't be easy.

Brows drawn tight, Bastian stared at his profile. "Azrad, if you're having second thoughts—"

"Bullshit." Baring his teeth, his brother spun on his heel. Navy eyes shimmered as he nailed Bastian with a hard look. "I'm not turning tail. Forget running. I'm in all the way, Bastian—all the way, but . . . fuck. Do you know what that bastard is doing?"

He shook his head. Silence was the better part of patience. Listening gave him more than talking right now. He'd get more information that way. Important in and of itself, but with added value. By playing the mute, he helped Azrad release the tension.

Big bonus. A win-win all the way around.

"He's hurting females, Bastian. Ivar's got HEs locked up, doing God only knows what to them." Brushing a hand over his Mohawk, he made twin fists, then unclenched his hands. Open. Closed. White knuckles to open palms. Rage sparked in his gaze. Azrad raised his arm, spread his fingers, and thrust his palm forward. "He's got five so far. *Five* innocent females imprisoned somewhere."

Terranon snarled. "Sick bastard."

No question. No doubt either. Bastian rolled his shoulders. "Any intel about the location?"

"Not yet." Bowing his head, Azrad palmed his nape with both hands. A muscle jumped, skipping along his jaw a second before he leveled his chin. "I have no idea where the main lair is located. None of the foot soldiers do. Only Ivar and his personal guards live there."

"Fuck." He'd hoped for more. Why? He didn't know. Ivar wasn't stupid. The male allowed few into his inner circle. Mind churning, Bastian turned and paced toward the road. His boots crunched over gravel. He completed a circuit, then stopped in front of the F-150, and scowled at the rust bucket. The urge to lift his foot and kick the thing jabbed at him. He pivoted instead and hopped up onto steel. His ass settled on the hood. Metal dimpled, warping beneath him. He bent his knees and banged his feet down on the front bumper. "I don't like it any better than you do, Azrad. No way females should be in the line of fire. But try to be patient, I've got an investigator working on finding them."

"He any good?"

"*She* . . . and yeah, Ange has serious skills."

Kilmar raised a brow. "You work with females?"

"When she's ex-SPD and mated to my XO?" Elbows braced on his knees, Bastian laced his fingers and eyeballed the pretty-boy blond. "Absolutely."

"Good." Settling alongside him, Azrad leaned his hip against the front of the truck. He scanned the horizon a moment, then threw Bastian a sidelong look. "She found anything yet?"

"Not much."

"Tell her to work faster."

"What's changed?"

"Everything," Azrad said, looking worried. "Ivar's setting up a series of war games—one in which Razorbacks will compete. Top five fighters win a week with an HE female."

Sloan sucked in a quick breath. "When?"

"At Meridian realignment . . . during the *hungering*."

"Fuck," Bastian murmured as epiphany struck. Ivar's plan bordered on diabolical. Hell, it was brilliant, highlighting Dragonkind's ultimate weakness. The *hungering* happened twice a year when the electrostatic bands realigned in mid-March and at the end of October. The cosmic twist scrambled a male's DNA, rendering him fertile for one night. Twelve hours of bliss. A glut of sexual conquest in which many males lost control in the mating frenzy. A night of singular purpose—to propagate the continuation of their kind. "He plans to breed the females with the strongest males."

"Yeah, and that's not all." Lifting his foot, Terranon kicked a stone. The round rock flew, zipping across gravel to slam into the boulders piled opposite him. A crack echoed, rushing toward the cone's dome. "There's a rumor in the Razorback ranks. Something about an experimental serum and the females. No one knows what it does, but—"

"Jesus." A *serum*. Bastian's brows collided. He'd heard that word before. From his mate after she'd treated Angela's injuries—wounds received while imprisoned inside a Razorback stronghold. Myst had described the needle marks on Angela's stomach. Concern hit hard, making his chest tighten. Only one conclusion to draw—whatever Ivar was doing to the females inside his lair had already been done to Angela. The news pushed urgency through his veins. Bastian hopped off the hood. "We can't wait. We need to know what the serum does now."

Wick shifted to flank him. "Only way we do that is by finding Ivar's lab."

"Keep investigating from your end," Azrad said. "I'll work it from mine."

Bastian tipped his chin. "How?"

"By qualifying for the games."

"All three of us will compete." One corner of his mouth curved up, Kilmar cracked his knuckles. "Win top placement and—"

"We get escorted right into Ivar's lair," Terranon said, finishing his friend's sentence.

"Kill the guards inside the bastard's lair. Locate the captives," Azrad said, a nasty gleam in his eyes. "The second we do, we'll get the females out. Hand each one off to you for safekeeping."

"And relocation." Secure each female. Find new places for them to live. Witness protection at its best. Already thinking ahead, Bastian made a mental note to get the ball rolling when he got home. Daimler knew all about rewriting a person's history. The Numbai had done just that for J. J., Wick's mate, less than a month ago. Fake IDs—passport, driver's license, new SSN—included. "Easy as pie."

Sloan grunted. "Tricky as hell. You get caught and—"

"We get dead." Expression nonchalant, Azrad pushed away from his perch. The buttons of his army jacket brushed the hood. Plastic rattled against rusty steel. "Well worth the risk to dismantle the Razorback nation."

"No arguing with that," Wick murmured.

"All right, then." With a nod, Bastian palmed his brother's shoulder. Giving him a squeeze, he treated him to solid slap, then turned toward the highway. He needed to walk away. Right now. Otherwise, he'd say "fuck it" and pull the plug on the entire operation. He didn't like the undercover sideshow. Direct and deadly suited him better, but well . . . he sighed. His strategy might be killing rogues, but it wasn't ending the war. Azrad's approach, however, just might. Scrubbing a hand over his head, Bastian stopped five feet away and glanced over his shoulder. His gaze skimmed over Azrad and his crew. "Meeting's over. Send us updates when you can, but be safe. Don't blow your cover."

Azrad nodded.

Boots crunching over gravel, Bastian shifted into dragon form. Unfolding his wings, he leapt skyward, heart aching, mind racing, hoping like hell he'd made the right decision. And wasn't sending his brother in too deep . . .

Or headlong into certain death.

Chapter Seventeen

He had a mole. A spy inside the Razorback ranks. Mind reeling, running shoes planted on wet pavement, Ivar stood on the edge of human calamity, watching chaos run amuck in the hospital parking lot. Flashing lights from emergency vehicles. Smoke billowing from the side of the building. Firemen at the end of water hoses snaking across the ground. He frowned as someone yelled and the crowd scattered in the wrong direction and . . .

His brow furrowed.

A traitor inside his pack. Un-fucking-believable.

Yet, nothing else made sense. Or explained the Nightfury presence in Arlington. No news reports. No call had gone out. No reason for the enemy to be here. Which meant someone with insider information had tipped them off. The idea left him cold. His temper solved the problem, flaring so hot it heated him through. Pink flame responded, circling the center of his palms. He shut the fire show down and skimmed the human horde panicking a few feet away.

Small town USA, his ass. The place felt far too big tonight. Betrayal-big. Battle-big. Fucked-up-big. Ivar clenched his teeth. *A spy.* Holy God. He could hardly wrap his brain around it. The concept seemed foreign, as though it belonged to someone else, not him. He pursed his lips. Stood to reason. No one, after all, had ever betrayed him before.

Frowning, he swept the crowd again. Man, what a mess. Police shouted instructions, trying to restore order, but . . . no such luck. Human civilians, it seemed, sucked at listening. Ivar cursed under his breath. Talk about inconvenient. Forget the traitor for the moment. He had a more pressing problem. One that began and ended with him getting back inside the hospital. Sooner rather than later. In others words—right fucking now. Otherwise, he wouldn't get what he needed to work in his laboratory . . .

Evelyn-of-the-gorgeous-energy's blood.

Her sample was in there—somewhere.

Probably in the medical lab awaiting testing. Ivar frowned. At least, if he got lucky. Who knew how far the humans had gotten? Maybe he was already shit out of luck. Maybe the lab tech had already used the entire sample. Maybe her results already sat inside a folder waiting for a doctor to look at them. He huffed. Such a waste of time. The female wasn't sick. She was a genetic anomaly with an extraordinary immune system.

One that would kill any virus it encountered.

Interesting. Fascinating. One hundred percent noteworthy on the sliding superbug scale. Not that he cared at the moment. His love of all things scientific would have to wait. He didn't have time to screw around.

He *needed* to get back in there.

Eyes on the human hive, he plotted his trajectory. Back door would no doubt be best. Avoid the mess. Find the lab. Steal the sample. Easy-peasy—

As long as Hamersveld answered his call.

Gritting his teeth, Ivar uncloaked and stepped forward. His soles scraped over a rough patch of pavement. He kicked at the crack with the toe of his boot. He wanted to say "screw it" and go in now. Just let loose, cross the lot, and shove the idiot humans out of his way. Prudence stopped him. Experience backed the play. Heading into the medical facility alone didn't qualify as smart. Not right now. Not with the building burning and Nightfuries within shouting distance. Ivar scowled. All right, so that was an exaggeration. The enemy might be close, but weren't cause for immediate concern. His soldiers were doing their jobs—and following instructions—hopscotching east, over thick forest toward mountain terrain, leading the Nightfury pack away from Arlington.

Great strategy. Even better outcome—distract on one end, slip in and get what he needed on the other. Now, if only his new XO would show the hell up.

Dragon half rising, Ivar sent out another call. The ping echoed inside his mind, then spiraled out, searching for a connection. He held his breath and listened hard. One second turned into more, ticking past with unerring accuracy. Nothing. No answer on the other end of the line. He bit down on a curse. Freaking Hamersveld. Independent bugger. Where in God's name was he? Good question—one without an adequate answer. A pity. If the male didn't arrive soon, impatience would get the better of him and something bad—or rather, worse—would happen.

Probably another batch of dead humans.

Siren wailing, another fire truck roared into the lot. Emergency lights painted the side of the building red. Spin away, then circle back for another go-round. A revolving light show without end. Come one, come all. More human calamity.

Ivar growled in frustration. As if there weren't enough to wade through already.

Crossing his arms over his chest, he watched a group of females run past. Total panic territory. Typical human behavior.

No doubt a flaw in their nature. Then again, what did he know? After his bonehead performance tonight, he shouldn't cast the first stone. Raising both hands, he rubbed his temples. The entire mess was his fault. He'd set the fire, KO'ing a hospital room in the process.

His gaze strayed to the shattered window. Shards of glass clung to the steel frame, looking like shark teeth in the smoke. An image of the explosion expanded inside his head. Ivar grimaced. Such a dumb-ass move. A momentary lapse in judgment, except for one thing . . .

Lighting the fuse had been so much fun.

Pleasure hummed as he replayed the look on Venom's face. The surprise in his eyes. Complete panic when the fucker unleashed his magic, then realized his mistake. Highly enjoyable. Beyond priceless. Well worth the mess in the aftermath. It wasn't often, after all, he surprised, then upended a Nightfury. The bastards played the game too well for that. Like master chess players, his enemy liked to control the board, never flew into a firefight unprepared, and rarely, if ever, made mistakes.

Tonight, however, proved an exception to the rule.

Lovely in so many ways. Brutal in others. Particularly since he was stuck here, growing more impatient by the moment while—

Rain splattered across his back. A lethal vibe followed, raising the hairs on the nape of his neck. Branches snapped. Shrubbery rustled behind him. Ivar's mouth curved as he glanced over his shoulder.

Hamersveld stepped out of the bushes and onto the pavement behind him. Expression set to thundercloud, his XO scowled. *"What the hell, Ivar?"*

"About time you got here." Relieved to see the male, Ivar growled at him. *"Where have you been?"*

"Setting up an ambush," he said, sounding as pissed off as he looked. *"I had a wide-open shot before you yanked my chain.* Hristos, *I could've had him this time. Was . . ."* He raised his hand and held his thumb and forefinger an inch apart. *"This close to nailing the whelp."*

Ivar raised a brow. *"Who—the Nightfury water-rat?"*

"Who else?" Muscle ticking in his jaw, Hamersveld glared at him. The pale-blue rims around his black irises flashed. He stomped his feet into his combat boots. The thud-thud echoed across the parking lot, sending a clear message. Irritation times a thousand. *"Wide open, Ivar. This close. Whatever you want, it had better be good."*

"Just back me up, okay?" With a quick pivot, he jogged toward the rear of the hospital. No time to lose, even less to explain. He'd fill his XO in on the fly. Skirting a fire truck, he rounded the back of the hospital. Pavement turned to grass. Frozen blades snapped, crackling beneath his shoe treads. *"We need to move before the Nightfuries come up for air."*

"What happened?"

"I fucked up."

"How?"

Well, by blowing the hell out of a hospital for one thing. By not testing the virus in his lab before unleashing it for another. *"The virus is attacking females. Males are not being infected."*

"None at all?"

Ivar shook his head.

"Silfer's balls," Hamersveld whispered, worry in his voice. An apt reaction considering the danger and the horde of dying females. Ivar upped the pace. Hot on his heels, his XO followed, the crunch of footfalls rippling off the brick facade. *"How do we stop it from spreading?"*

"Make an antivirus. Give it to human doctors as fast as possible."

"Before it reaches larger populations?"

"Da, *exactly."*

Muscles bunching, Ivar leapt over a boulder. Cold air whistled in his ears. Sighting the ground on the other side, he landed with a thump and slid down an embankment. His feet slammed down on another stretch of asphalt. He glanced left. Perfect. A loading dock, large doors open to receive transport trucks. Not wasting a second, he ran toward the concrete platform—while marveling at the irony. Unprecedented, but he planned to put his scientific genius to work and save human lives. Ivar frowned. A weird thought. Not something he'd ever imagined doing before. Yet, here he was, racing to find a cure . . .

Using an HE female's blood.

Her plasma—all those lovely, killer red and white cells—would do the job. Allow him to synthesize an antivirus in his lab to achieve the desired result—death of his baby, superbug number three, in the wilds of human society.

Reaching the wide alcove, he vaulted onto the concrete platform. With a mental flick, he opened the door and stepped over the threshold. He paused in the center of the large foyer. Hamersveld slid to a stop behind him. Ivar glanced at the wall signs to get his bearings and . . .

Yippee-ki-yay. Medi-lab . . . basement floor.

"This way," he murmured, jogging past a bank of elevators.

A door marked "Stairs" sat beside them.

Ivar cranked the handle, crossed the threshold, and descended the stairs. His Nikes slapped against concrete treads. Hamersveld's footfalls rose in tandem behind him, making Ivar's heart beat faster. The violent blood rush echoed in his ears, shooting him full of adrenaline. A few more steps, a couple of doors, and . . . please, let the sample be intact and usable. All he needed was a couple of vials.

Reaching the landing, he hammered the next door. Reinforced steel flew open with a bang. He strode into the subterranean corridor. A high counter stood opposite him. No one at the helm, just a solitary stretch of no-one's-home manning the entrance to the hospital lab. He took a run at it, and planting his hand on the hard surface, leapt over the attendant's station. File folders shifted, slipping to the floor. Ivar stepped over the pile and headed for a set of glass sliders.

Motion detectors went active.

The clear panels slid sideways, dumping him into a large laboratory. Organized environment. Clean smell. Long table stacked with papers to his right. Work stations full of samples to his left. Human lab tech decked in protective gear, absorbed in his work, sitting at a high counter, noise-canceling headphones on, a row of fridges behind him. Gaze narrowed on the lab rat, Ivar moved toward him. The doors closed with a hiss behind him. His soles squeaked on the industrial-grade floor. The male tech looked up from his microscope. Ivar rounded the end of the countertop.

Blinking like an astonished owl, the idiot stared at him. His brow furrowed, the human shoved the headphones off his head and set them on the counter. "Hey, man. You can't be in—"

Ivar struck. His hand closed around the tech's throat. The human squawked. He squeezed, lifting the male off his stool. "Where are the blood samples kept?"

Caught fast in his grip, the tech shook his head. Ivar flexed his hand. Fear sparked in the human's eyes. He pointed to the row of fridges.

"The samples from the quarantine patients." Needing more specific information, Ivar leaned in and looked him in the eye.

His pink gaze glowed, reflecting in the dark one staring at him in horror. "Which fridge?"

"Th-th . . ." Unable to talk, the male gasped for air. Ivar relaxed his grip. Toes dangling an inch off the floor, his captive sucked in a desperate breath. "Th-third one."

"From the left?"

"Yes."

"Sveld . . ." Glancing toward the door, Ivar shoved the human toward his XO. "Mind scrub him while I search."

Scraping him off the floor, Hamersveld slammed the tech into the wall. His black eyes started to shimmer. The male whimpered. Ivar turned away from the counter. Three strides put him in front of the third refrigeration unit. He grabbed the handle and pulled. The glass door opened with a suctioning pop. Glass vials rattled in metal trays. Focus on the fragile test tubes, he read each label, looking for—

Bingo. Evelyn V. Foxe. Name written on the side. White sticker standing out against the dark richness of her blood.

Pocketing all three vials, he spun toward the exit. Hamersveld met his gaze and released the lab tech. The male groaned and, eyelashes flickering, slid into a heap on the floor. Ivar nodded on the flyby, letting his XO know he had what he needed.

"Praise Silfer," Hamersveld muttered, Norwegian accent joining the hum of overhead fluorescents. "Let's go."

Indeed. Absolutely. The quicker he got home, the better.

He'd had enough of the small town. He needed to get airborne. Back to the laboratory nestled one hundred and fifty feet below 28 Walton Street. The second he landed, he'd go to work while Hamersveld went hunting. Smoke out the spy. Stop the leak. Create an antivirus and find a cure. Tall orders, but it didn't matter. Do or die. Now or never. Full steam ahead on all fronts.

Otherwise, his race would suffer and the traitor would slip away before he made him pay.

Chapter Eighteen

Evelyn flinched as Venom shifted in flight, banking into a wide turn. He settled into a smooth glide over thick forest. Supercharged with the threat of an oncoming storm, the wind tugged at her hair, blowing wayward curls into her face, rattling his scales, shredding her nerves. Wrapped inside his leather jacket, she breathed through the fear. In. Out. Catch and release. The trick usually worked like a charm, helping her think, putting things into perspective and logic front and center. Not tonight. Calm wasn't part of the package. Neither was catching her breath. No matter how many times she forced air into her lungs, she couldn't get enough. Which left her worse than afraid. It left her light-headed, in doubt, unable to believe what she was seeing.

God, it was surreal. She was flying. With a dragon. That could turn into a man.

The truth slammed through her, spinning her mental roulette wheel.

Venom descended through wispy clouds, losing altitude.

Her stomach bottomed out. Bile burned the back of her throat. Swallowing the awful taste, she searched the horizon. Thick forest thinned. City lights exploded across the landscape, popping up like mushrooms on the dark ground. Tucking her knees in tight, she snuggled deeper into Venom's leather jacket, fighting to control the psychological slide into panic. Job one? Put away her fear. Stop trembling. Control her reaction long enough to think straight. All terrific ideas. Completely out of reach considering where she sat—inside a huge dragon paw with razor-sharp claws.

Like Ginsu knives—the ones that filleted fish and never went dull—the black tips gleamed in the weak light. She swallowed. Her heart went into overdrive, trying to escape through her breastbone. Evelyn cupped the front of her throat. God help her. The hooked tips were far too close. Just inches away. Within shredding distance of her face or—she cringed—her jugular. One wrong move. A quick flick. A skin-splitting slice, and good night sweet prince.

Game over.

Angling his wings, Venom wheeled into another turn. Squeezing her eyes shut, Evelyn went back to breathing. Her lungs expanded, providing much-needed air, prompting her mind to unlock. Mental acuity sped into view, dragging logic along. Not that it mattered. It didn't matter what angle she looked at it from, the conclusions remained the same. She was screwed. Neck-deep in something she couldn't puzzle out, never mind understand. Dragons and humans. Violence and death. Explosions and ruined hospitals. She and Venom. Each piece belonged in a larger puzzle. And yet, she didn't know which piece to put where. How did it all go together? Where did she fit in? Why her . . . what reason did Venom have for coming after her?

Frowning, Evelyn played with the mental jigsaw puzzle. An ache expanded between her temples. Still nothing. No matter which way she turned the board, nothing made sense. The pieces didn't fit. Then again, what did she know? She was dealing with unknown factors and shifting variables. The biggest of which was dragons.

Dragons, for the love of God! The stuff of legend, one that belonged in a bedtime story.

Somehow, though, Venom hadn't gotten the you're-not-supposed-to-exist memo. He broke all the rules. Add in his ability to turn into a man, a gorgeous one with gentle hands, an incredible voice and . . . good lord. Evelyn shook her head. It didn't make any sense, but she couldn't deny the truth. Or keep from wondering who had dropped the ball and forgotten to alert the rest of the planet about the dragon infestation. A huge lapse in judgment on someone's part. Particularly since the realization left her out in the cold. Alone in Crazyland, on the wrong side of mental health, straitjacket and mind-altering drugs mandatory.

A shiver rolled through her.

Evelyn pulled the jacket tighter, closing thick leather lapels into a cocoon around her. Venom's scent drifted from the folds, reminding her of the Luxmore. She couldn't wrap her brain around it. He'd been so gentle with her, almost polite while holding her in his arms. Such a surprise. A welcome one, sure, but she hadn't expected a man who paid for sex to behave like a gentleman. Concerned for her welfare. Invested in her comfort. Willing to let her go with the money without taking it to the next level.

Nowhere near *john*-like in the high-end escort-slash-prostitution racket.

Heat bloomed in her face. Evelyn turned her warm cheek into his coat collar. Talk about embarrassing. Not her finest moment. A terrible first meeting too. She'd met Venom in a hotel room. Had been willing to sleep with him for money. For *money*!—God forgive her. The memory of him—the taste of his mouth, the strength of his body, the careful way he'd touched her, as though she was precious—made her heart ache and her eyes sting. Tears blurred her vision. She blinked them away as the water came into view.

Puget Sound winked beyond bright city lights.

Evelyn stared at the surface of the water. Whitecaps heaved, then dipped. Waves whispered, rolling into the shoreline as she replayed the debacle inside her head. The reason she'd done it surfaced like a whale in ocean swells. She drew a shaky breath. All right, so she'd been in serious trouble. In a desperate scramble, trying to outrun Markov and the Russian mob. Somehow, though, the reasons no longer mattered. She'd done the unthinkable to save her own skin. No doubt a normal response to a life-threatening situation, but that didn't make her feel any better. Or assuage her wounded pride.

Her behavior with Venom shamed her.

Now she didn't know what to do. Thank him for coming to her rescue—again, for the second time in as many days? Or nail him for scaring the crap out of her? Serious questions. An even bigger debate. Arguments rose on both sides. She weighed the pros and cons and . . . yup. She could go either way. Shut down and shy away. Or wind up and let fly.

Using her lashes for cover, she looked Venom over again. Ridged dragon scales. Sharp canines in the shape of fangs. Jagged horns jutting from the top of his head. Shimmering ruby-red eyes. She released a fractured breath. Air rattled from her lungs. Self-preservation kicked in. She grimaced. Well, all right then. Maybe yelling at him wasn't the best idea. Shutting down—staying quiet until she knew him better—seemed like a better option, the safe side of sane.

Too bad she didn't want to be reasonable.

Or safe.

She wanted to throw caution to the wind instead. It would feel so good to hold him accountable. To relieve the pressure and make him pay. For what? Well, turning into a dragon for one thing. For being the hottest, most generous guy she'd ever met for another. Her heart panged. The pitiful throb echoed inside her head. God, it was unfair. Totally ridiculous. He'd asked her to dinner, made plans with her, demanding exclusivity.

At the time, she'd been thankful, so damned relieved she wouldn't have to see other men to get what she needed to stay alive. Now she wasn't so sure. Instinct whispered in her ear, plying her with suspicion. She frowned. What was his game? He must be running one. Venom wasn't stupid. Far from it. Which meant he must've known. Must've guessed what would happen—that he wouldn't be able to hide his scalier side from her forever.

Or maybe he'd simply planned on lying to her . . . ad infinitum.

The thought tugged at her temper. An odd reaction. Not at all warranted. She didn't own the right to be pissed off at him. Anger didn't belong in the equation. She'd planned to use him for money. He'd wanted her for sex. A simple exchange. No fuss. No muss. And yet, the idea of him being dishonest with her woke something primal. Something dangerous. Something that shoved her toward the truth. The thought of Venom lying to her more than *bothered* her. It infuriated her, violated her sense of . . . of . . . well, she didn't know exactly. Right and wrong? Her sense of self-worth? A healthy dose of pride, maybe? No clue. But whatever the catalyst, it lit the fuse, setting moral indignation on fire, tipping the balance, making her throw caution to the wind.

Eyes narrowed, she scowled up at him. "Venom."

"Almost there, *mazleiha*."

"Where are we going?"

"Somewhere safe."

"Will your dragon friends be there?"

Her clipped tone made him glance down. She glared at him. A wary light entered his eyes. "No. It'll just be you and me for a while."

"Good," she said, hot sauce in her tone. "We need to talk."

"You gonna take it easy on me?"

"No."

He grimaced. "That's what I thought."

His leery expression warmed her insides. Her lips twitched. She shut her reaction to his wariness down. But it was hard not to find him charming. Big, bad Venom of the dark-green scales and vicious claws dreaded her reaction. Strange as it sounded, she could feel the unease in him. Could almost see his mind churning as he searched for a way to placate her. Not a bad plan, all things considered. He'd dropped a whopper on her tonight. Was even now flying her to some undisclosed location to—

Evelyn frowned. To do what exactly?

She stared at him harder. A buzz lit off in her veins. Warm sensation coasted down her spine, hooking her in to something vast. Connection sped through the cerebral space and intuition sparked, giving her a glimmer of his intent. Surprise battered her. Wow, that was weird. She could feel him now. Her heart paused mid-beat, then resumed pounding, keeping time with his, allowing her to read him. He was worried about something. Her reaction to his dragon half, sure, but something more than that too.

Her eyes widened as more of his concerns gained speed inside her head. The strange link flexed. The word *Razorback* whispered against her temples. Evelyn blinked. Holy crap. Hold everything. Put on the brakes. Back up the bus. What in God's name was that? No way she should be mainlining his thoughts. Pressing her palms to the sides of her head, Evelyn fought to control the cerebral flow—the thought exchange . . . whatever. She didn't care what it was called just as long as it stopped. The rush amplified, hammering her mental defenses, stealing more of her headspace.

Evelyn blew out a breath. "Uh, Venom?"

"Hold tight."

Angling into another turn, Venom flew over a beach. A skim of snow covered the sand in spots. Brown intersected with white, then tumbled into rock. The roar of waves rose on cold air as the surf rolled in, painting each stone black. Wings spread wide, Venom slowed and set down on the stretch of lawn fronting a huge house with a long stretch of dark windows. His back paws crunched against frozen blades of grass. Evelyn tensed and got ready for—

The hair on her nape rose. One moment slid into the next and . . . presto change-o. Venom transformed. Green scales turned to golden skin. Huge talons became hands and feet. Horns and sharp spikes disappeared. Long blond hair took its place, falling to his shoulders, framing his gorgeous face.

Evelyn sucked in a quick breath.

With a murmur, Venom wrapped his arms around her and tucked her in close. Her bare feet touched the icy ground. Big hands settled against her back as he dipped his head. Day-old whiskers grazed her temple. Pleasure whispered and bliss arrived, awakening deprived nerve endings a second before her brain turned over. Evelyn flinched. She needed to move. Distance was a requirement right now. Otherwise, he'd suck her in and scramble her thoughts. Which would result in what? Her ability to think straight wavered. Not a great idea. She had questions. He held all the answers. So no . . . becoming distracted, losing herself in him wasn't a smart move.

The second she gave in, it would be over. He'd win. She'd lose the high ground along with the opportunity to get what she needed—clarification on a large scale.

Reaching for courage, she squared her shoulders and went looking for her voice. She opened her mouth. Venom drew her closer. Her hands met the wall of his chest. He breathed her name, the whisper so full of sex her brain shut down. She blinked. Oh, no. Not good. She was losing the battle. He kept winning the war, screwing with her will to resist.

Evelyn shook her head. Crap. It was official. She was past pathetic and into needy. Which meant . . . she really needed to make up her mind—let him comfort her. Or pull a tilt-a-whirl spin out of her hat and break free. She couldn't do both. But even as she berated herself for enjoying his nearness, she damned herself by snuggling in and acknowledged her weakness.

She didn't want to fight with him right now.

Questions would be asked and answers would come. All would eventually be explained. For now, she bowed to a greater urge. She needed a hug. Wanted to be held by him—if only for a little while—and a chance to calm down. Topsy-turvy, total emotional upheaval, didn't sit well with her. She liked even. Enjoyed steady, for everything to add up in neat rows and orderly columns. Tonight didn't qualify as any of those things. So instead of shoving Venom away, she whispered his name—mind whirling, body pliant, protest nonexistent—when he kissed her temple, then raised his head, allowing her to take all the space beneath his chin. His heat rolled into her, and, just like that, it was over. She was done, field abandoned and battle lost.

"Sorry about all the hocus-pocus, Evie." His mouth brushed the top of her head, bringing more warm comfort. Feeding on his body heat, unable to find the words for what she needed, Evelyn showed him instead. She pressed closer. Venom tightened his grip and, pushing his hands under the hem of her jacket, hugged her harder. "I didn't mean to scare you."

The sound of his voice made her tremble.

"Shit," he said, lifting his head. "It's freezing out here. Let me get you inside."

She cleared her throat, trying to make her voice work. "Do you live here?"

"First time I've been." Gathering up her legs, he swung her into his arms.

"I can walk."

"Do you want to?"

Her bare toes twitched in protest. "Not really."

"Then be quiet and enjoy the ride," he said, a teasing lilt in his voice as he walked across the lawn.

"You always this bossy?"

"Part of my charm."

"You think?" she asked, loading the question with enough doubt to sink a ship.

He snorted. "You're lippy."

"Disappointed?"

Stepping onto a flagstone path, he glanced down at her. "Not even a little."

The heat in his eyes scorched her, lighting her up from the inside out. Blatant need. Unquenchable want. Burning desire. All three darkened his odd-colored eyes, telling her plainer than words he still wanted her. That he had big plans, ones in which she played the centerfold in his sexual fantasies. Her breath caught. An answering pulse of desire streamed through her. Wow. Crazy. Beyond fascinating. It wasn't about money anymore. Something had changed. Something monumental. He seemed more intent now. More focused on her . . . completely ravenous.

Awareness upped the ante, begging her to reciprocate. Her gaze strayed to his mouth. His lips parted in reaction, prompting memory, firebombing her imagination, igniting an internal flame. And she remembered . . . everything. The way he kissed.

How he tasted. How much she wanted to see him without a stitch on. All that golden skin on display. All those hard muscles under her hands. All his sexual focus riveted on her. Her hands buried in his long hair. His hips between her thighs. Her tongue tangled with his.

Her mouth went dry.

Red eyes shimmering, Venom's nostrils flared.

Dragging her attention from his mouth, she met his gaze. Hot lust shone in his eyes. Evelyn clenched her teeth. *Back away. Back away!* Her mind screamed the instruction, hammering reason home. She needed to remain even—and thinking. Putting the cart before the horse—or in this case, sex before the answers—would land her in serious trouble. More than she was already in, the kind a girl didn't come back from. Turning her head, Evelyn broke eye contact in favor of keeping her mind. Lord knew she'd just gotten it back. She wouldn't give it up again without a fight.

"Evie . . ."

She swallowed, working moisture back into her mouth. "Yeah?"

"You're thinking naughty thoughts."

"What?" Ah, frig. Busted. Guilty as charged. Her face heated. Prickles attacked her skin, warming her cheeks to a full blush. "No, I'm not."

His mouth curved. "Any time you want, *mazleiha.* Say the word, and I'll take you there. Make you come so hard, you scream my name."

Her body tightened. Evelyn twitched against her will. Oh God. Why did he have to go and say things like that? "Bossy and cocky. You really should get a handle on that."

He huffed in laughter.

She backpedaled into mental safety, grounding herself in the sound of his footfalls. The thump-thump echoed on the stone path, drifting on frigid air. Her heart picked up the beat. Blood rushing in her ears, Evelyn focused on her surroundings. The sound of waves rolled onto the beach behind her. A testament to architecture rose in front of her. Three stories high, the house boasted wide windows that looked out onto the Sound. Evelyn sighed in appreciation. Even with its boxy, modern shape, the place looked like it belonged. As though it had been planted centuries earlier, then left to grow out of the landscape.

A few things gave its true origins away. Wide cedar-plank siding on the upper levels for one. The complementing pattern of the uneven stone facade on the first floor for another. Evelyn's mouth curved. She recognized new-age old when she saw it. Built to look ancient, but in actuality state-of-the-art new.

Pace steady, Venom skirted the round fountain in the middle of the path and, dipping his head, brushed past sculpted cedars to reach the stone patio. Low-lying shrubs surrounded the elevated stone terrace. Deep and wide, the deck stretched end to end, taking up the entire back side of the house. Without breaking stride, he jogged up three steps and headed for a bank of tall windows on the ground floor. Halfway across, a lock snicked and a set of double doors opened. She expected to see someone standing on the other side, feet planted inside the house, hand on the handle. She searched the darkness beyond the doors.

Nothing and nobody.

Her brows collided. She glanced at Venom from the corner of her eye. "Did you do that?"

"I'm Dragonkind, Evie," he said as though that explained everything.

She blinked. *Dragonkind.* Weird, but all right. She bought that. Hard to argue the point after being flown here by Venom. "Which means—what, exactly? That you can move things with your mind?"

"Yes. Magic is part of my makeup. It's written in my DNA."

"Are you even human?"

"Half." Reaching the house, he stepped over the threshold.

The doors shut with a thud behind him. Halogens flicked on, then dimmed, throwing shadows across the open-concept setup—living room, dining area, and kitchen all in one. Skirting a large end table, he stopped in front of a wide-backed armchair. Or well, what looked like one. Hidden beneath a white sheet, the lumpy form reminded her of a ghost. Spooky. Floating above the wooden floor. Lying in wait to broadside an unsuspecting victim in the dark.

Kind of like Venom had done to her on the hospital rooftop.

An image of him transforming flamed in her mind. Silence spun in the picture's wake, rising hard between them. The quiet settled, whirling through the room, stripping her already-frayed nerves. Wariness spilled into the void, obliterating ease, silencing earlier banter, making her skin feel three sizes too small.

Discomfort spun its witchy web.

Shifting in his arms, Evelyn cleared her throat.

Hard muscle flexed around her. Venom exhaled and, with a gentle draw, slipped his forearm from beneath her knees. Her feet dropped to the floor. She leaned away from him. The shift wasn't much. Barely there displacement, but Venom got the message. Honoring her tension, understanding her silent request for space, he took his hands from her waist and retreated. One step turned into more. Boot soles scraping over wood floors, he stopped opposite her, in front of the long couch six feet away.

Evelyn should've been grateful. He'd done what she asked, after all, and backed off. Somehow, though, the move didn't make her happy. Loss cranked her tight instead, urging her to call him back. To bridge the distance. To ask to be held and for more comfort.

Something else that didn't make sense. Yet, for all her confusion, the urge rang true.

Like it or not, having him close soothed her. Without him, reality set in, making her forget his gentleness in favor of remembering his fangs. Understandable. No doubt a normal reaction—that felt all wrong. Surprising as it seemed, she didn't want to be afraid of him. Didn't want to look him in the eye and see a threat. She wanted a friend, not a new enemy. Someone to help her navigate the strange new world she'd landed in the middle of.

Dragonkind. Her throat went tight. Dear lord, it still sounded unreal.

"So half dragon, huh," she said, forcing her voice out of hiatus.

Venom nodded. "My mother was human, my father, Dragonkind."

"Oh, well . . ." Stood to reason. Made perfect sense in an imaginary world.

And yet, there he stood, looking positively lick worthy—like her favorite flavor of fantasy man, six and a half feet of wide-shouldered, hard-bodied perfection. She met his gaze. Her brain bottomed out, sinking into a cerebral muck hole. Beautiful man to vicious dragon—one and the same, part and parcel of the same pie. A switch-up that defied the natural order of things. She frowned. Didn't it? She ran her gaze over him again and shook her head.

"We're a different species, Evie, that's all."

"That's all?" she echoed, incredulity making her voice rasp and the words wobble. Dear God, she sounded like a mental patient—half-confused, half-hysterical. "Doesn't that seem like enough? I mean . . . God. How is that even possible? How is it no one knows about you? You're flying around, blowing stuff up, starting fires and—"

"I didn't start the fire in the hospital. Ivar did," he said. "And we've stayed hidden from humankind to protect your race. Better for us. Safer for you."

"Why? Afraid of our history as dragon slayers?"

His lips twitched. "Something like that."

"Who's Ivar?"

"My enemy." His gaze went flat. Evelyn tensed, recognizing the violence in him. "A male who will imprison and hurt you if he finds you, Evie. A distinct possibility now that he's seen you."

Panic drilled deep, jabbing at her lungs, making it hard to breathe. "I don't . . . why would he . . . that doesn't make any sense. I'm nothing to him."

"You're a high-energy female," he murmured, his regret unmistakable. "Tremendously valuable, a prize among my kind. Many would die to possess you."

"You included?"

"No." Ruby gaze pinned on her, he shook his head. "I would die to protect you. The possession part is entirely up to you."

"Oh my God. You're talking in circles," she whispered. Pressure built behind her eyes. Bowing her head, Evelyn pressed the heels of her palms to her orbital sockets. The clampdown didn't help. Pain tightened its grip instead, refusing to abate, making her temples throb. "What the hell is going on?"

"I know you're scared. What you saw tonight is shocking, but—"

"It's not that." Leveling her chin, Evelyn rubbed the sore spot between her eyes. "I mean it is, but . . ." Drawing a choppy breath, she flicked her hands, the gesture one of helplessness born of fatigue. "It's more than that too."

"Tell me."

She shook her head.

"Come on, *mazleiha*," he said, tone so soothing her heart panged. Tears rose in reaction, pooling in her eyes. Concern on his face, Venom stared at her a moment, then closed the distance. He stopped in front of her. Raising his hand, he cupped the side of her throat. He tugged. Evelyn didn't resist. She went without protest, letting him pull her into his arms. Heat prickled over her nape. Relief washed in, arriving on a warm wave of sensation. "I was meant to find you, Evie. I mean to protect you. Please, talk to me. Let me help."

His entreaty obliterated her will to resist.

The dam broke, cracking her wide open. The truth spilled out before she could stop it. "It's too much—the last straw, you know? I've been holding it together with a shoestring, trying everything I can think of to stay in one piece. But no matter what I do it keeps getting worse—first my mom, then Markov and the money, my job too. Now Mema and the whole dragon thing. It's too much, Venom. I can't handle any more."

"I understand, Evie."

"No, you don't."

One hand caressing her back, he slid the other to her nape. "You're not alone, love."

"Then why do I feel like I am?"

"Because it always feels worse in the moment than it actually is."

"Maybe," she said, half huff, half hiccup.

He could say anything he liked, but nothing changed the facts. With Mema gone, she was alone in the world. Without family. Without a lifeline. One hundred percent on her own. Funny thing, though? Venom was right. Talking to him helped. Admitting her problems—facing her fears—made her feel less afraid. More optimistic too, something she needed more than a paycheck. Closing her eyes, she allowed herself to hope. Maybe things would get better. Maybe her problems weren't insurmountable. Maybe she could do something else, change tack, find other solutions, concentrate on figuring out her life instead of running scared.

The idea took root.

Belief and conviction collided, dragging possibility into the picture. Muscles twisted by stress loosened. Evelyn relaxed with a sigh, welcoming relief as the knot in the center of her chest unraveled.

"Feel better?"

"A little," she whispered. "You've got serious Dr. Phil skills."

He smiled against the top of her head. "I'm a fix-it ninja."

Evelyn snorted. The urge to laugh surprised her. She smiled anyway. Good lord, he said the strangest things. Funny things. Charming things. Which equated to big trouble for her. He became more appealing by the moment. His sense of humor added to the sexy-as-sin vibe he carried around like cargo and . . . boy, oh boy. Watch out world. She was headed for a fall. One that would end with her flat on her back while Venom stripped her bare.

"Hey, Evie?"

"Uh-huh."

"Markov I've figured out. Who's Mema?"

"My grandmother." Her heart clenched. Grief spilled out as an image of Mema rose inside her head. Flower apron on, wooden spoon raised, eyes twinkling in merriment about something while she fried up a batch of to-die-for chicken. Evelyn always thought of her that way—talking, laughing, in her favorite spot in front of the stove. A sob caught in the back of her throat. The tears she struggled to contain rolled over her bottom lashes. "She died at the hospital tonight. The doctors wouldn't let me see her. I didn't get to say good-bye."

"Ah, hell." His hand flexed on her nape. Turning his head, he pressed his cheek against hers. "I'm so sorry, Evie."

"It's a nightmare, Venom . . . a *nightmare*." Another sob escaped her. Not knowing what to do, Evelyn fisted her hands in his shirt and hung on hard. Her chest heaved on hiccups. Tears continued to fall, cascading into an avalanche of emotional ruin. "I can't make it stop. My situation keeps going from bad to worse."

"Not anymore." he said. "I'm here now. It's going to be okay, *mazleiha*. Don't worry about anything—Markov, the money . . . nothing at all. We'll figure it out."

Nice thought. Beautiful dream. An even softer place to land.

Too bad it was too good to be true.

Evelyn knew it. The world had taught her well, and history liked to repeat itself. So no. She couldn't allow Venom to solve her problems. Dependence brought nothing but trouble. Reliance could be a shackle in the same way love could be a curse. Her father's struggle to save her mother underscored that awful fact. Which meant she must find a way out on her own. Do it while standing on her own two feet, or not at all.

Here today. Gone tomorrow.

As amazing as he seemed, Venom equated to a bad idea. He was hit and run. Nothing but collateral damage, a Dragonkind guy caught up in the middle of her mess. Sure, she might like the look of him. He might want the hell out of her. But the attraction wouldn't last long. The flame that burned the brightest always went out the fastest. The light never lasted. Darkness would return. Well-laid intentions rarely went to plan, and present circumstances kept pointing out the chasm that sat between her and Venom.

Two different species. Two worlds apart.

His interest in her would fade. Hers in him would fizzle out too.

Natural law. Unbreakable order. The way of the world.

And yet, as he held her, she wanted to believe. Pretend she meant something to him—that she was special somehow and that things would get better. Foolish to hope. The height of stupidity to wish. Fruitless faith leading her astray. Knowing it, however, didn't make her release him. She held on tighter instead, drawing out the embrace in the hopes of finding solace. If only for a little while. One night or a thousand. It didn't matter, just as long as he didn't let her go.

As quiet drifted through the living room, Venom released a pent-up breath. Thank God for huge favors and a dash of foresight. For an empty house and the silence that went with it as well. Black Diamond never approached quiet. It was loud and lived-in. Comfortable and full of family. But as he held Evelyn close, tucking her against him, he didn't miss his brothers-in-arms in the least. The loud bunch could go to hell and tweak his tail another day. He could stand silent with his female forever. No need to talk. No reason to move. Sure in knowledge he'd met his match. Finally. At last. She was here, 100 percent real.

No longer a figment of his imagination.

His mouth curved. Call it perfect, then call it a day. She fit in his arms as though she'd been made for him. Sheer perfection. A dream come true as she snuggled in, allowed him to hold her, accepting the comfort he offered . . . ripping him apart with her tears. Trying to be strong, she held on hard, hands fisted in his T-shirt, head tucked beneath his chin, no longer crying, yet still breaking his heart with each hitching breath she took. Mouth brushing her hair, he kissed the top of her head, waiting her out as she trembled in his arms, struggling to recover. From grief and loss. From the turmoil of losing someone she loved. Which meant . . .

Nothing was *perfect.*

Not her present circumstances. Not the strength of his arms around her. Nor his need to soothe her. He couldn't will her to calmness via hug alone.

The thought made his chest go tight.

It wasn't fair. He'd wanted it to be perfect. Had dreamed of getting her alone—of having the chance to talk and laugh and . . . make love to her. Mutual satisfaction, however, was nothing but a distant hope now. She needed a friend, not a lover. Comfort instead of passion. Someone to help mend her heart and make her laugh. Someone who looked exactly like him. But not yet.

She wasn't ready to face him yet.

He could tell by the way she clung to him. He blew out a regret-filled breath. Despite the pleasure of having her in his arms, her anguish tore him apart, fracturing him in ways he hadn't thought possible. Now he bled for her, aching so hard her loss became his. As she hiccuped, he took it all, drawing the agony out of her, absorbing it himself, willing to take every ounce of pain to lessen hers. It was only fair. He dealt with loss all the time. Knew death well and understood it even better. And right now, he'd do anything to help. To somehow—some way—ease her burden and make it better.

"You are making it better," she whispered, shifting in his embrace. Her soft mouth brushed his throat. "I don't know how, but you are."

Her voice drew him tight. His body did the rest, taking the compliment to heart. Arousal hit him full force, sending the wrong signals. He hardened behind his button fly. Venom clenched his teeth. Goddamn it. He'd been doing so well—controlling his reaction, denying his urges, refusing to think about the softness of her skin, the lush curve of her behind, the gorgeous—

"Hell," he muttered, trying to get himself back on track.

The safe side of sanity sounded good right now. Too bad the prick behind his button fly refused to agree. The no-more-tears effect was getting to him, making him imagine things he shouldn't. He bit down on a curse. Rock hard and willing, 100 percent ready to please her. A bad state to be in with his female in his arms. But even as he told himself to behave, naughty images sped into his head. Of Evelyn naked above him, thighs spread, nipples furled, body rolling as she rode him. Without mercy . . . or end.

His mouth went dry.

Trying to distract himself, he stared at a picture hanging on the wall opposite him. A bistro scene. Midnight in Paris, maybe. Cobblestone avenue next to a street-side patio. Street lamps aglow, two glasses of red wine, one table. A pretty sturdy-looking piece, inviting a male to sit his female on the edge, flip up her skirt and—

Venom blinked. Shit. Bad brain. Wrong thought. Again.

He really needed to get a handle on his obsession and stop fantasizing about being buried deep inside her. About what she would sound like too. He swallowed, working moisture back into his mouth. Would she be loud—moan his name, beg for release, scream when she came? Or was she the silent type, demanding but quiet in pleasure. God, he'd give anything to find out. Now. This minute, but well . . . lord save him from lusty thoughts. Sex wasn't on the menu and might not be for a while.

Inhaling deep, Venom filled his lungs to capacity. He held it a moment, let the pressure build, then released the air in a rush.

Breathe in. Exhale out. Repeat. The exercise helped to focus him. Control settled in, calming his body, downgrading the tension, moving his brain in a different direction. Rushing Evelyn wasn't wise. Patience would get him further. He wanted her to trust him. Needed her to feel safe despite his nature and what she'd seen. Most females took time to acclimatize and accept new situations. The one his female faced was bigger than most.

Good-bye, human world. Hello, Dragonkind.

Evelyn might not know it yet, but she wouldn't be returning home. It wasn't safe for her anymore. Not with Ivar in the mix. A master scientist, the bastard was hunting HE females. Something to do with a breeding problem and a nasty serum. Which put Evelyn in the bull's-eye, smack-dab in the rogue leader's line of sight. The asshole would learn her name, find out where she lived and—

Venom growled. No way in hell. He refused to leave Evelyn vulnerable. Would never allow her to be taken. She belonged to him now. Was part of his pack. His to nurture. His to protect. His to please the moment she let him.

Nothing else would ensure his success. Or help her accept his claiming.

But it was hard to be patient. He wanted her so badly. Hadn't dared hope he would ever find someone like her—his equal, a female able to flourish in his presence and thrive under his touch. Awe tightened his throat. The need to treat her right slowed the sweep of his hands along her back. He shouldn't be touching her right now. She needed time and space—for him to back off while she figured out what she wanted. A heart-wrenching thing to do. An even more difficult action to implement, but . . .

He needed to step away. Right now. Otherwise, he'd screw up. Make her uncomfortable. Do something stupid—like dip his head and claim her mouth while he raised her skirt.

Easing his hips away, he cleared his throat. "Evie?"

"Can you feel that?"

Oh, man, could he ever. Somehow, though, Venom didn't think she meant the hard bulge behind his fly. "What?"

"It's like a hum inside my head." Sliding her hands up his back, she stroked the tops of his shoulders. Venom tensed. She lifted her cheek from his chest. Dark-brown eyes met his. Need thumped on him. He slammed the door, keeping lust locked on the other side as he searched her face. Lashes spiked by tears, a single drop rolled down her cheek. His chest tightened at the sight. Raising his hand, he wiped the moisture away. "Strange, but I can feel you."

"Not so strange," he murmured, knowing he played with fire.

He'd already decided to back away and give her room. Treat himself to some too. But instead of embracing smart, he plunged headlong into stupid and caressed her again, marveled at the softness of her skin, loving the contrast—her dark to his light—as the buzz filled his own veins. No, not odd at all. Startling, maybe. Incredible, for sure. Not the least bit *strange*. Her ability to feel him stemmed from energy-fuse: powerful, unbreakable, the Meridian's gift to Dragonkind. And yet, the strength of the connection surprised him anyway. He hadn't expected it to happen so fast. Or for Evelyn to accept his dragon half so easily.

Unable to resist, he dipped his head. She tipped her chin up. His mouth touched down, brushing the corner of hers. "We're fated, you and I."

"I'm not sure I believe in fate."

"Consider me your wake-up call—the universe's way of telling you different."

"That I'm wrong, you mean?"

"You said it, not me."

She laughed. "God, you're funny. I really like that about you."

"A compliment," he said, glancing behind him. The couch sat six feet away, the perfect place for a midnight chat. Lacing his fingers with hers, he tugged on her hand and retreated a step. She resisted, then gave in to the gentle pull. Skirting the coffee table, he walked backward. The soft thud of his boots echoed, rising toward the high ceiling as she followed him across the living room. "I'm moving up in the world."

"Maybe." She shrugged. His leather jacket fell off one of her shoulders, exposing more soft skin and her dress. Smudged by soot near the hem, pale silk shimmered in the low light, hugging her curves, showing off her shape, making his mouth water. "Or maybe you just caught me at a weak moment."

His legs hit the front of the couch.

Holding her gaze, he sat down. The dustcover sighed beneath his Levi's. Thick cushion conformed to his body, inviting him to settle in and stay a while. Not a bad idea considering his companion tonight. Evelyn. God, she was beautiful. All lithe curves, dark skin, and sassy attitude. So touchable. Beyond gorgeous. Made for loving. His for the taking—if only she asked. He swallowed a groan, let go of her hand, and patted the cushion next to him. Evelyn took the hint, accepted his invitation and—

Hiked up her skirt, revealing a gorgeous length of leg.

Venom sucked in a quick breath. Her knee hit the cushion next to his knee, then slid along the outside of his leg. Surprise blindsided him, locking him down, holding him immobile, making his brain short-circuit. His mind went blank. Pressing her hands to his chest, she pushed, asking him to lean back, then threw the other leg over. His back touched the backrest. She set her exquisite ass in his lap and, straddling his hips, settled in, her core pressed to his erection.

Her heat scorched him through denim.

Venom bit down on a curse.

Shifting her weight, she squirmed, adjusting their fit. "Hi."

"Hey," he said, trying to sound calm. Put together. Like a male who'd had his fair share of females. Not one about to lose his mind.

"So," she said. "I was thinking."

"About what?" Sex . . . please let it be hard-core, body-rocking sex.

"You promised me something earlier."

"Did I?" he asked, forcing his brain to turn over. Synapses fired, speeding mental acuity along, giving him hope then—ah, hell—sputtered and died. Eagle eyes on him, Evelyn rocked her hips. Ecstasy burned through his veins. The traitor behind his button fly twitched in warning. Gritting his teeth, Venom swallowed hard, losing more brain cells as blood rushed south, leaving him empty-headed. He drew a desperate breath. "You're teasing, Evie."

"You would know." Her fingertips played across his collarbone. With a sexy swirl, she sent one dancing beneath his shirt collar. Her skin caressed his. Desire curled, sank deep, rushing heat through his veins, making his muscles clench. "You're the biggest tease of all."

His eyes narrowed. "It's not teasing when you plan to follow through."

She raised a brow. "And are you going to—follow through?"

Head resting against the seat back, he stared up at her. One second ticked into the next. When she didn't shy away, he slid his hands up the outside of her thighs. Up. Up. Smooth skin whispered beneath his calloused palms. And then up some more . . . until her hem brushed his fingertips. She didn't flinch. Bold as ever, she met his gaze with a challenge in her own.

Venom hummed in approval. Well, all right then. Game on. No turning away.

He needed to meet her head-on. Match her move for move. Give as good as she gave to win the round and come out on top. Brushing a stray tendril of hair away from her temple, he studied her a moment, weighing the pros and cons, trying to guess her game. Loose curls clung to his fingers, slipped in between, tempting him to linger. Unable to resist, he played in the soft strands and tried to decide.

Make love to her now or make her wait.

It was a toss-up. A real tug-of-war.

He didn't want to rush her. Or help her run headlong into disaster. She'd suffered a shock. Was contending with tragic loss. Which left her feeling unmoored, in need of an anchor. He equated to a good one—solid, strong, gentle yet supremely skilled in bed. Tapping into her bio-energy, Venom mined her mood. He huffed. Nice. He could actually hear her thinking.

Each word. Every bit of logic. The clash of opposing values too: the good girl she'd always been versus the bad one she wanted to be.

The latter would give her what she needed—peace and stability, reason in a world gone topsy-turvy on her. Understandable. A pretty good strategy too, despite the fact he found himself in the hot seat. He couldn't find fault with her approach. She craved comfort. For someone to relieve the steady pressure building inside her. Making love with him would do that—exhaust her body, calm her mind, stop the turmoil. Question was . . .

Did he want his first time with her to be that way?

Winding one of her curls around his fingertip, he tugged her closer. "My following through depends on one thing."

"What?" she asked, her mouth a hair's breadth from his.

"You."

She frowned and leaned away, not understanding.

Venom almost said to hell with it. Giving her what she wanted—a fast fuck followed by mind-blowing orgasm—after all, played into his plans. She was his mate. Made for him. Meant for him. The only female he would sleep with from now on. The only one he would please and be pleased by in return. Which should've unleashed him—given him permission to claim her. Somehow, though, it didn't. What he wanted no longer mattered. This was about her, not him. So despite her bold move—and assertive nature—he needed to make something clear. And she needed to understand how it would be if she continued toward him, instead of away. Fast. Hard. Deep. Animalistic and intense the second he flipped her over and took what she offered.

"Venom?"

"Be sure, Evelyn," he said with a growl. "I want you too much. Once we start down this road, I might not be able to stop."

"You would never hurt me."

"No. Never."

"Then unlock and let go."

"Jesus." His hands flexed on her thighs. "You don't know what you're asking."

"Yes, I do," she whispered, rocking her hips, inviting him to lay her down and lose control. "I want you, Venom. I have since the moment I saw you at the Luxmore."

Truth stacked upon truth, and lust on top of lust. His more than met hers. But God, he needed to be sure. Of her. Of himself. Of the situation too.

Undulating against him, she moaned his name.

He seized her hips and pressed down, controlling her ride. "God, Evie. I can feel you through my jeans. You're so hot."

"Very wet too," she whispered against his mouth. "I'm slipping against my panties."

Holy God. Gorgeous tease. The things she said turned him inside out.

With a hum, she licked his bottom lip, teasing him with a wet stroke, making him imagine the soft flesh between her thighs. Venom groaned. She captured and swallowed the sound, kissing him harder. Deeper. Stroke for stroke. Tangling her tongue with his before retreating again. "It may not be wise, but I need you—to feel good and forget the hurt for a while. Please, Venom."

The entreaty cranked him tight. Chest heaving, still unsure, he hesitated.

She flicked her tongue over his teeth. "Hmm, I love your hair."

"It's too long." Unable to resist, he picked up her rhythm. Fast and furious. No holds barred. She was magic, moving against him with one aim in mind—his pleasure and her eventual victory.

"No. It isn't." Fingers playing, she stroked through the long strands. Her nails grazed his scalp, sending shivers down his spine. "It's perfect."

"Another compliment," he murmured, trying to keep it light. A good plan. Maybe if he kept talking, he'd maintain some restraint. Do it right. Love her well. Make her come before he lost control. "Jesus, Evie. You're beautiful."

"You should see me without my clothes on."

She smiled, all imp, no mercy.

Her expression, the teasing lilt of her voice, unleashed him. With a snarl, Venom reversed their positions, putting Evelyn on her back. She bounced against the couch cushions. He bared his teeth and shoved at her skirt, warning her without words. Screw right. He was headed straight into wrong. She wanted him. He longed for her. Flawless symmetry. The perfect storm. Nothing standing in his way. Desire surged, funneling into a single thought. He needed to see her naked . . . right now. Kiss her soft skin. Caress her gorgeous curves. Taste the slick flesh between her thighs. Now. This instant. Before Evelyn pushed him over the edge of reason, and he lost what little remained of his mind.

Chapter Nineteen

Flat on her back beneath Venom, Evelyn tried to catch her breath. Great idea. Perfect in theory. Totally impossible to pull off. Determined to drive her wild, Venom controlled her completely. Rough hands pinned her to the couch. Strong thighs spread her legs. His dominant nature made her pant as thick cushions gave beneath her, bowing in deference, obeying his command, keeping her comfortable in the face of his strength. The rough press of his body should've scared her. Maybe even backed her up a step. Started her thinking about self-preservation and possible exit routes.

Excitement flooded her instead.

Hmm, he was gorgeous. So strong. Beyond beautiful as he unraveled a thread at a time—for her . . . because of her—a lethal Dragonkind guy on the verge of losing control. She saw it in his eyes. Felt it in the wildness of each caress. Read it in the way he moved—his singular focus driven by ravenous need. Reason enough to call it a night and race for safer ground. Undulating beneath him, Evelyn purred his name instead, egging him on, showing him her need . . .

Fueling his desire one breathy whisper at a time.

He snarled at her. Shimmering ruby eyes met hers. He shoved her skirt up. The sheath dress slid on her skin. Excitement erupted into anticipation. Her nipples tightened in reaction, begging to be sucked and . . . oh God. She could hardly wait to have him inside her. He was going to feel so good. Ride her hard. Treat her well. Show no mercy while he made her burn and beg and . . . come so hard she screamed in bliss.

Shameful, really. Not that she cared how it sounded.

Desire didn't negotiate. And need was a double-edged sword. Beautiful one minute, a ravenous beast the next. And yes, she needed him that way. No holds barred. No regrets or looking back. Just skin on skin, and glory upon glory.

Fighting the lockdown, Evelyn surged beneath him. Venom cursed, but loosened his grip, allowing her some leeway. She took every bit, pushed her hands into his hair, and licked into his mouth. Pressing her down, he deepened the kiss, delivering his taste with a delicious stroke. Pleasure shivered through her. Desire grabbed hold. Whimpering in desperation, she begged him for more. He tangled their tongues, blowing her mind, lashing her with delight before lifting his head.

His mouth left hers.

She keened in protest.

He bared his teeth and held her gaze. A warning flashed in his eyes. Evelyn got the message—stay still, behave, and . . . get what you want. Breathing hard, she tried to obey, but couldn't keep from moving. Her hips churned, rising off the cushions, setting a rhythm, begging him without words to fulfill her needs. His mouth curved as he shifted forward, thrusting his leg between her thighs, giving her something to ride. She moaned as bliss sparked, spiraling into a powerful wave of sensation.

Watching her move, he fisted his hand in the cushions sitting along the back of the couch. Taut muscle flexed. He flung his arm out and let go. Plump pillows flew over the coffee table and across the living room. The roll of her hips slowed. Her breath caught, stalling in her lungs as each one hit the far wall with a thud, then slid, falling to the floor.

"Eyes on me, Evelyn."

The low growl snapped her attention back to him.

Planting one hand beside her ear, he fisted the other in her skirt. "Lift up."

Glory, glory, hallelujah. Thank God. Time to get naked. "Rip it."

Her throaty request rose in the quiet. He paused and glanced at her, surprise in his eyes. It didn't last long. Arousal hit full force. Venom's nostrils flared, and she got ready. Oh, yeah. Here it came. The moment of truth, his strength about to be unleashed. Caressing the back of her calf, he stared at the hem of her dress. Shifting on soft cushions, Evelyn tilted her hips and spread her thighs, giving him a glimpse of what lay beneath off-white silk. His breath hitched. She hummed in satisfaction, knowing what he was seeing.

Pink lace panties, wet with arousal.

Wonder on his face, he reached out. His hand slid between her thighs. A gentle caress across the damp lace. A maddening caress over her mound, then lower where she needed him most. Gaze on his hand, he traced the frilly trim. Evelyn held her breath and stayed stock-still, hoping, praying, ready to beg for the pleasure of his touch. Her muscles quivered. Please . . . please . . . *please—touch me.* The chant throbbed inside her head. Over and over. Again and again. With a groan, Venom obeyed and slid beneath the edge of her panties. He stroked in. She arched up, moaning as he caressed her folds with a fingertip.

Rapture threatened. Her body clenched, demanding release.

"Hmm, *mazleiha*." Fingers sliding in her slickness, he drew a deep breath. "You're so soft. So slick. Beautiful."

"Venom, please—*please*, rip it. Get it off me," she said, silk feeling like sandpaper against her skin. He delved deeper between her thighs. His thumb brushed the top of her sex. Once. Twice. A third time, making her pulse deep inside. "Oh God, please. I want to be naked with you."

He stroked her again, then retreated. Gaze riveted to hers, he raised his hand. His tongue flicked out. The pink flash held her prisoner, shackling her in surprise as Venom licked his fingertips. He hummed in delight, the sound so naughty Evelyn forgot about her clothes and, unable to look away, watched him suck her cream from his skin.

"So good," he murmured. "You taste like peaches."

Overwhelmed by him, Evelyn quivered in response.

Dark and unreadable, his gaze roamed her a second before he slid his hand beneath her bottom. He lifted. She complied, raising her hips, holding still, waiting for him to rip the dress in half. A hard yank would do it—split the center seam, shred the silk, leaving her half-naked beneath him.

"Just tear it."

"No, I like this dress. I'm going to make you wear it again sometime. Bend you over. Take you from behind. Stroke deep while silk slides across your skin."

His words made her shiver. The promise in his tone made her moan.

Doing as he pleased, he pushed the dress up her torso. The hem caught on the undersides of her breasts. She raised her arms. He tugged, pulling the dress over her head. Cold air caressed her skin, making her sigh in relief. Venom froze, going stone-still above her. Satisfaction soared, and Evelyn swallowed a laugh. God, that felt good. His reaction soothed her impatience. Waiting had been worth it. She knew what he'd expected—a pink bra, one to match her racy panties.

What he got sucked the air out of his chest.

Bare breasts instead of frilly lace. Soft skin and tightly furled nipples.

"Oh Jesus."

"Surprise," she whispered.

Venom didn't bother to answer. He dipped his head instead. Fine by her. She'd rather have his—

He licked her nipple.

"Oh, yes—finally."

"Impatient."

"Yes." Definitely. Without a doubt. She wanted him inside her. Right now.

Venom flicked her again, bathing her in bliss. "Wait a little longer."

"No."

He smiled against her breast. Nipping the tip, he settled in and suckled hard, rolling tender flesh against his tongue. She arched as he shifted alongside her, trapping her between the couch back and him. Exposed. On display. Bared to him, she gasped as he tongued her other nipple. Watching her reaction, he sucked softly and, holding her still with one hand, sent the other exploring. Calloused and hot, his palm skimmed her skin, stroked over her hip, then across her belly, raising goose bumps, drawing out bliss, driving her mad with desire until—

His hand pushed beneath her panties.

A gentle tug on lace. An even slower draw down her thighs, and he stripped her bare, leaving her naked in his arms while he remained fully clothed.

Lifting his mouth from her breast, Venom slipped his hand between her thighs. His fingers pushed into her folds. He stroked deep. Bowed in supplication, begging for release, she rose on a pulse of ecstasy. Her hands slid into his hair. Her lips brushed against his. A little sip. A gentle nip. She purred and, lips parted, offered him her mouth. Playing in her heat, he hovered a breath away, watching her as he slid his finger inside her. She gasped in delight, tightening around him. Pushing deep, Venom upped the pace, testing her tension, stretching her with each thrust, preparing her for his possession.

"That's it, *mazleiha*. Ride my fingers," he whispered against her mouth, thumb circling her clitoris, feeding her bliss one hand pump at a time. "You're so tight, Evie. Open up. Let me in."

"Please," she rasped, delight hovering a breath away. "I'm so ready for you."

"Right now?"

"This second."

"Clothes on or off?"

"Off."

"As you wish," he murmured.

His clothes disappeared, leaving him naked against her. Golden skin and thick muscle surrounded her. Her mouth fell open. Evelyn sucked in a startled breath. Holy God. What the hell had just happened? How had he done that? Dressed one second, naked the next. Weird. Crazy. Incredible in a way that—

Venom stroked her again.

Surprise fell away, dying in the burn of approaching release. She gasped his name. Staring at the dark curls between her thighs, Venom shifted down her body. He pushed her knees up and out, spreading her wider, then settled in-between. His mouth joined his hand. He traced her folds with his tongue. With a shout, Evelyn twisted beneath him. Holding her still, he delved in. Her muscles clenched as he licked deeper, pushing her hard, making her beg and plead beneath him. Shifting focus, he flicked the nub controlling her pleasure. Air stalled in her throat. She lost the ability to breathe. He growled and sucked harder. Rapture bit. She gasped. Her body pulsed, raging into orgasm. Bliss bowed her spine. Ecstasy threw her head back, raised her hips and—

Evelyn screamed as she came.

Lifting his head from between her thighs, Venom rose above her. The tip of his shaft nudged her core. He surged forward, possessing her in one thrust. She clenched around him. He snarled in answer and showed no mercy. Spine flexing, he rocked her hard. Made her his. Stretched her wide. Filled her full as he drove her toward another climax. Helpless in the heated rush, Evelyn wrapped her legs around his hips and held on. God. Finally. At last. She had him deep. Was being worked hard and ridden fast. Just what she wanted from him. Better than she imagined. Everything she needed wrapped up in one man.

Possession. Surrender. Passion-fueled oblivion without end.

Tensing against her, Venom shouted and throbbed, coming deep inside her. An answering pulse picked her up, threw her high, rushing her over the edge and into rapture a second time. She went weightless in her own skin, falling fast, skipping across time and space like a shooting star. But as Venom relaxed—warm and trusting in her arms—emotion welled, making her chest go tight and her heart feel too full. Powerful truths spilled into the open. Profound happiness. An undeniable sense of belonging. Bright and shiny hope as Venom sighed her name and held her close. Unbelievable tenderness. Dangerous connection. Devastation in full effect. And yet, Evelyn ignored the danger and nestled in, risking her heart by hugging him back.

Foolish, perhaps. Reckless, without a doubt.

The purest thing she'd ever felt.

Forget the damage. The danger too. It might not be wise, but she refused to shove Venom away. Or shut him out. She might not be his forever, but Venom was hers for the moment. Hers to hold. Hers to treasure. Hers to remember when the situation turned and life forced her to let him go. Good. Bad. Neither applied anymore. Making love with him had driven the truth home. She loved the way he made her feel—bold, beautiful, strong, more like herself than she had in months. Which meant serious trouble, and that she was done. Cooked. Invested now, and, wise or not, she planned to enjoy Venom for as long as fate allowed and her time with him lasted.

Sitting next to Evelyn at the kitchen island, Venom watched her slather peanut butter across the top of a soda cracker. The smell of nutty goodness made his mouth water. The sight of her dressed in his clothes made his body burn. Hmm, she was incredible. A goddess in baggy sweatpants and an oversize tee. So goddamn beautiful with her messed-up hair and nonchalant attitude, she slipped past his guard and stole his heart without even trying. Strange, really—to become so attached to someone after such a short time.

A welcome realization in some ways. Startling in others. Scary as hell too.

He'd never felt this way about anyone. Not even the other Nightfury warriors, all of whom he loved without hesitation. Evelyn, though, elevated his game. She fell into a different category. What he felt for his female—the depth of his need for her—crossed emotional boundaries, surpassed normal, ass-planting him in no-man's-land. Foreign territory for him. Now he didn't know what to do. Or how to act. What to say escaped him too.

He wanted to tell her what was happening and how energy-fuse worked. About the bond connecting her to him and what it meant. Lovely goal. The right thing to do. Too bad he kept clamming up. Every time he opened his mouth, something other than "We're mated for life. I'm keeping you forever" came out. Granted, what information he'd shared with her—after carrying her from the living room to his bedroom, after making love to her so many times he lost count, and lying curled around her in the aftermath—was all good. Important stuff. All things she needed to know to navigate his world. How Dragonkind functioned. About the Nightfury pack and the males he called brothers. What living at Black Diamond was like and how Daimler kept the peace in a houseful of volatile personalities.

Somehow, though, it wasn't enough.

Piling small truths—one on top of the other—to avoid telling her the bigger one smacked of cowardice. The thought left a bad taste in his mouth. Leaning his forearms on the countertop, he watched Evelyn prepare another cracker. Venom clenched his teeth. He didn't like being afraid. Or thinking that she'd leave the moment she found out. And yet, that's exactly what he imagined she would do. Freak out. Run scared. Leave him before he got the chance to put things in perspective and convince her of his worth.

An irrational fear? Maybe. Maybe not. All Venom knew was that he didn't want it to end. He wanted more time with her. More of her sass. More of the smile. More of everything and then more after that. To hear her laugh and give him attitude for as long as possible. So he stayed quiet, heart pounding and body tight, and watched her eat instead of starting the conversation. A total pansy-ass move. Particularly since his inability to come clean shamed him. It was sad, really. But not knowing, living with the tension and uncertainty—horrible as it felt—seemed better than knowing for sure and losing her forever.

With a hum, Evelyn licked peanut butter off her fingertip.

An image of her *licking* him slammed into his head. Venom bit down on a groan. Holy shit. She was hot. Unbelievably sexy, and he couldn't get enough. Or forget the way she'd looked in bed earlier. Nipples furled tight. Head thrown back. Spine arched as she rode him into ecstasy on cotton sheets. Skimming her face, Venom absorbed every detail. Each nuance of her expression. The hidden depths in her eyes. The hard-core intelligence she possessed, but never flaunted.

God, that drove him wild—the way she looked when she put her brain to work. Smart and sexy, an attractive combination. One that shoved him closer to the edge, making desire rush back into view. Muscles tightened across his abdomen, pulling at his hip bones, and temptation circled, urging him to toss decency aside and drag her back to bed.

Fantastic idea. One huge problem.

He didn't have enough time.

With night falling, duty called. Now he needed to put himself in gear and get outside before—

"You asked about my ring earlier."

Surprised by the comment, his gaze strayed to the ring on her middle finger. Set in an intricate pattern, a trio of rubies winked beneath the kitchen lights. "You didn't want to talk about it."

"I rarely do," she said, setting the knife down next to the jar of peanut butter. Metal clicked against marble countertop. Head bowed, she fiddled with the gold band, spinning it around her finger. The third time around, she paused to run her thumb over the gemstones, then looked up and met his gaze. "Good memories tangled up with bad."

He could understand that. Hell, he lived the same thing day in and day out—pride for his roots ruined by horrible memories of his father. "More good than bad, I hope."

"Depends on the day," she said, self-mockery in her tone. "Sometimes I remember the good. Most of the time I remember the bad."

"You should probably turn that around—do the opposite."

"Probably." Pursing her lips, she turned the ring. Antique gold flashed against her dark skin. One rotation spun into another. She fisted her hand, tucking the rubies against her palm, and frowned at her knuckles. A furrow between her brows, she flexed her fingers and shook her head. "The ring's a family heirloom. It's been passed down for generations, mother to daughter. I'm the fourth to wear it . . . including my mom."

"It became yours after the accident?"

"No. I've had it for years. Mema gave it to me when I graduated."

"A good memory."

"The best. Now, here's the bad." With a tug, she pulled the ring off her finger and handed it to him. Warm from her skin, the delicate band settled in his palm. "When I was eleven, my mother did the unthinkable."

"What's that?" Perched between his fingertips, he examined the setting more closely. Stellar workmanship. An incomparable piece—pretty, expensive, just the right size for Evelyn's hand.

"She pawned it."

Venom hummed in sympathy. "She needed the money?"

"Yeah. My dad had a great job, but that wasn't enough for her. She always wanted more, and well . . ." she trailed off with a shrug, her eyes glued to her ring and his hand. "An addict knows no shame."

"What was she into—drugs?"

"Gambling . . . the compulsive kind." She held out her hand, palm up . . . the gesture saying "Give it back, please."

He complied without hesitation. His fingers slid against hers as he turned her hand over. She clutched at him, holding on hard, not wanting to let go, and Venom understood. Talking about her mother was difficult for her. No doubt one of the hardest things for her to reveal. Particularly since she believed it signaled weakness—a flaw in her DNA, the genetic equivalent of a ticking time bomb. He could tell by her tension. The wariness in her eyes too—as though she feared her confession would push him away. Make him judge and find her lacking.

"Evie," he murmured, wanting her to understand. Nothing about her—good, bad, or ugly—could turn him away. Running his thumb over the points of her knuckles, he slipped the ring back on her finger. "You don't have to—"

"You know the funny thing, though?"

Chest so tight his heart hurt, he shook his head.

"Of all my childhood memories, that one's the sharpest." Clinging to his hand, she drew a circle in the center of his palm with her fingertip. Pinpricks exploded up his arms, making him shiver even as she cleared her throat. "I remember everything about that day—getting in the car with my grandmother, driving down to the pawn shop, the musty smell inside the store. The look of relief on Mema's face when she got the ring back, and my mother's irreverence." Moisture made her eyes glisten. Blinking away tears, she stared at the ring. "She didn't care that she'd sold a piece of our history. All she wanted was her next fix and yet . . . I loved her anyway. I don't know what that makes me—a fool, probably, but I can't seem to help it."

"You're not a fool, Evie. Loving her makes you normal."

"Normal," she whispered. "Right. I haven't felt *normal* since the fifth grade . . . since the moment Mom left."

"I'm so sorry, *mazleiha*."

"It is what it is. Even though it still hurts, I've come to terms with it." Dragging her focus from their hands, she met his gaze. "I'm the reason she's dead, you know."

He frowned. "I don't believe that."

"Believe it," she said, her grip on him tightening. "It's my fault. After my dad died, the life insurance settlement came to me." She huffed, half sorrow, half resignation. "Lord knows he couldn't trust Mom with it. Not with her addiction and all the money problems. After the dust settled, Mom banged on my door. She was sweet as pie at first, but when I refused to give her the money—"

"You fought."

"A real knock-down, drag-out. She said terrible things, Venom. Screamed the most horrible things, but I just . . ." Her voice cracked, breaking his heart. "I couldn't go against Dad's wishes."

"What happened?"

"I bought Mema a house in Granite Falls with the money. My mother retaliated by driving her car into a tree."

"Jesus."

"Exactly," she whispered, looking so lost he ached for her. A tear slipped down her cheek. He brushed it away, cupping her face, soothing her the best he could. Leaning toward him instead of away, she accepted his touch and blew out a shaky breath. "Lovely family history, don't you think?"

"Mine's no better."

"It can't be any worse."

"It is," he said, thumb tracing her cheekbone, debating how much to tell her. Everything down to the last detail? Only a smattering of the facts? The truth held the power to push her away. A single moment in time, and he might lose her forever. And yet, he wanted to believe. Needed to hope that Evelyn would accept him—no matter what. A lot to ask? Maybe, but knowing her past gave him hope for their future. His female understood struggle—the mind-twist of screwed-up family dynamics and what it was like to have a parent who didn't love you. He stroked her again, drawing as much comfort from her closeness as she did from his touch. "You may believe you're responsible for your mother's death, but I know I killed my father."

"What are you saying?"

"I killed him, Evie. His blood is on my hands."

"There's more to it than that." Confusion in her eyes, she tipped her chin, inviting him to talk. "Tell me what happened."

Dropping his hand, he let her go and leaned away, settling back on his own stool.

"Venom?"

"It's complicated," he murmured, searching for the right words.

Speechlessness.

Venom blew out a strained breath. A forever affliction around her, it seemed. A throwback reaction from his upbringing, maybe. The fear of losing her—certainly. The inability to trust without the assurance of complete acceptance first—absolutely. And yet, he knew he needed to tell her. Before he explained about energy-fuse. Before he crossed the line, and she agreed to be his without knowing the whole truth.

And so he did what he'd never done before. He started to talk, spilling secrets, sharing intimate details, telling her about his father. And Evelyn listened without interrupting. All the while holding his hand. Under normal circumstances, he would've scoffed, said to hell with comfort, and played the tough card. He couldn't with her. She tore down his walls without even trying. So instead of hiding behind humor—his weapon of choice when dealing with difficult issues—Venom told her the truth.

"He hurt you."

"All the time. Every day."

"And that night . . ." she trailed off, prompting him.

He drew a deep breath. "He took me to our country estate. It was way out of town, in the middle of nowhere . . . a party was in full swing."

He shook his head, not wanting to remember the orgy. Or the fight club set up in the back garden. It had been awful. A terrible thing to witness. And his sire? The sadistic bastard had been proud—of the outrageous depravity and orchestrated butchery. But worse? He'd expected Venom to jump in and take part. Bet on the fights. Drink himself into oblivion. Revel in debauchery while younglings fought and died.

Bile rolled up the back of his throat.

An image flashed in his mind's eye, taking him back to that night.

Boys—eight, maybe nine years old—locked in combat, knives raised, circling onstage while elite members of Dragonkind looked on. The smell of blood and urine in the air. The smile on his sire's face. Venom grimaced. Even now, all these years later, he couldn't shake his disgust. Couldn't forget what his sire ordered him to do at the end of the night either.

Load a dying Wick onto a truck bound for Tanzenmed.

"That was the last straw," he said, trying to find the words and make Evelyn understand. Maybe if he confessed, said it all out loud, got it out once and for all, he would feel better. Maybe then the shame would fade and his guilt would go away. "I looked at Wick locked inside that cage and saw myself—all the years of abuse and torture. All the unfairness. How wrong my sire was and—"

"You refused to do it," she whispered, shifting on her stool. Her knee brushed his as she settled sideways in her seat. Raising her hand, she brushed the long strands of his hair away from his temple. "What did he do?"

"Hit me . . . per usual. But this time, I got angry back." Unable to look her in the eye, he glanced away. Overhead halogens glowed, throwing light over high-gloss cabinets. Frowning at the fancy cornices, he clenched his teeth. "I'd just gone through the *change*, and through some quirk of fate, I came through my first shift bigger and stronger than my sire. So when he raised his fist again, I shoved him." How many times? Venom didn't know. His sire never backed down—or cried defeat. His pride had been too thick. And after years of having the upper hand, the bastard hadn't been able to accept that his son not only outweighed him, but could beat him in a fight too. "He wouldn't stop. Just wouldn't, and I . . . God, Evie. I don't know how many times he came after me. Or how many times I hit him, but when it was over, he was impaled on a spear and I had blood all over me."

"Oh, Venom."

"I know." He shook his head. "I didn't mean to shove him that hard. I didn't know the weapons were there, but it doesn't make me any less responsible."

"It doesn't make you guilty either."

Venom flinched as surprise slammed through him. He opened his mouth to retort. To tell her she was wrong. That he was to blame. Shock closed his throat instead as his gaze snapped back to hers.

"Sounds to me like it was you or him. Self-defense, not murder," she said, tone soft, yet somehow firm too. Not understanding, Venom stared at her. She gazed back, holding the line, refusing to back down, pushing her assertion. Eyes full of compassion met and held his, making his throat go tight. "You did what you had to do to protect yourself, Venom. And you got Wick out too . . . shielded him when no one else could."

"Yeah." He frowned. True enough, although all in a fit of blind panic. The second his sire died, he'd known he would be next if the Archguard managed to pin the murder on him. So instead of taking his father's place among Dragonkind elite, he'd torn the collar from Wick's neck, dragged him out of the cage, and run for his life . . . with his future best friend in tow. "We hid out in Europe for a while until good luck hooked us up with Bastian and Rikar. After that, we jumped the pond and came to Seattle."

"Hunting for Ivar and the Razorbacks."

Venom nodded.

"But the fight with your father still bothers you."

"Every day."

"Don't let it, Venom." Cupping his jaw with one hand, she sent the other skating over his shoulder. The gentle caress reached soul-deep, unraveling his tension one thread at a time. "I know it's hard, but I want you to do something for me."

"What?"

"Accept what you did was necessary and move past it."

"I don't know how."

"Practice makes perfect. Take it one day at a time, and it'll come," she said. "If you let it, peace will come."

Maybe. Maybe not. But for Evelyn, he would try. Hope like hell he could leave the past behind. Let it go. Start fresh. *Move past it* into healthier territory, just as she asked. All while praying that the day didn't bring new nightmares, the night any more recriminations, and his female stayed with him—forever.

Before sharing his sin, he hadn't been sure of his chances. Evelyn was a strong female. Smart. Self-assured. More than capable of taking care of herself and returning to the human world on her own. Now, though, with her so close, nothing but understanding in her eyes, he held a glimmer of hope. Maybe he wasn't giving her enough credit. Perhaps all she needed was a gentle push. More information. More conversation. More openness on his part to help her accept his claiming and—

A car door slammed outside in the driveway.

Venom clenched his teeth. Well, shit. Talk about bad timing. No more baring of souls tonight. The cavalry had just arrived. So . . . time to shift gears and get a move on.

"Hey, Evie?"

"Yeah?"

"Thanks."

"For what?"

"Being so incredible," he murmured, taut muscle loosening as he let the last of his tension go. "You're amazing . . . you know that, right?"

"Princess Awesome, that's me," she said, pure imp as she lightened the mood. He grinned. She picked up the abandoned butter knife, grabbed a cracker, then dug more peanut butter out of the jar. Plopping it on the saltine, she spread it across the top, then glanced his way. Her eyes met his. Desire shoved thoughts of his past out of the way. His body went haywire, twitching with the need to make love to her. Reading his expression, she blinked in surprise a second before her mouth curved. "You're thinking naughty thoughts again, Venom."

"Your fault."

"Sure it is." The devil in her eyes, she raised a brow. "I think you're just horny."

More sass. How perfect. "And you aren't?"

"Maybe."

"Minx." She huffed in laughter. One ear on the crunch of footsteps outside in the driveway, Venom pushed away from the countertop. Leather whispered beneath his jeans as he turned on his stool and grabbed the base of hers. Forearm bunching, he tugged. Metal feet scraped across floor tiles, sounding loud in the quiet as he pulled her between the spread of his thighs. The side of her stool touched his. She swayed toward him, bumping into the wall of his chest. Dipping his head, he kissed the curve of her bare shoulder. "Gorgeous female. I want you again."

"Nice. Good answer." Her smile widened into a grin. "More brownie points for you."

His lips twitched.

She leaned toward him. Her mouth brushed his. Once. Twice. A third time before she settled in and kissed him—softly, sweetly, with so much affection his heart went AWOL and he forgot about the male outside. Drawing away, she drew a swirl in peanut butter with the tip of her knife and lifted her hand. He opened his mouth. She fed him the saltine. Kraft's finest hit his taste buds, making him hum in gratitude. Gaze locked on his lips, she watched him chew. And Venom knew what she was thinking. Despite her teasing, she wanted him again too. Was ready to forsake her snack in favor of feasting on him.

A thump drifted into the kitchen. Metal rattled. Hinges hissed as the door from the garage into the house opened.

The sound made Evelyn jump. "Did you hear that?"

"Relax, *mazleiha*." Brushing her hair aside, he cupped the side of her throat. A gentle tug turned her back toward him. His thumb drifted, brushing over her pulse point. "It's just Daimler."

"Right," she muttered, her focus split—half on him, half on the corridor. "Ever notice that when you use the word *just*, I get blindsided?"

"Like when?"

"Like when you kidnapped me at the hospital—"

"Rescued, you mean."

She ignored his interruption and sailed on. "And that crazy-looking black dragon was sitting on the roof glaring at me."

"Wick wasn't glaring at you."

"Total evil eye. He gave me one," she said, treating him to a you-bet-your-ass-he-did look. "I saw it."

"When—before or after you freaked out?"

"Oh, shut up. My screaming was totally justified."

He chuckled, enjoying her tart tone. Big surprise there. He adored everything about her—attitude included.

Her eyes narrowed on him. She pointed the knife at his nose. "Listen, mister, I—"

"Hello!" Full of pep, Daimler's shout drifted down the hall. "Anybody home?"

"In here," Venom said.

The quiet click of a closing door drifted into the kitchen. Plastic rustled. Paper crinkled. Quiet footfalls sounded a second later, rushing the Numbai out of the corridor and around the corner. Eyes bright, elfin ears peeking through his dark hair, and loaded down with shopping bags, Daimler slid to a stop. His gaze landed on Venom, then bounced over to Evelyn. Taking in the cozy arrangement—the fact she nearly sat in his lap—he smiled, gold front tooth winking in the low light.

Venom tipped his chin. "Thanks for coming."

"Of course, Master Venom. I am delighted to be here." With a happy hop, Daimler stepped up to the island and set the bags on the marble countertop. A pleased look on his face, he met and held Evelyn's gaze. "And you must be Evelyn. I am so very pleased to meet you, my lady."

Evelyn blinked. "My lady?"

"Go with it." Taking her hand, Venom pushed off his stool and stood. Lacing his fingers with hers, he tugged Evelyn off her seat. Her palm sliding against his, she tucked in, standing so close pleasure erupted in a wave of glory, glory, hallelujah. Venom shut it down, forcing his body to cool and his mind to work as she raised a brow in question. He shrugged. "It's just easier to go along."

"There you go again . . . using the word *just*," she said, tone hushed before smiling at the newcomer. "It's great to meet you too, Daimler. Venom's told me so much about you."

Not an exaggeration. He'd extolled the Numbai's virtues. Told Evelyn all about his wizard-like culinary skills. Daimler's wicked triple-decker to-die-for chocolate cake too.

"Oh, good, then there is no need for me to explain." Popping up on his toes, Daimler hunted through the collection of bags. Paper rasped against plastic, shuffling into each other across the countertop. With a soft *a-ha*, he grabbed one with "Macy's" printed on the side. "I brought you a gift."

Evelyn sucked in a breath. "Clothes?"

Daimler nodded. "Running shoes too."

"Bless you," she said. "Venom's right. You're the best, Daimler."

Clasping his hands in front of his chest, the Numbai blushed.

Gaze on the bag, she shook free of Venom's hand. The loss made his chest go tight. He let her go anyway, mourning the distance as he watched Evelyn step around the edge of the island. Thanking Daimler again, she accepted the shopping bag full of goodies. Handles hanging from her fingertips, she glanced over her shoulder and smiled at him. "I'm going to have a shower. Wanna come?"

Venom blinked. Muscles roping his abdomen clenched and . . . oh, baby. Talk about a double entendre. His stomach flip-flopped, somersaulting into a quadruple backflip. *Wanna come*, indeed. He bit down on a laugh. Little minx. Gorgeous tease. Of course he wanted to come—in the shower or anywhere else she asked him to please her.

Too bad he couldn't. Not right now.

No matter how much he longed to love her again, he needed to go. His brothers-in-arms awaited his call. Were already in the air and headed his way. Fine-tuning his sonar, he reached out with his mind. A soft buzz swirled against his temples as his dragon half rose. Six males. Five miles out. And closing fast. Venom glanced over his shoulder. His gaze skimmed the living room, over the couch and a pair of armchairs to reach the wide bank of windows along the back wall. Magic rippled across glass, individual panes moving from opaque to clear in the moonlight. Which made it official. Dusk had fallen, and now duty called. Granite Falls wouldn't wait much longer, never mind another night. Neither would the humans who called the small town home.

Which meant playtime was over. At least, for the moment.

"Evie."

Reacting to his serious tone, she turned toward him. Intuition sparked in her eyes, downgrading the pleasure of Daimler's gift. "What's wrong?"

"Come here for a second."

With a whispered "Excuse me" to Daimler, Evelyn skirted the kitchen island. Sidestepping one of the stools, she stopped in front of him. "You're leaving, aren't you?"

"For a little while."

"How long will you be gone?"

"A few hours. Maybe more, but I'll be back before dawn."

She frowned. "That's why you called Daimler, isn't it—to keep me company?"

"I didn't want you to be alone in the house."

"I could come with—"

"No, *mazleiha*, you can't." He shook his head, backing up the words with action. Super-strong immune system or not, he didn't want her anywhere near Granite Falls. Jesus. Just the thought sent him into a tailspin. "I need you to stay here. Inside the house with Daimler. Don't go outside. I'll come back as fast as I can."

"But—"

"Promise me, Evie."

Worry in her eyes, she stared at him. "What aren't you telling me?"

"It's nothing serious," he said, lying through his teeth. Tell her . . . *tell her* about energy-fuse. He'd revealed so much already, trusting her with a secret only Wick knew. Still, the words refused to trip off his tongue even as honor urged him to be honest. Down and dirty. Quick and clean. The truth tied up in a neat little bow. Venom cleared his throat. He opened his mouth. Nothing came out. Goddamn it, he was pathetic. In need of a good ass-kicking or something. A boot to the balls. A fist to the head. The method didn't matter just as long as it allowed him to move forward. Away from the fear of her rejection. "Really, it isn't, but I've still got to go."

Her brow furrowed. "Why are you lying to me?"

"I'm not."

"You're asking me to take a lot on faith, Venom." Raising her hand, she stroked a finger along his jaw. "To trust you without proof or knowing why."

"I know."

"A tall order."

"It is, but . . ." He trailed off, struggling to find the right words. Again. Like always, but like it or not, he needed her to stay put until he got home. Her safety wasn't optional. It qualified as a must. Especially now that Ivar knew her name. The rogues weren't stupid. Masters of technology, the bastards pulled intel off the Internet in the same way Sloan mined human databases. Personal information—address, job history, friends, bank account numbers—ranked as important when hunting prey. Which meant his enemy would already be tracking her credit cards, looking for patterns and preferences in the hopes of finding her favorite haunts. "Do this for me, Evie. Stay here. It's not safe for you in the city after dark."

Chewing on the inside of her lip, Evelyn held his gaze. One second ticked into more. Silence spun into tension. Venom stayed quiet, forcing himself to be patient, waiting her out, praying she fell in line.

After what felt like forever, she blew out a breath. "Okay. I'll stay here . . . on one condition."

Relief hit him like a wrecking ball. "Name it."

"When you get back, you tell me what's bothering you. No pussyfooting around."

"Deal." Thank God. He'd just bought more time. Enough maybe to find a way to explain without freaking her out. "We'll talk when I get home."

"And you'll be honest." Dark eyes narrowed, she leveled him with a no-nonsense look. "One hundred percent straight with me."

Venom nodded. "About everything."

"All right, then go," she said. "Daimler and I—"

"Will bake cookies!" The excited chirp echoed across the kitchen. A thunk followed as Daimler set a mixing bowl in the center of the island. "Maybe watch some movies too."

Laughter chased the worry from Evelyn's eyes. "Kind of like a slumber party."

"Exactly! Now . . ." With a jubilant hop, Daimler disappeared behind the mound of grocery bags. Cupboard doors banged. Metal rattled against metal. A second later, he popped back into view with an armful of baking trays. Setting them down with a bang, he waved a hand, flicking his fingers at them. "Kiss Master

Venom good-bye, my lady, then sit down. I will make tea and we'll talk."

"No chance of that." Holding her hand up to keep Venom at bay, she took a step back. And then another, punishing him with distance. "No kissing until I have the whole truth."

"Shit," he grumbled. "Unfair, Evie."

"Within bounds, Venom."

"Fair warning then, love," he said, picking up the gauntlet she threw down. "I'll make you pay for it later."

"You've got to come back to do that."

The provocation cranked him tight.

Venom growled. She held her ground, crossing arms over her chest. Well, all right then. His female refused to back down, and he wasn't going to get his good-bye kiss. A frigging pity. A total kick in the pants, but . . .

No sense pushing the issue now.

She was entrenched and ready for a fight. One Venom knew he couldn't win. Not right now. Not without a winning approach and the right words. Frustration grabbed hold. Blowing out a breath, Venom tore his gaze from hers and, with a quick pivot, headed for the door. Pace steady, boots thumping, and mind churning, he strode across the living room.

Seconds before he reached the door, Venom glanced over his shoulder. "Prepare for the fallout, *mazleiha*. There's gonna be some when I get home."

She leveled her chin. "Bring it on."

No need to worry. He would. Nothing would keep him away.

The promise of his female's kisses was too much to resist. So was accepting her challenge. No kissing, his ass. No way would she be able to hold out. Which meant the game was now afoot. And he planned to come out on top—literally, by spreading her beneath him before he told her the truth. Just to make a point.

Stubborn, maybe, but well . . . hell. He didn't like manipulation of any kind. So yeah, *bring it on*. Let her try to hold out. Let her use desire like a weapon. Let her believe she would win in the end.

Venom clenched his teeth, then shook his head. Her strategy wouldn't work. With a mental flick, he turned the handle, flung the door open, and stepped out into cold night air. And she wouldn't last long once he started the seduction. The thought energized him. Venom upped the pace, making tracks beneath huge trees to reach open lawn. More space made for a better launchpad, and he needed to get airborne. Must meet the others. Do his job—quick, neat, and clean, 'cause . . . yeah. No question. The sooner he killed the contagion in Granite Falls, the faster he'd be on his way home to prove his female wrong.

Chapter Twenty

Stretched out on the floor, Gage struggled to wake up. He told his body to move. His muscles disobeyed, brushing off the direct order. Sticky cobwebs held him down instead, pressing him back toward slumber. Now he lay captive, suspended between layers, one level up from dreams, one down from wakefulness. Struggling against the muscle drag, he forced his eyes open. Soft light whirled into pinpricks of mind-spinning blur. He blinked, hoping to stop the light show. Nothing. A total no-go. No improvement at all. No matter how many times he reached for clarity, the druglike feeling refused to abate.

With a grumble, he allowed his eyes to drift closed again.

Fuck. Not good. He was way too groggy. Completely off his game, stuck in the hazy layers of sleep instead of alert and ready to fight. Unusual for him. Gage grimaced. Most evenings, he surfaced fast, bolted out of bed, feet hitting the floor before his brain acclimatized to his body being upright. Which pointed to one inescapable fact. His sluggish reaction signaled trouble. The kind he didn't want to be anywhere near. Something was off. Screwed up in a big way, but—he frowned—damned if he could touch on the problem.

Or figure out if there even was one to begin with.

He didn't feel threatened. Wasn't shackled or tied down. No buzz of electricity surrounding him either. Just a steady sway and an odd vibration that rocked the floor beneath him. Dragging his hands off his chest, he pressed both palms to the floor. Solid. Soft. A carpet, maybe? Muscles squawking, body throbbing, he explored further, stretching his arm out to—

A big hand landed on his shoulder.

Instinct grabbed hold, pumping him full of adrenaline. With a snarl, Gage jacked upright. His head brushed a low ceiling. His feet thumped down on the floor. Vision a mess, seeing nothing but blur, he raised his fists and spun around.

The fuzzy outline of a male stood behind him.

Gage bared his teeth.

Raising his arms to the sides, the guy turned his hands palm up. "Easy. It's just me."

Swaying on his feet, Gage blinked. "Haider?"

"Yeah."

"What the hell?" Frowning, Gage rubbed his eyes. His vision cleared a little, giving him a quick snapshot. A familiar silver gaze met his. Relief hit him like a body shot, making him sag and reach out. His friend grabbed hold, keeping him upright. "Where are we?"

"On the plane."

Hanging on to Haider like a lifeline, Gage blinked again and looked around. Narrow space. Rounded roof. Oval windows with the shades pulled down. Comfortable wide-backed chairs and a long couch hugging the curved wall on the far end. "Holy fuck. We made it."

"Thanks to you." Supporting his weight, Haider shifted, turning him toward one of the chairs. Gage sank into the leather seat back with a grateful sigh. "You got us to the airplane hangar in daylight—crazy son of a bitch."

He snorted. Some things never changed. Most notably? His friend's bad attitude. Mouthy male. Honest to a fault, Haider never pulled any punches. He struck fast and hard instead. Called it like he saw it too, hammering him with so much truth Gage didn't want to hear it half the time. Thank God. He loved that about his friend. Never say quit equaled big fun on the fighting scale.

Leaning his head against his backrest, Gage grinned.

Haider smiled back.

Stretching out his legs, he tipped his chin. "Where are we?"

"An hour from home."

Which meant they'd just crossed the border into Washington State. Perfect. Less than two hundred miles away from Black Diamond. "Shit, I've been asleep awhile."

"You've been pretty out of it. You were in Connecticut too."

Gage exhaled in surprise. "We landed in Connecticut?"

"In Hartford to refuel," Haider said, settling into his own seat. "And feed."

Brows drawn tight, Gage racked his brain, trying to remember. His eyes narrowed. Okay, he remembered the drive after busting out of Rodin's pleasure pavilion. The wheel of the Bentley in his hands, the dust in the rearview mirror, and the pain of sunlight on his skin. Not surprising. That kind of agony was hard to forget. So were multiple injuries thanks to time spent in an Archguard kill room. Funny thing, though. Gage rolled his shoulders. He wasn't in pain now. Exhausted, sure, but not hurting anymore.

Rubbing his jean-clad thigh, he glanced down at his bare chest. No cuts. No burns. Nothing but smooth skin poured over heavy muscle. Another round of relief rolled in. Gage relaxed, letting his tension go. The mental ease-up unlocked his memory. Images streamed into his head. Fuzzy, indistinct, and short of a full load in places, but . . . hmm. He remembered the late-night pit stop now. A crowded bar on a busy street. Beer on tap—three-dollar pitchers, ladies' night out.

"Pretty little barflies."

"Super-fun night." Haider grinned. "You liked the twins." Gage huffed. Made sense. Blonds were his favorite, but a pair at the same time? God. Absolute paradise. Although, the redhead he'd pleased after exhausting the twins hadn't been bad either. Tipping his chin, he met his friend's gaze. "You okay?"

"Right as rain. Ready to go home."

Reaching out, Gage flipped the window shade. Vinyl hissed as the thin covering rolled up to reveal wispy clouds and a clear night sky. "Osgard?"

"Still asleep in the rear cabin. Nian's in the head."

"Well, hell," he said, disappointment in his tone even as he breathed a sigh of relief. The kid had come through okay. Was none the worse for wear. No need to worry. "So much for hoping you'd already thrown the namby-pamby overboard."

"Bastian's call, Gage, so hands off." Amusement sparked in his friend's eyes. "Nian stays alive until B green-lights him."

Oh, man. Pretty please with sugar on top. He wanted the green light. So fucking badly. Something about Nian put a wrinkle in his radar. Now his dragon senses screamed, warning Gage not to trust the aristocratic prick. Too bad Haider was right. Bastian wouldn't bring Nian on board without a good reason. Which meant a great scheme was in the works. Gage knew it. Accepted it even, but that didn't mean he couldn't dream about ass-planting the pansy . . .

Every single day, for the foreseeable future.

A lovely thought. Something to keep him warm during long winter months.

Pushing to his feet, Gage stretched out sore muscles. "Does B know we're an hour out?"

With a nod, Haider popped to his feet. Shoulder to shoulder with him now, boots planted in the narrow aisle, he flicked at the sleeve of his motorcycle jacket and glanced at his watch. "Wake Osgard and get ready. I'll rouse Nian. We bail out in five minutes."

Heading for the sleep cabin, Gage glanced over his shoulder at the cockpit. Door closed. His dragon senses sparked, reading heat signatures through the wall. Two males seated up front. "You in control of the pilots?"

"Yeah." Showing off, Haider leaned left. Magic shimmered in the air around him, making Gage's skin prickle. The plane turned, banking left as the humans in the cockpit obeyed his friend's unspoken command. Shifting again, Haider returned to normal, weight evenly distributed on his tall frame. The plane leveled out, flying fast across clear skies. "You strong enough to fly?"

Gage rolled his shoulders, testing his muscles' responsiveness. Fatigue poked at him. Discomfort followed, streaking down his spine. Shoving it aside, he gave his friend two thumbs up and continued down the aisle. A narrow door stood at the end. Gaze fixed to it, he reached out with his mind. His magic flared. The latch clicked. He shoved the panel to the sleep cabin open and, dipping his head, crossed into the small space.

He scanned the surface of the bed.

Empty. Not a kid in sight.

"Osgard?" Searching for the male, his gaze bounced around the room.

Nothing. No response. Not many spots to hide in the tiny excuse for a bedroom either. A total of two—the narrow cupboards bookending either side of the headboard. Skirting the end of the bed, Gage came around the corner of the mattress and—

Stopped short.

Ah, hell. Not good. Osgard, curled up on the floor, knees tucked against his chest, sleeping in the narrow space between the curved wall and the wooden frame . . . instead of on top of a nice, soft mattress. Gage's chest went tight. He knew what the kid's position meant. Understood what prolonged abuse did to some males. Degraded a kid's worth. Shredded self-esteem. Obliterated trust until suspicion became the norm, instead of the exception. Made him sleep in tight spaces that offered maximum protection and little opportunity for attack.

Goddamn Archguard pricks.

How dare the assholes treat a defenseless kid with such brutality? Gage shook his head. Such senseless violence. A complete tragedy. Absolutely no reason for it. And yet, Osgard's dysfunction stared him in the face. Rage spiked, rolling through him like thunder. Gage stopped the roll, tucked his fury away, and, watching Osgard sleep, made himself a promise. The Archguard would pay for hurting a helpless kid. And Zidane would die. He would make sure of it. But . . .

First things first.

He must get Osgard home. Telling the kid he was safe wouldn't work. Showing him constituted a better plan. Actions spoke louder than words, and seeing was believing. The youngling needed experience—to live with and be accepted by a normal pack—in order to understand the difference between right and wrong. Give him a month or two at Black Diamond, with him and the other Nightfury warriors, and . . . yeah. Gage nodded.

The kid would come around. Eventually.

Hitting his haunches at the end of the bed, he flicked his new ward's foot. The gentle touch jacked Osgard upright. With a yelp, he scrambled backward. His back slammed into the cupboard door. Gage didn't move. He stayed still instead, his body language nonthreatening. His intent spilled into the cabin, his message clear—*trust me, I mean no harm.* Chest heaving, eyes round with terror, the kid stared at him. One minute stretched into another. Gage waited. Slow but sure, Osgard calmed down, ragged breaths leveling out until he relaxed, releasing his death grip on the blanket.

The second the male evened out, Gage pushed to his feet. "Come on. Time to go."

He didn't wait to see if the kid obeyed. He turned and left the room instead. After a moment of hesitation, Osgard followed him into the main cabin. Standing beside Nian, one hand on the lever that opened the outside door, Haider tipped his chin. Gage nodded, giving him the go-ahead. With a grunt, his friend slammed the latch into the unlocked position and shoved. The door pushed out, then opened wide.

Wind raged into the plane.

Cabin pressure dropped.

Gage braced himself as the jet wobbled in mid-air. Steel wings seesawed. Newspaper blew off a nearby tabletop. Haider growled and took control, leveling the plane as Gage grabbed Osgard and headed for the open door.

Fresh air hit him in the face.

Osgard sucked in a startled breath.

Gage didn't stop. One arm around the kid, he leapt from the plane into the night sky. The kid flinched. Gage shifted into dragon form, snarling as stiff muscles stretched and relief came calling. His bronze scales rattled in the wind rush. He bared his fangs. Osgard laughed, free-falling with him an instant before Gage tucked the younger male into his paw, folded his wings, and dove toward mountainous terrain. Speed supersonic, the spikes on his tail hissed in his wake.

Haider growled behind him.

Gage glanced over his shoulder and watched Haider and Nian clear the jet's underbelly. The plane banked into a wide turn, veering south high above him. Both males transformed—Haider flashing silver scales, Nian sporting burnished gold. Gage's mouth curved. Hmm, it felt so good to be flying again. To be free and clear. No threat in his rearview mirror.

Night vision sharp, he searched the horizon. Forty-five minutes tops, and he'd land at his front door. Eagerness punched through to reach his heart. Tears stung the corners of his eyes. Gage blinked the moisture away and stayed on course. Less than an hour, and he'd be home. Surrounded by his pack and safe with his brothers. Back in the only place he'd ever truly belonged.

Chapter Twenty-One

Talons planted in a deserted parking lot, Venom settled on his haunches and stared at the building less than fifty feet away. He folded his wings, tucking the black webbing against his sides. The familiar move should've made him feel better. His spiked tail twitched instead, elevating nervous tick to whole new levels. Swallowing the bad taste in his mouth, he wrapped the scaled length around his front paws. Classic move—very catlike, and one that normally helped him relax. No such luck. Comfort wasn't in the cards tonight. He grimaced. Forget comfortable. He would've settled for painful to get rid of screwed.

A muscle along his jaw twitched as he looked over the setup again.

Venom sighed. Goddamn. Guess that made it official. His mission had just gone from doable to difficult in under three seconds flat.

He should've known it wouldn't be easy. Hell, he *had* known the moment he flew into town. The toxins in his blood reacted that quickly, locating the source of the virus without effort. Tipping his chin up, he put his nose in the wind and inhaled. His lungs filled. His nostrils flared, filtering chilly night air. Ultrafine olfactory senses twitched. He snorted, the sound full of disgust.

God, that stunk. Putrid and thick, the odor hung over Granite Falls like fog, slithering in to spoil everything it touched.

Not that any of his brothers could smell it.

Choking on the stench, Venom glanced skyward. Bright stars looked down from a blanket of black, telling secrets, revealing patterns, keeping time with the moon. As he watched, the rest of the Nightfuries rocketed overhead. Night air warped, jetting white off multiple wing tips as his pack fanned out, looking for threats, setting up a security grid, waiting for him to call the play and pull the trigger.

Venom returned his attention to the building.

Of all the horrible luck.

Trust Ivar the Asshole to do the unthinkable and contaminate Granite Falls' water supply. Infection via precious resource. Viral load delivered via drinking glasses. Crank the tap, let it flow, take a sip: instant health issues packaged inside nature's purest offering—something every living thing needed to survive. It was brilliant. A plan with long-reaching consequences and loads of bite. Venom shook his head. Scales ruffled like feathers, sending a symphony of clickety-click-click through the quiet.

The familiar sound settled him down.

He scowled at his target.

The water treatment plant rose like an eyesore in the large clearing. Square construction. Solid design. Set on the outskirts of town in a spot most humans would've enjoyed building a house. Dragon senses seething, he scanned the tree line again. Tall pines sat alongside huge cedars, lording over the human facility, giving the place an ancient, lived-in look. Venom swallowed his distaste. Pretty spot. A total travesty given what lay inside the state-of the-art death trap.

"You have got to be kidding me," he muttered, internal alarm system flickering.

Taking a deep breath, Venom shut down his unease. Freaking out wouldn't solve the problem. Or get him home any faster. But God, it was hard not to react. To forget a lifetime of fear in favor of moving forward—into the teeth of something that still made his skin crawl. Not surprising considering what he'd been through, but . . .

He suppressed a shudder.

Of all the rotten luck. A building full of water—tons of it. His least favorite thing in the world.

Memory surged, forcing him to remember. His stomach clenched. Bile sloshed into the back of his throat. Venom swallowed the acrid taste. Against his will, he relived the sheer force of sensory burn. Could still feel the scrape of rough rope around his wrists as his sire tied him to the pole at low tide. The chilly crush of ocean waves rolling in. The smell of brine as salt water filled his lungs. The slow rise of suffocation and the awful panic that followed.

A shiver rattled through him.

Rolling his shoulders, Venom shrugged it away. Time to go. He couldn't stay in the parking lot all night. His brothers-in-arms were counting on him. So were the humans who called Granite Falls home, so . . .

Enough. No more hesitating.

The past didn't belong in the present. And he needed to move on. Champion the cause. Do his duty. Face his fear, once and for all. Otherwise his sire would win, and Venom would never be able to let the hurt go.

Raising his paw, he flexed his talons. Black razor-sharp claws winked in the moonlight. The sight unlocked his lungs. With a snarl, he shifted into human form and conjured his clothes. His favorite leather jacket settled across his shoulders. Heavy. Familiar. Perfect as Evelyn's scent drifted from the collar, teasing his senses, calming him down, helping him relax. His mouth curved. Hmm, so good. His female always smelled so damned amazing.

An image of her rose in his mind's eye.

Resolve settled deep. His gaze narrowed on the building. *"I'm going in."*

"Not without me."

A black blur streaked into view.

Wick banked hard and circled around. He folded his wings. Gravity took hold, yanking his friend out of the sky. Black amber-tipped scales rattled as he landed with a thump in front of him. Gravel skittered sideways, pinging off the base of a lamppost.

"No need, Wick," he murmured, hoping his friend stayed out of it. *"Stay outside. I'll holler when I'm done."*

Excellent plan. He didn't want any help. Any witnesses either. It was safer that way. Easier on his pride too. No matter his resolve, it would take him a while to work up enough courage to hop into one of the tanks. Total body immersion would equal victory. Or, rather, a dead contagion instead of a live one. Contact with his skin combined with the manipulation of his magic would strip the contaminant of its core components. Break down the bug. Kill the disease one molecule at a time by pushing the antidote through the network of pipes into human homes and . . .

Presto. Safe, clean, filtered water—that he would be standing up to his gonads in. Then again, maybe he'd have to go deeper. Chest-deep? Chin-deep? Venom cringed. He really didn't know. Didn't want to think about it either. But as he strode across the parking lot toward his best friend, nerves got the better of him, making his mind scream and him imagine the worst.

Water filling his lungs. Death by drowning.

Golden eyes narrowed on him. *"Venom—"*

"I'll be fine."

"Bullshit." Magic sparked. Wick transformed. Inferno-like heat blew into the sky, killing the cold air as his friend nailed him with a pissy look. Venom growled at his best friend and set a course to the front doors. Wick snarled back and, with a quick pivot, followed him across the lot. *"I'm going in with you."*

"And that makes three."

Venom cursed under his breath. *"I don't need your help, Mac."*

"Double bullshit." Smooth, blue-gray scales flashed in his periphery. Tucking his wings, Mac landed on top of the building. Sharp claws shrieked against steel. Venom clenched his teeth, stepped onto the walkway, then glanced up. Hanging over the roof edge like a gargoyle, the male frowned at him. *"I'm a water dragon, dumb-ass. You're about to fuck with water, ergo . . ."*

Mac trailed off, the *duh* in his tone unmistakable.

Okay. Fine. The guy had a point. Maybe he did need Mac on standby. *"Jesus, you're both major pains in the ass."*

"Fuck off," Wick said, using his favorite phrase.

With a grin, Mac somersaulted off the roof. Halfway down, he shifted into human form. His boots slammed into the ground beside large windows. Glass shuddered in steel frames, vibrating in protest. *"Lead the way."*

"Perimeter's secure. Nothing's moving out here. We'll stand post," Bastian said, deep voice rolling through mind-speak. *"Yell if you need us."*

Venom nodded and, pace steady, strode up the walkway. Concrete pavers led the way, rolling out like a red carpet, pointing toward the front entrance. He slid to a stop and grabbed one of the door handles. Icy metal grazed his palm. He yanked. The door flew open and unease squawked. He kept his feet moving and crossed the threshold, his chest so tight it hurt to breathe. Pressure banded around his rib cage. Acid swirled in the pit of his stomach. Ignoring the churn-up, he paused in the foyer to get the lay of the land. Locked up tight for the night, an office-slash-reception area sat to his left, rubbing shoulders with the corridor running alongside it. A picture gallery of the facility in different stages of construction sat to his right.

He scanned each one, looking for the layout.

A photo of two rectangular water tanks caught his eye. He stared at the pair a moment, trying to make his brain work. Right size. Perfect shape. Full of running water. The tanks would do. He'd be able to hop in, get good and wet, then—

His heart clenched, shutting down reason.

"*Relax.*" Stopping next to him, Wick bumped his shoulder. The love tap made Venom sway on his feet as his friend met his gaze. "*Don't worry. If it goes wrong in there, I'll pull you out.*"

"I know," he said, dropping mind-speak, coaxing his lungs to unlock.

Oxygen rushed into his body. His muscles shuddered, then released the clampdown. Flexing his hands, Venom forced himself to move. One foot in front of the other. Shoulders rolling. Knees bending. Stride after heart-pounding stride down the wide corridor. Pale walls raced past. His friends' footfalls thumped in his wake. Boxy fluorescents buzzed overhead, lighting up industrial-grade floors, making his skin crawl, as he paused on the lip of an intersection. Only two options—turn right, or go left.

The reception photo flashed in his mind's eye.

Venom turned left and headed for a set of solid double doors. Raising his hands, he hammered both panels. Well-oiled hinges swung inward, dumping him into the large rectangular room. A walkway ran around the outside, hugging the exterior walls, only to drop away in the center. The gurgle of rushing water joined the hum of machinery. Gaze on the sturdy railing bolted to the edge of the mezzanine, Venom moved in for a closer look. Reaching out, he grabbed the steel banister and glanced down. His stomach dipped. His muscles twitched. The old fear struck, closing his throat as he stared at two long trough-like tanks made of concrete. Water churned along each length, pouring into a narrow spillway sitting between the two.

White-knuckling the rail, Venom glanced over his shoulder. He met Mac's gaze. "Stay out of the water. Don't come in unless I ask you to."

Mac opened his mouth to argue.

Wick shut him down. "He'll be pure poison in there, Mac."

"Could he kill me?"

"Probably."

"Definitely," Venom said, his voice overlapping Wick's. "Give me some time. Make sure no one interrupts. This may take a while."

Both males nodded.

Gritting his teeth, Venom leapt over the rail. Chilly looking water swirled eight feet below, taunting him with its movement. Damp air slapped him in the face. Sucking in a quick breath, he braced for impact. Four feet to go. Now three, two, and—

Splashdown!

He plunged into the tank feetfirst. Heavy water dragged his boots into the swirl, then flowed over his legs. His waist went under. And then his chest. A load of cold-wet-and-nasty hit him in the face. Off balance, Venom struggled to plant his feet. His soles slid on the slimy bottom. With a curse, he thrashed. Waves splashed up and out, arching through the air, rolling over the lip of the tank and into the narrow spillway. His feet slipped again, then found traction. Hammering his internal gearshift, he put himself in reverse. Water dragged against his back. One second ticked into the next and—

He rammed, spine-first, into the side of the tank.

Concrete gouged his skin. Pain bit, curling around his torso.

Wick cursed from his vantage point on the walkway.

Gasping, trying not to throw up, Venom threw his arms out. He must stay in control and on his feet. The second he panicked, he'd go under and it would be over. He'd be done. Finished. In complete freak-out mode instead of on task. Needing an anchor, he grasped at the concrete wall. His hands found the square top. He grabbed hold, clinging to the lip, fighting the raw burn of fear, and stared at the cinder-block wall a few feet away.

Breathe. Just breathe.

Short and sweet. Simple, yet effective. The command whispered through his mind. Venom listened. Forcing each breath, he sucked air in through his mouth. In. Out. Catch and release. Inhale, exhale, then repeat . . . go at it all over again. In the sixth round, still clinging to the wall, Venom pushed past panic. Relief slid in, then spread wide, and attacked tense muscle. As the taut threads unraveled, he unwound, relaxing the cradle of his body. His mind came back online.

Soaked to the skin, shivering in the cold, Venom let go of the wall. Hands curled into twin fists, he planted his feet. His weight settled back on his frame. Small waves slapped at his chest. The wet tendrils stroked over exposed skin. Ignoring the provocation, he shuffled toward the center of the tank. Almost there. Just a little farther, and he'd be in the thick of it. In a prime virus-killing position. Able to unleash his venomous side and burn Ivar's plan to the ground.

Taking another deep breath, he counted off each inch. One turned into more, and then into feet, propelling him to the middle of the trough. The sound of rushing water echoed between his temples, joining the physical push of ebb and flow. Ignoring the waves, Venom sank inside his own head. His dragon half rose.

The current changed direction, swirling into a whirlpool around him. His magic flared. All went silent. The hum of machinery faded away. The slap and burn of water ceased to exist. His focus narrowed, allowing him to see individual water molecules with his mind.

He bared his teeth. "There you are."

Nasty little bugger. Deadly. Able to multiply in human blood. A viral masterpiece, multiple chemical compounds spliced together for one purpose—to infect fast and kill without mercy.

With a growl, Venom unfurled his fingers. Water flowed over his open palms. Digging deep, he dipped into his core energy to feed his magic. His venomous side responded, rising hard, working fast, speeding through his veins. He held onto it, allowed the intensity to build, then unleashed it in a hellish rush. Deadly toxins poured from the surface of his skin into the icy swirl. Like an invading army, poison pierced the sidewalls of H_2O molecules, decimating the virus in the tanks, then went hunting for more.

Time spun away. Seconds tumbled into minutes and then sped into hours.

Feet planted, body swaying in the eddy, Venom didn't notice. He controlled the magic instead. Bled poison. Monitored toxicity levels. Spread his antidote through the system, pushing the cure down pipe after pipe, infiltrating human homes. He reached into house after house, scrubbed the water supply clean, refusing to stop even when he weakened. Fatigue hit him hard. An ache bloomed inside his head and . . .

Goddamn. He hurt . . . everywhere.

Agony streamed down his spine. His muscles quaked, threatening to give out.

Flexing his hands, Venom locked his knees. No. God, no . . . not yet. He couldn't quit yet. Bowing his head, he bore down, struggling to hold on. He was so close. So damned *close.*

Moments from closing the deal. One more street to finish. A few more human homes to make safe. But as he infiltrated the last one, his left knee buckled. Off balance, he fought the backward slide into water. Unable to breathe, he gasped in agony and sent his magic out in one last burst of energy. The toxic wave slammed into a house on the far side of town. The antidote sped through the plumbing, killing the last of the virus.

Satisfaction gripped his heart as realization struck. It had worked. He'd succeeded, ensuring the safety of those who called Granite Falls home.

A whole town of humans out of harm's way. Back on the right track once more.

So weak his muscles shook, Venom turned toward the side of the tank. Time to get out of the water. Thank God. Bless whatever deity was listening. He couldn't wait to pull himself free, but as he moved, his life force ebbed. The last of his strength drained away. Agony streaked down his spine, and he lost control of the venom in his veins. Magic detonated like a nuclear bomb. The toxic cloud blew up and out, spreading like radiation. Steel pipes shattered like glass. Metal shards exploded across the room. Wick and Mac shouted in alarm. His legs gave out. Unconsciousness hit and, sinking like a stone, Venom went under, disappearing beneath the surface of the water.

Unable to wait outside a second longer, Bastian cranked the front door open and jogged into the water treatment plant. He scanned the main lobby. Empty. Nothing and nobody. Not a human in sight. Just miles of pale walls made more interesting by photographs in plain steel frames. Not that he cared. He hadn't left his perch—and Rikar in charge—to fly in and check out the décor. Something was wrong. Way, way out in left field.

It had been hours. Five fucking *hours* since his warriors entered the building. A bad sign. He'd thought for sure Venom would be finished by now.

Or, at the very least, would've sent him another update.

The last one had come half an hour ago. All clear. Two thumbs up. Venom chest-deep in water, venomous side rampaging, but still alive and kicking. The news should've comforted him. Dragged satisfaction to the surface in the face of a job well done. Worry thumped on him instead. He had a bad feeling. One that refused to leave him alone, raising instinct, jabbing at him, telling him to haul ass. Bastian upped the pace. Footfalls thumping, he sprinted down a wide corridor. Man, he didn't like what he was sensing. Maybe it was the silence. Maybe it was the godawful smell in the hallway. Maybe he was losing his mind, but—

Boom!

The explosion rocked the building, throwing him sideways.

His shoulder slammed into the wall. He bounced off, careening toward the other side of the hallway. Arms and legs churning, Bastian fought to stay upright. Boot treads sliding across high-grade linoleum, he crashed into the wall. His elbow bashed through gypsum, leaving a hole in the painted finish. Plaster dust puffed into his face. As he coughed, thick smoke billowed around the corner in front of him.

"What the fuck?" Rikar's snarl blasted through mind-speak, hammering his temples. Pain raked the insides of his skull. *"Bastian—"*

"Get airborne. We've got trouble." Finding his balance, he slid to a stop at the intersection. Magic rolled in on his left, mixing with smoke. More lethal than a load of hard-core radiation, the toxic wave sucked oxygen out of the air. Choking on the

fumes, Bastian pressed his forearm to his face, covering his nose and mouth, and tried not to breathe. *"I think Venom just went nuclear."*

"Shit."

"Where are Mac and Wick?" Forge asked, worry making his accent thicker than usual. *"I cannae sense either one anymore."*

"Jesus. H. Christ. I can't either," Sloan said, his voice mixing with the sound of flapping wings. *"Get in there, B. I'm on my way."*

"On the move."

Pivoting left, Bastian headed for a pair of solid doors. Hanging off twisted hinges, one of the panels swayed, squeaking in the haze. Venomous swill thickened, making him cough. His eyes started to sting. He kept going, hunting for his warriors in the smoke, stepping over debris, forcing his sonar to work. His magic pulsed. The cosmic burst rushed out, coated the walls, and scrubbed the air, allowing him to breathe while he got the lay of the land. Up ahead. Just a few more feet and he'd step inside a room. A large one with water tanks and—

A shadow moved through the smoke. "Motherfuck, he's heavy."

"Hang on to him, Mac."

Water splashed, joining the sound of voices and . . . thank God. Two warriors alive and pissed off, one still down for the count. Heart thumping hard, Bastian tore the broken door off its hinges. As he kicked debris out of the way, the smoke cleared a little. With a quick glance, he took in the scene. Thick pipes blown wide open. Puddles pooling on smooth concrete. Soot smeared across cinder-block walls. And Mac and Wick, standing at the railing, working to haul Venom onto a narrow mezzanine.

Soaking wet, blood running from a cut above his eye, Wick turned to face Bastian. "He's alive, but—"

"Weak." With a grunt, Mac grabbed the back of Venom's jeans and yanked. Rancid water flew in a dirty arc. A nasty gash on the male's shoulder opened, dripping blood down his back. "We need to get him out of here."

Pale as death, Venom groaned as his feet hit the floor. Half out of it, he murmured Bastian's name. Bastian's heart tightened in reaction, thumping the inside of his chest. God love Venom. The male never said quit, even when it meant risking his life. Swallowing a curse, Bastian stepped over a pile of debris and moved in tight. He grabbed his warrior's arm, slung it around his shoulder, and turned toward the exit. Wick took the other side, helping him carry Venom over the threshold as Mac jogged into the hallway ahead of them.

A quick right turn put them in the main corridor.

Smoke swirled in their wake. The glass front doors flashed up ahead.

Feet barely moving, Venom tried to lift his head. "Home."

"Okay, brother," Bastian said. "No problem. Myst'll patch you up and—"

"No," Venom rasped, his voice barely audible. "To Evelyn. Home to Evie."

He glanced at Wick over the top of his warrior's head. "The safe house?"

Wick nodded.

Mac made tracks, punching through the doors. Holding both open, he waited for them to reach him. "I'll take him."

Bastian shook his head. "I got it."

"I'll fly point," Rikar said, rocketing overhead in a flash of white scales.

"The rest of you—go home." Boots crunching over gravel, Bastian muscled Venom into the middle of the parking lot. "Rikar and I will handle it from here."

Wick balked.

Bastian backed up the order with a don't-fuck-with-me look. "You're injured, Wick. Go home to J. J. I'll make sure Venom reaches his female."

Wick glanced down his chest. A nasty gash ran along the side of his abdomen. Bleeding like a sieve, he weakened with every breath he took. Gaze on his injury, Wick cursed through clenched teeth. And Bastian waited for him to decide: Be smart and return home to his mate? Or risk his life rather than allow Bastian to protect his best friend? A hard choice for Wick. He could see it in his warrior's eyes and understood his hesitation. Shit, he felt the same way. No one wanted to leave Venom. The male was important, a valued member of the Nightfury pack. And yet, Wick's commitment to Venom ran even deeper than that. Love. Friendship. Trust. The two males shared a bond that had been forged in the heat of battle and tested by time.

But that didn't change the facts.

Wick needed to be skin-to-skin with his female—to feed in order to heal. Which meant returning to Black Diamond while Bastian took his best friend in the other direction. A tough pill to swallow. Wick did it anyway, releasing his hold, stepping away, trusting Bastian to take care of Venom. He nodded, praising his warrior without words, and, with a gentle shrug, adjusted his grip on Venom.

Wick shifted into dragon form and leapt skyward.

Bastian followed suit and transformed. His claws scraped over gravel. Cradling his warrior in his paw, he unfurled his wings and took flight.

Venom gasped in pain. "She's mad at me."

Gaining altitude, Bastian rose above the treetops. "Who—your female?"

"Won't kiss me anymore."

Bastian blinked. Well, all right. Too much information on the sharing front. Not that it mattered. Or that Venom noticed. Deep in sensory overload, his mind was stuck on replay, mired in one thing—the well-being of his mate.

"I'm hungry, B." Shimmering ruby-red eyes met his. "Don't let me hurt her."

"I won't," he said, banking south, heading for the city.

But as the words left his mouth, Bastian didn't know if he could keep his promise. A hungry male could be a dangerous thing—and energy-greed equaled unpredictable on a huge scale. He should know. He'd nearly killed his mate once while hungry. But then, their coupling hadn't yet been complete. Which had left her vulnerable. Energy-fuse changed all that. Now, the intensity of his hunger didn't matter. Myst held all the power, controlled the flow of each feeding—had tamed his dragon half—which meant he couldn't hurt her anymore.

No matter how desperate he became.

Welcome knowledge. A beautiful thing. A bond without equal.

One he hoped Venom now shared with Evelyn. God, he prayed Venom was right. That he'd found his mate and that the bond had already taken root. Otherwise, the second he landed and placed his warrior in the female's arms, things would get out of hand fast, and Evelyn would end up hurt in the aftermath.

Chapter Twenty-Two

Curled up on one end of the couch, Evelyn snuggled beneath a homemade quilt and settled in to watch another round of Jason Bourne. Well, all right, not quite *Jason* this time around. Already on the fourth in the series, her movie marathon now included some other actor. Nice-looking man, as kick-ass as his counterpart in the earlier movies. A bowl of popcorn in her lap, she watched the new guy fight off a pack of wolves. With nothing but a branch, fire blazing from one end. Her mouth curved. Pretty cool stuff . . . made even better by a sixty-inch plasma screen TV.

Munching on her snack, she shook her head.

Unbelievable. She hadn't thought watching her favorite box set could get any better. High definition coupled with primetime surround sound proved her wrong. The picture clarity was stunning, the sound even better, throbbing through the living room, making her believe she stood right alongside the guy, struggling to stay alive. Her heart panged as she watched him fight. She knew how he felt, all alone out there in the wilderness. Beyond help. Beyond hope. In need of some luck and a clear break. She had, after all, lived through a battle of her own. But now, for the first time in months, in the blue light thrown by a TV that wasn't hers, in a house she didn't own, Evelyn allowed herself to unwind.

Strand by taut strand. Worry giving way beneath a wave of relief.

With a sigh, she nestled deeper in the couch cushions. Thank goodness for expensive toys. The entertainment system was doing its job tonight, helping her forget her troubles, if only for a little while. Venom, though, refused to leave her alone. Like a soft sweater, he surrounded her, lying thick and heavy on her skin, warming her even while away. It seemed strange to think of him that way after so little time, as though he'd somehow become her home: a place of comfort, the most solid thing in her life. But only a fool denied the truth, and after months of upheaval, she didn't want to be foolish anymore.

She wanted to be brave instead.

What that kind of courage entailed she didn't know. No matter how many times she puzzled it out, she still didn't know what Venom wanted from her. Or what he intended in the long run. A brief love affair? Nothing more than catch and release on his part? The thought made her grip the popcorn bowl harder. She didn't want it to be that way—to be brushed aside, sent away, and left behind . . . thrust back into a life with little meaning and even less joy. Strange as it seemed, she wanted to stay with him. Make a go of it. Explore the connection she sensed growing between them and figure out what it meant. What that made her, she didn't know. A pawn in a Dragonkind game? A woman without the sense God gave her? Maybe, but . . .

She understood her own heart. Felt the yearning. Registered the risks of getting too close to Venom with every breath she took.

And knew exactly what it meant.

Evelyn sighed. Drat self-awareness, anyway. She would've preferred to remain oblivious. Then again, she always called a spade a spade. No sugarcoating the truth. No side trips into self-delusion. Just straight-up logic couched in hard-core honesty. So . . . no sense lying to herself. Somehow, some way, she'd fallen head over heels for Venom. Now she felt the stir. Recognized the compulsion as her I'm-made-for-you gene went into hyperdrive.

Until he walked into her life, she would've sworn soul mates didn't exist. Were nothing but made-up fairy tales. Poppycock designed to drown people in the illusion of happiness. Tonight, she realized her mistake. Her father had been right. Love was real. So was finding *the one*—the right man to share her life. And as she watched Jason number two leap from one cliff to another, Evelyn wanted to make the leap too. To let go, be brave, feel the rush as she fell, and allow Venom to catch her.

"How's the movie?"

Dragging her gaze from the screen, Evelyn glanced at Daimler. Pep in his step, slippers whispering over hardwood, he pranced toward her. Her lips twitched. Wow, he was funny. Over-the-top fantastic—an incredible combination of exuberance, entertaining anecdotes, and honest-to-God mischief. Right now, though, his outfit held her attention. She swallowed a snort of amusement. Tartan pajama pants a la Scottish Highlands coupled with a purple T-shirt that read "Try me"—insert sparkly cupcake here—"I'm delicious!" Toss in a jar of peanut butter and the bar of chocolate he carried and . . .

Yes. It was official. He was now her favorite person in the world.

"Good so far," she said, replying to the movie question. She eyed the bar of Cadbury's finest.

Dark eyes twinkling, he smiled at her. "I come bearing cinematic gifts."

Leaning forward, Evelyn plunked her popcorn bowl on the coffee table. Stopping alongside her, he handed her the jar and the bar. With a hum of gratefulness, she accepted both. Cracking the package open, she dipped her treat in the peanut butter and took a bite.

She moaned in delight. "You're a god."

Daimler grinned. "Would that it were so."

Raising her hand, she pretended to wave the chocolate like a magic wand. "I anoint thee Master of the Universe."

With a snort, he grabbed the blanket folded over the back of a chair and, skirting an end table, took up residency on the other end of the couch. She stared at him a moment, then returned to the movie. He was good company. Chatty without being intrusive. Cheerful without being annoying. Incredibly inquisitive too. He asked more questions than anyone had a right to, and yet, she hadn't felt threatened once. She'd answered instead, watched him bake, munched on warm just-out-of-the-oven chocolate chip cookies, and told him all about her old job. Explained business management and corporate structure, laid out investment strategies and wealth management tactics as well. Daimler never missed a beat, and she'd been grateful.

Talking about her field made her feel almost normal again.

And speaking of normal—something wasn't quite right. Just a little bit off, odd in a way that defied description, but drew her tight just the same. Now her skin felt two sizes too small, as though she'd been stretched thin within seconds. A bad case of the shivers hit, raising goose bumps on her nape. Her gaze on the plasma screen, Evelyn frowned. Tilting her head, she struggled to control her reaction and—huh. Weird, but . . .

Sensation spiked, turning into prickles.

Pinpricks raced down her spine. Alarm closed in, engulfing her without warning. Tossing the quilt aside, Evelyn popped off the couch and onto her feet. As her bare soles settled on the hardwood floor, a signal morphed inside her head. Her heart paused mid-beat, then rebounded, keeping time as awareness thumped on her temples and fine-tuned her senses, making her hunt for the source.

She glanced toward the ceiling. "Do you feel that, Daimler?"

In a flap of movement, her new friend bounced to his feet. "I'll make up some more beds."

Evelyn blinked. *Make up more beds?* What the hell for? An excellent question. One she would've liked answered. But as Daimler hightailed it across the kitchen and disappeared from view to make beds for some unknown reason, the signal intensified. A buzz lit off, scraping the inside of her skull.

A bang sounded outside.

Pivoting toward the glass sliders, Evelyn stared out into the night. Nothing yet. No movement beyond the wide bank of windows. No reason for the violent thud. No one approaching the—

A blond guy became visible in the gloom.

Long legs pumping, he vaulted from the walkway, over three steps, and landed on the stone patio. The loud thump echoed, competing with the surround-sound system. Surprise struck, gluing her feet to the floor. The blond didn't break stride. Moving like a freight train, he ran toward the door. A second before he reached it, glass sliders slid open all by themselves. Cold air rushed over the threshold. Flurries swirled in its wake, blasting into the living room. Awareness hit along with the chill. She tensed. Oh, boy. Watch out. Not even close to good. The guy might be nice looking, but the vibe he wore screamed lethal.

Boots pounding, he sprinted into the room.

Evelyn flinched and took a step backward.

His head snapped in her direction. He paused mid-stride and slid to a stop in front of the TV. Pale eyes the color of ice chips met hers. "Evelyn?"

Inching backward, she nodded. "Yes?"

"I'm Rikar, a friend of Venom's." The intensity of his tone put her on edge. "We've got a bit of a situation, and I need you to—"

A snarl drifted in through the open doors.

Evelyn stared out into the night. Her gaze skipped over the terrace, then beyond to search the high hedges. The ominous growl came again. Nasty. Brutal. A sound with bite and even more danger embedded in it. And yet, she recognized the tenor. Had heard it before while making love with Venom. When she'd moaned and pleaded, begging him for the pleasure while he moved deep inside her, a snarl just like that had come from his throat.

"Where is he?" Focus on the outdoor patio, Evelyn stopped retreating. Hitting the forward button on her brain, she skirted the coffee table and headed for the door. She knew what the signal meant now. The hum in her veins cranked her tight, clued her in, making instinct and intuition collide. Venom was out there . . . somewhere. Hurt? Maybe. Weak with fatigue? Certainly. Tapped in now, she could feel him struggling to get his feet underneath him. Her gaze narrowed on Rikar. "What happened?"

Raising his arms, Rikar blocked her path to the door. "Listen, I need to—"

"Move." Her pissy tone struck like an open palm.

His eyes widened in surprise. "Evelyn. Hold on a second. I need to explain—"

"Get out of my way," she said, slipping between two chairs to get around him. She needed to reach Venom now. She knew it. Sensed it. Felt the urgency building inside her with every breath she took. It didn't matter that she didn't understand what she was feeling or why. Only one thing mattered. "He needs me."

"He does." Dancing the dance, Rikar kept himself between her and the door, pissing her off. Making her wish she'd learned to be a linebacker so she could turf his ass and be on her way. "Listen carefully, Evelyn. When he touches you, I want you to control the flow."

She paused mid-step. "Excuse me?"

"Venom needs to feed, and you must control the flow of energy. Feed him a little at a time. Calm him down. Control the *flow.* Understand?"

No, she didn't understand. The guy wasn't making any sense. Par for the course, she knew. Dragonkind equaled confusing on a grand scale. Even after spending all day talking with Venom about his kind, she struggled to understand the ins and outs—all the differences between his race and hers. But as a dark-haired man helped Venom mount the steps, all that fell away. Concern struck instead. Her heart clenched. God, he looked so pale. So tired—beyond exhausted—as his friend half-carried, half-walked him across the patio.

Gaze glued to Venom, worry out in full force, she tried to sidestep Rikar again.

He shook his head. "Let Bastian get him inside."

She growled at him. Rikar's mouth curved, but he refused to move. So she waited, fingers flexing, breath rasping in her throat, almost coming out of her skin as Venom raised his head. His gaze met hers. He whispered her name. Tears filled her eyes. *Come on. Come on. Cross the threshold*, her mind screamed. The second that happened, she knew Rikar would move aside. The shift would release her, free her to do what she wanted and . . .

Touch Venom.

With a grunt, Bastian hauled him into the house.

The sliding glass doors closed with a hiss.

Rikar retreated, shifting to one side to get out of her way.

Not wasting a second, Evelyn leapt into action. Bare feet flying, she bridged the distance and slid to a stop in front of him. Venom bared his teeth on another snarl. His ruby-red eyes started to glow. She didn't care. Wrapping him up, she hugged him close. No rhyme or reason. No proof or even a hint of logic. And yet, she knew what he needed—her skin against his. Instinct showed her the way. Caring pushed her hard against him. Necessity shoved her hands beneath the hem of his T-shirt.

Her palms touched his back.

Venom arched, reacting like he'd been struck by lightning, and came alive in her arms. Hard muscles flexed around her. One hand gripping her nape, he yanked at her sweatshirt. The hem rose. Cool air washed over her stomach. Dipping his head, he pressed his mouth to her temple and his other palm to the small of her back. Electricity sparked beneath the surface of her skin. Heat streamed through her body. Desire moved through her veins. A snick echoed inside her head, opening a fissure somewhere deep inside her. Luscious and thick, high current rushed through the gap, moving from her into him.

With a moan, Venom's mouth jumped to her throat.

His teeth grazed her neck. Bliss bloomed, burning through her as he flicked her with his tongue. Settling in, he suckled her skin, drawing hard on her pulse point. Ecstasy careened out of control, bursting through the crack, widening the seam, making her spine bow under the pressure.

Her heart stalled mid-beat.

Fighting for breath, Evelyn gasped in shock.

Venom groaned in delight. The pressure increased, making her head spin.

"Fuck," someone said.

"Concentrate. Control it, Evelyn. Slow him down."

Edged by command, the deep voice reached through the mind-fog. Evelyn blinked, understanding now. *Control the flow.* She felt the burn. The hard rush of a rising current. The overwhelming stream as energy flowed from her into Venom. He was feeding, taking from her in order to sustain himself . . . renewing his strength by stealing hers. The idea should've alarmed her. It intrigued her instead. Despite the pressure, she liked him like this—out of control, needy, completely focused on her. Evelyn swallowed a moan. The intensity was incredible. Beautiful. Addictive. Pleasure-pain in the burn of physical chaos. Mind-numbing arousal and the promise of sexual release.

But only if she controlled it.

Rikar was right. She needed to tame Venom and control the flow. He was too hungry. Being too greedy, losing himself in the taste and feel of her. *Concentrate.* The word whiplashed inside her head, waking neural pathways. Clarity poured like water from a pitcher, filling her full, giving her strength, allowing her to turn inward. Closing her eyes, she tapped into the current and grabbed it by the tail. She bent it end over end, turned the tap, slowed the flow, making him jerk against her.

Fighting the slower pace, he snarled against her skin.

Fisting her hands in his hair, she locked him down, feeding him small sips instead of frantic swallows. He shook his head. With a gentle tug, she pulled him away from her throat. He fought the separation. Tightening her grip, she insisted. His chin came up. She invaded his mouth, licking between his teeth, kissing him deep to calm him down. Little by little, he obeyed and opened his mouth wider, welcoming each caress, respecting her pace as she gave him what he needed. High-voltage current downgraded, moving from dangerous to delicious.

She gentled the kiss.

He sighed against her mouth. "Thought you weren't going to kiss me anymore."

"I lied," she whispered between kisses, continuing to feed him.

"Thank God," he murmured, swaying on his feet.

She caught him mid-wobble. His friends did the rest, helping her walk Venom across the room. He stumbled over his feet. Rikar and Bastian steadied him. She continued to kiss and caress him, never breaking contact, enticing him with her taste, making him follow her retreat. Out of the living room. Past the kitchen island. One left turn and a length of corridor later, she stood with him inside a bedroom.

Rikar closed the door, leaving her alone with Venom.

Running her hands over his shoulders, she walked him across the room. The back of his legs bumped the side of the mattress.

His eyes drifted closed. He sagged in her arms. "I'm so tired, Evie."

"I know." Kissing him one last time, Evelyn laid him down and stripped him bare, leaving his damp clothes in a heap on the floor. "You need to sleep now."

"You'll stay?"

"Yes."

"Kiss me again?" he asked with a sleepy murmur.

Ditching her pajamas, she slid in next to him. The mattress sighed beneath her. Cool cotton brushed against her side as she settled next to him. Bliss whispered her name. Evelyn hummed. Oh, boy. Total body contact—skin on skin, all of her pressed up against all of him—the absolute best. On the verge of slumber, Venom curled his arm around her, tucked her closer, and turned his face into her hair. Her heart hitched, kicking the inside of her breastbone as she did as he asked and leaned in to kiss him again.

A soft touch. A small taste. A hint of explosive passion.

"I love you, Evie." Muscles lax, eyes closed, he sighed. The sleepy sound drifted through the quiet, hanging like a promise in warm air. "I love you."

Her chest went tight. She blinked in astonishment and glanced at his face. Fast asleep now, he remained oblivious to her reaction. *I love you, Evie.* The words slammed into her temples, then resonated, finding a place in her heart so fast Evelyn flinched. Good lord, she hadn't expected him to say that. Staring at his gorgeous face, she frowned. Had she heard that right? Did he even know what he'd said? Or was it just . . . just . . .

A lie.

An easy out brought on by fatigue. And the fact she'd fed him.

Good question.

Ruinous results—a pox upon her heart, a threat to her future, devastation times a thousand—if he didn't mean it. An outcome firmly entrenched in the realm of possibility. Which meant she should probably leave now. Make a break for it and save her pride. But as dawn arrived, she held him close instead of turning away. Damned herself by nestling in and closing her eyes. Wrecked all chance of escape—and a clean getaway—by settling into sleep with Venom in her arms, all while praying she wasn't making a huge mistake. One that would force her to leave in the morning. Run hard, hide fast, and never look back.

Chapter Twenty-Three

Holed up in bed, surrounded by quiet and the stillness of his room, Venom lay on his side, watching Evelyn sleep. Gaze locked on her, he roamed her face, memorizing every facet, refusing to miss even the tiniest detail. The thickness of her eyelashes. The fullness of her mouth. The gorgeous hue of her skin. The beauty of the loose inky curls falling to her bare shoulder. All things he'd taken note of before. Hard to miss given that his attention remained riveted on her whenever she was in the same room.

Today, though, brought a multitude of new surprises.

With her eyes closed, he noticed others things. Details he'd missed with her smart mouth and saucy attitude distracting him. The small freckle sitting beneath the curve of her bottom lip. The tiny scar marring the underside of her chin. The way one of her eyebrows curved up a little more than the other in the center. Insignificant details on their own; all Evelyn when put together to create a whole.

God. She was precious.

Beautiful in slumber. So warm and sweet next to him. So trusting and soft in his arms. Gratefulness made a home inside his heart, rousing thick emotion. His throat went tight. Venom battled a moment, fighting to stay even, forcing himself to remain on track. But it was hard. He'd dreamed of this day. Of waking up next to his mate. Of having a female to call his own. Now, the promise of it sat within reach. Just inches away. One question from becoming a reality. All he needed now was for Evelyn to agree.

By no means an easy feat. Or a done deal.

Particularly since he couldn't remember what had happened last night.

He frowned. Well, at least, not all of it. Which amounted to a big problem. No way he wanted to wake Evelyn—never mind ask her the all-important question—without knowing what the hell he'd done to her last night. She wasn't hurt. He could see that, but, well . . . he needed a baseline. A jumping-off point to guide him when he started the conversation.

Forcing his brain out of neutral, he stared at the wall above her head. Recall murmured, pointing him in the right direction. He remembered the water tank and the explosion, Bastian flying him home as well. After that? His brow furrowed. Shit. He didn't know. Digging deep, he pushed harder, reaching for the memory. An image of Evelyn dressed in flannel pajama bottoms and a sweatshirt rose in his mind's eye.

His gaze strayed to her mouth.

Yes. Definitely. He remembered kissing her. Or rather, Evelyn invading his mouth, tasting him deep, taking control. Wonder washed in on a wave of surprise. He drew a soft breath. Thank God. She wasn't angry, which meant . . . time to wake her up. He ran his gaze over her face again. Man, he almost hated to do it. She looked so peaceful in slumber. Like a content kitten curled up next to him. Venom debated a second, then shook his head. Stalling wouldn't solve the problem. Or elevate his growing tension. He needed to talk. He wanted to know. And the only one who could tell him what he longed to hear was fast asleep beside him.

Raising his hand, he pushed a stray curl away from her temple. She stirred. He continued to caress her. Gentle touches. Soft strokes. A quiet murmur. Enthralled by the feel of her, he brushed his thumb over her bottom lip, traced the tiny freckle, then turned his hand and cupped her cheek. "Evie . . . *mazleiha*, wake up."

She sighed, the sound more hum than exhale. Her eyelashes flickered, then rose. Sleepy brown eyes met his. Her mouth curved, making his heart jack-rabbit inside his chest. As the thump-thump-boom got going, she stretched, undulating beneath the sheet, making another part of his anatomy throb. Rock hard for her now, Venom clung to self-restraint and issued a mental order, telling his prick to hold-the-hell-on and get-the-hell-in-line.

"Hi," she said, with a husky murmur.

"Hey back."

She blinked, trying to wake up. "What time is it?"

Her tone made him shiver. His body hit the gas, roaring at full speed into dangerous I-want-her territory. Venom swallowed a curse. Holy God. She had the sexiest bedroom voice he'd ever heard. "Late. Mid-afternoon."

"Oh. Wow. Guess I've been sleeping awhile." Less than a foot away, she stretched beneath the sheet one more time. Muscles across his abdomen twitched, tugging at his hip bones. She settled quick, curling on her side to face him. "How long have you been up?"

"Awhile," he said, wondering how to start the conversation. Ease into the subject? Blurt it out and hope for the best? Excellent questions. Both valid approaches, although—Venom swallowed—despite his nervousness, leaping in and getting it over with sounded like a better strategy. At least, right now. With

Evelyn less than an arm's length away, the most direct route held more promise. Was way more expedient considering Evelyn didn't have a stitch on. Naked, soft, and warm beneath the covers—his favorite combo when it came to his female. Holding her gaze, he shoved uncertainty away, took a fortifying breath, and jumped in with both feet. "Did I scare you last night?"

"No." Evelyn frowned. "Not really, but . . ."

"But?"

Straight white teeth flashed against her lower lip. She chewed on it a moment, as though trying to decide, then broke eye contact. The loss made his stomach clench. Trying to read her, he searched her expression. Not much to go on. Even less to reassure him.

A pucker between her brows, she shifted beneath the sheet.

Cotton sighed as she retreated, moving away from him. Venom swallowed his protest. The urge to reach out and stop her jabbed him. He shut down that inclination too. Crowding her wouldn't get him what he wanted. Neither would holding her prisoner. Then again, allowing her to put more distance between them didn't seem like the way to go either, but, well . . . hell. He didn't know what else to do. Or what to say as she reached the edge of the bed, grabbed something off the floor, and stood. He caught a flash of lithe curves—a gorgeous length of her thigh, the taut lushness of her backside, the graceful sweep of her spine—a second before she covered up, wrapping the quilt around her.

His internal alarm system came online.

The warning shrieked inside his head, Venom sat up, but forced himself to stay put. She didn't want him close right now. He could tell by the look in her eyes. Guarded. Unsure. Maybe even a touch afraid. Swallowing past the knot in his throat, he scanned her face, searching for the reason behind her unease and . . . oh, so not good. Evelyn had the best poker face around. Now he couldn't get an accurate read on her. Her bio-energy, a perfect match for his, locked him out. Which left him adrift, at sea, unable to read her mind or hook in to her emotions . . . unless she permitted him to. But one thing for sure? Something was wrong.

Really, *really* wrong.

Her posture—the rigid way she stood—gave him another clue. Her uncertainty, the jumbled tumble of her energy, did the rest, telling him to talk fast and be honest too. Screw his nervousness. Forget his pride. Evelyn needed him to tell her the truth. Lay it all on the line. Otherwise, she'd retreat some more, and he'd lose her for good.

"Evie . . ." Unable to stay still a moment longer, he slid across the mattress. She took a step back. And then another, breaking his heart as the distance between them grew. Not wanting her to feel threatened, each of his movements slow, he sat on the edge of the bed. Sheet bunched at his hips, feet planted on the floor, he leaned forward and, planting his elbows on his knees, laced his fingers together. "Talk to me, *mazleiha*. Tell me what's wrong."

Clinging to the quilt, she tucked her hair behind her ears. "What are we doing, Venom?"

"What do you mean?"

"What I mean is—what's happening here? Between you and me?" Bare feet brushing over hardwood, she retreated some more, then stopped to adjust the quilt. Securing it beneath her arms, she waved her hand, gesturing to him, then pointing to herself. The move hinted at vulnerability. Of raging insecurity and the helpless need to know. "Are you just playing? Is this all a game to you? Am I just a bit of fun to pass the time before you go back to your world?"

Venom's chest seized. *A bit of fun?* Nothing but a *game*? The thought sent him sideways inside his own head. Temper bled through, making him want to kick his own ass. God. How could she think that? How could she possibly believe that he would—

"Because I've got to tell you, if that's what you're doing, it's pretty crappy."

Venom opened his mouth to respond.

Evelyn cut him off. "And you know what else? I haven't been playing. Not for a second. From the moment I saw you in that hotel room, I knew something was up. That you were different and, well . . ." Squaring her shoulders, she leveled her chin and stared him down. The look was all about being tough. Acting strong. Telling him off, giving as good as she got. The sheen of tears in her eyes, however, belied her show of strength. Right now . . . in this moment . . . Evelyn wasn't tough. She was hurting, mired heart-deep in insecurity. "I know the dragon stuff should freak me out. I *know* it should, but it doesn't. Nothing about you scares me, Venom, and now, I don't think I can go back to my life. To the status quo, to normal—whatever that is. I just . . . I don't think—"

"Jesus, Evie. I would never send you back. *Never.* I want you with me." Shoving the covers aside, Venom vaulted off the bed. His feet hit the floor in front of her. He reached out, needing to hold her, wanting to soothe her, desperate to chase her fears away. Raising her hand, she kept him at bay. His chest went tight. Goddamn it. He was losing her. *Losing her* without knowing why. "What happened last night? What did I do to upset you?"

Tears pooled in her eyes. Looking everywhere but at him, she blinked them away. "You said something."

"What?"

"That you love me."

Venom blinked. Well, shit. So much for easing into the whole love-match, mated-for-life thing. "I did?"

"You don't remember?"

He shook his head.

Her throat worked as she swallowed. "Yeah, well . . . you were pretty out of it."

No kidding. He'd been a mess. Ravenous with hunger. Weak from energy overload. Impatient as hell too. But obviously not far gone enough to shy away from the truth.

Gaze riveted to her face, he held out his hand, palm up in invitation. "Come here, Evelyn. I want to tell you something."

Releasing a shaky breath, she hesitated a second, then complied, bridging the distance to slip her hand into his much larger one. He reeled her in, craving the connection, needing the closeness, and raised his free hand. He traced the curve of her cheek. She turned in to the gentle touch, giving him what he longed for—instant connection, stunning acceptance, the incredible gift of her trust. Sighing in relief, he traced the fine arch of her eyebrow with his fingertip. "Wanna know a secret?"

"Yes," she whispered, the uncertainty in her eyes breaking his heart.

"I wasn't lying. I meant it. Every word, Evie," he said with conviction—with everything he felt for her—in his voice. "I love you."

Her breath hitched. "God, I was so worried you didn't . . . that you wouldn't . . ."

"Wouldn't what—want you to stay with me?"

She nodded. "We haven't talked about it, and you haven't asked me, but I love you too and really want to try, Venom." A tear escaped, rolling down her cheek. Heart so full of her he could hardly breathe, he caught the droplet. He brushed it away, caressing her soft skin as she pressed her palm to his chest. Right over his heart, claiming it by unspoken agreement. "I'd really like to—"

"Stay." *Please stay.* He wanted her so badly. Had waited so long to find her. Had loved her an entire lifetime without knowing it. And she loved him back. Now, no matter what happened, he'd never let her go. He needed her in his life—in his bed each morning, in his arms every day, waiting for him to come home at the end of a long night. "*Stay* with me, Evie."

"I want to, Venom, but . . ." She smiled through her tears. "You know my life is a mess, right?"

"It doesn't matter. Not anymore." Hooking his arm around her waist, he tugged her closer. She nestled in, her heat and sweet scent a gift as he breathed her in. "In my world, you get a fresh start."

"With you."

He nodded. "With me."

"Thank you."

"For what?"

"For finding me," she said, a hiccup interrupting the words. "For coming after me. For loving me . . . and everything else in between."

"Sweet love, you were mine from the moment I saw you. And now, I'm yours." Dipping his head, he brushed a kiss to the curve of her bare shoulder. "I love you, Evelyn. Come home to Black Diamond with me."

"Love you too." She grinned against the side of his throat. "When will we go? Today?"

"Tomorrow's better," he said, a teasing lilt in his tone. "Right now, I have plans that don't include traveling."

"Is that so?"

"Uh-huh," he murmured, more hum than answer. "I'm going to take my time with you. Love you so well, make you come so hard and so often, you forget how to walk. And then . . ."

With a snort, Evelyn retreated enough to look at him. She arched a brow. "And then?"

"I'll take you home."

"To meet your family?"

"To initiate you into the Nightfury pack."

"Sounds ominous."

"Oh, it is," he said, fingertips swirling along her back. Her lips parted on a rush of pleasure. Unwrapping her like a gift, he tossed the quilt aside. Soft skin met his. He hummed and sent his hands south to caress the curve of her bare bottom. The sexy sound ramped arousal higher. With a growl, he gripped the back of her knee. He tugged, parting her thighs before lifting her feet off the floor. Satisfaction soared when she took the cue and wrapped her legs around his hips. Turning with her in his arms, he walked toward the bed . . . and an evening full of mutual satisfaction. "Daimler will do a jig of joy and bake cookies in celebration."

She laughed and slid her hands into his hair. Nails grazing his scalp, she leaned in to tease him with a gentle kiss. Her lips brushed over his. "Okay. I'm in. Two thumbs way, *way* up."

His mouth curved.

Praise his good luck. Thank whatever god was listening. He'd found his mate and claimed her for his own. At long last, once and for all. He wasn't alone anymore. Evelyn had stepped into the breach, filling his heart to bursting. With her laughter and charm. With her grace and beauty. With the wonder of her presence in his arms. Nothing left to do now but hold on tight, treat her right, and celebrate with the female he'd waited his entire life to find.

Chapter Twenty-Four

Three dead. Four injured. A garage full of devastation.

All in all, not a good day.

Boots planted on the edge of the loading dock, Zidane looked over the slaughter. Hunks of twisted steel littered the floor. A veritable rainbow of wreckage—yellow and orange, blue and gray, black, white, and red—lay strewn across scorched concrete. Maseratis dead beside vintage Mustangs. Mercedes mangled beside one-of-a-kind Corvettes. Garage doors blown wide open, right off heavy-duty hinges. Moonlight flooded through gaping holes in the facade, shining a spotlight on the destruction.

He clenched his teeth.

A muscle twitched in his jaw as he skimmed the mess again. His gaze landed on the guard room. Well, at least, what remained of it. Equipped with nothing but the best, his favorite Dodge Ram—the one he'd imported all the way from New Hampshire and waited months to receive—sat in place of the office. Front end smashed against the back wall. Truck bed bent beyond repair. Office walls half destroyed. The Ram's rear tires hovering above crushed gypsum and shattered windowpanes. A hint of smoke and the smell of motor oil hung in the air, driving the truth home.

He'd screwed up. In unforgivable ways.

Rage rumbled through him. The burn spread, raging like wildfire, knotting his muscles as regret sped through his veins. Pressure built between his temples. Discomfort expanded. Swallowing a curse, Zidane funneled the flow, channeling fury in more productive directions. Anger wouldn't solve anything. Neither would losing himself in heart-wrenching loss.

Brows drawn, he toed a shard of debris with his boot. Glass skittered across concrete, clanging against a chunk of steel, joining the buzz of industrial fluorescents. His throat went tight. *Kristus.* His best friend lay dead. Was nothing but a pile of ash now. Much like the collection of automobiles inside his palatial home.

Entirely his fault.

One hundred percent his mess to clean up too.

Asshole Nightfuries. Bane of his existence.

Literally. No word of a lie.

He couldn't escape the bastards. Inside his home. Around the dinner table. While attending the fights at the club every week. No matter where he went, he lived with his sire's paranoia. The yakety-yak-yak never stopped. Morning, noon, and night, it went on and on . . . and on—Bastian this, the Nightfury pack that. Ivar, and the problems brewing a world away in Seattle. Rodin's preoccupation bordered on obsessive. One driven by fear—and the sure knowledge that if Bastian made a play for the Archguard, it would be over. Done. Close up shop and call it a decade. No matter how powerful, Rodin wasn't well loved and couldn't compete. Not with the likes of the Nightfury commander. Hence his sire's unhealthy fixation and the never-ending chatter. All the warnings too.

Which meant he didn't have an excuse.

Not a real one anyway.

He'd heard the cautionary tales for years. *Never trust a Nightfury. The only good Nightfury is a dead one.* How many times had he listened to his sire say things like that? A hundred? A thousand? *Hovno*, he didn't know. He'd lost count eons ago. Scowling at a decapitated Porsche Spyder, Zidane blew out a long breath. He should've known better. Ferland had been lethal in a fight, but, well, not the brightest Skittle in the pack. He swallowed a snarl. Another mistake to lay at his feet. He never should've asked his friend to handle Gage on his own.

And Osgard? An image of the male rose in his mind's eye.

Zidane bared his teeth. "Traitor."

The hiss in his voice slithered over the wreckage. Fucking youngling. The playback of video footage damned the brat, branding him a traitor in picture-perfect quality. He'd led the Nightfuries to freedom. Shown them the way through the underground tunnels. Set up members of his own pack—allowed their slaughter—while jumping ship to join another. The realization should've surprised him. Somehow, though, it didn't. Osgard might've been his favorite plaything—fun to torture, great to bend to his will—but the male wasn't easy. The brat had never broken. Or begged for mercy. He'd remained silent instead, fighting his possession without ever saying a word.

He frowned.

Guess he should've paid better attention. If he had, Osgard would already be dead, instead of out there . . . somewhere . . . providing insider information to the Nightfury pack and—

Broken glass crackled against concrete behind him.

The sharp sound rose in the quiet.

The deep voice followed, making his skin tingle. "Zidane."

Dragging his attention from the wreckage, Zidane glanced over his shoulder. Eyes more black than brown met his. "Father."

Dressed in a dinner jacket, expression set in hard lines, Rodin shook his head. Shined to a high polish, his wing-tip shoes gleamed as he picked his way through the debris and walked across the loading dock. Speculation in his dark eyes, he stopped beside him. Six inches shorter, a great deal slighter of frame, his sire broke eye contact to take in the destruction.

Zidane tensed, but remained silent. No sense speaking before spoken to. His sire enjoyed claiming the first word. Fine by him. Rodin could have it. Every. Single. Time. Zidane always preferred having the last word anyway.

His sire raised a brow. "Care to explain?"

"The bastards had help, but the fault is mine," he said, owning the mistake. Much as he hated to admit guilt, he refused to back away from the truth. The Nightfury escape—the responsibility along with the failure—sat squarely on his shoulders. "I underestimated Gage."

"Will you make the same mistake again?"

"No." Conviction rang in his tone. Rage made another appearance, making a home inside his heart. Zidane rolled his shoulders, easing the tension, fighting the seductive pull of anger, and cleared his mind. He needed a plan. A good one. Something to feed his sire and keep the peace. Mind churning, he searched for an angle and . . . hmm. Yes. That one would do. Huge bark. Brutal amount of bite. A strategy full of retaliatory effect. Exactly what he required to soothe the leader of the Archguard's pride. "Give me a second chance, Father. Allow me to make it right."

"How?"

"By going after them."

"Where are the Nightfuries now?"

"Gone," he said. "We tracked the Bentley to an airstrip twenty miles from here. The bastards boarded a private jet long before we got there."

"With Nian?"

"Osgard too."

"A problem." Worry in his eyes, Rodin frowned. "Nian knows too much. Bastian will use him against us."

"Maybe, but not if we strike first." Zidane tipped his chin toward the mess. "See all this? Tremendously useful. A perfect way to discredit Nian before he points a finger at us. If we can link him to the Nightfury pack, we can frame Bastian. No one knows about Scotland, so—"

"We twist the truth to our advantage." A consummate strategist, his sire stared at him. His eyes narrowed in thought. "Inform the high council of the attack. Say that the murder of my personal guard was an attempt on my life and that Bastian ordered the hit in hopes of overthrowing the Archguard. Demand the entire Nightfury pack be charged with treason."

"Reinstate *Xzinile*, Father, and we will have the law on our side."

"And a clear shot at Bastian."

"Sanctioned assassination . . . signed, sealed, and delivered," Zidane murmured, eagerness in his voice. He couldn't help it. Or stem the tide of anticipation. Just the thought of getting his hands on Gage again sent his mind reeling. Oh, the possibilities . . . all the lovely *possibilities*. "No one need know about the kidnapping."

"Or of the Nightfuries' stay inside our kill room."

"Gage and Haider can't prove anything. Neither can Nian." Excitement tingled through him. His mouth curved. "It'll be your word—esteemed leader of the Archguard, head of a respected family—against theirs."

Flexing his hands, Rodin growled. "I will call the high council and pack commanders to order immediately."

"Good." Already preparing his plan of attack, Zidane threw his sire a sidelong look. "But before you do, I would ask one thing."

"You wish to lead the death squad to Seattle?"

"I want revenge."

"For Lothair?"

Mention of his younger brother made his heart clench. Fucking Nightfuries. First Lothair, now Ferland. Both murdered, dead long before their time. A muscle twitched along his jaw. Zidane cleared his throat. "For Ferland too, Father."

"Done." With a quick about-face, Rodin strode toward the hallway at the back of the loading dock. A second before he disappeared into the labyrinth, his sire paused. Dark eyes shimmering, his gaze burned through the gloom, reaching out to warn him. "Choose your warriors with care, son. Prepare yourself accordingly. You leave as soon as the vote is complete and the council signs off."

Hot damn. The sweet, sweet taste of victory.

If all went according to plan, he'd be airborne within weeks. One if he got lucky, more than a few if he didn't. Not that it mattered. He didn't have time to bask in the glow of his sire's approval. Or dwell on what the future would bring. Bragging belonged to fools. Warriors, on the other hand, prepared for every eventuality. Rodin was right. Actions spoke louder than words, and he didn't have a moment to waste. Running down a list inside his head, Zidane pivoted toward the tunnel and walked away from the garage. The cleanup could wait. Preparations for travel could not. Whatever the timeline, he must be ready to move—the members of his death squad chosen and trained—the instant the high council reinstated *Xzinile* and put a bounty on each Nightfury warrior's head.

Chapter Twenty-Five

Wearing nothing but an oversize T-shirt, Evelyn tiptoed past floor-to-ceiling bookcases. Soft cotton brushed the tops of her thighs. Wide-planked floorboards creaked. She tried not to notice. A hard sell, considering Venom lay belly down on silk sheets across the room, fast asleep after an afternoon spent in bed with her. Her mouth curved. Poor baby. She'd worn him out—ridden him hard and put him away wet. Not that she would ever admit it out loud. Oh, no . . . not her. She possessed more pride than that. And honestly? After making her moan and plead for the pleasure of his touch, Venom's ego was out of control.

No need to feed that beast. He already knew he was fantastic in bed.

"Thank God for that," she murmured, running her fingertips over colorful book spines.

Sighing in contentment, Evelyn slowed her pace and, trying to be quiet, bypassed another bookcase. She paused to read the titles. As she skimmed each one, she shook her head. Incredible. So many choices. Another shelf cramped with books she'd never heard of before. The whole room was like that—full of literature that ran the gamut, hopscotching from crime fiction and historical treatises to Shakespeare, ancient leather-bound texts, and an impressive collection of novels.

She ought to be accustomed to the two-story library by now—or rather, Venom's bedroom inside Black Diamond. Lord knew she spent enough time in it.

Somehow, though, she wasn't.

Almost a month with him, and, still, she marveled at the changes. In her life, sure. But mostly in the way she felt. Safe. Secure. Relaxed, well loved, and accepted. Toss in the fact she'd never slept better and . . . bingo. She owned a recipe for success. One that had her up and energized before Venom opened his eyes and got up for the evening. And yet, despite all the improvements—the smoothing out of her once-screwed-up life—she couldn't wrap her mind around it. A bunch of Dragonkind guys. One Numbai. And four incredible women. Sounded like a movie title. The effect, however, was all too real. Particularly since Myst, Angela, Tania, and J. J. (or the Fab Four, as she liked to call them) had become her best friends in the space of a few weeks. Had she said incredible earlier? Well, slap surreal on the situation instead.

The gift of friendship. A man to call her own. A safe haven far from Markov and the mess her mother had left her.

All in a month's time.

Her throat went tight. Unbelievable, yet totally real. Evelyn shook her head. God was good, and she was thankful. So damned glad Venom had found her, she didn't know how to control the emotional fallout half the time. Sometimes, she didn't. Sometimes it overcame her, and she went from steady to teary eyed in a heartbeat. Venom disliked seeing her that way. Hated her tears almost as much as the Razorbacks. Not that it mattered. Even though she tried, she couldn't always hold it in. Gratefulness, it seemed, always took prisoners, caging her on the weepy side of thankful.

Skirting the spiral staircase to the mezzanine—and the library's second level—she glanced toward the bed. Stretched out in the center of the mattress, Venom slept on: head half-buried beneath his pillow, top sheet bunched around his hips, arms flung wide, an ocean of golden skin on display. A shiver of pleasure ghosted down her spine. Evelyn swallowed a hum of appreciation. She wanted to wake him up—kiss her way between his shoulder blades, nuzzle his ear, flip him over and . . .

Make love with him again.

A great plan but for one thing. She wasn't ready yet. She needed more time. Not a lot. Hardly any at all. Just enough to shore up her courage before she caressed Venom awake and asked the question. Broached the subject . . . whatever. She didn't need to label it. What she wanted was answers. Some clarification too. Curiosity demanded it along with her pride, 'cause . . . yeah. Ever since meeting the other girls, she'd been wondering about something. Taboo subject matter, no doubt, but . . .

Butterflies attacked her stomach.

Ignoring the flutter, she walked past the stone-clad fireplace, stepped around the leather couch, and drifted to a stop next to the bed. Her gaze strayed to the night table. Stacked high, books littered the surface, hiding an expanse of glossy mahogany before spilling onto the floor. More books. Bigger piles. Untold variety on a wide range of topics. Evelyn smiled, loving the fact Venom liked stories . . . and often read aloud to her before bed each morning.

She enjoyed that almost as much as his lovemaking. Hearing the deep rumble of his voice while lying snug in his arms, warm under the quilt as he tilted the book so light fell on the page. Funny, but she never would've guessed that about him. Or that being read to was such a luxury, one she'd missed growing up in her household.

Dragging her gaze from the messy stacks, she returned her attention to Venom. He stirred in his sleep. Evelyn drew a deep breath and, mind whirling, went over what she wanted to ask. Again. For what seemed like the thousandth time. But, well, she couldn't help it. Practice made perfect. Phrasing was important. She needed it to come out right when she finally voiced her concern and—

"*Mazleiha.*"

Husky with sleep, the warmth of Venom's voice washed over her. Pinpricks of pleasure exploded across her skin. Desire welled in the pit of her stomach as he turned over. Hard muscle flexed. Silk slid over his hip, across his ribbed abdomen, then settled, molding to the front of his body, showcasing intimate details, making her mouth water. Which was . . . well, disconcerting to say the least. Downright gluttonous, to say the most. She'd already had him—countless times—and yet, she wanted him again. Right now. Screw the question along with her curiosity. Except . . .

Her attitude was all wrong.

There were too many things left unsaid. And she needed to know.

Stuffing a pillow behind his head, Venom resettled on the mattress. Back against the headboard, bare chest on display, sheet riding low, sleepy ruby-red eyes met hers. He studied her a moment, then tipped his chin. "What has you worried, Evie?"

She pursed her lips. The moment of truth. Time to dive in and find out. "I have a question."

He crooked his finger, asking her to come closer. The second she stepped within range, he grabbed her hand. His calloused palm played against hers. Anticipation twisted the screw, urging her away from conversation and toward desire. She shivered, loving the feel of him, but held the line, refusing her body what it wanted in favor of satisfying her mind. Lacing their fingers, Venom tugged, drawing her onto the mattress. Her knees touched down beside his hip and . . . ah, to hell with it. She threw her leg over and straddled him. He sucked in a quick breath. She hummed. God, she loved being like this with him. Almost skin-to-skin. So close, yet still too far away. Nothing but a thin, silk sheet between them as she settled in his lap, pressing her core to his erection.

"Goddamn," he said, appreciation in his tone. Sitting up a little straighter, he slipped his hands beneath the hem of her shirt, palmed her bare bottom, and adjusted their fit.

She wiggled, settling in, making him groan. "So . . . my question."

"Shoot. Ask me anything."

"When are we going to get married?"

Surprise sparked in his eyes. Venom blinked. He opened his mouth—once, twice . . . a third time—before closing it again, as though he'd fallen into speechlessness.

"I mean . . ." She trailed off, nerves getting the better of her. Chewing on the inside of her lip, she searched for the right words. All the ones she'd practiced. None arrived. Each well-practiced word abandoned her. She cleared her throat, stalling for time, then blurted, "I've been talking with the other girls, and they all have mating marks, but we haven't talked about it. Or about the mating ceremony, and I just . . . well, I want to know if . . . if . . ."

"You want to get married?"

"Yes."

"Thank God." Relief relaxed his expression. Raising his hand, he cupped her cheek. As he caressed her skin, Venom murmured something in Dragonese. A prayer? Words offered up in gratitude? Evelyn didn't know. Didn't much care either, just as long as she hadn't overstepped her bounds and pushed him too far, too fast. "I've been waiting . . . hoping that—"

"I would ask?"

He nodded. "I don't want to rush you, Evie. I want you to be ready. The mating ceremony is heavy-duty shit. No take-backs. Once it's done, the binding spell can never be broken. I wanted to give you time. The chance to decide . . . to be 100 percent sure I'm what you want."

"Venom." Turning into his touch, Evelyn nestled her face against his palm, soothing him the only way she knew how—with her acceptance. Lord love him. He was the most complicated man she'd ever met. One moment confident, the next, completely unsure. The insecurity—his desire to protect her, even from himself—simply made her love him more. Her need for him tightened its grip on her heart, infusing her with everything she felt for him. "I don't want a *take-back*. My decision was made the moment I met you. I might not have known it then, but I know it now. I'm yours, love. I want a mating mark of my own."

"Well, in that case . . ." A smile surfaced in his eyes as Venom trailed off. He shifted beneath her and reached toward the bedside table. With a flick, he pulled the drawer open and withdrew a blue box topped with a frilly black bow. Evelyn's breath caught as he cupped the back of her hand and placed the gift in her palm. "Open it, Evie."

A frisson of excitement skittered down her spine. Evelyn didn't hesitate. She tugged on the bow, watched it unravel, lifted the box top and—

"Oh, my." Air left her lungs in a rush. Awe circled deep, dragging tears to the surface and . . . ah, crap. Here she went again, tumbling into weepiness. "Oh, Venom."

"Do you like it?"

Did she *like* it? Was he insane? The ring was a masterpiece, one without equal. Set in white gold, a huge yellow diamond winked from a bed of white ones. Wonder closed her throat. Joy lifted the corners of her mouth, blooming into a wide smile. "Oh my God, Venom. It's incredible . . . the most beautiful thing I've ever seen."

Pleasure in his eyes, Venom plucked the ring from the box. Gaze locked on hers, he slid the band on her ring finger. The gemstone settled, looking as though it belonged next to her skin. "Evelyn Victoria Foxe, I love you. Marry me, *mazleiha*."

"Yes." A tear slipped down her cheek. "When?"

"Tonight."

"Perfect."

And it was. Simply *perfect*.

Nothing better in the world. No one better than Venom.

And as he drew her into his arms and held her close, Evelyn felt the weight of the ring on her finger and a startling lightness in her heart. At last. Thank God. She'd finally come home. Was exactly where she longed to be, committed to the man she was meant to love . . . forever.

Acknowledgments

Some books are harder to write than others. *Fury of Obsession* was one of those books. The writing of it challenged me in new and unexpected ways, making me dig deeper, helping me understand the living, breathing quality of a story better, forcing me out of my comfort zone and into the truth of my characters. I fell head over heels for Venom, hero of this book, the moment I met him. He made me laugh and cry and hope for something better. I'm so glad he found that *something better* in Evelyn and finally arrived at his happily-ever-after.

Tremendous thanks to my literary agent, Christine Witthohn. You are, without a doubt, the best of the best.

Many thanks to my editors, Helen Cattaneo and Melody Guy. Thank you for all your hard work. Your support and enthusiasm for my books make the entire process an absolute pleasure. And to the entire Amazon Publishing team whose talents and commitment are second to none. You amaze me constantly. It's fantastic working with all of you!

To my friends and family—thank you for dragging me out of my office and away from Storyland every once in a while for some much-needed R & R. I love you all.

Last, but never least, to Kallie Lane, fellow writer, critique partner, and friend. Thank you for all the BS sessions, early morning phone calls, and being so honest. You make me better. You always have. Thank you!

I raise a glass!

About the Author

Photo © 2009 Julie Daniluk

After growing up as the only girl on an all-male hockey team, Coreene Callahan knows a thing or two about tough guys and loves to write characters inspired by them. After graduating with honors in psychology and taking a detour to work in interior design, Coreene finally gave in and returned to her first love: writing. Her debut novel, *Fury of Fire*, was a finalist in the New Jersey Romance Writers Golden Leaf Contest in two categories: Best First Book and Best Paranormal. She combines her love of romance, adventure, and writing with her passion for history in her novels *Fury of Fire*, *Fury of Ice*, *Fury of Seduction*, *Fury of Desire*, *Knight Awakened*, *Knight Avenged*, and *Warrior's Revenge*. She lives in Canada with her family, a spirited golden retriever, and her wild imaginary world. Visit her at www.CoreeneCallahan.com.